Ginger Rice
Oct. 2005

# mindy starns clark

# the trouble with tulip

HARVEST HOUSE PUBLISHERS

EUGENE, OREGON

*Cover by Terry Dugan Design, Minneapolis, Minnesota*

**THE TROUBLE WITH TULIP**
Copyright © 2005 by Mindy Starns Clark
Published by Harvest House Publishers
Eugene, Oregon 97402

ISBN 0-7394-5667-9

**Printed in the United States of America**

With tremendous gratitude and affection,
this book is dedicated to the Smart Chicks in my own life,
those women who have always known how to dish out
not just good food and good housekeeping, but also good sense:

Lucille Dickerson,
Mildred Taylor,
Fan Starns,
Alma Beard,
June Ann Murphy,
Alice Clark,
and
Joyce Hammel.

Ladies, your love and care has helped
to shape my world.  Thank you!

## ACKNOWLEDGMENTS

Many special thanks to…

John Clark, my husband and best friend. Thank you, honey, for working with me in so many ways to bring these books to life. You're amazing!

Debbie Clark, for sharing your heart in helping me to find the character of Jo.

Fran Severn, for giving me Chewie.

Robert Bruce Thompson, Mary C. Chervenak, and Paul B. Jones, for incredibly brilliant (and devious) minds.

David Starns, for giving me much-needed humor injections.

Robert M. Starns, M.D., for excellent medical advice.

Jackie Starns, for eagle-eyed proofreading.

Russ Jones, for teaching me about the wide world of professional stock photography.

Steve Brewer, for an insider's look at being a newspaper columnist.

Shari Weber, for guiding and assisting in ways too numerous to count.

Emily and Lauren Clark, for story help, character names, and endless encouragement and love.

Kim Moore and all of the amazing folks at Harvest House Publishers.

Dave Sharpes and the ministerial staff of FVCN—especially Tracy Tucker and Doug Moister, for answering all of my crazy questions.

Ned and Marie Scannell, for incredible hospitality when I needed it most.

The members of Murder Must Advertise and DorothyL, especially those whose ideas and suggestions made it into this book, including Alison Moore, Sharon Wildwind, Maria Hudgins, Jayne Barnard, and Kate Bulman.

To ChiLibris, for unwavering support, ideas, suggestions, information, and brainstorming. You are such a blessing!

# TIPS FROM TULIP

**Dear Readers,**

My wedding day is almost here! Trust me, when you're 27 years old and have found the man of your dreams, there's something amiss about being a "miss." Therefore, tomorrow I'll be walking down the aisle to become a "Mrs."

Before I do, I want to pause and thank you, faithful readers, for being a part of my life for as long as I can remember. This column, as you probably know, was created by my dear grandmother when she was just a young housewife eager to share new and better ways to deal with the daily chores of cooking, cleaning, and laundry. After learning at her side, I was able to take over the column upon her retirement three years ago. And though my precious grandmother died last winter, Tips from Tulip is her legacy, and it continues to live on.

Of course, though much has changed since the first column appeared in 1948, readers still keep asking questions. As the Italians say, *"La gente è stata sempre stupido nella cucina,"* which means, roughly, that the search for domestic excellence is a noble tradition. (Actually, I think it means "people have always been fools in the kitchen," but, hey, who's translating? We all have a lot to learn!)

For the next week, as I take time off for my wedding and honeymoon, I have decided to feature some of my favorite letters from the past. The phrase that my grandmother first coined back in the '40s, "Be a Smart Chick!" is just as apt now as it was then. I hope you'll enjoy the letters from these clueless questioners of years gone by as we attempt to solve their problems. Until I return, may we all wise up, open our eyes, and be Smart Chicks.

*Lovingly,*

*Tulip*

Jo Tulip was suffocating.

As the digital clock glowed 11:48 P.M. from her bedside table—fully two hours after she had climbed in bed and turned out the lights—Jo finally threw off her covers and sat up. Her mind was so full of thoughts and her house so full of people that she felt as though she could hardly breathe.

Air. She needed to get some air.

Jo pulled some clothes on over her pajamas, slipped her feet into her sneakers, and grabbed the rechargeable flashlight from the plug across the room. She tiptoed through her small house, passing one snoozing body in the spare bedroom, another on the couch, and more in sleeping bags on the floor of the living room. Quietly, she continued to the back door, grabbed her key ring from the hook, and stepped into the cool September night, pulling the door shut behind her.

Already, just being outside, she felt better.

Inhaling deeply, Jo tucked the keys into her pocket, clicked on the flashlight, and made her way along the side of the house to the driveway. She followed it forward to the road, intending to take a short walk around the block. It was a cool night, very peaceful, and her hope was that the air would clear her head and help her relax.

It was no wonder she was feeling crowded. When her fiancé, Bradford, had asked if she would mind hosting a few of his relatives for the wedding weekend, she didn't know he would be sticking her with the intrusive branch of the family. They were friendly enough, she supposed, but they had scattered their belongings from one end of her home to the other, and their three boys were so wild that they had already broken the doorbell, a planter by the back door, and the towel rack in the bathroom.

Those same boys had looked so innocent as they lay dreaming on the living room floor, but Jo knew looks were deceiving. Come morning they would no doubt be at it again, probably setting her house on fire as their beleaguered mother tried to make cheese omelettes.

Oddly, though Jo was barely tolerating them, the whole family had really taken to her, which made it even more difficult to deal with their chaos. The boys were constantly fighting for her attention, and their mom seemed eager to become friends and confidants. Already, the whole family was trying to make elaborate plans for Jo and Bradford to come up to Connecticut and visit with them. Jo was pleased that they saw her as a welcome addition to the family, but if she had her way, that visit wouldn't be happening any time soon.

Autumn leaves crunched under her feet as she walked down the sidewalk, her stride taking on a soothing rhythm. She practiced some deep breathing: in, out, in, out. Jo usually preferred in-line skating to walking, but if anyone were to glance out of their window at this hour and see her whizzing past on a pair of 'blades, they might think she was crazy! Better to be out for a simple stroll. And it was a lovely night. She reached the end of the street and turned right, careful not to trip where the sidewalk buckled near the big maple tree.

Jo lived in a neighborhood that stretched for many blocks, a series of modest two- and three-bedroom homes with tidy yards on streets that were all named after trees. The town of Mulberry Glen (also named after a tree; the founding fathers hadn't exactly been a creative bunch) was a quiet place where neighbors mostly knew each other and a trip to the pharmacy or dime store sometimes took twice as long as necessary because of all the friendly encounters along the way. Jo loved living there, and though Bradford hoped eventually to convince her that they should move to New York City, where he worked, she didn't think that would ever happen. Better that he try to find a job a little closer to Mulberry Glen, Pennsylvania, which was a good three and a half hours from New York. Where they lived was just one of the issues that remained to be worked out between them once they were married.

*Married.*

Tomorrow Jo was getting married—well, technically, *today* she was getting married. A strange wave of apprehension rolled through her at that thought, but she swallowed the feeling away, as she had all week. She didn't know why she was feeling so anxious about it. The event was planned out thoroughly to the most minute detail. Jo assumed her midnight anxiety was simply standard prewedding jitters—and that as soon as she stood at the altar with Bradford and they were pronounced husband and wife, all would be well.

*Husband and wife, husband and wife,* she told herself in a simple cadence as her feet struck the pavement. The air felt so good and the night sky was so soothing that when she reached the next block, she kept going straight rather than turning to round the block toward home. She would just make a bigger square, looping down Weeping Willow to where it met Dogwood. Wildly, Jo wondered for a moment if she could simply keep walking all night. She could stroll all over town and finally walk right to the church and all the way down the aisle. The deed would be done and all of this worrying about it would have been for naught. Then again, her absence from the morning appointment at the hairdresser might send her mother into heart failure—not to mention that showing up at the altar in jeans over pajamas would be a sad waste of a really pretty wedding dress.

Jo reached the next corner and turned on Weeping Willow Way, the sound of her steps causing a cat to dart out from behind a trash can. Startled, Jo faltered a bit and then kept walking, glad that Mulberry Glen was such a safe town. She had taken plenty of late night walks last January, when her grandmother had been slowly dying and Jo's only solace was to wait until the night nurse arrived and then head outside to burn off some steam. Jo had walked almost every night back then, slowly coming to appreciate the darkness, the calm, the quiet.

Sometimes, as she went, she tried prayer-walking, where she would lift up to God the members of the households she passed. But invariably, her mind would become distracted: *Oh, Lord, please bless the family who lives in this house, and I wish they knew that they could clean that filthy siding simply by using a long-handled car washing brush attached to an ordinary garden hose...* Try as she might, Jo always had trouble keeping her mind from drifting toward household hints.

She was thinking of some other housecleaning techniques when, up ahead, she heard voices. As she kept going, she could tell that they were coming from a home on the left. Jo couldn't hear what was being said, only that someone was shouting in angry tones. Most of the other houses in the neighborhood were dark, but this one was lit up like a Christmas tree. The shades were all drawn, however, so as she walked past, she couldn't catch a glimpse inside.

From what she could recall, an older woman named Edna Pratt lived there. Edna was a fan of the Tips from Tulip column, though she and Jo's grandmother had never exactly been friends beyond a hello in the grocery store and an occasional chat about cleaning methods. Jo tried to avoid the woman when she could. Edna's daughter, Sally, was important in politics—a senator or a congresswoman or something like that—and it was always a bit tedious to hear Edna go on and on about Sally's latest accomplishments.

Jo kept walking, the sounds of the voices fading away by the time she reached Dogwood Drive. She turned right, feeling not a hint of tiredness, wishing she had taken four blocks instead of two. As she turned on to Oak Street and reached her own house, she decided to go around once more, this time at a slow jog. Maybe that would wear her out. Holding the flashlight a bit higher, she began jogging, passing her own dark home and those of her neighbors. Turning the corner, she took a big hop over the buckled sidewalk and kept going. The running felt good, and by the time she reached Weeping Willow a second time, her heart was pumping strongly, her breathing even and hard.

As she took the corner, she realized a car was coming up Weeping Willow in her direction, moving much more quickly than it should have been. Jo hated that, hated the way someone would willfully break the speed limit in a nice little neighborhood, just because it was late at night and they thought no one was watching. Well, she was watching. She glared at the car as it came toward her, aiming her flashlight directly toward the driver. It was probably some teenager, thinking he had the road to himself.

Suddenly, the car screeched to a stop.

The action was so odd that for a moment Jo slowed. She glanced to her right and then her left, but the street was deserted except for her.

The car continued to sit in the middle of the road, lights on, engine running. Jo felt a shiver begin at the base of her neck. Were they waiting for her?

Or did the fact that they were sitting there in the middle of the road, engine running, have nothing to do with her at all?

Feeling very uncomfortable but trying to act nonchalant, she made a simple U-turn on the sidewalk and began jogging in the opposite direction, toward home.

Turning left at the corner, she listened for the car but it still hadn't moved forward. She kept glancing back as she ran, but it wasn't until she was two blocks away, at the corner of her own street, that she noticed the car finally pulling out onto the main road. It made a right turn, away from her, and in the darkness she couldn't even tell what kind of vehicle it was.

Jo slowed to a walk for her cooldown, and as she covered the half block to her own house, she tried to think of different reasons a car would just stop in the middle of the road like that for what had to have been four or five minutes. She decided it was one of two things. Either they needed to pause and consult a map, or they had spilled something, like a soda or a cup of coffee, and they had to stop and clean it up. (Jo always suggested keeping a hand towel under the passenger seat for just such an emergency.)

By the time she reached her own home, she thought of the most likely scenario: *They* had been scared of *her!* After all, what kind of nut goes running at midnight—and then has the nerve to shine a flashlight in your face? Smiling to herself, Jo put the incident out of her mind. There were more pressing events going on there, and they all had to do with a certain guy at a certain church at a certain time, to whom she would say a certain "I do."

Suddenly, a wave of tiredness swept over Jo, and she thought she might finally be able to sleep. She decided not to go back to her bedroom but instead to the little building out behind her house, the one that served as her home office. There was a perfectly good couch inside, and she might do better to catch some z's there. She just couldn't face the crowd sleeping in her living room.

Jo crunched through the leaves in the driveway, used her key to unlock the door, and stepped inside without turning on the light. She had been in there only a few hours before, doing some final paperwork, so she knew everything was neat and clean and put away until after the honeymoon.

The couch was against the back wall, between the modified test kitchen to the right and the desk area to the left. Breathing in the sweet, spicy smell of her favorite room in the world, Jo crossed to the side closet, dug out a pillow and a blanket, and arranged them on the couch. This room was such a familiar, beloved place that she felt herself relax almost instantly. She pulled off her clothes, still wearing her pajamas underneath, and did a few stretches to complete her cooldown.

Finally, she laid down on the couch and pulled the blanket up to her neck. Despite the tensions of the day and all the thoughts that had been swirling around in her mind, Jo began to drift off almost immediately. In the quiet and the darkness, her breathing grew even and soft as she left behind the stresses of her world and slid into the deep, deep sleep that had been eluding her all week. She slept soundly, unaware that all was not well in Mulberry Glen.

Two blocks away, Edna Pratt lay dead on her dining room floor.

# TIPS FROM TULIP

*Dear Readers, this week as we feature classic letters from the past, enjoy this exchange from 1949.*

---

**Dear Tulip,**

My husband works as a funeral director and has to comfort people a lot, so he's always coming home with women's lipstick stains on his collar. What's the best way for me to get them out?

—*Stumped in Sarasota*

**Dear Stumped,**

Lipstick creates an oil-based stain, so water will only make it worse. Try rubbing in some vegetable oil and letting it sit. After 20 minutes, sponge the area with some ammonia, then finally scrub with some dish soap. Launder as usual.

And may I add: Be a Smart Chick! Ask other funeral directors' wives if they're facing the same laundry problem you are. If not, then you might need to wise up and realize that your husband's idea of giving comfort to the bereaved is dead wrong.

—*Tulip*

# 2

Danny Watkins stood over the corpse, thinking he had never seen anything quite so grisly in his life. As the coroner and the cops watched and waited, Danny carefully leaned forward to shoot pictures of Edna Pratt, who lay dead on the floor in front of him. Though he wasn't a cop himself, Danny was a freelance photographer, and this morning he was working in the employ of the Mulberry Glen Police Department. The police had hired him to photograph crime scenes before, once when a fellow had taken a bulldozer to his brother's cornfield over a property line dispute, and another time when the local high school's mascot, a giant papier-mâché cow, had been stolen and put upside down in the cupola over the town hall. But in this community, public humiliation of a synthetic domesticated animal was usually about as violent as crime got.

If this turned out to be a murder, then as far as anyone could remember, it would be the first murder the town had ever had. It was certainly the first one Danny had ever photographed. In fact, this was the first time he had ever seen a dead person other than a few friends' grandparents all dressed up and laid out nicely in their coffins for the funeral.

This was different and quite disturbing, but somehow Danny knew he had to find a way to stay emotionally disengaged from the appalling sight of this woman sprawled out in such a bizarre fashion. So far, he was just glad he hadn't had time to eat breakfast before getting the call that had brought him here.

The police chief, Harvey Cooper, had warned Danny that it was going to be bad. Once inside, Danny had taken in the shock of the scene with as much professional detachment as he could muster. Still, as he snapped away with his Nikon DX1, he had to keep swallowing down the bile in his throat. The whole scene was disgusting, both the way it looked and the way it smelled.

Edna Pratt had died in her own dining room, probably from a head wound from what Danny could see. Now she lay in a heap on the floor in front of the bay window, wearing a simple faded housedress, her feet bare. In between each of her toes were small white blobs that looked suspiciously like Styrofoam packing noodles. On each of her hands was a white athletic sock, and another sock had been stuffed with something and duct-taped around her neck. Edna's face was smeared with some sort of whitish green paste, and though her head was coated with blood, a clear plastic shower cap had been put on over the blood, almost as if to hold it in. The red blood met the white paste along the edges of the shower cap, creating an inch or so of pink ooze.

A strange chemical odor hung in the air, and after Danny had taken photos of the body from every conceivable angle, the coroner pointed toward a bucket nearby, the source of the smell, so that Danny could photograph it. When he was finished, a cop in rubber gloves tagged the bucket and carried it outside, taking the smell away with him.

"I hope you've got a lot of film in there," Chief Cooper said to Danny, " 'cause we have some weird things all over this house that need photographing."

"I've got plenty."

"Good. Either this lady was nuts or some real sicko was messing with her."

Chief Cooper led the way, and for the next hour Danny shot up four rolls of film, taking pictures in closets, in the bathrooms, and especially all over the kitchen. A cooling rack on the counter held a pie—from the look of it, a peach pie—which appeared to be normal except for the three ziti noodles that protruded vertically from the top crust. On the counter were the two vegetable drawers from the inside of the refrigerator, empty except for several layers of bubble wrap. Nearby, four orange halves sat side by side on a cookie sheet, and each of them had been hollowed out and filled with what looked like salt. Had the woman been senile?

An old piece of furniture, a baker's cabinet, lined the far wall, and a glow seemed to be coming from inside one of the drawers. With a gloved hand, the chief slid the drawer open to reveal a small lamp, turned on, lying on its side with its lampshade removed. As Danny snapped a photo, something began to tickle the back of his mind. He wasn't sure why, but something about a lamp shining in an empty drawer rang a bell.

Strangest to Danny was the sight of even more shower caps, which were all over the house on the bottoms of every hanging plant. As Danny photographed them, he had a feeling the editor of the local paper would end up dubbing this the Shower Cap Killing. With a shudder he wondered how the woman's head wound had been inflicted—and if she had been wearing the shower cap when it happened, or if the killer had put it on her head after the deed was done. There didn't seem to be any blood anywhere else, so probably it was the former. Then again, maybe she hadn't died from the head wound at all but from strangulation by the sock around her neck.

On the back porch was an ashtray where four cigarettes had obviously been burned from beginning to end without being disturbed—not a single puff having been taken from any of them. Danny was with Chief Cooper, photographing the ashtray, when a female cop appeared in the doorway. She opened her mouth to speak, spotted Danny, and then hesitated, a shy smile suddenly teasing at her lips. She was cute, that was true, but Danny wasn't going to pursue it. There was simply too much else going on today to throw flirting into the mix as well.

"Spit it out, O'Connell," the chief said to the cop, obviously noticing the way she was looking at Danny. "And don't even think about getting mixed up with this guy. He's working his way through every eligible female in town."

"Hey!" Danny said. "That's not true. I—"

"Don't worry, Chief," she interrupted. "I need a little more spit and polish than that. I don't really go for the artsy type, even if he does have soulful blue eyes and sexy hair."

"Yeah, he's divine," the chief replied dryly.

Danny could feel himself blush even as he resented being talked about as if he wasn't right there.

The chief said, "Now, what do you need, O'Connell?"

She turned her attention fully to him, all business now.

"We, uh, we have an interesting twist here."

"A twist?" he replied with a heavy sigh. "What is it?"

"The coroner checked under Miz Edna's shower cap."

"Yes?"

"That red stuff all over her head? It's not blood. It's tomato juice."

"Tomato juice?"

"Yes, sir."

*Tomato juice.*

"Chief!" Danny gasped. "I think I know what you should do."

"Oh?"

"Yes, sir. There's a person you need to call. Her name is Jo Tulip."

"Jo Tulip? Who's that? Girlfriend? Ex-girlfriend? Next girlfriend?"

"No," Danny replied. "None of the above. She's just a friend. And I can almost guarantee she'll know exactly what's going on."

Jo opened her eyes and tried to remember where she was. The sun was streaming through the window onto her face. She shifted her position to look around, and with the creak of the couch, she remembered: She was in her home office.

It was now officially her wedding day.

Jo inhaled deeply, glad she had made the decision to go for a walk last night and then come in there. Finally, she had gotten some decent sleep! And though she woke a full hour before she really needed to, she hoped there wouldn't be bags under her eyes as she walked down the aisle. Just to be sure, she got up from the couch, took a potato from the bin in the test kitchen area, and cut two big slices from the middle. Then she laid back down and put a slice over each eye. Five minutes like that should take care of any swelling she might have. It was one of her grandmother's oldest tricks—and Nana had been the queen of clever tricks.

Jo pulled up the blanket and forced herself to relax as the potatoes went to work. In all her childhood dreams of the perfect wedding, it had never crossed Jo's mind that her sweet grandparents would be absent from the festivities. They had been a huge part of her life—more important to her, really, than her own parents had been. But Pap had died a few years ago, and Nana had passed last winter. She felt so alone. Sometimes she missed them with a fierceness that caused her physical pain.

Jo took a few deep breaths, focusing on the woman who had been such a wonderful influence in her life, trying to have only happy thoughts on this important day. Nana had been the original Smart Chick, an intelligent woman far ahead of her time. She created the well-known Tips from Tulip, the daily question-and-answer newspaper column that provided readers with household hints and just a bit of sassy attitude thrown in for good measure. Though Nana had never exactly been a celebrity, the column was quite popular; in its heyday it had appeared in more than 200 newspapers across the country. Nowadays, Jo was continuing her grandmother's legacy by researching and writing the column herself, though the numbers had dropped considerably. The last time Jo talked to her agent, he was trying to get her a syndication deal, or at least a contract with a news service, so that she wouldn't have to worry so much about self-syndicating to individual markets. Until then, the money she made from the column, combined with the income from her part-time job teaching home economics at the local high school, kept her comfortable enough. It also helped that she had no house payment. Her home—and the little backyard office behind it—had been a loving bequest from her grandmother.

Jo liked the house well enough, but she really loved the office. Even as a small child it had been one of her favorite places, perfect for sitting on the rug in front of the couch to read picture books or play with her paper dolls. Jo's grandfather was a chemist by trade, and he would frequently help Nana with the more complicated household questions that came her way. Like them, Jo could be a quiet person, not given to chatter, appreciative of peaceful silence. "A *statue* makes more noise than the three of you combined," her mother had once complained, but Jo didn't understand what was so wrong with that. Her parents made an enormous amount of noise, and they rarely said anything useful at all.

Nana and Pap had brought Jo into the world of household hints early on, starting the day she was tall enough to stand on the step stool between them and listen quietly as they showed her how soap was created by mixing fat with lye. Jo had been hooked ever since. To her mind, there had never been any question that one day she would follow in her grandmother's footsteps—despite the fact that her own parents had done everything they could to talk her out of it. Of course, they weren't on board with much of anything Jo chose to do.

At least they approved of her choice of Bradford for a husband—as well they should, since they were ones who set them up on a blind date in the first place. Bradford was a protégé of Jo's father, an up-and-coming young executive who served as Kent Tulip's right-hand man. The day Bradford and Jo announced their engagement—a quick two months after the day they met—Jo's mother had actually cried with joy.

Jo took the potatoes from her eyes and sat up, the sound of a siren barely detectible in the distance. As she listened to the far-off wail, she felt a surge of sadness sweep over her, taking her by surprise. Today of all days, she shouldn't be feeling this way. The loneliness was supposed to go away now that she was getting married! Instead, she had the overwhelming feeling that walking back into her house and going through the motions of the day was going to feel like diving into the roll of a giant wave.

*Please, God, don't let me drown.*

Jo took the potatoes to the sink and ran the water, grinding them up in the disposal and telling herself she was being silly. She tried to recall a psalm about waves, something about "breakers and waves sweeping over me." Jo couldn't remember it exactly, but that was how she felt about the wedding—like waves were sweeping over her and she was helpless to stop them.

The siren sound grew louder, and as it did, Jo hoped her guests wouldn't wake up from the noise and wander all over the house looking for her. Drying her hands on a towel, Jo had to admit that there was no way they weren't awake now, as the siren sounded as though it were coming up her street. Soon, the noise was so close that it sounded as though it was right in front of her house. The siren suddenly stopped, only to be followed a moment later by pounding on a nearby door.

In an instant Jo was at the window, trying to see what was happening. Maybe the little hooligans really *had* set her house on fire!

"Lord, help me," she whispered as she quickly grabbed her clothes and headed for the house.

By the time she ran across the patio, opened the back door, and stepped inside, there were two uniformed policemen in her living room, standing awkwardly among the sleeping bags of her houseguests.

"There she is!" one of the boys cried.

"Jo Tulip?" a cop asked, stepping forward.

"Yes," she said, clutching her clothes to her chest. "What's wrong?"

"I'm afraid you're going to have to come with me."

"Come with you? Why?"

"I just have my orders, ma'am. Please come with me."

"I'm not even dressed."

"We'll wait, then. But please hurry."

Jo hurried down the hall to her bedroom, brushing past Bradford's bewildered cousins on the way. In her room she quickly ran a brush through her hair, pulled off her pajamas, and got dressed. After a quick stop to brush her teeth, she reappeared in the living room.

"What's this about?" she demanded, reaching for her purse. "Is this some kind of joke? A wedding day prank?"

"No joke, ma'am," the officer replied. "I'm afraid there's been a murder. And it involves you."

# 3

Danny paced in the front yard, dreading the moment when Jo Tulip would pull up in a police car. He knew she would be furious, that today of all days she wouldn't have a moment to spare. Worse, he felt certain she would think he had orchestrated something to get her here, to throw a hitch in her well-laid wedding plans.

But it wasn't his fault.

Yes, Danny was against the wedding, always had been. And, yes, it was Danny who told the police that Jo Tulip should be brought to the crime scene. But one had nothing to do with the other. He could only hope she would understand that once she went inside and saw the body of Edna Pratt.

Still, he wouldn't blame Jo for jumping to conclusions at first. After all, ever since she had announced her engagement four months before—just two months after she and Bradford *met,* for goodness' sake—Danny had done everything within his power as her best friend to talk her out of it. A few days ago, he had given his best you're-making-a-huge-mistake speech one more try. Jo had pleaded with him to let it drop, that this wedding was going to happen no matter what he said or did. She repeated her plea again last night, and so, finally, Danny had agreed. Like a dutiful friend he planned to hold his tongue from here on out. Jo had asked him to shut up, so he was going to shut up. But that didn't change how he felt about it.

In the distance, he could hear a siren, and he had a feeling it was her.

"You hear that?" Chief Cooper demanded, coming out on the lawn. "What an idiot."

"Sir?"

"Running the siren at this hour. Is he nuts? It's seven o'clock in the morning!"

"Well, you did tell him to hurry."

"Did I say use the siren?" the chief demanded, reaching for the radio. "Did I say wake up the entire town?"

The question was obviously rhetorical, so Danny did not reply. Instead, he waited a beat and then announced the sudden need to get another piece of camera equipment from his car. Anything to get out of Jo's line of sight when they pulled up to the house.

With the sounds of the siren coming closer, Danny hustled down the street—past four police cars, an ambulance, and the coroner's private vehicle—to his little red Honda. He got inside and leaned over, rifling through his spare camera bag. When the police car screeched to a stop and the siren turned off, Danny could hear the chief yelling.

Quietly, Danny got out of his car and stood beside it. All the noise had drawn even more neighbors from their homes, and a small crowd was gathering on the street. In the midst of everything, he could see Jo climbing from the backseat of the police car, her thick blond hair curling in the early morning mist, looking upset and bewildered.

*Father,* he prayed silently, *be with her right now. Please keep the problems of this home from overshadowing her special day—even if her special day is a really big mistake.*

Suddenly, it didn't matter to Danny if Jo would be angry or not. She needed a friend.

"Jo!" he called, quickly striding toward her.

"Danny!" Jo replied, her big green eyes near tears. "What's going on?"

Before he could reply, the chief finished his tirade at the deputy and turned his attention toward Jo.

"Miss Tulip? How do you do? I'm Chief Harvey Cooper."

"Can someone please tell me what's happening?" Jo asked, turning from the chief to her friend. "Danny, are you okay?"

"I'm fine," he replied. "I'm here as a photographer."

"A photographer! But you're *my* photographer today."

"It's okay. I'll be done in plenty of time."

"Miss Tulip," Chief Cooper said, "what you're about to see is pretty disturbing. But according to Danny, here, your, uh, area of expertise might shed a lot of light on what's going on."

"My expertise?"

"Household hints," Danny said. "Tips from Tulip, specifically."

Jo's face always clearly mirrored her thoughts, and now was no exception. Danny watched as she went from confusion to suspicion to anger.

"Danny, what have you done? Is this some misguided attempt to stop my wedding?"

Danny shook his head.

"Jo, listen. A woman was found dead in there this morning. It was looking suspiciously like a homicide, but now they're not so sure. They need your help to figure out what happened."

"Dead?" Jo asked, her eyes wide. "Who? Edna Pratt?"

"Yes," the chief said. "Did you know her?"

"Only in passing," Jo replied. "She was a friend of my grandmother's."

"Well, the next-door neighbor came over this morning and found Mrs. Pratt dead on her floor, with all sorts of weird things on her body and in her house."

"The police were trying to decide if she was crazy or if some psycho did all this," Danny interjected. "I offered a third alternative. Tips from Tulip."

Jo opened her mouth to speak, but before she could say a word, Danny continued.

"She's got tomato juice in her hair, Jo, some kind of cucumber-smelling paste smeared all over her face, and Styrofoam packing noodles between her toes."

"Sounds like she was beautifying herself."

"Beautifying herself?" Chief Cooper asked, leaning forward. "What do you mean?"

"The column has offered a lot of homemade facial treatments over the years, but if the stuff on her face smells like cucumber, it's probably cucumber and honey. Is it lumpy and greenish white?"

"Yes," the chief said, getting excited. "Why was her head covered with tomato juice?"

"Tomato juice takes chlorine out of hair. Was she a swimmer?"

To Danny's surprise, the chief barked out a laugh and slapped his thigh.

"Yes!" the man cried. "She swam every day! That's why the neighbor came over. They drive together every morning to the Y."

"Well, that's it, then," Jo said. "The packing noodles were probably to keep her toes separated after a pedicure. Are her toenails freshly painted?"

"I didn't notice," the chief replied. "Let's go see."

Danny held Jo's elbow as they went inside. He was afraid the sight of the dead woman might be too traumatic for her, but she remained calm.

"Is that the smell of death? she asked Danny as they crossed the threshold.

"No, that's the smell of whatever was in the bucket next to the body. It's gone now."

"It still stinks."

"You should've been here an hour ago. It was almost unbearable."

Jo greeted the coroner and then stepped close to the body and looked down intently, careful to follow his directions not to touch anything.

"Poor thing," she said softly. "I'm sorry I never took the time to get to know her better."

"She obviously knew you," the chief said. "According to Danny, your influence can be seen all over this house."

"That's true," Danny told her. "The thing that clued me in was a low-wattage lamp burning inside a wooden drawer. I knew it was familiar, and then I remembered you talked about that one in your column just a few weeks ago."

"A lamp in a drawer dries the humidity out of the wood and stops the drawer from sticking."

"I told you," Danny said to the chief and the coroner. "All of this. This entire home is like a living tribute to Tips from Tulip."

"Well, not completely living," the chief amended, looking down at Edna Pratt, whose toenails were indeed a freshly painted pearly pink.

To Jo, the whole situation was quite surreal. Here she was on her wedding day, touring the home of a dead woman, a neighbor she barely knew, offering simple explanations for all of the seemingly inexplicable things this woman had done. From the rice-filled sock duct-taped around the woman's neck (put in the microwave first, it would serve as a portable heating pad) to the shower caps under the plants (to catch the drips when she watered the plants), Jo had an explanation for everything. The only one that confused her was the ashtray on the back porch with the four unsmoked cigarettes. But then, as they walked to the living room again, she figured that out as well.

"The cigarettes," Jo said, pausing at the coffee table, where several white rings marred the dark wood surface. "If I had to take a guess, I would say she was burning the cigarettes to use right here."

The chief bent down to study the rings.

"Why?"

"To get rid of water rings on wood, you can sand them down a little and then make a paste of cigarette ashes and vegetable oil to rub into the wood. As long as it's not too big of an area, it should nicely darken the wood so the rings don't stand out as much."

"Incredible," the chief said.

"This was her sander," Jo added, reaching for a heavy brick that was covered in felt and had a little steel wool taped to the bottom. "For an older woman who doesn't have a lot of hand strength, the weight of the brick provides the force needed to sand the surface."

Jo looked up, realizing she had actually gathered an audience of cops, as they all listened, rapt, to her explanations.

"What about the orange halves with salt in them?" someone asked.

"For deodorizing the refrigerator."

"The noodles in the peach pie?" from another.

"To let out steam so the crust doesn't crack."

"The bubble wrap in the veggie drawers?"

"To keep fruit from bruising."

"Enough, enough," the chief said, waving his hands. "I'm the one asking the questions."

The cops grew quiet, though they continued to listen.

"Miss Tulip," the chief said, "you haven't told us about the socks on her hands. Let me guess—she was moisturizing?"

Jo put a finger to her lips, considering.

"Either that or cleaning her miniblinds."

"Excuse me?"

"To clean miniblinds," Jo explained, walking between the body and the window, "you can put socks on your hands. You dip your right hand in a bucket of cleaning liquid and run it along each slat this way, then use your left hand to dry, running it along each slat that way. See? Wipe, dry, wipe, dry. You just work your way down the blinds."

The chief stepped closer to the window and eyed the blinds.

"You're right!" he exclaimed. "They're clean about halfway down and then they're all dusty."

"That explains the bucket," the coroner said, rocking back on his heels and then standing. "It also explains her death. Good news, Chief. If I had to guess, I'd say this was definitely not a murder." He peeled the rubber gloves from his hands.

"It wasn't?" the chief asked skeptically.

"Don't think so. My best guess as to what happened here is that Ms. Edna was doing some beautifying and housecleaning, passed out from the fumes in the bucket, and hit her head against the windowsill, probably about here."

He pointed to the bottom of the frame of the bay window, where there was a small dent and a few missing chips of paint. Though it did look like the obvious spot, Jo didn't quite see how striking her head there would cause the woman to end up flipped around the other way.

"Sadly," the coroner added, "the accidental blow was fatal. I'll still do an autopsy, but I feel certain the cause of death is an intracerebral hemmorhage secondary to trauma from a fall."

The chief was silent for a moment.

"What was in the bucket that made her pass out?" the chief asked finally. "What kind of fumes?"

"My guess is that the woman mixed together a couple of different housecleaning chemicals and they reacted with each other. It's not unheard of, especially with someone like this who did things in a rather, uh, homemade fashion. What happened was that she probably mixed the wrong chemicals, the fumes got the best of her, she passed out, fell down, hit her head, and died. It's sad, but it's not murder."

"But if the fumes were so toxic," Danny asked, "why didn't all of us pass out when we got here?"

"The worst of the fumes would have dissipated overnight," Jo said softly. "Though the stench remained." She considered again the positioning of the body in relation to the bump on the windowsill. "So how do you explain the direction she's lying in?" she asked the coroner. "If she passed out and hit her head there, how did she end up here, like this?"

He looked down at the dead woman for a moment, considering.

"Good point," he said. "If I had to guess, I'd say the blow wasn't instantly fatal. She might have hit the ground and sat there for a few minutes, and then she fell back in the other direction. No way to know for sure. But I have no doubt it was an accident."

Jo was surprised he seemed so sure about it, especially because she knew it was murder.

# 4

Simon Foster was waiting at the bank when they unlocked the doors. In his wallet was a withdrawal slip for $400,000, the full amount that was in the account he had opened two days before with Edna Pratt. He didn't know if he would get away with this or not, but he had to give it a try. After all of his hard work, it was worth a shot.

Simon's shiny black shoes clicked against the marble floor as he crossed to the row of tellers. Sizing them up, he went with the youngest, prettiest one—not because he thought he was youthful or good-looking enough to charm her, but because in his experience pretty girls were never quite as thorough as their plainer sisters. It was as if life came so much more easily to the beautiful that they didn't bother with the small details.

He slipped one hand into the pocket of his suit, glad he had worn the Armani he had bought last spring off his friend Vinny for fifty bucks. It was a well-known secret among certain circles that at the Shady Ridge Cemetery in West Palm Beach, Florida, some of the richer, more well-dressed corpses had actually been laid to rest in just their undies. Vinny had found a profitable side business stripping down bodies just before he buried them and then selling the fancy suits and shoes on the side. Some of the guys didn't go for that, even if it was a bargain, but Simon had no qualms. What did a stiff need with Armani once he was in the ground, anyway?

"May I help you?"

Simon stepped forward and gave the pretty teller a practiced nod, slight and professional, communicating efficiency.

"Yes, I'd like to close out an account, please," he said, pulling the slip from his wallet and sliding it to her across the narrow counter along with his driver's license.

She took the paper from him and looked at it.

"For an amount this large, I'll have to give you a bank check," she said.

"No problem."

But there was a problem. After entering the information on the computer and then consulting a manager, the teller gave Simon back the withdrawal slip and his license.

"I'm sorry, sir, but this money isn't available to you yet. The deposit just went in two days ago."

"Yes, I know."

"The checks haven't cleared. As soon as they clear, then you can withdraw the funds."

"How long will that take?"

"Could be up to seven days. Why don't you check back on Wednesday?"

Wednesday. By then, he'd be a thousand miles away and the cops would be all over this thing. He might as well kiss the cash goodbye.

So close and yet so far.

"I, uh, I'm moving away," he said. "Can I close out the account via long distance?"

"Oh, sure," she said, glancing past him to the line that was already forming in the queue. "We'll just need a notarized letter telling us where to send the funds. Or, if you'd like, we can arrange that right now. Do you have your new address?"

Simon hesitated.

"Um, no. I'll have to get back to you on that."

"Well, here," she said, reaching into her drawer for a small card. Glancing at her computer screen, she jotted some numbers on the card. "This is our automated system. You can call it twenty-four hours a day and just enter your account number and this code. It'll tell you if the money is available yet or not. Once it is, all we need is that notarized letter telling us where to send the bank check."

Simon thanked her and took the card. He walked out of the bank, his heart heavy and his wallet nearly empty. He would change into his travel clothes at the bus station, and then he needed to get out of town fast, before the police started looking for him. He supposed he had enough cash to get a ticket as far as Baltimore.

From there, he'd just have to wing it.

Jo presented her case for the chief as the others stood nearby, listening. In the first place, she explained, there was no way on earth that a cleaning aficionado like Edna Pratt would accidentally combine a lethal mix of household chemicals.

Secondly, Jo continued, there was something important they needed to know about last night.

"Something was going on here," she said, "around midnight. A big argument."

"What do you mean?"

"I was out jogging in the neighborhood, and as I came past this house—"

"You went jogging last night?" Danny interrupted. "Why didn't you stop by? I would have gone with you."

Danny lived directly behind Jo in a house he had bought from his grandparents. A real night owl, he was always up late. Though he hated jogging, he would have gone along for Jo's sake. He had certainly accompanied her plenty of times last winter, when her grandmother was dying and Jo got in the habit of walking or running almost every night.

"Wait a minute!" said the chief. "Who jogs at midnight?"

"I couldn't sleep," Jo explained. "I'm getting married today, remember?"

The chief didn't look convinced, but he gestured for her to continue.

"Anyway," she said, "I was jogging past this house when I heard people arguing. All the lights were on, but I couldn't see in any of the windows."

"You tried to look in the windows?" the chief asked.

"No, but you know how it is. I heard voices and glanced over here, but I couldn't see who was fighting. Then something really weird happened."

She went on to describe how she made the block a second time, coming face-to-face with a speeding vehicle that screeched to a stop in front of her, unsettling her enough that she turned around and ran back home the other way.

"They sat there so long, I just figured they were looking at a map or something," Jo said. "But what do you want to bet it was the murderer trying to get away?"

Danny nodded enthusiastically, swept up in her tale.

"They probably stopped coming forward so that the lights would be in your eyes and you couldn't see the make and model of the car."

"Or the driver's face," Jo replied.

"Or the license plate," Danny added.

"Enough!" Chief Cooper cried. "That's all the speculation we need for now. Miss Tulip, I'm afraid you're going to have to come down to the station and give a statement. This does complicate things a bit."

Jo glanced at her watch and swallowed hard.

"Can we do it here, Chief?" she asked. "I'm supposed to be at the hairdresser's in fifteen minutes. The wedding starts at two, and I've got every minute planned out between now and then."

The chief reluctantly agreed, taking Jo's statement there at the scene, asking her questions and taking note of her answers, moving as quickly as he could step-by-step through her version of the events of last night. After a few minutes, Jo excused herself to call Marie, her maid of honor, to tell her to proceed with events as planned, minus one bride.

"I'll explain when I get there," Jo said into the phone. "Just tell the hairdresser to do everyone else first."

When the police were finished with Jo, she had them bring her straight to the salon. Jo's father had insisted on providing full limo service for the entire day, and, sure enough, there was a big white stretch limousine parked out in front of Hair's What's Happening.

Jo walked into the salon braced for the rapid-fire questions that were bound to greet her. Sure enough, as soon as they all saw her, everyone started talking at once. Before she explained what happened, however, she wanted to make sure things were moving along as smoothly as possible. The hairdresser assured her all was well and that there was still plenty of time to get her hair and makeup done.

"What about my mom?" Jo whispered to Marie, looking around the salon until she spotted the woman near the back, at the shampoo sink, eyes closed, head covered in lather. "Did she freak?"

"A little," Marie replied. "It all worked out, though. She just breathed some fire, ate a few maidens, and then went back into her cave."

Danny walked into his house, tossed his keys onto the table, and stepped over the basket of laundry waiting to be folded by the couch. He was exhausted, and it was only 9:30 in the morning.

He was also starving, so after he stashed his camera equipment down the hall in the darkroom, he came back to the kitchen and started digging around in the refrigerator. He decided to cook bacon, scrambled eggs, and toast, though the frying pan needed washing first; it was still on the back of the stove, dirty from last night's hamburgers.

As he made room in the sink and scrubbed the pan, he looked out of the window across his backyard toward Jo's house. He wondered if she had made it home in time to keep herself on schedule. He sure hoped so, as he had learned a long time ago that Jo Tulip did *not* like being thrown off her timetable.

The fence that divided their backyards was merely for ornamentation, a low split rail that had been there so long they weren't even sure which house it belonged to. All either one of them could remember was that one day twenty-some-odd years before, Danny had been outside with his grandmother hanging up the laundry and Jo had been outside with her grandmother weeding the garden. The two children had spotted each other through the fence, met at the middle, and become lifelong friends.

Women came and went from Danny's life with what even he had to admit was a steady frequency, but Jo was the one presence who remained throughout. Certainly, she was beautiful and smart and everything a man could want in a woman, but they had never even considered taking things to a romantic level, probably because their friendship wasn't worth risking. Over the years they'd had to defend their relationship as "just friends," but the word "just" bothered him. They weren't "just" friends. They were real friends. True friends. Best friends. Whatever they were, it was a lot more than *just*.

In any event, Danny took great joy in knowing his favorite person in the world was only a short walk away. With the backs of their houses facing each other, they had a clear view of each other's homes, and Danny would catch glimpses of Jo as she went from the house to the test kitchen or to set up elaborate experiments in her backyard. He worked from home sometimes too, and when he did they spent a lot of time waving to each other and eventually popping back and forth for coffee breaks.

Danny wondered how Bradford felt about that—or if he even knew. Considering the warp speed at which Jo and Bradford had gone from introduction to engagement to marriage, he doubted they had had time to talk about much other than the flavor of the wedding cake. As far as Danny was concerned, Jo Tulip had scored the land speed record for the fastest dash between meeting someone and marrying them. Only six months ago she and Bradford had gone on their first date—and a blind date at that? Just because Jo's parents knew Bradford and were the ones who arranged that first date didn't mean Jo had to fall in love with the guy *or* accept his proposal *or* meet him at the altar in record time. It was too soon!

With a heavy sigh, Danny stirred up a couple eggs in a bowl and dumped them in the frying pan. As the eggs heated, he balanced the bowl precariously atop the pile of dirty dishes in the sink. He thought he might try to get to them later, before it was time to put on the monkey suit and take part in this afternoon's farce of a wedding. In the meantime, what he really wanted to do was meet Jo at the back fence and try one last time to talk her out of the big step she was making today.

But not only did she not have time for that, he had promised her he would lay off. And so he would. Instead, he would spend the rest of the morning getting the crime scene photos processed and over to the police station. Though the coroner remained convinced that Edna Pratt's death had been an accident, the chief seemed to be leaning more toward Jo's opinion that it had been a murder. Either way, Danny needed to finish the job he had been hired to do.

After that, he would just have enough time to get cleaned up and dressed up and over to the church. The wedding was to begin at two, so he needed to be there by noon to get set up and start taking shots of the bride and the bridal party.

Could this day get any better? Surely, it couldn't get any worse.

Simon Foster had exactly twenty-three dollars in his pocket. In the privacy of a dirty gas station bathroom in Baltimore, he counted it out again, just to make sure. Who would have thought he'd end up like this? Especially when things had been going so well. It was his bum luck. He always had bum luck, when it came down to it. This mess with Edna was just the latest in a long line of good deals gone bad.

At least he managed to get out of Mulberry Glen without incident. But now he needed seventy-five dollars for the bus if he wanted to continue on to Jacksonville, where he could crash with a friend and wait to see if he'd be able to get that money out of the bank on Wednesday. If that didn't pan out, Simon figured he could still hide out there and probably get in on whatever action his Florida buddies had going on. He always had been a valuable member of any team.

For now, though, he would have to go solo. Gingerly, he balanced his suitcase on the bathroom sink and opened it up. The valet bit would have to do. There wasn't really time for anything else.

From the hastily packed jumble of clothing he pulled the red valet jacket, black pants, and white shirt. Once he was dressed, he fished around in the front pouch for the blank address forms and slipped them into his pocket. Everyone pulled the valet trick, but his came with a twist. He always had been a cut above the rest.

He closed the suitcase and unzipped the back, where he kept the folded valet sign. Luckily, he hadn't ditched it the last trip. He just never knew when it was going to come in handy.

The mirror over the brown-crusted sink was cracked, but he did the best he could combing his hair. He had already taken the time to shave that morning, thinking of his father's old adage: A clean-shaven man is always more likely to be trusted.

Simon had already scoped out the perfect spot, a corner right up the street near several swanky restaurants. If the right mark came along, he could be done and out of there in a matter of minutes. One of the restaurants, called the Tea Parlor, seemed especially promising. Who but old ladies would be going out for tea?

He needed somewhere to stash the suitcase. Walking out of the bathroom, he went behind the gas station and slipped it between a thick row of bushes. Then he carried his sign to the corner, opened it up, and waited.

# 5

"Who's writing your column while you're on your honeymoon?" the hairdresser, Lola, asked, poking Jo in the head with a bobby pin. "Surely you won't be dashing off helpful hints from the beach in Bermuda?"

"We're running some old classics all week," Jo replied, watching her reflection in the mirror as her elaborate hairdo was slowly taking shape. "It's been kind of fun, going through the archives."

Though Jo's mind was still on Edna Pratt's murder, once everyone else had gotten their questions answered, they seemed eager to change the subject. It was as if no one wanted to taint Jo's special day with talk of death or murder. Instead, they were hopping from subject to subject, mostly related to the wedding.

Now Lola had brought up the column. Despite Jo's modest success—and modest income—the girls at the salon always seemed to think of her as a celebrity. She supposed she was one, of sorts, though she doubted the competition she presented was keeping Heloise up nights. Jo didn't mind the "celebrity" part of her work: the personal appearances, the occasional television spot, and her once-a-week radio show. Mostly, though, she just liked writing her column, helping people get a handle on clutter and mess, and experimenting with new cleaning methods. That was the best part.

"What's up with your mom?" Lola asked Jo under her breath. "Looks like she's driving my girl nuts."

Jo glanced back toward the manicure area, where her mother was pointing at one of her nails, berating the manicurist.

"My mother is kind of a perfectionist," Jo whispered.

"Understatement of the year," Marie added.

"I guess that's why we're all glad she lives in New York," another bridesmaid quipped softly.

"Well, at least she sprang for a limo," Lola said. "That thing makes my joint look swanky just by being parked out front."

"You should see the driver," Marie giggled. "He's a real cutie-pie."

Though Jo's maid of honor, Marie, was not a raving beauty, there was something very attractive about her. Marie and Jo had been friends since high school, and even back then, the short, buxom brunette had been turning heads. Marie dated some, but she hadn't yet found anyone she wanted to settle down with. She didn't seem to mind; these days her bigger focus was in trying to get her real estate career off the ground. So far, Marie had listed three houses but had yet to sell one. Jo wondered if the housing market in their town would ever be robust enough to support another full-time Realtor. Mulberry Glen wasn't exactly a hotbed of commerce and growth.

"I didn't see a ring on his finger," one of the married bridesmaids commented.

"I noticed that," Marie replied, grinning. "He's so yummy I almost skipped my hair appointment just to sit out there in the limo and keep him company."

Jo's mother, Helen, joined them at that moment, her manicure finished, her hair ready for the final step.

"Don't be ridiculous, Marie," she chided. "At your age you should never date a man you aren't willing to marry. You never know when you might fall in love."

Helen sat in the chair at the end of the row. Her stylist removed the curlers and began working with her hair.

"Why wouldn't I want to marry him?" Marie asked. "We'd have some gorgeous kids, that's for sure. And just think, we could go on all our dates in a limo. How romantic."

"Oh, that's silly," Helen said, squinting her eyes at the mirror. "As I've always said, it's just as easy to fall in love with a CEO as it is a plumber."

"Hey!" Lola cried. "My George is a plumber."

Jo felt her face burning red. Leave it to her mother to insult her hairdresser and friend.

"No offense, darling," Helen said. "Some plumbers make a very nice living, I'm sure. But I know Marie's mother would rather see her with a doctor or a lawyer than a limo driver."

"My mother wants to see me with someone who will treat me right and love me forever," Marie replied, surprising Jo with her forthrightness. Marie had always stood up to Jo's mom better than anyone. "As for how he earns his living, I'm quite sure she wouldn't care."

"I don't know about that," Helen said, tossing her head regally. "Ask her some time how much she *really* enjoys living on a fireman's income."

If Jo's face got any more red, she thought she might explode. Every nerve longed to berate her mother, to say *Enough!* Instead, she held her tongue, clenching her teeth. She rarely stood up to her mother.

She certainly didn't need to get into it today.

Simon turned down the first two customers who pulled up in front of him with their blinker on. One was a couple and the next was a teenage girl. In both cases he apologized and said the valet lot was full.

Finally, something looked promising. A gorgeous black Caddy pulled over and the passenger window smoothly rolled down. Inside were two elegantly dressed, silver-haired women.

"Good morning, ladies," he said, putting on his most charming smile. He might be in his sixties with gray hair of his own, but he knew how to work a pair of old biddies. Soon they would be putty in his hands. "Will you be coming to the Tea Parlor today?"

"We're doing some shopping first," the driver said, leaning toward him. "But that's where we'll be ending up."

"That's good enough for us. I can take your car from here, or I can drop you at your choice of stores."

"Ooo, that sounds nice," the passenger said. "Let's get him to take us to Wellington's."

"Wellington's it is," he said, discreetly kicking down the valet sign and then coming around and opening the driver's door. He helped the woman climb out and move into the backseat, and then he slipped behind the wheel, taking the time to buckle his seat belt and adjust the rearview mirror. Above all, he wanted to give the impression that he was a careful individual not prone to recklessness.

Fortunately, there was some heavy traffic in the downtown strip that gave him more time to work it. He chatted them up for a few minutes, making plenty of eye contact and paying several compliments. By the time they were halfway up the block, he had indeed won them over.

"Oh, before I forget," he said, reaching into his pocket. "The Tea Parlor is having a drawing today. A free trip to Can—to Canada."

He had almost slipped, saying Cancun. But that wouldn't appeal to these women. He went on to describe a lovely weekend getaway to Banff and Lake Louise.

"You just fill out this form and give it back to me. The drawing's in about three hours. Will you be at the Tea Parlor by then?"

"I'm sure we will," the passenger said, passing one of the slips to her friend in the back and filling out her full name and address on another. "We just have an hour or two of shopping planned."

"Well, if by some chance you win and the manager needs to notify you right away, will there be someone at this address to answer the phone?"

"My son lives with me," the passenger said. "He should be home all day."

*Scratch that one,* Simon thought, trying not to wince.

"No one will be at my house," the woman in the back volunteered. "I live alone. But I could give you my cell phone number."

"That would be fine," he said. "Whatever way we can reach you best."

He pulled to a stop in front of Wellington's and helped them both out of the car.

"You ladies have a lovely morning of shopping and we'll see you back at the Tea Parlor in a few hours. Take your time."

They thanked him and one of them slipped him a five.

He grinned as he drove away, loving this particular con. It never ceased to amaze him that folks would actually tip him to steal their car and rob their house.

"These came out great," Chief Cooper said, flipping through the series of 8 x 10 photos that Danny had brought in. "So much detail."

"Yeah, that's the new Fujichrome film I've been trying. Very sharp."

"These are works of art," the chief continued. "Very impressive. Like something outta *Ranger Rick* magazine. Do they even make *Ranger Rick* anymore? My kids always loved that. Lots of close-ups of frogs and squirrels and stuff." The chief set the pile of pictures on the desk, an image of the smeared-white face of Edna Pratt on top. "The autopsy's almost finished," he continued. "Pretty soon we'll know for sure if it was murder or an accident."

"Jo's convinced it was murder," Danny said.

"I know," the chief replied, "but as nothing was stolen, I'm having trouble finding a motive. According to all of the people we've spoken with, Mrs. Pratt didn't own anything of real value other than a few small pieces of jewelry—and they're all accounted for."

"How about what Jo saw and heard last night?" Danny asked. "Have you questioned the other neighbors?"

"We've canvassed the whole neighborhood," the chief replied, "and no one else heard the fight or saw anyone coming or going. From what I can tell, Edna Pratt was just your typical sixty-year-old woman. Lived in a modest house, belonged to a few women's groups, kept up her health with a daily swim."

"What about assets? Insurance?"

"Nothing special going on there. She was widowed six years ago and living on her late husband's pension and social security. According to the next-door neighbor, Pratt kept her hedges trimmed, watered her flowers, and lived a nice quiet life. Frankly, I'm a little stumped as to who might have been arguing with her, much less why someone would want to kill her. She didn't seem to have any enemies."

"Does she have relatives in the area? Maybe it was a family squabble."

"One daughter, but she lives in Texas. I just talked to her a few minutes ago."

"Is she coming up?"

"Flying in tomorrow morning. She's a politician smack in the middle of an election, so I get the impression the timing of this was a little inconvenient for her."

Danny looked at the chief, one eyebrow raised.

"A mother's death? Inconvenient?"

The chief shrugged.

"Let's wait for the autopsy before we go speculating about people's character. In the meantime, how 'bout we cut you a check for these pictures?"

Chief Cooper pushed out his chair, stood, and led Danny to the desk of the man who handled the money. Danny was glad to get it, as his bank account was already groaning from the strain of this month's bills. His wedding gift to Jo and Bradford was the deluxe bridal photography package, and he needed to pick up some supplies.

As the guy loaded the information about Danny's fee into his computer, Danny looked around the small station, a little depressed at the thought that he was twenty-eight years old and he was still having to supplement his meager income with jobs like this one.

"Sure was nice of you to get all dressed up just to deliver these," the chief teased, tearing Danny from his thoughts. "You weren't hoping to run into a certain female cop, by any chance, were you? Maybe show her you clean up good? You even got the shaggy hair under control."

"Actually, getting the pictures printed took longer than I expected, so I had to go ahead and get dressed for Jo's wedding. I'll be driving straight from here to the church."

"Uh-huh," Chief Cooper said, obviously not buying it. "Don't worry, you're like a walking magnet. If she's here, she'll find you."

"I don't *want* her to find me. Listen, Chief, what you said earlier today, about working my way through the eligible women in town, did you really mean that? Do I have that…reputation?"

The chief laughed, slapping his hand on a chair.

"Nah, I was just kidding. But you do seem to have more than your share of dates. Every time I see you, you're with a different gal."

Danny ran a hand over his chin and exhaled slowly, not sure why this conversation bothered him so much.

"Well, for what it's worth, I'm always a gentleman," he said at last. "But maybe I do have a hard time narrowing things down a bit."

"You draw women like flies to a picnic, that's all I know. Though for the life of me, I can't figure out why. I guess it's that starving artist thing you got going on, the creative soul and everything—not to mention that you're a musician on the side. Some women really go for that stuff."

Before Danny could reply, a nearby printer sprang to life and started spitting out a check.

"Hey, speaking of being a starving artist," the chief continued as he tore the margins from Danny's check, "didn't I hear that you were gonna be a photographer for *National Geographic* or *Scene It* magazine? Whatever happened with that?"

"Nothing yet," Danny replied as he took the proffered check and slid it into his pocket. "I've just got big dreams in a very competitive field. I'm still trying to break in."

"Well, good luck with it. Maybe you should call Ranger Rick himself. Think there is such a fellow?"

Reading the "entry form," Simon saw that the woman lived at 563 West Chambers. The stupid city map had cost him five bucks in the mini-mart, but at least he had been able to easily find the address. As he pulled up the quiet, tree-lined street and turned into her driveway, he was glad he had ditched the red jacket ahead of time. He was much less conspicuous in just the shirt and pants.

He calmly parked the Caddy, got out, and strolled to the back door. Then, discreetly trying several keys on her ring, he unlocked the door and stepped inside.

He had to work fast, so he started with a quick walk-through, checking each room for small valuables. The woman was obviously moneyed, and she had exquisite taste in Chinese porcelain. If he had more time and a local fence, he might have helped himself to a few of her vases.

No time or opportunity for that, though. Simon didn't like outright thievery, except when it was absolutely necessary. In his own personal code of ethics, stealing was wrong. Cons, on the other hand, were different. After all, a key ingredient to every con was the greed of the mark. They brought it on themselves—and usually deserved whatever they got. *Still, desperate times call for desperate measures.* Considering all that Edna had said to him yesterday, these were indeed desperate times! He needed to find the woman's stash of cash, something she was sure to have around somewhere. Old biddies like her always did. Simon searched all of the usual spots, finally finding a wad of money in one of the dress purses on a shelf in her closet. He took it without counting it, certain that it added up to at least several hundred dollars.

The woman's jewelry box was also in the closet, and he slid it out, put it on the bed, and opened it. Though there weren't any precious jewels there, she did have several substantial gold items, including a very chunky bracelet. Perfect.

Simon pocketed the best of the lot and put the box back on the shelf. His final stop was the bedside table drawer, and then the medicine cabinet in the bathroom. Old ladies were always suffering aches and pains, and he thought he might score a bottle of prescription painkillers, which were always good for a quick sale. No dice, though. All he found were Advil and a bottle of blood pressure medicine.

After that, he was ready to fly. Without missing a beat, he got out of the house, into the car, and within minutes was back on the main road, no one the wiser.

The Caddy was so nice he toyed briefly with keeping it and driving himself to Florida. But that would be asking for trouble, as he was sure to get spotted on the interstate and brought in by the police.

Instead, he drove to a parking lot near the original place he had acquired the car. Finding a spot on the end, he gathered his belongings, tossed the keys under the mat, and locked the door.

His knocked-over valet sign was still there on the side of the road, lying flat in the grass. He scooped it up and kept walking, first to get his suitcase from the bushes behind the gas station and then three blocks over to the bus stop.

He caught a bus to the main station in Washington, D.C., just to confuse any trail the cops might be following. In D.C. he could get lost in the crowd and buy another ticket there for the rest of the way to Florida.

Simon didn't count the cash until he was on the bus, in the last row, with no one around to observe him. Much to his excitement, he saw that he had scored a little more than twelve hundred dollars. Twelve hundred dollars!

Simon tucked the money away, leaned back in his seat, and grinned. His father had taught him years ago how to land on his feet.

Now it looked as though that was exactly what he had done.

## 6

W e're here," Helen said, peering out of the window of the limousine as they pulled to a stop in front of the church.

Between the salon visit and getting dressed for the wedding, Jo, her mother, and her bridesmaids had made up for the morning's lost time by forgoing the leisurely lunch they had planned and grabbing some quick sandwiches instead. Now it was 1:00 P.M., exactly one hour until the ceremony was slated to begin. They were back on schedule.

Too bad all Jo could think about was the investigation into Edna Pratt's murder. She was dying to talk to Danny and find out what he knew. Though her girlfriends might think her morbid for worrying about this on her wedding day, she couldn't help it. Her mind was filled with the image of poor Edna Pratt sprawled out on the floor with cucumber on her face and tomato in her hair.

"Ladies?" the handsome limo driver said as he opened the door with a flourish.

They climbed out one at a time—the bridesmaids, the flower girl, Helen, Marie, and then Jo. Though the driver held out a hand to assist Jo, he only had eyes for Marie.

Jo stepped forward and heard the rip before she felt it, a slick sliding of metal against fabric followed by a distinct tug at her waist. She froze, knowing immediately what had happened: The guy had closed the car door on her wedding gown.

"No!" Helen cried, and when Jo carefully turned to see, sure enough, the train of her dress was caught in the closed door of the limo, a torn piece of lace drifting to the ground beneath it like a feather. Marie looked from the dress to Jo and then burst into tears.

"Oh, no!" Marie wailed. "That was my fault. I'm so sorry!"

"No, I'm sorry," the driver said. "I wasn't paying attention."

Everyone sprang into action, quickly opening the car door, pulling out the fabric, and assessing the damage. The tear was significant, but Jo was more worried for Marie, whose sobs were escalating.

"You idiot, look what you've done! It's ruined!" Helen screamed, bending down to finger the layers of linen and netting, each of which sported about a six-inch gash. A line of black grease ran along the top of the tear.

"Let it drape," one of the bridesmaids said. "Maybe it won't show."

Jo just stood there while the women fussed about her, trying to see what could be done. As they did, Jo reached out to the sobbing Marie and placed a hand on her arm.

"Marie," Jo said softly, and then again, more loudly. "Marie! It's okay. We can fix it. Stop crying."

"We can't fix it! It's ruined!"

"She's right. It's ruined," Helen pronounced, straightening up.

"It's pretty bad," the driver said. "You'll either have to go down the aisle like that or cut the whole dress off just above the tear."

Marie clamped a hand over her mouth.

"Marie!" Jo said, focusing in on her. "Look who we're talking about here. It's me. Jo Tulip. Has there ever been *anything* I can't fix?"

Slowly, Marie's eyes widened. She shook her head from side to side.

"That's right," Jo continued calmly, glancing up at the clock tower of the stately white church. "We've got fifty-eight minutes before the wedding starts. Plenty of time to repair the damage that's been done."

Helen pursed her lips.

"Jo, you've got two layers of fabric here, with a grease stain on ripped linen and torn netting. I know you're the Smart Chick and all that, but this'll take a miracle."

"No, it won't," Jo said, holding up her fingers and then counting off. "It'll just take an egg, an iron, a bottle of clear nail polish, a toothbrush, and some corn meal."

"Okay, look right here and smile," Danny said. "Last one."

Bradford and his parents stood up straight and flashed their perfect teeth as Danny captured the moment on film.

"Thanks," he said. "I think that'll do it."

They clustered together, speaking softly as Bradford crossed to Danny and held out his hand.

"Thanks for doing this, buddy," he said. "Jo and I sure do appreciate it."

"No problem," Danny lied, shaking his hand. "My pleasure."

His heart heavy, Danny gathered up his equipment and carried it to an empty side room where he could switch out some lenses, load film, and organize his bag before photographing the women. The longer he had spent posing and photographing Bradford and his clan, the more upset he became about the impending nuptials. What was Jo doing? *Was she out of her mind?*

It's not that there was anything wrong with Bradford per se. It's just that he and Jo hardly knew each other. Having grown up with three sisters of his own, Danny thought he understood women pretty well. But Jo had always been an enigma in some ways—and in this way most of all. She deserved a lifetime of love and happiness with someone who knew her to the depths of her soul, not just some executive type who happened to meet all of her "Mr. Right" requirements on the surface.

Danny checked the batteries on his light meter as he recalled their biggest argument about it, just a few days before. They had met at the back fence, Jo weeding her flower bed as they talked.

"Bradford is a nice guy," Danny had said, "and I know your parents were pushing him on you pretty hard, but it's irrational to think you can make a decent marriage out of a six-month relationship. And a long distance relationship at that!"

"Bradford and I have been soul mates since the day we met," Jo insisted as she ripped up a dandelion root. "You can't even imagine how many things we have in common."

"With an occasional date here and there, all well planned and thought out and meticulous, how could you even know? I mean, that makes for a nice dating arrangement, but it's hardly the basis for a marriage. Have you ever had a single argument? Does he even really *know* you?"

"Know me?"

"Like," Danny sputtered, his hands forming circles in the air, "how you spend your free time, what movies you like to watch, what ice cream you choose when there are thirty-one flavors to choose from."

"Danny, come on. Those things aren't important—"

"But they are, Jo! Some would say they are the most important things of all. What do you know about him? How does he spend his money, do his laundry, study his Bible? What brand of ketchup does he like, what sort of trips does he dream of taking? Did he have a childhood pet?" He was grasping at straws. Thrusting a finger into the air, he added, "Does he love or hate mime?"

Jo stood and put her hands on her hips.

"You want me to cancel my wedding because I don't know my fiancé's stance on *mime?*"

"Yes! No couple should ever get married without knowing that!"

"You're being ridiculous, Danny. And who are you to talk anyway? You've never had a relationship that lasted more than a week."

"This isn't about me, it's about you. All I'm saying is that if you had any faith in this guy, you'd be eager to take it slow, not fast. You'd want to explore every good thing you have in common and every bad thing that might pop up to cause problems down the road. You'd make plans, negotiate the tougher issues, figure out what each of you will have to do to make this marriage work."

"We'll cross each of those bridges as we come to them."

"Have you even decided where you'll live when you come back from the honeymoon? I can't imagine Bradford's going to commute from here to New York City—it's more than three hours each way! From what I can tell, that means you're really only going to have a husband on the weekends—that is, unless you're willing to give up your home and live there."

"You're talking about logistical problems," Jo said, avoiding his gaze and bending again to tend to the weeds. This time, as she pulled on them, her knuckles were white. "We're working it out. For the time being, yes, we're keeping my house *and* his apartment."

Danny studied the top of her head as she bent over the flowers. If she ripped those weeds out any harder, she'd break through clear to China.

"What about spiritually?" he said. "Is Bradford really a man of faith?"

"We're the same religion."

"I'm not talking about religion. I'm talking about where he is in his personal walk. Is he mature spiritually? Because if he's not, you're making an even bigger mistake than I think you are."

"He's a Christian," Jo said defensively. "He gets to church when he can. He's so busy all week, he needs Sunday to rest."

"Do you hear yourself? Do you know what you're saying? How can you even consider yoking yourself with a man whose faith is at a different level than your own? Do you understand the kind of problems that can produce?"

Jo didn't reply, so Danny lowered himself there on his side of the fence, down on his knees until they were face-to-face. Then he reached out through the fence and put his hands on top of hers, forcing them to be still.

"Jo," he whispered, practically pleading. "Have you asked yourself what you're running away from by marrying this man?"

The conversation had ended there. In tears, she had jumped up and run back into her house. Then she avoided him for two days.

Finally, last night, just before the wedding rehearsal, she stopped by his house and gave a short and obviously rehearsed speech about how she appreciated his concern but that she knew what she was doing and she didn't ever want to hear his thoughts on the matter again. For the sake of their friendship, Danny had finally agreed.

Sighing deeply, he slung a camera strap over his shoulder and headed toward the bridal room, knowing that it still didn't mean he had to like it.

Simon Foster chose the busiest line in the D.C. terminal, the one with the most harried and distracted-looking teller. When he asked for a one-way ticket to Jacksonville, he was careful not to make eye-contact or to do anything memorable. Though he doubted the Baltimore cops would do much more than take a theft report from the old biddies, it never hurt to cover his bases. It might also be smart to unload the gold jewelry as soon—and as locally—as possible.

The bus didn't leave for two hours, which gave him enough time to go out and find himself a pawn shop or a jeweler. As he made his way outside and down the grungy sidewalk, Simon marveled at how different working a con had become since he got older. With his silver temples, wrinkled face, and neat mustache, people were more inclined to trust him than they ever did when he was young and handsome. No one expected old folks to lie. Be cranky, maybe, or snap at nearby children.

But they were generally considered trustworthy. As a professional grifter, he found that his age had become one of his biggest assets.

Simon passed a jeweler with a sign in the window that said "We Buy Gold." As he went in, he stooped a bit, slowed down, and shuffled his steps. The more they thought he was an honest old fellow selling off his widow's bangles, the less trouble he'd have—and the more likely he was to get a decent price.

It took a bit of haggling. But Simon was educated about gold and jewels, and once it became obvious that he knew his stuff, the jeweler offered him a fair amount. He paid Simon in cash, which added another five hundred to the cash he'd already acquired. All in all, this wasn't shaping up to be such a bad day after all.

If only he could know how things were playing out with Edna in Mulberry Glen.

Danny knocked on the door of the bridal room. Jo was usually so organized and calm and efficient that Danny was surprised to find total chaos inside.

"I've got the egg and the cornmeal!" the pastor cried, brushing past Danny and coming into the room with a brown paper bag in his hand. "My wife wanted to know if we were cooking up some fried catfish."

The women laughed. Jo took the bag from him and Danny watched as she set it on the counter next to a bottle of nail polish and an iron. Jo looked beautiful from the neck up, but instead of a wedding gown, she was wearing one of the church's choir robes. Her gown was hanging nearby, and Danny gasped when he saw a giant rip and a big black stain halfway down the skirt.

"Don't panic," Jo said, hearing his gasp and looking up at him. "We had a little accident, is all."

"What about the photos?" he asked.

"We'll have to do them after the ceremony. Right now I've got some threadless mending to do. Everybody, if you can't get quiet, then get out."

They all settled down and watched, fascinated, as Jo went to work. She began by spreading the netting over an ironing board and then, using fingernail polish, she glued the tear back together again.

"What are you doing?" someone asked softly.

"You can't sew netting or it makes an ugly seam," Jo explained. "So I'm using this instead. The fingernail polish acts like a glue. Once it's dry, the tear will be almost invisible."

Danny began to snap photos of Jo in action, thinking a few candid shots might be useful down the line. She might even be able to capitalize on this in the paper: "The Smart Chick Uses Household Hint Knowledge to Save Her Big Day."

By the time Jo was finished with the netting, the iron was hot and ready for the next step. Jo cracked the egg, separated the white, tossed the yolk, stirred it up, and then used the spoon to paint the egg white on the back of the fabric, right over the tear. She cut a small strip of matching linen from an inside seam of the dress and then placed it on top of the gooey wet area, and pressed it with the hot iron.

"I call this invisible mending," she said simply, glancing up to see everyone's eyes on her. "It works on certain fabrics as long as you do it before there's been much fraying."

Danny shook his head, proud of the odd storehouse of knowledge inside Jo Tulip's astounding brain. It was no wonder her column was on the verge of national syndication. She could do anything, often with nothing more than a few ordinary household items.

When she finished and turned the material over, the repair was, indeed, nearly invisible. Jo attacked the stain last, smoothing out that part of the material on the ironing board and then pouring cornmeal all over the big black smudge.

"The milled grain should absorb the grease," Jo explained, this time not even looking up to see who was watching. "We'll give it as long as we can to just sit there and absorb, and then we'll scrape it off and work at the stain with the toothbrush. Hopefully, we'll get it all. In the meantime, Danny, may I speak with you in the hall?"

He nodded, a sudden hope surging in his chest. *Please, God, has she decided to call this wedding off after all?*

She took his elbow and led him from the room, an urgency to her stride. They walked together to the end of the hall, out of earshot, and then she spoke.

"Danny, I have to ask you something."

"Yes?"

"The police. Have you talked to the police? I'm dying to know the final word on Edna Pratt's autopsy."

Jo made Danny call Chief Cooper for the autopsy results, but as she listened to Danny's side of the conversation, her heart sank.

"I guess you heard from my end," Danny said as he hung up. "Edna Pratt's death has now officially been declared an accident."

"Why?" Jo demanded, knowing they were wrong.

"Several reasons. First, the fatal head wound matched the shape of the indentation in the windowsill. Second, she had no other bruises or marks that would indicate she had been pushed down. She had to have fallen on her own."

"What if someone else mixed those chemicals when she wasn't looking?" Jo said. "That would've been murder."

"I'm sorry, Jo. The chief says no go. There were no signs of breaking and entering, no indications of violence at all except the dent in the window frame. Like the coroner said, that was probably from Edna passing out and falling. The only thing out of the ordinary with this entire case are the things you heard and saw—the argument and the car. That's not enough."

"I refuse to believe it," Jo replied, crossing her arms in front of her chest. "Edna Pratt knew too much about cleaning to mix together the wrong chemicals. What were the chemicals in that bucket, anyway?"

"I don't know."

"Let me borrow your phone, would you?"

She took it from him before he could respond and pressed the redial button.

"Chief Cooper?" she demanded once she had him on the phone. "Jo Tulip here. What was in the bucket that made Edna Pratt pass out?"

"I don't think it's necessary for you to know that, Miss Tulip," Chief Cooper replied. "The case is closed."

"I just want to know. Please? I think you owe me that much."

The chief grunted.

"Fine, hold on."

She could hear him flipping through papers and then he spoke.

"Bleach and ammonia."

"Bleach and ammonia?" Jo repeated. "That makes chloramine gas! At best, it would be highly irritating to the lungs. At worst, it would be lethal."

"Well, she's dead, isn't she?"

"But Chief, that's like housecleaning *101!* Edna Pratt would *not* have done that."

"I'm sorry, Miss Tulip. There's just not enough evidence to call this a murder."

Jo wanted to argue her case, but she suddenly caught sight of her mother marching determinedly down the hall toward her.

"I'll call you later," Jo said into the phone and hung up just as her mother reached her.

"You're supposed to walk down the aisle in eleven minutes," Helen hissed. "I think you need to get in there and finish getting out that stain!"

"Fine," Jo replied. "I'm coming."

Helen spun back around and marched away.

"I've got to get to the sanctuary anyway," Danny said softly, taking back his phone. "I'll see you in there."

Jo reached out and caught his hand and gave it a squeeze.

"Thanks, Danny," she said softly, looking into her friend's warm blue eyes. He had to know she was thanking him not just for helping out this morning, but for all he did as her friend. He was more important to her than he could ever know.

"No sweat," he replied. He squeezed her hand back and released it. "Now get dressed, why don't you? After all this work, I'd hate to see you getting married in a choir robe."

Jo raced back to the room and worked at the stain, finally declaring it good enough to go. The grease wasn't completely gone, but it would do.

She pulled on the dress, and as her mother worked the tiny buttons up the back and the bridesmaids fluffed the train where the repairs had been made, Jo checked her image in the mirror, straightening the pearl tiara that held her veil in place. She usually wore her hair down, where it hung several inches past her shoulders, or pulled back in a ponytail. Today, however, her mother had talked her into an updo. Though the elaborate hairstyle did look quite elegant, Jo was wishing she hadn't been so easily swayed. Behind the fancy hair and the professionally applied makeup, she didn't quite feel herself.

"You look beautiful, honey," Helen said, stepping back after the last button had been fastened. "A vision."

Everyone agreed that she looked lovely and that the dress repairs weren't even noticeable.

"So tell us, Jo," Marie said, gathering everyone's flowers from the box. "Will you put all of this in your column?"

"Oh, that stupid column," Jo's mother interjected before she could reply, checking her own image in the mirror. "Please tell me you'll be giving up that foolishness once you're married."

Some of the bridesmaids gasped, but Jo merely held her tongue. Helen had always been vaguely embarrassed by Tips from Tulip, first when it was written by her mother-in-law and then when it was taken over by her daughter. Many a time she had chided Jo for squandering a perfectly good college degree on "trivial household matters" that were, as she said, better left "to Heloise or Martha Stewart."

A knock at the door saved Jo from having to reply.

"Ladies?" Pastor Beacon said. "Are you decent?"

Marie let him in, and he stepped inside, his face lighting up at the sight of them.

"I trust everyone's ready?" he asked. "Crisis averted?"

"Yep. We have it under control."

He led them in prayer and then told them that it was time for them to go out the side door and around to the front of the church. As Jo walked among the small crowd of giggling, excited women, she thought not of the groom who waited for her at the altar or even of the music that was ringing majestically from the organ.

She thought, instead, of a bucket of bleach and ammonia. Jo promised herself that as soon as she got back from her honeymoon, she was going to pay a visit to the police chief in person and insist that he figure out who killed Edna Pratt and why.

# 7

J o!" her father whispered sharply. He was waving from the top of the stairs and pointing at his watch. "Come on. It's time!"

Jo looked up at her dad, who was strikingly handsome in his tuxedo. Her mother gave her a final hug and then hurried to move to the front of the line. As Jo mounted the steps herself, she couldn't help but smile. The big moment was finally here.

"You look stunning, dear," her father said, giving her a peck on the cheek. She looked into his eyes, surprised to see he was tearing up a bit. As Marie arranged Jo's train into place behind her, Jo slipped her hand into her father's arm and gave it a squeeze, feeling oddly touched by his show of emotion. She doubted he had ever shed a tear over her before.

"It's showtime," Marie whispered once the train was set. "You ready?"

"Ready as I'll ever be," Jo replied, taking a deep breath.

Marie ran up to take her place in line just as the organ music swelled from inside. As Jo held onto her father's arm and waited her turn, she thought about her parents and her own difficult childhood.

Though Jo's paternal grandparents, the Tulips, had been humble and loving, her maternal grandparents were quite another story. The Bosworths were an old money, industrialist family who fully expected their only daughter, Helen, to marry a man capable of stepping into the family business and serving it well. Kent Tulip had not disappointed them. Starting in his twenties as a district manager, over the years he had worked his way up the position he now held, that of CEO of the entire company. In the meantime, Bosworth Industries had bought and sold so many other companies and businesses that it was now a world-wide conglomerate.

As a child, Jo had lived an odd and isolated life, relocating with her parents from country to country as her father worked to establish Bosworth's international holdings.

He always brought his wife and child with him on these long-term assignments, so consequently Jo had spent much of her youth starting over—new home, new school, new friends, often after only six months. And though there was usually an American-centric place to live and go to school wherever they ended up, Jo always found herself among children who were a lot like her: friendly, but afraid to form lasting bonds. Unable to connect. The only consistent people in her life were her grandparents and her best friend back home, Danny Watkins. More than anything, Jo treasured the times between foreign assignments when her father would work out of the main office in New York City, her parents would live in their apartment there, and Jo was allowed to stay with her father's parents in Mulberry Glen.

The summer after Jo graduated from the eighth grade, she asked her grandparents if she could live with them year-round. Much to her relief, they embraced the idea enthusiastically. Armed with their consent, she approached her parents and told them she was tired of moving, she wanted a normal high school experience, and she wanted to live with her grandparents from here on out.

Jo had expected fireworks, as both of her parents were rather stubborn and difficult people. Instead, once they had worked through a few of the details, they agreed that it might be a good idea. Jo moved permanently to her grandparents' house, into the bedroom that had always been hers anyway. And though she'd been glad to get what she wanted, she had also felt oddly hurt that her mother and father hadn't put up more of a fight to keep her.

After high school came college, and Jo attended locally there in town, content to continue living with her grandparents. She had planned to move out on her own once she graduated, but by then they were in poor health and she needed to stay for their sakes. Once they had both passed away, of course, the house became hers. After today it would be hers and Bradford's, the perfect place to begin their new life together.

"Here we go," her mother whispered when it was her turn to head down the aisle. After that went the bridesmaids. Jo watched them slowly make their way to the front as Danny took each photo in turn.

He was so utterly adorable in his tuxedo—and so completely clueless as to his own adorableness. Jo treasured him in a way that was different from how she felt about anyone else in the world. That's why it was so difficult for her to hear his objections to her marriage.

Jo watched the flash of his camera, forming a final response in her mind. *So what if Bradford and I rushed into things? After today we will be husband and wife. And then we can spend the rest of our lives together, learning everything there is to know.*

The music changed and the congregation stood and turned.

"We're on," Kent said softly.

Together they walked down the aisle toward Jo's future.

Bradford was standing tall at the front of the room, looking more handsome than any movie star. From his precisely cut blond hair to his tan skin and square jaw, he really did look as though he could have stepped straight from the big screen. As she walked forward, Jo studied his face and tried to lock onto his gaze, but he wouldn't quite meet her eyes.

The moment Jo reached the altar, she knew something was wrong. At first, she blamed it on the heat. The lights. The attention. Maybe Bradford wasn't used to being up in front of a crowd, especially not in a tuxedo, about to be married, so it wasn't terribly surprising that his eyes were darting about, his skin pale. But as Jo's father gave her away and she stepped into place beside the man who was about to become her husband, she couldn't help thinking it was more than that, that Bradford looked as if he were ready to faint.

Jo could see the sweat on his forehead, the shaking of his hands, the panic in his eyes. Briefly, she considered stopping the ceremony to ask if he needed a glass of water or to sit down and put his head between his legs. *Maybe a whiff of camphor on a cotton ball or a cool compress to the pulse points at his wrists would do the trick,* she thought, remembering one of her past columns, "Tips for Conquering Stage Fright."

"Dearly beloved," the minister said, snapping Jo from her thoughts. "We are gathered here today to unite this man and this woman in holy matrimony."

The minister opened the ceremony with a few words of greeting and then a prayer. Jo closed her eyes for the prayer, asking God to calm the heart of the man beside her.

Still, she could practically feel the tension radiating from Bradford. He was breathing heavily, little huffs that kept getting stuck in his throat. She opened one eye to steal a glance at his face, half expecting him to be crying. But, no, he was just standing there with his head bowed and his eyes closed, his lips puffing together, opening and closing, like a fish. Were he not such an incredibly handsome man, the mannerism would have looked ridiculous. As it was, Jo couldn't help thinking how very much she wanted to comfort him. He needed to relax and enjoy the ceremony.

She reached out to slip a calming hand into the crook of Bradford's elbow, but as she touched him he jerked away, almost as if he had been electrocuted. Jo quickly retreated, placing her hand back on the stem of her bouquet and feeling her face flush with heat. As the prayer ended, she kept her eyes on the minister, blinking back tears. While he proceeded with the ceremony, Jo could hear Bradford softly clear his throat repeatedly, his breathing even more rapid than before.

Deep in her heart, then, she wasn't really surprised when everything fell apart. They were at the point in the ceremony where the minister asked Bradford if he took this woman to be his lawfully wedded wife. Bradford hesitated in his answer long enough to earn gasps from some of the bridesmaids.

"Do you take this woman to be your lawfully wedded wife?" the minister prodded a second time, his eyebrows lifting just a bit.

Biting her lip, Jo turned to look directly at Bradford, and the expression on his face told her all she needed to know. He looked first at her, and then he turned and directed his gaze toward her father.

"I'm sorry," he whispered, shaking his head. "But I don't."

Then he dashed out the side door of the church, the same way he had come in.

Danny wanted to deck the guy! This whole event had been a nightmare, from pulling on a monkey suit to keeping his mouth shut about the wedding to watching Bradford slowly decompress at the altar. Now, as two of the groomsmen ran out after Bradford, Jo just stood there with her big green eyes full of tears. And though Danny was thrilled the guy was gone and the wedding obviously wasn't going to take place after all, he was enraged that Bradford had let things get this far.

*Had he actually just dumped her at the altar?*

Danny looked at Jo, having no idea how to comfort her. He hesitated, trying to decide whether to go after Bradford or stay there with her. The pastor seemed similarly torn, and a buzz was starting up among the congregation. Finally, Danny knew someone had to take action.

"I'll go see what's up," he said. Then he ran from the sanctuary.

Danny had been a member of Trinity Church for most of his life, so he knew the intricate hallways of the old building like the back of his hand. He ran first to the room next to the pastor's study where the groomsmen had been stationed prior to the wedding. It was dark and empty. Danny thought of the parking lot, so he ran down the hall and out the back door just in time to see Bradford speeding away in his Corvette. The best man, Bradford's younger brother, was standing there watching him go.

"Did he say why he ran out?" Danny asked, trying to catch his breath.

"No," the kid replied, shaking his head. "He just kept saying 'I gotta go. I gotta go.'"

"Go where?" Danny demanded. "He's got the most perfect woman in the world standing there waiting to marry him and he takes a powder? Is he crazy?"

"Cold feet, I guess. Better he figure it out now than after the deed is done, you know?"

"What an idiot!"

Danny took his anger out on a discarded soda can, kicking it as hard as he could. It struck a nearby stone wall, bouncing back toward the two men and splashing their legs with the cola that was left in the can.

"Aw, man, I'm sorry," Danny said, feeling the anger inside him evaporate like the fizz from the can. The anger was replaced by despair and a heavy heart. He had known all along that this relationship was doomed—had hoped for it, in fact. Now that this had happened, though, all he could feel was Jo's pain and embarrassment.

"Don't worry about it," the fellow said, shaking out his legs. "The suit's just a rental." He ambled back toward the building.

"Wait," Danny called after him. "What do we tell Jo?"

He held out both hands and shrugged.

"She's your friend, Danny," he said. "I'm sure you'll think of something."

Simon settled back against the seat of the bus, gazing out of the window as they crossed into Virginia. He was glad to have the wad of cash in his pocket—both the money he'd stolen from the lady's house and the bills he received from selling her gold—but mostly he lamented the fortune he might never be able to get out of Mulberry Glen. Four hundred thousand dollars!

All of it gone. All of it wasted. All of his hard work shot to pot.

All because of Edna.

He closed his eyes, thinking of his buddies down in Jacksonville. If he could round up the gang, there was no limit to the games they could get going. They might even try the same one he'd had running in Mulberry Glen, but using the lessons he'd learned this time to get it right.

Four hundred thousand dollars, probably out of his reach forever.

The very thought of it made him sick.

# 8

Jo sat on a stool in front of the mirror, her mind racing in a million different directions. Just beside the sanctuary, this was the room where she and her bridesmaids had worked so furiously to fix her dress before the wedding began. Now it looked as though the wedding might be over before it had barely started. What on earth had gone so wrong?

"Here's some water," Marie said, handing her a paper cup, as if that would somehow help to save the situation.

Jo took it from her absently just as organ music swelled from the other side of the wall. A moment later the pastor appeared in the doorway.

"Jo, I asked the organist to play a few songs. I'm going to talk to Bradford and see what's going on."

"What did you say to the congregation?"

"I just asked for their patience and suggested that they enjoy the special music."

Jo nodded, wondering how she was ever going to live this down. She was an idiot, a complete and utter fool who had been humiliated at the altar. With an inner groan, she thought of her column from the last few months, all of those handy wedding tips. Here was a handy wedding tip she obviously forgot to mention: *Pick a groom who won't bolt when it's time to say the vows.*

"Uh, Jo?" She looked up to see Danny in the doorway. "I'm sorry," he told her, "but Bradford left. He's gone."

"Are you sure?"

"I watched him drive away."

Jo stood, setting the cup of water on the table in front of her, spilling a bit of it into an open tray of face powder.

"Everyone out, please," she said. "I need a moment. Danny, you come in."

The bridesmaids silently filed out of the room. Danny stepped inside and pulled the door shut. He sat awkwardly on a nearby stool, looking as if he'd rather be anywhere else in the world.

"What did he say?" she asked quietly.

"I didn't talk to him. His brother is under the impression that Bradford had cold feet. All he said was 'I gotta go, I gotta go.' And then he left."

The room was silent between them. On the other side of the wall, the music swelled to a crescendo.

"Maybe he just needed a bathroom," Jo said.

Danny smiled in spite of himself.

"I'm afraid that's not what he meant."

As Jo closed her eyes, twin tears spilled down her cheeks.

"Ah, Danny," she whispered, "It's not like you didn't warn me…"

There was a soft knock at the door. It opened and the pastor leaned into the room.

"I guess you've heard from Danny. Bradford's gone."

"Yes."

He stepped into the room and looked about for a chair. Danny surrendered the stool he was sitting on and leaned uncomfortably against the wall.

"Here is how I suggest we proceed," the pastor said. "I'll say a few words to the congregation and try to minimize the embarrassment of what has happened as much as possible."

"Oh, gee," Jo said, swiping at her wet face, "that'll be simple."

"It will," he insisted gently. "I'll just say we need to be respectful of the bride's feelings and trust that we can bring some resolution to the relationship one way or the other very soon. In the meantime, let us not condemn or throw stones or place blame. The kindest thing everyone can do is offer encouraging words and leave the whys and hows to the couple involved. Sometimes these things just happen."

"Has it ever?"

"What?"

"Happened. To you. While you were performing a wedding for someone."

Pastor Beacon ran one finger under the tight collar at his neck.

"No, not really. But there's a first time for—"

"Where is he?" Jo's father demanded, swinging open the door. "I'm gonna kill him."

Jo stood, her full gown knocking over the stool behind her.

"Daddy, no," she said, reaching out to touch her father's arm. He jerked away, which only served to remind her of Bradford's similar gesture at the altar. He was furious, the vein along his temple bulging out the way it did whenever he got worked up. He usually saved his temper for his coworkers and associates, yelling into the phone about market shares and shipping problems. Jo had no doubt that if Bradford were here right now, her father would pulverize him on the spot. Maybe it was best he had driven away.

"This isn't helping anything, Mr. Tulip," Pastor Beacon said. "Let's speak in the hall." With a firm hand he pulled Kent from the room, shutting the door behind them.

*It just figures,* Danny thought, *that Jo's dad is acting this way. For a man who doesn't seem to care about his daughter any other time, suddenly he's trying to pull the concerned father act? Give it a rest!* Mr. Tulip would bluster and fume for a while, sure, but Danny would take bets that the man would be on a plane by nightfall, flying off to his next business appointment whether the situation was resolved or not.

"Maybe I should change clothes," Jo said, sniffling heavily and not making a move toward the outfit hanging in the corner. "I feel like a complete dope sitting here in my wedding gown."

"Do you want me to get Marie to help you?" Danny asked.

Jo looked at him, her eyes brimming with fresh tears.

"Why'd he do it, Danny?" she whispered.

Danny could feel his heart flip-flop in his chest. He had a number of opinions as to why Bradford had done it, but the honest truth was probably that the man had realized just in the nick of time what a big mistake the two of them were about to make. That was the silver lining in this very dark cloud, that at least Bradford's actions had saved Jo from what would surely have been a lifetime of misery. Any fool could see that this had not been a match made in heaven; unfortunately, up until

Bradford took off, both he and Jo were just fools enough to think it could work.

"Jo, look," Danny said, reaching for her hands with his, feeling suddenly uncomfortable in the small, intimate setting. "We will get this sorted out. In the meantime, just be glad it happened before the wedding and not after. What if he had become your husband and *then* abandoned you?"

Danny's words sounded empty and hollow even to himself. After a moment, as he struggled to come up with something to say that would be a bigger comfort to his friend, the door opened and the pastor stepped into the room again.

"Your father is outside getting some air," he said to Jo softly. "We have discussed the situation, and here's how we'll proceed, if it's okay with you."

Soon, everyone was on their way to the reception hall—everyone except for Jo, who was sitting in the back of the limousine, on her way home by herself. Since there were so many out-of-town guests, the pastor had suggested that the reception go on as planned, albeit in a modified form. Jo's parents would serve as hosts, the wedding party would see to it that the event flowed smoothly, and the modest buffet dinner at a nearby restaurant would still be held.

"Certainly, you can go to the reception if you think you're up to it," Pastor Beacon had told her. "Otherwise, it's probably best to remove you from the church now, while the congregation is still seated inside. The limo can pull around back and take you home."

Several of the girls had offered to go with her, but Jo insisted that she wanted to be alone. Now, she felt ridiculously small in the back of the gigantic vehicle. She closed her eyes, knowing the whole thing was simply pathetic. She thought of the fancy hotel suite in nearby Moore City where she was to have spent her wedding night, not to mention the flight she and Bradford were to have taken the next morning, their honeymoon trip to Bermuda. Right now, Bradford was probably headed back to his apartment in New York. The hotel suite would sit empty tonight, as would their two seats on the flight to Bermuda tomorrow. No one on the plane would understand or care what had happened to those two passengers.

*Why?* The question pulled at her, filled her mind, overflowed her eyes with tears. Fumbling with the little compartments and doors around the minibar, she finally found a slot that dispensed tissues. She dabbed at her face, trying to imagine what her grandmother would say if she were here right now.

*It will all be sorted out in time, Jo Jo. The Lord can bring good out of every bad thing.*

That's what she would have said, but it sounded a bit simplistic now. Where was the Lord when her groom dumped her at the altar?

*For that matter,* Jo thought, *where was the Lord last year when my precious grandmother died slowly from cancer? Where was the Lord when my grandfather dropped dead five years ago from a stroke?*

The bottom line, Jo knew, was that she had been alone through most everything in her life. And while she believed in a benevolent Creator, she suddenly doubted very much that He involved himself with the day-to-day concerns of anyone. If He could make good come from every bad thing, then why was her life such a mess?

*The reception isn't as bad as it could have been,* Danny thought grimly as he stood near the punch bowl. Jo's parents had turned on the charm, glad-handing the guests as graciously and smoothly as they probably handled their numerous business clients. Mr. Tulip had grown up in this town, and though he had long since moved away, almost everyone knew him or at least knew of him. He moved easily through the crowd, seeming to be everywhere at once, chatting people up, making sure they had food on their plate. Mrs. Tulip lent a quiet elegance to the event, her striking beauty and expensive attire bringing a level of class to the small-town setting. Danny knew she was usually a petty and bitter woman, but she was putting on the charm tonight. Danny would be able to report back to Jo that her parents had done her proud.

The band was pretty good too. A few people even got up to dance now and then. Fortunately, the gossip seemed to be at a minimum. There was an odd mood to the room, but with the pastor's very visual presence among them, most folks were keeping their thoughts to themselves. The general consensus seemed to be that the reason Bradford had taken off was because the entire engagement process had been rushed along so quickly. Bradford and Jo had only met six months ago; it had obviously been far too soon to culminate their whirlwind romance into a wedding. Danny knew that much was true, but he also knew it was more than that, much more.

To his mind, Bradford and Jo had not really been in love with each other at all, but merely in love with love. Jo's vision of a handsome groom to sweep her off her feet and make her dreams come true and her troubles go away was merely that: a vision. The reality was that Jo Tulip had probably never let anyone into the inner recesses of her heart, with the exception of her father's parents and Danny. She didn't have a clue what real love was. She had been hurt and rejected so many times in her life that she had created walls around herself. At this point those walls were so thick that Danny doubted anyone else would ever get through. Even her relationship with God—though important to her—suffered because of her past. She didn't know what true spiritual intimacy was, settling instead for so much less than the rewarding wholeness the Lord had to offer.

At least maybe those walls would serve her well now. If Jo had never really let Bradford in, then it wasn't going to hurt very badly for very long as she got over him and worked out her feelings for him. Danny's bigger concern was what this would do to Jo in the long run. If she already kept people at a distance, what was this hurt, this rejection, going to do to her? He thought of Pharaoh in the Bible and how every trial and tribulation wrought by God through Moses had hardened the ruler's heart.

*Don't let Jo's heart be hardened, Lord*, Danny prayed. *Keep her receptive to You.*

By 4:00 P.M., Jo was going stir-crazy. She had heard from Danny once, when he called to say that the reception was lovely, gossip was minimal, and her parents were doing a great job of keeping the party rolling. Marie had also called, from her cell phone, but Jo let that one go to voice mail. No one else had called—especially not Bradford.

In the meantime, Jo had spent an hour on her hands and knees, scrubbing the floors with a hard-bristle brush. When all else failed and the world was crumbling down around her, she usually turned to prayer. This time, however, that wasn't going to happen. She resorted to cleaning instead, as she could always find peace in cleaning. And though her intrusive houseguests had been as good as their word—repaired everything they'd broken and moved out all of their stuff—they had still left behind plenty of crumbs and spills. In a way, Jo was glad. It gave her something to attack.

Eventually, though, her work was finished. The house sparkled. Her heart ached. She changed into clean jeans and a shirt, pulled on her helmet and pads, grabbed her Rollerblades, and wrote out a note to Danny: *Went to the park.*

She went out the back door and across the grass, stepping over the split-rail fence into Danny's yard. The grass had worn down to dirt where they always cut through. She made her way to the front, to the flower bed beside the door. Among the weeds nestled a little garden gnome Jo had bought for Danny years ago when she was living with her parents in Germany. Though it looked tacky now, at the time they both thought it was simply magical. The gnome's hat was hinged at the back so that it could be opened, and the hollowed-out head made a little container, perfect for leaving secret notes. Over the years the gnome had become a point of communication for them both, and they still used it frequently.

Jo put the note into the head and then rolled down Danny's driveway to the sidewalk and made her way to the end of the block, turning right along Maple Street. In the eight months since her grandmother had died, Jo had rediscovered in-line skating with a passion. The town park was on the other side of Maple, and it featured a long, beautiful bike path that allowed Rollerblading. Jo headed there now, but she hesitated just one block later as she reached Weeping Willow Way.

On a whim, she curved to the right and rolled toward Edna Pratt's house. Had it really been less than twenty-four hours ago when she jogged past this home and heard an argument while trying to calm her prewedding jitters? It seemed a lifetime ago.

For Edna, it *was* a lifetime ago.

Jo rolled to a stop and sat on the curb across the street from Edna's house. In the afternoon light, the place looked empty and forlorn, one piece of yellow police tape still hanging from the chain-link fence that surrounded the backyard. Jo wished she could remember more about what she had heard and seen last night. She had been so consumed with herself and her own anxieties at the time that she hadn't even realized a woman was in jeopardy right behind those walls.

"I'm sorry, Mrs. Pratt," Jo whispered. "I would have tried to save you if I had known."

In her mind Jo went over the different conversations she'd had with Edna Pratt through the years. They had discussed gardening and closet organization and minor household repair. They had talked about Edna's daughter, Senator Sally Sugarman, and all she had accomplished down in Texas. Jo had even met Sally once, at a party, and when she told her that her mother was always singing her praises, Sally had looked at her oddly and changed the subject.

Otherwise, there had been nothing of note for Jo to remember from Edna Pratt's life. She was a nice woman, if a little reserved, and devoted to the pursuit of a clean house. Whenever someone could quote to Jo complete sentences from her own column, she knew they were indeed a fan. Edna Pratt had been such a person, which was why Jo knew the woman had been murdered. In a million years she would not have mixed bleach with ammonia. Whenever Tips from Tulip mentioned either substance, a warning was always included at the bottom of the column stating that the combination could be lethal.

*So who killed you? Who were you fighting with? Why are you dead?*

Jo's life was certainly in a shambles around her feet right now, but maybe she could dedicate herself to answering those questions. Chief Cooper and the coroner both felt certain that the woman's death was an accident, but deep in her gut Jo simply knew better. Maybe it was just the way her brain worked, but she was convinced that a kindred cleaning spirit like Edna Pratt wouldn't have made that fatal mistake. Last night's argument and speeding car only lent more weight to Jo's certainty that Edna had been murdered.

*I'm the only one who believes it,* Jo thought, *so maybe I'm the only one who can prove it.*

Heart pounding, she stood, suddenly determined to find justice for Edna Pratt. *Can I do it?* Jo wondered. *Can I uncover the truth myself?* An internal dialogue ensued as she considered how her skills as a household problem-solver might extend themselves to a murder investigation.

"I'm Jo Tulip," she said out loud, confidently, as she pushed off with her Rollerblades. "I have a solution for *every* situation."

Just as quickly she stopped again, one house over, and looked back at Edna's place, wavering just a bit.

"Correction," she said to herself, more softly this time. "I have a solution for every situation…except my own love life and, oh yeah, the dead body next door."

# 9

Danny was exhausted. He pulled into the driveway, turned off the car, and then just sat there. Somehow he had to find the energy to go inside, change into something more comfortable, and then walk across the back lawn to face Jo. What a day.

By the end of the reception, he'd practically had to pry himself loose from one of Bradford's female cousins. She had set her sights on him halfway through the party and wasn't happy about taking no for an answer.

*Why does this always happen to me, God? Do I lead these women on? Do I flirt and encourage them without even realizing it?*

Before the chief's comment that morning, Danny had never given his success with the ladies a second thought. But now he had to wonder: Was his love life out of control?

Currently, he had two women on the line, not counting Bradford's cousin. There was Tiffany, his coworker, with whom he'd gone out for one lousy cup of coffee and she took it to mean they were officially a couple. Then there was Marci, a friend of one of his sisters, who had needed a date for a business function. Danny had obliged as a favor, but Marci took it as something more. In the past three weeks, she had called about five times to ask him out again.

What was he doing wrong?

*I'm not interested in these women, God. Please show me how to live more honestly so they'll understand that from the get-go. And if You do have a special someone in mind for me, bring her into my life. I'm tired of playing the field, of looking for something that simply isn't there.*

Feeling frustrated and confused, Danny climbed out of the car and went inside, suddenly realizing he was starving. He went straight to the kitchen eager to make himself a big ham sandwich with mustard and

Swiss. As he sliced open a roll, he paused to grab the phone and hit the speed dial for Jo's house.

She didn't answer, so he left a message that he was home now and he'd be over in a minute. It was more like fifteen minutes by the time he had eaten and changed, but she hadn't called back. He tried calling again, and still he got no answer. She was probably just laying low, but before he went over there anyway, he checked the gnome. Sure enough, she had left a note.

Danny felt a surge of some emotion he couldn't identify as he read the words she had scribbled. Deep in his heart, he longed to comfort her. She'd had too many rough knocks this year.

He decided to go over to the park and find her. He didn't skate, but he could take his bicycle. The path was several miles long, but Danny had a feeling he knew exactly where she would be.

"How you doin', Miss Tulip?"

Jo glanced up, not surprised to see Angus Young sitting on the loading dock of the main building at the Golden Acres Retirement Village, smoking a cigarette. She often cut through their back parking lot to reach the head of the biking trail, and Angus was a familiar sight there. His full-time job was as the janitor of the high school where Jo taught home economics, but she knew he made ends meet by working here at the retirement community on the weekends.

"Hey, Angus," she said, slowing to a stop.

"I thought you'd be on your honeymoon by now."

Angus was in his fifties, hardworking and hard-faced, with a scar that ran under his nose to his chin, splitting his lips. Angus was built like a Mack truck, which made him a valuable employee both at the school and at the retirement village. He was the one who did the heavy lifting, and Jo knew he was popular with the residents here. According to him, he was often called in to move around furniture or boxes—and then gratefully rewarded with homemade soup or cookies.

"I guess you could say things didn't turn out exactly as I'd planned," Jo said.

"Problems at the airport?"

"Problems at the altar," she told him. "To put it simply, the wedding is off."

There. That wasn't so hard to say. Except that once she said it, out loud, to someone who hadn't been there, it made it seem so very real.

They chatted for a few minutes about the wedding disaster. As she described what happened, Angus grew indignant for her sake, assuring her it was Bradford's loss, not hers.

"No offense, Miss Tulip, but if I were thirty years younger, I'd be in line to take his place in front of that preacher. He was an idiot to pass up that opportunity."

"Maybe I was the idiot," she said, "for letting it get this far."

Their chat was interrupted by Angus' walkie-talkie, which crackled to life at his belt, telling him he was needed in another building.

"Gotta go," he said, stubbing out his cigarette. "You have a nice evening. Just remember: You deserve better than that. You deserve the best."

Danny pedaled slowly down the path, thinking about Jo Tulip as a little girl. He could still remember the day they met, the way she seemed so mature and in control even then. She was different than the other kids in town, and not just because she had lived all over the world. Jo was smart in ways that seemed new and different and exciting to Danny in his limited childhood experience. She was gifted in chemistry, like her grandfather, but she was also grounded in common sense, like her grandmother. As the heir apparent to their little newspaper column, Jo couldn't have been a better fit—or a more dedicated granddaughter.

Danny was still thinking about Jo as a child when he spotted her up ahead, now all grown up. Watching her roll toward him, he was struck—as he often was—by her beauty. She was tall but petite, with wavy blond hair that she could never quite keep under control and pretty hands that fluttered around like little birds when she talked.

"Hey," he said, as soon as she spotted him. "How are you doing?"

"I'm okay," she replied, slowing down and giving him a brave smile.

He turned his bike around so that they were both headed in the same direction. They rolled along, side by side, as Jo talked about how the autumn was slowly coming on and the days were already getting shorter. Danny let her talk, knowing she was dancing around the issue of the day. It wasn't until they neared the bottom of the hill that she stopped jabbering and got to the point.

"Thanks," she said finally as she skated.

"For what?"

"For not saying I told you so."

They were silent a bit longer as Danny struggled for the right words. He wanted so much to make this easier for her. *Lord, show me how to help her with this burden.*

"I wouldn't do that, Jo. It's not that kind of situation."

"Well, I appreciate it. More than you know."

He switched the gears on his bicycle as they started up a slight incline.

"The reception went very well, considering," he told her. "Your folks really know how to put on the charm."

"Of course," Jo said. "It's what they do best."

He glanced at her and then straight again.

"What?" she said.

"What what?"

"What is it you're not telling me?"

He pursed his lips, knowing he could never keep anything from her.

"I'm sorry, Jo. Your parents are leaving town tonight, as scheduled."

She nodded, a blank look coming into her eyes, but he knew what she was thinking: On what had to be one of the worst days of her life, her parents were not going to be there for her. Again.

Jo didn't speak for a while. They reached the part of the path where they would cut over to the cemetery, so Danny stopped the bike, climbed off, and started walking it instead. Silently, they made their way from the trail, through the bushes, and into the graveyard next to the park. Jo's grandparents were buried in a double plot near the end of a row. When they got there, Danny stood back and Jo did as she always did. She knelt beside the headstones to pull out the weeds that were trying to grow around the bases.

"This stupid milkweed," She said, grabbing frantically. "Why does it always grow back?" She ripped at the grass with desperation until she started crying. Then she just sat there on the ground and sobbed.

Despite having grown up in a house full of women, Danny wasn't good at these things. Finally, when it didn't look as though she was going to stop any time soon, he laid his bike on the grass and went to sit awkwardly on the ground next to her.

"Hey," he said, wishing that the perfect words would pop into his mouth. "Hey."

"I'm sorry, Danny," she said, sniffling. "It just hurts so bad!"

He put an arm around her and pulled her close as she buried her face into his shoulder.

"My parents have never cared, never worried, never paid one bit of attention, have they?" she asked as she sobbed.

"They're jerks."

"They live for themselves and no one else. I'm just a blip on their screen."

"Less than a blip."

"I'm less than a blip!"

She broke into fresh sobs. For a long time, they just sat there in the graveyard, the sun giving a muted late-afternoon glow to the rows of marble stones. It was pretty there, and peaceful and quiet. Danny could only wish Jo's grandparents were still alive to comfort her.

"At least you had your grandmother," he said, realizing that maybe just the mention of her would help. "She and your grandfather gave you twice as much love as both of your parents should have, combined."

That seemed to help. Jo nodded, swiping at her face with her hands.

"I know they're not here for you anymore," he continued, "but they were here when it was most important. They were here when you were growing up."

"You're right."

"They helped make up for the qualities your parents lacked."

"They did, didn't they?"

She cried a little bit more. Danny held her and slowly her sobs gave way to sniffles. Finally, when it was almost dark and she was silent again, he closed his eyes and prayed out loud.

"Father," he said softly, "we know that what happened today can be used by You for good. Please be with Bradford as he figures out what he wants. Be with Jo as she struggles with the ramifications of his actions. Be with me, as her friend, to show me how I can help. And keep our eyes only and completely on You."

He left off the "amen" in case she had anything to add. She was quiet for a moment and then she finished the prayer.

"Lord," she said, her voice sounding strangely determined, "please help me to learn who murdered Edna Pratt. Amen."

# TIPS FROM TULIP

*Dear Readers, this week as we feature classic letters from the past, enjoy this exchange from 1964.*

———————

### Dear Tulip,

This may sound crazy, but I'm writing to ask if too much house dust can kill a cat. This morning we buried our fourth pet in six months, and every one of them passed in exactly the same way, suddenly choking and wheezing until they couldn't breathe at all. My husband thinks maybe the house isn't clean enough, but I think he's wrong. After all, some animals live outside in the dirt and do just fine.

I am enclosing a photo of our beloved Spiffy, who was the first to go. I thought you might like to see a picture of him in the living room with our family, in happier times.

*Signed,*
*Mourning My Four-Legged*
*Friends in Ohio*

### Dear Mourning,

*I'm so glad you enclosed a photo, or this is one mystery that might never have been solved. In the lower right corner of the picture I noticed a lovely pot of dieffenbachia, a houseplant commonly known as dumb cane. You may be shocked to learn that dumb cane is poisonous to pets! My suspicion is that each of your four cats somehow ingested some and that's what killed them. Dieffenbachia paralyzes the vocal cords and can eventually asphyxiate.*

*My advice: Ditch the plant and then visit the pound to give it one more try. In the meantime, you might reach for that feather duster anyway and put it to work around the house. Dust may not be lethal to cats, but it has been known to kill a relationship or two.*

*Signed,*
*Tulip*

# 10

Jo woke up early on Sunday morning, glad to have an excuse for not going to church. There was simply no way she could face a room full of people so soon, many of whom had been there yesterday for her wedding and would still be wagging their tongues about it today. Last night she had poked around online until she found a phone number for Sally Sugarman down in Texas. Jo called and offered her condolences, and when Sally mentioned that she was flying in this morning, Jo had quickly offered to pick her up at the airport in nearby Moore City.

Of course, Jo realized, the irony was that she was supposed to have gone to the airport in the morning anyway to begin her honeymoon flight to Bermuda.

What a difference a day makes.

As Jo sailed up the highway on the 40-minute drive to the airport, she thought about the brief visit she'd had with her parents the night before, when they'd stopped by her house to say goodbye on their way out of town. They had described the reception in detail and gone on and on about the food and the wedding cake and the band. But when Jo said all she really wanted to know was what had gone wrong with Bradford, her mother surprised her by saying, "Oh, your father's already talked to him, dear. He's all right."

"He's all right?" Jo had said, stunned. "He's *all right?*"

"Cold feet," her father explained dismissively. "We're going to discuss it further at the office on Thursday."

"You're going to discuss it further? What does this have to do with you, Father? Why isn't he here discussing this with me?"

"Jo, calm down," her mother said.

"I won't calm down," she said, surprising even herself. "Why are you in the middle of this?"

Her father paced in the small living room, looking about, obviously wishing that somehow a wet bar or a liquor cart might magically appear. In times of stress he always reached out for a drink.

"Jo, like it or not, Bradford is my employee. He knew I would be upset with what happened, so he called to let me know that he was sorry but that he just got cold feet and he would explain further next week."

The conversation with her parents had degenerated from there, but the bottom line was that Bradford had thought a conversation with his boss should take priority over a conversation with the woman he had publicly humiliated by abandoning at the altar. Unbelievable.

Once her parents were gone, the entire group of bridesmaids had shown up to offer comfort and to talk about the reception, but there wasn't really all that much to say. Between all of them, they polished off a gallon of ice cream, and then they took one of Jo and Bradford's engagement photos and set it on fire, watching it burn in the empty fireplace as they sang "Na na na na, hey hey hey, goodbye."

It didn't help.

What did help was when they went through every single wedding present, card, and check, and organized them all for returning. Two of Jo's friends split the load between their cars, insisting that this was one of the official duties of wedding attendants—to make sure the gifts got returned in the case of a cancellation.

With that burden off her shoulders, Jo was determined to make the most of the next few days—the days she had already planned to be off work and out of town for her honeymoon. She didn't expect to hear from Bradford anytime soon—and she had no intention of trying to contact him herself. So for now, her derailed love life was utterly on hold. In the meantime, Jo planned to share the facts about Edna's death with Sally. Maybe they could put their heads together over who might have wanted Edna dead.

Jo reached the airport a few minutes early, found a parking spot, and made her way to the central area. She sat on a bench there and watched people milling around, both those coming out of the terminal and those in line to go through security to get in to the terminal.

She was feeling a little sorry for herself, imagining how different this morning would have been had yesterday not gone so horribly wrong. In her imagination, she could almost see Bradford's tall, blond form as he worked his way through the line for security, and she knew she would have been right there with him—as his wife.

Suddenly, she stood up, wondering if that *was* Bradford's tall, blond form working his way through the line for security. She moved forward, trying to get a better look at the man she had spotted, until a uniformed officer told her she could go no further without valid identification and an airline ticket.

She wanted to yell, to call out Bradford's name and see if the man would turn around, but he was too far away—not to mention that she knew such an act might get her in trouble with security.

"Bradford!" she called halfheartedly, her hands cupped around her mouth. "Bradford!"

The man didn't turn, but his line did move forward, around the corner, and then he was out of her sight completely.

"Jo? Jo Tulip?"

Jo spun around to see a woman in her forties, brown hair pulled back into a neat French twist, her navy suit a cut above usual travel attire.

Sally Sugarman.

Jo shook her hand, forced a smile, and tried not to seem as though she were dying inside. Had that been Bradford, getting on a plane?

More importantly: Had he been alone?

Heart pounding, Jo asked if Sally had any checked bags.

"Yes, two." she replied.

"Do you mind going ahead to baggage claim?" Jo asked. "I'm sorry, but there's something I need to do. I'll meet you down there."

"Sure," Sally said. "No problem."

Trying not to run, Jo made her way to the American Airlines counter, where she waited in a short line and then stepped forward when it was her turn. She explained she had a flight that morning to Bermuda that she wasn't going to be able to take, and she wondered what could be done about a refund.

Confirming her worst fears, the woman pulled up her reservation and stared at the computer screen with a puzzled look, typing in several different entries before finally looking up at Jo.

"I'm sorry, but this reservation was exchanged."

"Exchanged. For another person?"

The woman typed a few keys and then studied her screen.

"Not exactly. You were to be traveling with a Mr. Bradford Quinn?" she asked.

"Yes."

"Looks like he cashed in the two coach tickets and bought a single ticket to Bermuda, first class."

"He *what?*"

As the woman went over it again in detail, everything became remarkably clear: Though the wedding was off, Bradford had decided to take the honeymoon anyway. The agent explained Jo's options at this point, but finally she just held up a hand to stop her.

Rather than going all the way to New York City last night as Jo had assumed, Bradford must have driven to Moore City and stayed at their wedding night hotel and then shuttled over to the airport this morning to catch their honeymoon flight to Bermuda. Unbelievable!

"It doesn't matter," Jo said numbly. "Let him have it. I don't care."

Almost in a state of shock, Jo wandered through the terminal toward baggage claim. As angry and hurt as she was, she had to admit that Bradford was the one who had paid for the honeymoon in the first place. The tickets had gone on his credit card, as had the deluxe hotel, so in a way he was right to have taken the trip himself.

Oh, who was she kidding? It was all she could do not to run down the hallway and throttle him. Luckily for him, there was just a little matter of airline security standing in her way.

"Hey, Mac, ain't this your stop?"

Simon snapped awake, his eyelids scraping across his eyes like sandpaper. The bus was sitting idle, and the fellow who had been on board and sitting across the aisle since Charleston was poking him.

"This Jacksonville?" Simon asked, running a hand across his face.

"Yep. Just pulled in."

"Very good, then. Thanks."

"No problem."

Simon gathered his things and climbed off the bus, waiting beside the luggage compartment as the driver opened it. He pulled out his suitcase, gave the driver a nod, and headed for the nearest pay phone.

Before he got a meal or even cleaned himself up, Simon wanted to touch base with Wiggles. Wiggles was the only one of the gang who kept a steady address and phone number. He lived in a tiny, one-bedroom bungalow his mother had left to him when she died years before—not that the joint was any big prize. In fact, the place was so close to the tracks that a passing freight train could rattle the dishes right off the shelves. But at least it was permanent. Wiggles lived off disability, spent his days walking the beaches with a metal detector looking for lost change, and served as a sort of ad hoc clearing house for the comings and goings of Florida's grifting underbelly.

Simon got Wiggles' answering machine, so he hung up without leaving a message, feeling at loose ends. The growl in his stomach told him he was long overdue for a meal. He used the bus station bathroom to wash his face and brush his teeth, and then, wanting to make the money in his pocket last as long as possible, he started walking in the general direction of Wiggles' house. Simon knew he would come across a grocery store in a few blocks, and that he could probably make do with a box of crackers and some sardines or tuna or potted meat—whatever was on sale. Maybe if he slipped Wiggles a twenty, Wiggles would let him crash at his place tonight. Maybe for a hundred, he'd let him stay there all week.

At church Danny's mother was the first to corner him when he walked in the door.

"Did you see it?" she asked, eyes wide. "Why didn't you tell me?"

"See what?" he replied, motioning for her to hold the door open so he could carry in his heavy drum bags. Their family group was performing in the service, and they had just enough time to set up and run through the song before the sanctuary was opened to the congregation for early arrivals.

"The newspaper!" she said. "You didn't tell me about Jo and the dead body. Poor dear. I can't believe she had to deal with all of that on her wedding day. Well, her *almost* wedding day."

She held out the paper and Danny took it, skimming the article that was front and center of page 1. "Household Hints Expert Guides

Detectives in Investigation," the headline read. The paper had probably played up the household hints angle because Jo's column was one of their regular features. Danny read the story, which was about how Jo went around the crime scene and explained the oddities to the police. It said nothing about her experience the night before, nor did it mention any suspicion of murder.

"Hi, Danny, how's it going?"

He glanced up to see his sister Denise and her husband, Ray.

"Hey, Danny," Ray said, "we watching the game at your house tomorrow?"

"Sure. You bring the dip."

"Are you kidding? You think I'd eat something out of that penicillin factory you call a refrigerator?"

"Oh, yeah," Danny replied. "You got no qualms about eating all my chips though, huh, Ray?"

Denise opened her case and pulled out her guitar.

"Danny, when are you going to give Marci a call? She really had a good time on your date."

Danny rolled his eyes.

"I took Marci out as a favor, Denise. Please don't expect me to do it again."

"You didn't like her?"

"She was nice. But there were no, uh, sparks, you know?"

"Fine. I'll tell her to stop calling you."

"Thanks. Just don't hurt her feelings."

Their mother hurried over, microphone in her hand.

"All right, no more chatting," she said. "They'll be opening the doors in half an hour, so we have to hustle if we want to run through the song."

One by one, Danny's other sisters came in as they worked to set up their instruments. Forming the group known as Regeneration, the entire family had been making music together for years. When Danny was a boy, his mother's dream was to be like a Christian version of the Partridge Family, a sort of roving band made up of her and her four children. All five of them sang beautifully, though mom Riva sang the lead. The rest of them provided backup vocals, and Danny was percussion, Denise was guitar, Diana was bass, and Donna was keyboards. Danny's dad, a jovial fellow who hadn't a musical bone in his body, served as their manager and number one promoter.

Their family band was good, but they had never found much success beyond the local level. As the kids got older, one by one they lost interest and became involved in other extracurricular activities. Rather than dissolve the group completely, they changed its focus. Nowadays, instead of trying to pursue big dreams of stardom, they were simply committed to practicing one night a week and performing three or four times per month at churches and local festivals. It made for a nice hobby for all of them, and it also served as a way to keep in each other's lives on a steady basis, week after week. Danny enjoyed it because he had a feeling that otherwise too much time might pass between visits. His sisters were all married with kids or kids on the way, and they were a busy bunch.

"Everybody ready?" Riva asked, stepping in front of the microphone. "Let's praise the Lord through song, shall we?"

Danny gave them a downbeat and they were off, launching into the smooth vocal harmonies that truly were a joyful noise.

"Is your car new?" Sally Sugarman asked as they rolled along, running one hand along the shiny leather arm rest.

"No, it's about six years old," Jo replied.

"Wow, it's so clean. You should see the inside of my car. Most of the time it looks like a tornado came through. But even when it's neat, it's not clean. Not like this."

"The secret is saddle soap."

"Saddle soap?"

Jo watched the speedometer reach sixty-five, and then she clicked on the cruise control and took her foot from the gas.

"I have a whole routine I go through, but my best trick is cleaning the seats with saddle soap and a damp sponge. Works great."

"What else is in your routine?"

"Well, you know those little scratches you can get in the clear plastic?" Jo asked, gesturing toward the dials on her dashboard. "If you rub in some baby oil, they disappear."

"Really."

"The biggest mistake I see people make is when they clean the inside of the windows. Most store-bought glass cleaners are ammonia based, but the ammonia can really dry out the plastic, rubber, and vinyl around the glass. For car interiors, I always recommend vinegar in water, like eight parts vinegar to one part water. It works just as well, but it doesn't hurt the lining."

"I see."

"There are a lot more steps when you get down to it, but you should always finish off the dashboard with a silicone-free UV-blocking interior protectant. That prevents cracking and fading."

"Oh."

Sally seemed to have lost interest, and for the next few miles they rode along in silence.

"I'm sorry," Jo said finally. "Here you are coming to town to handle your mother's funeral arrangements, and I'm rattling on about car care."

*I'm also trying to keep my mind from Bradford and my own anger,* Jo thought but did not say.

"No," Sally replied, shaking her head. "Don't be sorry, Jo. It helps to take my mind off this tragedy."

"It can't be easy for you."

"It's not. And it comes at a really bad time. I'm up for reelection in two months. This is the last thing I have time for right now."

Jo blinked, startled by the harshness of her statement. Her mother's death was a tragedy because it was...*inconvenient?*

"At least the funeral home has been very helpful," Sally said. "We made most of the arrangements over the phone yesterday, and if we can get the final details ironed out this evening, they're going to go ahead with a small memorial service tomorrow morning."

"That's fast."

"Well, I'm not expecting a big crowd. I just want to get it over and done with as soon as possible."

Over and done with as soon as possible. Was that a fitting end for anyone?

"I didn't know your mother very well," Jo said finally.

"She sure knew you. She knew your column, at least. She never missed it."

"I gathered as much. What was she like, as a person?"

Hesitantly at first, Sally began sharing about her Pittsburgh childhood. Jo was surprised to hear her describe Edna as an unaffectionate, remote woman who was more concerned with keeping a clean house than with showing love to her only child. According to Sally, her father had a bit more parenting skills, though he, too, was dead now.

"My dad passed away about ten years ago," Sally continued. "My mom ended up in Mulberry Glen when she remarried a few years later, and then her second husband died of lung disease a few years after that. She's been alone since. He didn't have any children, so the house went to her and now to me. Her lawyer agreed to meet with me this afternoon. I'll know more of the details then."

"What will you do with the house?"

"Sell it, of course. You think I want to move to Mulberry Glen, Pennsylvania?"

Jo didn't respond, and after a moment, Sally seemed to realize how she had sounded.

"Oh, gosh, I'm sorry," she said. "There's nothing wrong with your town. It's just that I have a whole life down in Texas. I'm happy there. I've got a strong career and a great husband and two wonderful kids. It's just very difficult right now to take time out from my campaign to come up here and settle all of these details. My mother was in perfect health, so I doubt she had done much to prepare for her death. I guess I'll have to hire someone local to clear the house out for me, sell her car, things like that."

"Sometimes it can be therapeutic to clear out the possessions of a loved one who has passed away," Jo said. "After my grandmother died, I handled all of her old papers and belongings, and it gave me a real sense of closure. I even came to gain a whole new picture of her. I found a box of love letters in the attic to her from my grandfather, and I treasure them."

Sally took a deep breath, held it, and then let it out slowly.

"Ah, but that's the difference," she said softly. "You treasure them because you obviously treasured your grandmother. My situation's a lot more complicated."

"Complicated how?"

"Because I most certainly did not treasure my mother. Didn't even like her very much. It's a lot harder to follow up behind someone who's died when your overall feeling is that you just want to be done with it and out of there."

# 11

Simon sat on Wiggles' porch for hours, waiting for the man to get home. Simon knew he could have easily picked the lock and made himself at home inside, but he didn't want to start things off on the wrong foot. He really needed a friend right now.

Finally, he heard the distinct rattle of Wiggles' old station wagon. He stood and waited as it rumbled up the street, over the patch of weeds that served as a driveway, and to a stop beside the bungalow.

"You still got that old heap of junk?" Simon asked with a grin as his friend got out of the car.

Wiggles looked the same as always, short and stooped and pasty, with a few long strands of hair that fought to cover his white head. True to his name, Wiggles' body nearly vibrated from head to toe with steady tremors, the aftereffect of a bad case of childhood meningitis.

"Well, Simon," Wiggles said, slamming the car door. "Ain't seen you in months."

"Yes, I've been busy. But that's over now. Thought I'd see what's going on here in Florida."

Wiggles came up onto the porch and began the long, excruciating process of pulling out his keychain, finding the house key, and sliding it into the lock. Simon learned a long time ago not to rush Wiggles or offer to do it for him. In certain ways, the man could be very stubborn.

"You looking for somewhere to crash?" Wiggles asked, never one to beat around the bush. " 'Cause it don't come free and your word ain't worth the sound it makes coming out of your mouth."

"I know, I know," Simon said. "Sorry about that. I really did mean to send you what I owed you."

"It's never too late to pay the piper."

Simon reached for the wad of cash in his pocket, most of which he had already taken out and slipped into a few well-placed, hidden pouches in his suitcase. He peeled off a twenty from what was left and held it out to Wiggles.

"Nice try," Wiggles said, glancing toward him and then returning his attention to the door lock. "You owe me sixty. Plus another hundred up front if you're planning on staying here this week."

"You drive a hard bargain, my friend."

"And I know darn well you don't show up here unless you got no place else to go. A hundred sixty pays back what you owe me and gives you a week's lodging. Deal?"

"How 'bout a hundred fifty?" Simon said. "For old times' sake."

Wiggles eyed him suspiciously.

"Sure," he said finally. "A hundred fifty. But that means you gotta take out the trash and do all the dishes—the whole time you're here."

"Danny, what's wrong with you today?"

He looked up at his sister Denise and shook his head.

"What?"

"You're so distracted. What's going on?"

Danny and his sisters and their children were in The Depot, an ice cream parlor in downtown Mulberry Glen. The far end of the room housed a full electric train set, and the kids thought working the buttons on the train was a bigger treat than the ice cream. Danny and his sisters came here sometimes on Sunday afternoons because it entertained the kids and gave the grown-ups a chance to chat. Right now, the place was empty except for their group and the novel-reading teenager behind the counter.

"I don't know," he said finally, dipping his spoon into caramel sauce and whipped cream. "I'm worried about Jo. She didn't come to church this morning and she's not answering her phone."

"Can you blame her? If I were her, I'd be so embarrassed I wouldn't show my face around town for at least a week."

Danny shook his head.

"No, Jo's not like that. She's just…"

His voice faded off and he shrugged. He didn't even know what he wanted to say. Truth be told, Danny always got a little agitated when he couldn't find Jo; he figured it tapped into all those times when they were children and she would disappear on him without any warning. Rarely did they get a chance to say goodbye back then. He could remember waking up and throwing on clothes and running over to her house to play—only to be told by her grandmother that Jo's parents had whisked her away on yet another extended trip.

"I'm sorry, dear, Jo is gone," the kindly woman would say. "But she might be back by Christmas."

Crestfallen, Danny would make his way home, kicking the dirt as he went, feeling so hurt by her horrible parents who disrupted his little world without a second thought. He was a grown man now, but sometimes he still felt like that lost, brokenhearted little boy.

"I wouldn't worry about Jo," Donna said. "She's the most resourceful woman I know."

"You're right," Danny said. "But this was a pretty big blow in a year that was tough all the way around."

The sisters looked at each other, some undercurrent of understanding passing between them. He squinted, looking from one to the other. All three had the same attractive features, big hair, big eyes—not to mention the same strange look on their faces.

"What?" he asked finally. "What are you not saying?"

Denise shrugged.

"I don't know, Danny. Just that now that the fiancé is out of the way, maybe it's time for the real romance to begin."

"The real romance?"

"You and Jo," Donna said, stifling a smile.

Danny put down his spoon, picked up his napkin, and wiped his mouth.

"Jo is my best friend," he said calmly. "She has always been my best friend."

"Call it what you want, bro," Denise said. "But I hate to tell you: You've been in love with her for a while now."

Danny looked over at his nieces and nephews, who were arguing about whose turn it was to push the button that would raise the bridge. Over the years he and Jo had had to defend their friendship plenty of times, but never to his own family.

"What makes you think I'm in love?" he asked. "That's crazy."

"Is it?" Diana pressed. "Why did you buy Grandma and Grandpa's house when they wanted to move to the retirement home?"

"Because it was cheap! They gave me a great price."

"They gave you only slightly less than market value and you know it. You bought that house because Jo encouraged you to do it. She wanted the two of you to be neighbors. Just like when we were kids, the way you used to stay at Grandma and Grandpa's whenever she was in town."

"I used to stay there because she and I had fun together. It seemed easier to sleep over at Grandma and Grandpa's than to have Mom drive me over there day after day."

"Uh-huh."

"Do you know what it's like to be the only boy in a house full of sisters? Going over there was the only way to keep the three of you from interfering with my life!"

"Whatever."

"Besides, Jo and I aren't kids anymore," Danny said. "We each have our own lives."

"Who do you call when you have a problem?" Diana said.

"Who do you run to when you have good news?" Donna added.

"Why do you think you're feeling so funky today?" Denise concluded. "I'll tell you why. Because you can't find your true love. You're lost without her."

The women giggled hysterically.

"Lost without her," he said, growing angry. Suddenly, Danny's appetite disappeared. He set down his spoon, put his napkin on the table, and pushed back his chair. "Let me tell you something."

They waited respectfully, listening, biting their lips to hold in their smiles.

"Jo Tulip is one of my favorite people in the world, that is true. But we are just friends. We always were just friends, always will be *just friends*. Think whatever you want, but my relationship with Jo will never be anything more than it is right now."

With that, he stood and grabbed his jacket.

"I gotta go," he said. "See you at Tuesday's rehearsal."

Angrily, he stomped out of the ice cream parlor. As he went, he expected to hear at least one of them calling after him. Instead, not surprisingly, they all burst into giggles. Good grief.

Just like he said, the three of them were always interfering with his life!

Jo sat at the desk in Edna Pratt's bedroom, flipping through a photo album. She put it back and pulled out the next item on the shelf, a small scrapbook filled with memorabilia. Jo had been at Edna's house for most of the morning, helping Sally get a handle on the job at hand and getting a good look at Edna's "stuff," all in a fruitless attempt to find some sort of sign of foul play. Jo hadn't found anything suspicious, and she still hadn't brought up the subject she most wanted to pursue—the notion that Edna had been murdered. Somehow, the mood had not yet been right for introducing such a radical thought.

For the last hour, Jo had concentrated on the bedroom, clearing out the closet and then the dresser, making neat piles on the big bed. Sally was in the dining room with her mother's lawyer, where they were going through estate papers. From what Jo could hear, nothing sounded complicated or surprising. It seemed much like when her own grandmother had died.

She hoped Sally and the lawyer would be finished soon, and by then Jo would have gotten up the nerve to approach the subject of murder. Jo wasn't sure why she hadn't brought it up already. It was just that Sally seemed so bereft when they finally arrived at the house. Despite all of her bravado in the car, she had started crying, and after that Jo hadn't had the heart to talk about it.

Jo put back the scrapbook and pulled out another one, surprised to find that it was filled with newspaper and magazine clippings—mostly Tips from Tulip columns. Edna had highlighted some parts, circled others, and even made notes in the margin. Jo smiled as she went through them, pleased that Edna had taken her work so seriously.

The dining room chairs scraped back, which was Jo's cue that the lawyer was ready to go. She listened as Sally walked him to the door. He again expressed his shock and dismay at learning of Edna's death, saying he knew now why Edna had never shown up for their appointment on Saturday.

"Appointment on Saturday?" Sally asked. "You mean yesterday?"

"Yes," the lawyer replied. "Your mother called me Friday night and said she wanted to see me the next day, even if she had to pay extra for a weekend appointment. We scheduled it for noon, but she never showed. I later learned of her death, of course, and then it made sense."

"Do you know what she wanted to see you about?"

"No, I don't. I assume she just wanted to make sure her affairs were in order. Fortunately, they were, even without the appointment. Your mother was extremely organized."

As she showed him out, they said a few more things Jo couldn't quite hear, and then, a moment later, Sally appeared in the bedroom doorway looking drained.

"Well, that was exhausting," she said. "But at least it looks like everything's in order."

"Did I hear him say your mother had an appointment with him yesterday?"

"Yes. What do you want to bet he'll bill me for the time even though she never showed?" Sally sat on the bed and leaned against the headboard.

"But don't you think that's odd?" Jo pressed. "Why would she call him on a Friday night and insist on an appointment the very next day?"

Sally shrugged.

"That's how my mother was," she said. "The minute she was ready to make a move on something, she expected everyone else to jump."

*I think your mother was murdered*, Jo wanted to say. But something inside made her tone it down.

"You know, I overheard something here on Friday night. Your mother was having an argument with someone. A very loud argument."

"My mother? What were you doing here?"

"I wasn't. I was out jogging. But as I ran past the house, I could hear yelling."

"Who was it?" Sally asked, seeming genuinely intrigued. "What were they saying?"

"I don't know. I couldn't tell. But I have to be honest. When I learned the next morning that your mother had died, my first thought was that she had been murdered."

Much to Jo's surprise, Sally threw back her head and laughed.

"Murdered!" she cried. "My mother? I tell you what, if anybody was going to kill that old broad, it would have been *me* years ago."

She was kidding, but suddenly Jo felt rather uncomfortable. "Listen, Sally," she said, leaning forward. "There's been enough fishy stuff here to warrant a closer look by the police, but to them it's a done deal. Your mom's death was an accident, case closed. I happen to disagree."

"Fishy stuff? Like what?"

Jo tried to explain, repeating her story about the argument, her strange encounter with the car, and then the utter implausibility of Edna making such a rudimentary mistake with the cleansers. When she was finished, she had hoped to see suspicion alive in Sally's eyes as well. Unfortunately, that wasn't the case.

"In a way, I think how my mom died is very symbolic," Sally mused, shaking her head.

"Symbolic?"

"She lived to clean. Now she has died by cleaning as well."

Jo hesitated, studying Sally's face. Why wasn't she buying into her theories?

"I'm sorry," Sally added. "Obviously, my mother and I had plenty of unresolved issues."

Jo waited a beat, understanding that Sally obviously wasn't willing to entertain the thought of murder. Jo decided to drop it for the time being. Maybe she would bring it up again tomorrow, after the funeral.

"I must be nuts," Sally said softly, "inflicting all of this on you. I hardly knew you before today, and now here you've gone and done all of this for me. I don't know how I can ever repay you."

"It's okay," Jo shrugged. "I guess the Lord put our paths together for a reason. This wasn't exactly the best day of my life, either."

She began to tell Sally the story of the aborted wedding, followed by the sad tale of her trip to the airport. The more she told, the funnier it all began to sound, and by the time she finished, they were both crying from laughter. Though there was at least a twenty-year difference in their ages, they shared the common bond of having been raised by truly reprehensible mothers. Somehow, that made them sisters.

"Oh, Jo, you're not kidding," Sally said, "you're almost in as bad a shape as I am."

"I know!"

They laughed again, and it felt good, in a sad sort of way.

"Can I make a crazy suggestion?" Sally said. "You don't have to answer me right now, but think about it."

"Okay."

"As you know, I have to fly home tomorrow afternoon. To be honest, Jo, I'd like to hire you to clear out my mother's things."

"Clear out your mother's things?"

"Yes. Clear out her closets, pack up her papers. Ship me whatever you think might be important or valuable, and get rid of the rest. I really don't want to fool with all of this. Financially, I could make it very worth your while."

Jo sat back, thinking she couldn't have asked for a better opportunity to solve the murder.

"What can I say, Sally? I'd be happy to do it."

Danny spent the evening locked in his darkroom, making prints from some shots he had taken last month at Gettysburg. Though his color photos were processed at a lab in town, he preferred to develop and print the black-and-white film himself, using the equipment he'd gotten as a college graduation gift from his parents. His darkroom was very well stocked, and he loved nothing more than to lose himself in the creative process of printing pictures.

The final series was very exciting, the view from atop Cemetery Hill. He had taken several hours to set up the shot, and when he was finally ready, the setting sun had burst through the clouds, creating an amazing image. Danny had snapped up two rolls in ten minutes, capturing the scene in a way he'd never been able to do before. Now, as one print after another sprang to life in the developer tray, he knew this was some of the best work he had ever done.

If only his income could keep pace with his output.

Danny worked until midnight, glad to have the distraction of his photography to keep him from thinking about Jo. His sisters were so far off the mark it wasn't funny. Danny *did* love Jo, but not that way. Too bad for them if they didn't understand that.

And even if he did love her, it could never work. He was a slob; she was a neat freak. He was a creative spirit; she was scientific. He was gregarious; she was more of a loner. They were just too different.

Danny hung the last dripping print over the sink, made sure his paper was sealed up tight, opened the door, and breathed in the fresh air of the hallway. A few hours spent in close quarters with all those chemicals was a bit stifling.

Rubbing his sore back, he walked down the hall to the kitchen, realizing he was suddenly ravenous. He hadn't eaten since the ice cream parlor, so he went to the freezer and pulled out a frozen dinner. He was too tired to cook, but he could certainly pop something in the microwave.

As he waited for the ding that would tell him it was done, he stood at the window beside the kitchen table. He couldn't see much in the darkness, of course, but a light was on in Jo's office. After being unaccounted for all day, was she finally there?

Danny reached for the phone. Though it was getting late, he dialed her number.

"So you're home?" he said when she answered, hating the tight sound of his own voice. "I was worried about you."

"Yes," she said, "I'm here. You wanna come hang out? I'm just going through some old papers."

"I guess," he grunted. Then he hung up the phone, a surge of frustration overtaking him.

Was he being too clingy? Or was she wrong to simply disappear and not expect him to be upset? Was one of them taking the other one for granted?

He left his meal cooking in the microwave and stomped over, ready to yell at her for being so inconsiderate. All he wanted was to know she was okay. Was that too much to ask? Instead, she had simply disappeared, leaving him to worry all day for no reason.

"What am I doing?" he muttered as he got to her door. She had been inconsiderate, yes, but he was being ridiculous. Suddenly, "hanging out" while Jo went through old papers was the last thing he wanted to do. He knocked on the door, told her he wasn't feeling well, and that he had changed his mind.

"I'll see you tomorrow," he said. "Unless you decide to disappear off the face of the planet again, of course."

Then he turned on his heel and stomped back toward his house, not even giving Jo a chance to respond.

He wasn't even thinking about the fence, and the night was so dark he was upon it before he realized it. The rail caught him right at shin level, sending him toppling onto the ground with a thud. Muttering under his breath, he stood, brushed himself off, and then limped the rest of the way to his house.

In the kitchen he could see that he had scraped both knees and one elbow, drawing blood in all three places. Rather than tend to his wounds right away, he simply washed his hands, took his meal out of the microwave, sat down, and shoveled it into his mouth.

He wasn't feeling any less angry ten minutes later when Jo tapped lightly at his back door and stepped inside. She apologized for not touching base with him earlier in the day, and she thanked him for keeping tabs on her.

"With Nana gone, you're really the only one who cares if I'm coming or going," she said. "I'm sorry if I abused that."

Before he could form an apology in reply, she noticed his wounds.

Jo ooed and ahhed over the injuries, insisting that she help clean and bandage them. Making herself at home, she bustled around in his bathroom, not saying a word about what a mess it was the way she usually did. After a few moments she emerged with the items she needed to play nursemaid. Danny was silent through the whole exchange, his mind reeling from thoughts and feelings he didn't understand. Jo was so sweet and apologetic that he felt his anger melt into something else.

Something infinitely more disturbing.

She put everything on the floor and knelt at his feet, placing a small tub of soapy water just behind his ankle. She gently lifted one of his legs and then rinsed the scraped knee, using a clean washcloth to drizzle water over the wound. Once both knees were clean and patted dry, she applied antibacterial ointment and then wide Band-Aids.

When she finished tending to his knees, she started in on the elbow. That was a much smaller scrape, though she went through the same process as before. As she worked, her head was bent over his arm in concentration, close enough that he could smell the incredible scent of her hair. Were he to lean forward just a few inches, he realized, he could actually kiss her on the forehead.

Instead, he sat back and closed his eyes and admitted what his family had known all along.

Danny was in love with his best friend.

## TIPS FROM TULIP

**Dear Readers,** *this week as we feature classic letters from the past, enjoy this exchange from 1968.*

---

### Dear Tulip,

On the weekends my teenage son and his friends always get really hungry late at night after my husband and I have gone to bed. By morning, my refrigerator has been raided, the kitchen's a mess, and all of the leftover food has dried in the pots and pans. How can I get these pots clean? I've tried using steel wool, but the pads make such a mess on the sink when they rust that I hate to keep them around.

Do you have any suggestions? Also, these midnight food raids leave the strangest odor in our basement rec room. I'm wondering if we should install an exhaust fan.

—*Frustrated Mom*

### Dear Mom,

*To keep a steel wool pad from rusting, simply put it in a plastic bag and stick it in the freezer. The next time you need it, take it out and reuse; it will be rust free.*

*But, please, be a Smart Chick! Does the term "munchies" mean anything to you? I'm afraid your son and his friends have a problem, and it's a lot bigger than a few dirty pots. Actually, "pot" is more like it, since I have a feeling that's where the odor is coming from. I suggest you contact your pastor or school guidance counselor for help with your son's drug problem. Immediately.*

—*Tulip*

# 12

Jo sat in her car in the funeral home parking lot and watched people going inside. Edna Pratt's funeral was scheduled to start at 10:00 A.M., but before Jo had the nerve to slip into the back of the service, she wanted to know who else was going to be there.

She had kept a low profile since being stood up at the altar on Saturday, and she didn't relish walking into a crowd now where she might become the main topic of conversation and gossip. But she felt that she owed it to Sally and to Edna to be there. Since Edna was older and had belonged to a different church than her own, Jo didn't think she would know many of the attendees.

So far, it looked as if the service wasn't going to draw much of a crowd. Of the seven or so people who had already gone inside, Jo only recognized one, and she was just the woman who worked the counter at the dry cleaner.

As the time got closer, a few more people drifted in. Finally, a car pulled up and parked behind Jo. She watched in her side window as two women got out. Jo recognized them as Iris Chutney and Louise Parker, two ladies who went to her own church.

The two women walked past Jo's car, deep in conversation and obviously not aware that she was there. Though she couldn't make out everything they were saying, she thought she heard Mrs. Chutney say something about calling the police.

Jo froze, wondering if she had heard correctly.

"...not a word about the money," Mrs. Parker said. "Not yet."

Jo couldn't hear any more, but her heart was pounding. She waited a beat and then followed the women into the funeral home, choosing an empty seat directly behind them. They were so wrapped up in their conversation that they hadn't even noticed she was there.

"We just have to talk to Simon," Mrs. Parker whispered to her friend. "He'll tell us what to do."

"But I told you," Iris whispered back, "I've been trying to reach him since we found out Edna was dead. He's nowhere to be found! I don't think we can afford to wait."

Whoever this Simon fellow was, he hadn't come to the funeral. That was clear by the women's behavior as they craned their necks to study the small crowd, whispering back and forth. Mrs. Parker kept glancing toward the door, but only two other people came in before the service started, obviously neither of them the man in question.

Sally was seated by herself in the front pew, and Jo felt a surge of pity for her for having to do this all alone. At least when Jo's grandmother died, she had had both her parents and some aunts and uncles and cousins to sit with. Theirs wasn't a large family, but no one had to sit by themselves, not like this.

The service was short and sweet, and Jo realized about halfway through that the minister hadn't really known Edna Pratt at all. He spoke in vague, general terms about the Lord's will and seasons of life, but there was nothing of Edna's personality or her life details in his sermon. Jo thought about all the things Sally had said the day before, and she had a feeling it was true: Edna had had her daily swim at the Y and her household cleaning to keep her busy, but otherwise, it didn't seem as if she had used her time on earth all that well. Certainly, she hadn't been very loving or giving.

Suddenly, Jo had a vision of the future, a flash of how her own funeral might look. She'd had some good friends, of course, but in the end, what if she, too, died all alone, socks on her hands, cleaning miniblinds? The thought was enough to bring tears to her eyes, which she quickly wiped away. How pathetic was that, to come to someone's funeral but sit there and cry about your own?

"Look at the ducky!" Danny cried, shaking a bright yellow rubber duck above the camera. "He's saying 'quack quack quack'!"

The little boy saw the duck and grinned. Danny snapped the camera at just the right moment, capturing his expression perfectly.

"How about that one?" Danny asked, pointing toward the monitor.

The high-strung young mother studied it intently and then nodded.

"Good," she finally pronounced. "That's a keeper."

It was about time.

Danny had already taken nearly twenty shots of the kid, and this was only the third shot the mother had deemed acceptable.

"One more pose and then we're finished," he said, gesturing for her to pick up the little boy while he moved around the things under the blanket. He had suggested a variety of unique poses and props, but she wanted nothing but the standard sitting, just like the first two customers of the day.

Did no one have any imagination besides him?

The only reason Danny kept the part-time job at the studio—besides the fact that he needed the money, of course—was because it came with a fringe benefit that other part-time jobs didn't: use of the color printer.

As long as he supplied his own paper, he was allowed free access to the FSX 4000, a state-of-the-art color photo printer that put out the most consistently high-quality prints he had ever seen. For the sake of his career, he didn't mind waving around a few rubber duckies a couple days a week.

*At least I don't have to fool with the sales end of it,* he thought as he finally finished. He thanked the woman, patted the kid's head, and walked down the hall to the computer room. Tiffany would take things from there, sitting the mother down and pitching the full package. Tiffany worked almost purely on commission, so she was very persuasive. According to her, her own income had gone up significantly since Danny started working there because he was such a good photographer. The better the pictures, the more likely people were to buy.

Danny wasn't sure the sittings this morning were up to his usual standard, however. He was so distracted he could hardly think straight. The whole revelation about Jo last night had thrown him for a major loop.

*What am I going to do?*

All morning he had carried around a sick sort of feeling in the pit of his stomach. Why did it have to be love?

*More importantly, what is this going to do to our friendship?*

Danny had heard plenty of stories about friends who became couples and ended up breaking up, ruining both the love relationship and the friendship. He didn't think he could handle losing Jo. Their relationship was the single most important one in his life.

*Well, the* second *most important,* he amended. God came first, of course. Come to think of it, he hadn't brought this matter to God yet. As Tiffany and the customer interacted down the hall, he closed his eyes and bowed his head and began to pray silently to himself.

*I want Your will for my life, Father,* he prayed. *But does that will really include a different kind of relationship with Jo than what we have now?*

When the funeral service was over, the minister invited those present to come to the cemetery where Edna would be laid to rest. Jo offered to drive Sally, which made hers the first car in line behind the hearse.

Once they reached the cemetery, among the smaller crowd at the graveside were Iris Chutney and Louise Parker. When the service was finished, they offered their condolences to Sally upon the death of her mother.

"So how did you know Edna?" Jo asked as they were just about to walk away.

The ladies glanced at each other, something passing between them.

"We were in a club together," Mrs. Parker volunteered finally.

"A club?" Sally asked. "What kind of club?"

The women shared a glance yet again, this time with a panicked, deer-in-the-headlights look on their faces.

"Bunco!" Mrs. Parker said. "Edna was a great Bunco player."

The women quickly turned to go. Jo watched them leave with one thought on her mind: That bit about Bunco was a bunch of bunk.

"You okay, Danny?"

Danny glanced up to see Tiffany in the doorway of the computer room, one elbow propped on the doorframe. She was wearing low-riding jeans and a shirt that barely reached her waist, so when she stood like that, the effect was several inches of bare stomach and abdomen, lean and tanned. Danny looked away, turning his attention to the computer. He wasn't interested in Tiffany, but she was an attractive girl—and she had been making it clear for a while now that she was interested in him.

"I'm fine," he said. "Are they gone?"

"Yeah. She decided on the Pride and Joy package. Not too shabby."

Tiffany walked closer and slid the paperwork into the "pending" tray. Even from five feet away, Danny could smell her perfume—a cheap knockoff that reeked strongly of citrus.

"You seem really distracted today," Tiffany said, sliding onto the desktop and twirling a lock of hair around one finger. "Long weekend, maybe?"

"Tough weekend," he replied. "Jo's wedding didn't go exactly as planned."

He gave his coworker the basic rundown, leaving out the more personal details. The story was all over town by now anyway, so he wasn't exactly betraying a confidence. Tiffany seemed fascinated by the tale, but then again she was always quite attentive whenever they chatted, all eyes and ears no matter what he was saying. Sometimes he wondered if she was really listening at all, or if her exaggerated reactions were simply some sort of knee-jerk, man-catching response. A lot of what she did seemed quietly calculated, from the clothes she wore to the hints she dropped to the double entendres that filled every conversation. Danny had the secret notion that she kept the heads of her biggest conquests stuffed and mounted over her fireplace like a hunter.

"What do our appointments look like for the rest of the day?" he asked, changing the subject. "I've got some new shots of my own I need to get out to the Stock Shop."

"You've got a corporate sitting in half an hour," she said, "followed by a kid and his dog. Then I think you're free."

"Interesting," he replied. "I've had some ideas I want to try with a pet sitting."

Tiffany shook her head, her little bell-like earrings tinkling among her artfully teased hair.

"Keep it simple, hon," she chided him with a smile. "I keep telling ya, even as good as you are, you can't get too creative with this hometown crowd."

Sally invited Jo to lunch, so they drove back to the funeral home, parked there, and then walked halfway up the block to a small diner. As they waited for their food, Jo broached the topic, once again, of murder.

"Jo, do you really have suspicions about my mother's death?"

Jo put both hands in her lap and looked at Sally earnestly.

"I do. Sally, I'm convinced your mother was murdered. A woman who was so precise with all of her household knowledge would never do something as elementary as mixing chlorine bleach and ammonia. Never. A lot of folks might make that mistake, but not Edna Pratt. Not from what I've seen of her house, of her notes."

"But why would someone want to kill my mother? She didn't have any enemies."

"Are you sure?"

Sally had already told Jo that she only talked to her mother on the phone about once a month or even every other month. If they had such little contact, how would she even know?

"How about the name 'Simon'?" Jo asked, recalling the heated conversation she had overheard between the Mrs. Chutney and Mrs. Parker at the funeral. "Did your mother know anyone by that name?"

Sally shook her head.

"We used to have a relative named Simon, but he died when I was a child. I'm not aware of anyone else by that name. Why do you ask?"

"Just a conversation I overheard at the funeral. And speaking of the funeral, didn't you think those two women were a bit odd when we asked how they knew your mother?"

"Frankly, I didn't notice a thing."

The waiter showed up with their food. By the time he left the table, Sally had visibly collected herself. There was a hard glint to her eye, though she spoke in soft, staccato tones.

"Jo," she said, leaning forward, "let me tell you the only thing more inconvenient than having my mother die in the middle of a campaign."

"What's that?"

"My mother being *murdered* in the middle of a campaign. Something like this could derail everything I've worked so hard for."

"What are you saying?" Jo asked softly. "You're going to sweep this under the rug?"

Sally sat back, patted her mouth with her napkin, and set the napkin on the table.

"You'd better believe it."

"But Sally—"

"Jo, please. My mom was a normal, small-town gal who liked to swim every day and play Bunco with the girls and occasionally give herself a cucumber-honey facial. Who would kill someone like that? We've already determined that nothing was stolen from the house. I know my mother didn't have any big money or other valuable assets. What other motives could there have been?"

Jo closed her eyes, the certainty of a murder growing more firm in her mind, not less.

"Let's not discuss it anymore," Sally said. "Now, I have something for you."

She pulled from her purse a check, already made out to Jo Tulip, for fifteen hundred dollars.

"Tell me if you think this is a fair amount for the job I'm hiring you to do," Sally said. "Fifteen hundred up front, with another fifteen hundred to follow when you're finished. Plus half of anything you can get for my mother's belongings and a ten percent sales commission on her car. I just want to be rid of this stuff. I did a blue book search of the vehicle, and it looks as though it's worth about eight thousand dollars. So that alone would be another eight hundred in your pocket once it's sold."

Jo took the check from her, nodding.

"Of course," Jo said. "That sounds more than fair."

"Good. I want you to go through the whole house, send to me whatever you think might be important—papers, photos, items of that nature. Have her furniture appraised in case there's anything of value there. Sell the best, donate the rest. Maybe have a garage sale. List her house with a Realtor. Sell the car. That's it. That's what I would like for you to do. Are you up to it?"

"Absolutely, Sally. Even more than you could imagine."

# 13

Simon found the toy in a thrift shop: a wooden rocking horse so old and used that most of the paint had worn away. Perfect.

He paid the three-dollar price, carried it outside, and walked to the end of the block. There on the corner was a bar, a dump that didn't even have a name, just a few neon beer signs in the window. Simon went inside. Blinking as his eyes adjusted to the darkness, he walked to the barstool most visible from the front door, set the rocking horse on the stool, and then sat himself on the next one over. The bartender was chatting with a gal at the end of the bar, but after a moment he came to Simon, wiped the shiny wooden surface in front of him, and asked him what he was having.

"Jack Daniels," Simon said. "Neat."

Simon had never been much of a drinker, especially not hard liquor, but he needed to look as though he belonged there. Once the drink came, he slouched down and focused all of his attention on it. He wasn't rude, but he also attempted no conversation with the bartender or the lady at the end of the bar. He simply sipped his drink and occasionally glanced at the game on the television in the corner.

"Hey, buddy," the bartender finally said, gesturing toward the horse. "What's with the toy?"

Simon glanced at the horse and then back at his drink. He shrugged.

"I just bought it at that thrift shop down the street. Thought my grandson might like it."

The bartender chuckled and the woman giggled.

"It's lookin' a little used, ain't it?" the woman said.

Simon glanced at it and then at her.

"Yeah, well," he said, "maybe I'll slap a coat of paint on it 'fore I give it to him."

He was quiet again, focusing on his drink and the TV. They went back to talking to each other.

After about ten minutes, Simon stood.

"Hey," he said to the bartender, "you got a john?"

"In the back," the man gestured. "Second door on the right."

"Thanks. I'll leave the horse here if that's okay."

The bartender didn't reply but merely shrugged and returned to his conversation with the woman.

Simon followed the directions to the bathroom, pulling the door shut behind him. Checking his watch, he waited exactly five minutes, trying to listen. He couldn't make out the words, but he definitely heard a third, higher voice. Finally, when it was time, he flushed the toilet, ran the faucet, and came out.

When he got back to the bar, the bartender's demeanor had changed considerably, as had the woman's. They both looked at him with interest, exactly as Simon had anticipated. Everything must have gone perfectly with Wiggles.

"Listen, I was thinking," the bartender said, "that's a pretty good toy, actually. I bet my kid would like it."

Simon played dumb.

"That's too bad. I think it was the only one they had in the store. They had some other good toys there, though."

"I was thinking I might buy that one. From you. I'll give you ten bucks for it."

"Ten bucks?" Simon cried. "That's what I paid for it at the thrift shop."

"Fifteen, then," the man said. "Five extra bucks to make it worth your while."

Simon shook his head and took a sip of his drink.

"It may look faded and old to you," he said, "but I really think my grandson's gonna like it. I'm gonna paint a little face on it and every-thing. I couldn't part with it for a lousy fifteen bucks."

"Twenty bucks," the bartender said.

"No way, I—"

"Each," the woman added.

"Hey!" the bartender cried, looking at her. "You mind?"

She crushed out a cigarette and gave him a meaningful look.

"We said we'd go in on it to-ge-ther," she told him slowly. "How 'bout fifty bucks, mister? Final offer."

Simon looked at the horse and then back at them.

"Fifty bucks for this piece of junk?" he asked.

"Cash," she said. "Twenty-five from each of us."

"Plus my drink on the house?" Simon asked.

"Sure, why not?" the bartender replied, glancing at the door.

Simon stood, lifted the horse onto the bar, and held out his hand.

"You got it," he said as they dealt the dollars onto his palm. "The toy is all yours."

He walked out of the bar, down the street, and around the corner, where a rattletrap of an old car was waiting for him. Climbing inside, Simon sat and then grinned.

"Fifty bucks," he said, handing half of it to Wiggles. "What'd you tell 'em?"

Wiggles pulled away from the curb, shakily pocketing his share of the cash as he drove.

"That I was a rare toy collector and that it was worth two or three hundred dollars. They think I'm out looking for an ATM machine to get that much cash and come back and make you an offer."

"The greedy idiots tried to take advantage of me."

"Yeah," Wiggles said with a laugh, turning onto the highway. "Too bad I ain't coming back—and that the toy ain't worth more than a few bucks!"

After lunch Jo checked her voice mail and found a message waiting from her agent, Milton.

"Hey, doll, I know you're on your honeymoon right now, but I thought I'd leave this for when you get back. We got the final word on the syndication deal, and I wanted to talk to you about it as soon as it's convenient for you."

Of course, this was the moment Jo had been waiting for, the opportunity to recover her lost newspaper markets and vastly increase her income from the column. She called Milton's office right away and made an appointment for in an hour. That gave her just enough time to drive to Moore City, find a parking garage, and walk to Milton's building.

Jo had known Milton most of her life, and she trusted him implicitly. Her biggest dread was of his retirement, which would be coming in the next year or so. She had thought him old when she was a little girl. Nowadays, he was practically ancient.

A few months ago Milton had taken on a partner, a woman about thirty years his junior, to whom he was showing the ropes. Her name was Annette and their intention was for her to slowly take over the business. Jo liked Annette well enough, and she seemed to know her stuff, but no one could ever replace Milton. He wasn't just the man who managed Jo's column, he also did her bookings for television and radio, sort of an all-purpose literary/entertainment agent and publicist. There weren't too many guys like Milton around anymore.

Jo stepped into the office, greeting Annette with a handshake and Milton with a strong hug and a kiss to his cheek. It felt leathery and paper-thin, which made her sad.

"What are you doing in town?" he asked, sinking heavily into his chair. "Shouldn't you be on your honeymoon?"

"Canceled."

"Canceled the honeymoon or canceled the marriage?"

"Both. Bradford had a last-minute change of heart."

"You're kidding," Annette said, pulling up a chair on Milton's side of the desk. "Are you okay?"

Though Jo wasn't eager to discuss it, they seemed genuinely concerned. She gave them the short version of what had happened, knowing how pathetic it sounded in the retelling.

"I couldn't wait to hear the news about the syndication deal," Jo explained, "so here I am. Now that the wedding's a wash, I'm eager to get back to work on my column."

Their response wasn't exactly what Jo had expected. Rather than give her news that would match her optimism, they shared a glance that told her all was not well.

"Is something wrong?"

Annette averted her eyes and Milton sighed heavily, folding his hands on the desk.

"It's not working, kiddo," Milton said solemnly.

"Not working?"

"The household hints angle. The syndication deal fell through, but it's not just that. Your markets are down, Jo. We've had about ten more cancellations in the last month."

"Ten?"

"Honey," Milton said, looking as if this were breaking his heart, "in your grandparents' heyday the column was carried by more than two hundred newspapers." He reached for a file on his desk and opened it. "Right now, Tips from Tulip is in twenty-three."

"Twenty-three?" Jo asked in a small voice. "That's all?"

"I'm afraid so."

She looked away, feeling the terrible weight of her grandparents' legacy crashing to the ground around her. She had failed them. Miserably.

"I'll do better," she said hopefully. "What happened with syndication?"

Milton began paging through the file, reading out comments he had scribbled there.

" 'Old fashioned.' 'No interest level.' 'Not applicable to our readers.' They all basically said the same thing. This is the twenty-first century, Jo. Nobody cares about household hints any more—at least, not in any of the desirable demographics."

"Desirable demographics?"

"Young women, eighteen to thirty-nine. They don't care. We live in a disposable, use-it-and-toss-it age. Who has time to bother with the old-fashioned way of keeping house?"

"My column has plenty of regular readers," Jo protested.

"Yes, white-haired old ladies!" Annette said, obviously unable to hold her tongue any longer. She also reached into the file and pulled out some clippings of the Tips from Tulip columns. "Jo, last week alone you referred to witch hazel, borax, and glycerin. Who the heck even knows what those things are anymore? Women today are juggling jobs, kids, households. They don't have time to rinse out and reuse their baggies."

"It would be a better world if they did," Jo said softly.

"But they don't. You're out of touch. You've lost relevance to today's women. Sweetie, you don't even have a website!"

Jo nodded, stunned at this turn of events. She always had felt a little out of step with the rest of the world. This just confirmed what she'd known all along: She had no idea what "normal" really looked like. Maybe she never had.

"What can I do?" she asked finally. "Is it time for me to call it quits completely?"

Milton closed the file and sat back in his chair.

"You should probably start thinking in those terms," he said kindly. "At least start making plans for some alternative source of income. The column isn't going to be worth doing if you lose many more markets."

"An alternative source of income?"

"You teach home ec, don't you?" Annette asked. "Can you support yourself with that?"

"It's just part-time. For fun."

"Well, you have a little time, I think," Milton said. "You should be able to muddle through for a while."

"What about everything else?" Jo asked. "The speaking engagements? The radio?"

Annette nodded.

"Glad you asked. Your radio show has strong ratings, actually, and your television appearances have always gone well. I suggest you focus on those markets, capitalize on the fact that you're young and beautiful and smart."

"Oh, I don't—"

"The whole Smart Chick thing," Annette added. " 'Chick' is a good word, very *now*. If you could find the right angle, we could even pitch a book for you. You just need to find your focus, Jo, change your media, and come up with some way to offer relevance to young women."

"And if I can't?" Jo asked. "What if there's no relevance to be found?"

Milton leaned forward, putting a wrinkled old hand on hers.

"Then at least you could say you gave it your best shot, dear. You had a good ride."

"This business gets tougher all the time," Annette added. "You can't imagine how hard it is to carry a successful column for as long as you have. The failure rate for attempted syndication is tremendous."

Milton squeezed Jo's hand, and after a moment she squeezed back.

"Whatever you decide," he added, "I know this: You carried on as best you could for as long as you could. Your grandparents would be proud of you regardless."

Danny was just packing up to leave the studio when Tiffany buzzed and told him Jo was on line one. His heart did a flip-flop in his chest as he tentatively reached for the receiver.

"Yes?" he said, his voice sounding strained in his own ear.

"Danny, hi," Jo replied, her voice soft and far away. "I need a favor."

"Sure," he replied. "Anything." His plans for the rest of the day were modest: balance checkbook, pay bills, and straighten up a little before a couple of guys came over to watch the game. On second thought, they were all slobs too. Maybe he'd skip the straightening part.

"I'm in Moore City meeting with Milton, and it looks like it's going to take longer than I thought. Is there any way you could run by the school and pick something up for me? It's just some papers the secretary put together."

"Sure," Danny said. "I can do it right now. No problem."

"Thanks, Danny. I have to admit, even if I were in town, I think I'd be too embarrassed to show my face over there just yet. The kids are going to have a field day with my being stood up at the altar."

"I understand. Not a problem."

He hesitated, hearing something odd in her voice. Even as self-conscious as he was feeling, something told him she needed him right now.

"Is everything all right?" he asked. "You sound funny."

"Guess I'm just thinking about next week when I do have to show up and teach. How humiliating."

He tried to offer her some comfort, but she didn't sound convinced. After they hung up, he drove across town to the high school, parked in a visitor slot, and went inside, requesting the papers for Jo Tulip. The secretary gave him a brown manila envelope. As he came back out of the office, he nodded toward the janitor, a big man with a scarred lip who looked very familiar. Danny glanced back at him again to see the man staring oddly at him as well.

"Do we know each other?" Danny asked.

The man smiled.

"Just trying to figure that out," he said. "Oh, I know. You're Jo Tulip's friend. I've seen you with her at the park."

"Yes," Danny said, remembering now. "I thought you worked at Golden Acres Retirement Village."

"I've got two jobs," the man replied. "There and here."

"Well, nice to see you again."

Danny tucked the envelope under his arm and started walking.

"So how is Jo?" the man called after him. "I saw that article about her in the newspaper. Did she really have to go in and look at a dead body?"

"Edna Pratt," Danny replied, nodding. "It was really something."

"You were there too?" Angus asked, falling into step beside Danny.

"Yep. The police hired me to photograph the scene."

"Photograph?" Angus asked. "You took *pictures* of the dead body?"

"Yep. They weren't sure at first if it was a crime scene, so they brought me in to photograph it just in case."

"There was other people there?"

"Sure. Lots of cops. Neighbors hanging around outside."

"How 'bout a man, an older gentleman, silver hair, mustache?"

"I don't recall anyone like that. Why?"

Angus shrugged.

"Mrs. Pratt, she comes to the retirement village sometimes to visit friends. He's usually with her. Never knew if he was her boyfriend or what."

"I have no idea."

"But her death…it was an accident, right?"

"Yes, an accident."

"And she really is dead? You saw the body with your own eyes?"

Danny hesitated, wondering why it mattered so much to this man.

"I-I mean," Angus stuttered, "I was just curious, is all. Miss Tulip is a nice lady. I hate to think of her having to look at something like that."

"Jo's stronger than you think," Danny replied. "She handled it well."

"That's good. And Edna Pratt, she really was dead?"

"She really was dead," Danny replied. "Without a doubt."

Angus looked oddly relieved.

Danny puzzled over that all the way to his car. Then he promptly forgot about it as he headed toward home, wondering if he ought to pick up some bean dip for tonight, just in case Ray forgot to bring it. Popcorn might be a good idea too.

# 14

Jo felt guilty about lying to Danny, but she really didn't feel like getting into things over the phone. The truth was that her meeting with Milton had been finished for several hours. She just wasn't ready to leave the city yet.

She had come out of his office in a daze and simply started walking. Before she knew it, the sun had moved much farther along in the sky and she was several miles from where she had started.

Jo called Danny and asked him to run the errand to the school, and then she hung up the phone, turned it off, and started walking back the way she had come. After a while, she passed a small riverside park that seemed clean and safe, so she made her way to a bench there that overlooked the water.

She knew she ought to pray, but she couldn't. Right now, as far as she was concerned, God had done nothing in her life except, one by one, take away everything that was precious to her. Worse than that, not only had God failed her, she had failed herself. She had taken the legacy handed to her by her grandparents and driven it into the ground. There was no other way to see it. Not only had she not adapted to the changing times—she hadn't even realized the times were changing! As soon as Annette had explained, however, Jo knew that it was true. More and more, her letters were from little old ladies with no money but lots of time—the exact opposite of the "desired demographic." Her column had become obsolete.

Annette and Milton had encouraged her to forget the column and focus more on other media. Radio. Television. Maybe write a book. She would think about it, but thus far in her life, she had only done those things for promotional purposes. The column was the centerpiece of everything. Without that, what was the point of all the other?

Jo closed her eyes, remembering the period of time when she and her grandmother had written the column together. Her grandmother was ready to retire and Jo was eager to take over, but they had taken it slowly so Jo could learn everything step-by-step. First, Nana had taught her how to choose the best reader letters for the column. They usually selected the quirky, the unusual—and especially the clueless. Those made the best letters of all.

Next, they would comb through their past experience, combining knowledge with theory until they had solved the issue at hand. If it was a stain or something else chemically based that Jo couldn't figure out, she would work on the problem with Pap, who eventually found a solution for almost every problem.

Finally, she and Nana would construct the reply. Sometimes that was the hardest part of all, since it took a lot of work to sound so effortless. Nana said Jo had a real flair for humor, and that she should develop that. In the few years since Jo had taken over the column completely herself, she had found herself exploring humor more and more.

But there was nothing funny about her situation now. Jo closed her eyes, tears spilling down her cheeks.

"I'm sorry, Nana," she whispered. "I'm sorry, Pap. I'm sorry for letting you both down."

Simon pulled the card from his pocket and balanced it on top of the pay phone. According to the teller at the bank in Mulberry Glen, he could dial into their automated system and check the balance on his account. He had hesitated to do that in case the call set off some sort of electronic tracking system. Surely the account had been closed by now and the police were looking for any indication of his whereabouts.

But just in case...

Just in case the money was still there, ripe for the taking...

He had to do it.

Fingers shaking, Simon pressed the buttons that would connect him to the system. Once he was in, he held his breath as he entered his account number and then the passcode the teller had given him.

After a moment, an automated voice responded.

"Your balance is four hundred thousand dollars and zero cents. Funds currently available for withdrawal are zero dollars and zero cents."

The voice went on to offer him more menu options, but he hung up, heart pounding. Did that mean the account was still intact, still sitting there, just waiting for the checks to clear? Or did that mean the police had put some sort of "freeze" on the account so that they could track him down while he tried to get his hands on the money?

Simon slid the card into his pocket and stood there, tuning out the noisy sounds of the gas station behind him. So Wiggles wouldn't know what he was doing, he had walked half a mile to get to this pay phone. Now he wondered if there was one more call he wanted to make before returning to the house.

He decided to think about it for a while first. It had been in the back of his mind since he snuck out of Mulberry Glen. But would it be a mistake? If he made the call, would the phone lines point a trail directly back to him?

Across the street was a small diner, and in the window was a faded, dirty sign that advertised a three-dollar omelet twenty-four hours a day. As if in response, his stomach growled. He decided to spring for the three bucks, get some chow, and think about the call. If he made this particular call, one of two things would happen: Either it would solve his problems, or it would greatly compound the ones he already had.

Jo knew she couldn't sit in a park and feel sorry for herself all day. In her purse was the check from Sally for clearing out Edna Pratt's house, so that seemed like a logical next step. Besides, she had a murder to investigate.

Jo walked all the way back to the parking lot near Milton's office, feeling her spirits lift just a bit with the prospect of the project. Housecleaning was always her favorite antidote for whatever ailed her, so completely clearing out a house would probably make her feel much, much better. At least it would help keep her mind off her string of failures: Bradford, the column, her life.

*At least I have life,* Jo thought as she started up the car. *Poor Edna Pratt no longer does.* Jo was determined to do a good job clearing out Edna's things—and hopefully find some clues to what might've caused her death in the process.

Jo organized the task in her mind as she drove. Once she got back to Mulberry Glen, she decided her first stop would be to get some empty boxes from behind the shopping center. She would also have to hit the dollar store, where she could grab some packing tape and permanent markers.

Just thinking about all of that activity had her in much better spirits by the time she reached the main highway. She decided not to think about Bradford for now. Somehow, someway, she would deal with the fallout from her failed wedding later.

As for her column, Jo realized that what she needed most right now was time to think, to brainstorm. If her household hints weren't relevant to the modern woman as they were now written, what could she do to change them, to *make* them relevant? Ideas flowed through her mind, from cleaning computers to day care issues. Surely out there somewhere was the right angle for the Smart Chick!

Finding that angle would require careful thought and a bit of research, observation, and testing—and the more she thought about that, the more excited she became. Something would pop up soon, she just knew it. Household hints were still relevant. She just had to figure out how to communicate that to today's modern woman.

Danny sat at the computer in his home office, staring at the figure on the bottom line. He had just balanced his bank account, and the resulting number was so low he wondered how he could pay off the stack of bills sitting next to the keyboard.

Something had to change, and soon.

Danny was used to piecing together an income from an assortment of odd jobs (like taking photos for the police), his studio job, and the sales of his stock photography. He had all of his best photos listed with different stock photo agencies around the world, and in any given month he earned from several hundred to several thousand dollars from them, depending on the leasing of the rights to his photos. Stock photography would never make him rich, but unless he started landing plum assignments from *Scene It* magazine, it would have to do.

And it was quite fun sometimes. He never knew where one of his pictures might end up, whether in a corporate brochure, a glossy calendar, or a CD or book cover. As he slowly made a name for himself, he found that more and more of his photos were being accepted by the larger agencies for representation. Sales had been steady, but if he didn't land something a little more lucrative soon, he was going to have to give some things up, like cable TV or his cell phone.

He glanced up at the sign that hung over his desk: *God has promised to meet all of our needs. God has not promised to satisfy all our wants.* Cable TV was definitely a want. For that matter, so was the cell phone. He took a deep breath, let it out, and smiled.

*Thanks, God. Thanks for reminding me how it works.*

Before Danny started going through the bills, he printed out the first check, ten percent of last month's income for his Sunday tithe. His non-Christian friends thought he was nuts for giving money to the church when he could barely afford to feed himself, but he knew what his priorities were. Priority number one was to be a faithful steward of all the Lord had given him.

The rest usually fell into place, one way or another.

Jo used the key Sally had given to her to unlock the door to Edna Pratt's house. It was almost dark outside, so she walked through and flipped on most of the lights. Despite the fact that Jo had murder on her mind, she didn't feel frightened to be there. There had been no signs of a struggle or a forced entry surrounding Edna's death, so whoever had purposefully mixed the chemicals that killed her was someone Edna allowed into her home willingly. Jo figured she was safe as long as she didn't let anyone in.

On the way into town, she had filled her car with sturdy cardboard boxes, but before she unloaded them, she wanted to look around and size up the task in front of her. She studied each room, opening closet doors, sliding open drawers. It was a small, two-bedroom house, though the guest room doubled as a sewing room. In fact, Edna's sewing skills were on display throughout the house, from the curtains in each of the windows to the gingham skirts around the sink and tub in the outdated master bathroom.

Besides the two bedrooms and two bathrooms, the house had a living room, a dining area, and a small, tidy kitchen. Jo finished her tour at the back door, where she looked out on the porch, the little yard, and a shed.

The job seemed simple enough, though from what Jo could see, Sally had left town without doing much more than the two of them had accomplished together the day before. Edna's food was even still sitting in the refrigerator.

Jo decided to start there, finding a garbage bag under the sink, opening it up, and filling it with everything inside the fridge and the freezer. When she was finished, she continued on to the pantry, tossing everything except canned goods. Those she bagged up to donate to the local soup kitchen. Everything else, sadly, needed to be tossed for safety purposes.

The food completely filled the garbage bag, so Jo carted it to the back porch and then came back in, located Edna's stash of cleansers and rags, and went to work on the inside of the refrigerator. It was clean already, but Jo knew she might as well get it completely scrubbed out, even putting a washcloth over a butter knife to clean the rubber tracks around the door. When she was done, she found a pencil and some paper and started a shopping list with the first item being two boxes of baking soda, for clearing out any lingering odors.

After Jo had thoroughly cleaned the fridge, freezer, and pantry, she decided to take a break and do a little digging around. She knew that over the course of the next few days she would come into contact with all of Edna's stuff. But for now she just felt like looking in the more "private" areas of the house. Under the beds. In the tops of closets. In the backs of drawers.

She didn't know what she was looking for, only that she'd know it when she found it. Sure enough, at the back of the closet in the sewing room, hidden by a pile of blankets, was a small black trunk, sealed up tight by a rusty metal padlock. Maybe it would hold something important, something relevant to Edna's death.

Jo carried the trunk to the bed and then went digging for a key, which she found in the drawer of the sewing table. She had a feeling it was the right key, though when she tried to insert it into the lock, she realized that the lock was rusted completely shut. Undeterred, Jo carried the trunk into the master bathroom and balanced it on the corner of the tub. Then she went out to the kitchen, where she retrieved a shallow bowl and a can of cola.

Back in the bathroom, Jo knelt in front of the tub. She opened the cola, poured it into the bowl, and then held the bowl directly under the lock so that the lock rested down in the brown liquid. The substance bubbled and fizzed for a few minutes, and Jo knew that the cola was eating away the rust that was freezing up the lock. Finally, she set the bowl down in the tub, used a nearby towel to wipe off the lock, and tried again with the key.

This time it worked.

Jo pulled the trunk right down onto the floor in front of her and opened it. As she did, the smell of must and dust filled the room. The trunk was filled with papers and photographs, scrapbooks and mementos—all of it obviously quite old. Jo flipped through everything, seeing pictures of Edna Pratt as a young woman, a bride, a pregnant housewife. Sally would enjoy the shots of herself as a baby, then a toddler, and then a little girl, both by herself and with other children, other adults. There were dried corsages and snips of fabric and treasured letters and documents.

But there was nothing there that was relevant to now—or that could point to murder.

Disappointed, Jo closed her eyes and leaned back against the tub. As she did, her hand bumped something just behind the gingham skirt that surrounded the tub. Sitting up, she lifted the skirt to see what it could be.

What she found was very odd indeed.

Simon walked out of the restaurant, disappointed that the three-dollar omelet had been dry and overcooked—and that it hadn't come with anything on the side except a wilted piece of parsley and a soggy orange slice. Feeling full but not satisfied, he crossed from the diner back to the pay phone at the gas station.

More than anything, he wanted to call Edna.

Simon knew Edna's phone number by heart, but he made no move to dial it. Instead, he stood there for several moments, a hand on the receiver, considering the possible ramifications of making the call.

If Edna went to the authorities on Saturday as she had threatened to do, then calling her now would be a gross miscalculation. Her phone would be silently rigged, ready to track back his number and bust him on the spot.

But if she'd had a change of heart—if she hadn't gone to the police after all—then he needed to know. He needed to hear her voice, to hear her say, "Don't worry, Simon. Come on back. The money's still in the bank. Everything's okay."

Just imagining it, tears sprang to his eyes. Surprised, he gruffly swiped at his face. He had to admit it: He missed Edna, missed hearing her voice. In a life filled with upheaval and misery, she had been the only constant in his world. Over the years there had been times when he would dial her number only to hear her simple "Hello?" He would hesitate, not wanting to intrude, not wanting to bother, just needing that sound. Sometimes, somehow, she would know it was him.

"Simon?" she would say into the silence, a sudden softness coming into her voice.

When that happened, he would always answer, "Yes, Edna. It's me."

Other times, she would simply repeat, "Hello? Hello?" and those times he would gently lay the phone back on the cradle and walk away. He treasured her too much to be a burden.

In the last few months he had been able to spend real time with her, to get to know her all over again. He still didn't understand how she could have betrayed him there at the end, but there were many things about Edna he had never understood. At least she'd had the decency to offer him a fair warning and a good head start.

Maybe he *should* call her now. Maybe she'd had a last-minute change of heart but had no way to let him know.

Maybe she'd decided she loved him enough to leave the police out of things entirely.

Swallowing hard, he lifted the receiver and quickly dialed her number. It rang once, then again, then again.

"Hello?" a woman's voice said breathlessly. It wasn't Edna. Simon hesitated, wondering if he had dialed correctly. *Who else would answer Edna's phone?*

Simon cleared his throat and put on his best falsetto, trying to sound just like a woman himself.

"Hello, is Edna there?" he asked in a singsongy voice.

His question met with a pause, and instantly his radar was on full alert. Was this a female cop? The next-door neighbor? One of the club members?

"I'm sorry," the woman's voice said. "Are you a friend of hers?"

Simon's mind raced. Finally, without a reply, he disconnected the call. Obviously, Edna had proceeded exactly as she had warned him on Friday night. She'd gone to the police and told them everything. They probably already had this number and a possible lock on his location.

He took off running, despite the fact that he was far too old for that. A bus was just pulling away from the corner, and he reached it and pounded on the side. It stopped, the doors opened, and he climbed aboard. He dropped in the fare and found a seat, not even caring where it might take him next.

Jo stood in the kitchen and slowly replaced the receiver of the telephone. That was odd.

She realized she needed a better approach for future calls because Edna probably had friends who hadn't learned yet of her unfortunate demise. *When they call,* Jo wondered, *how, exactly, should I respond?* "I'm sorry, but Edna can't take your call right now. She's dead."

It just didn't seem right somehow.

Mulling it over, Jo returned to the bathroom, where she had just stripped the skirt from the tub to better see what it had been hiding.

The tub was the old-fashioned, claw-footed kind, and underneath it, right in the center where the tub sat several inches from the ground, was a section of false flooring Jo had accidentally knocked loose with her hand. The whole room was floored with what looked like self-sticking linoleum tile. But there under the tub, four of the tiles weren't on the floor, they were on a square piece of wood, which she now managed to lift up and slide away, revealing a secret cavity about two feet wide and a foot deep.

Jo resisted the urge to pull out the items that were inside until running to the cleaning closet and putting on a pair of rubber gloves. Then she came back to the bathroom and carefully took out the three items one by one.

The bathroom was small, but she laid everything on top of the closed trunk in front of her. When the hole was empty, she slid the covering back over it and watched it drop into place. If she hadn't bumped it with her hand, she would never have noticed that it was there.

Jo stood and carefully picked up the three items she had taken from the hole: a small painting, a manila envelope, and a worn, dusty book with a maroon velvet cover. She carried them into the dining area and set them on the table, eager to study the treasures that had been important enough to hide under a false floor in the bathroom.

# 15

Danny was just settling down in the living room to watch the game with his buddies when the phone rang. He passed the bowl of popcorn to his brother-in-law, Ray, and then answered it.

"You busy?" Jo asked, never one to beat around the bush.

"Why? What's up?"

"I need your expertise as a photographer."

"Now?" He got up and strode into the kitchen, looking out the back window. There wasn't a single light on at Jo's house. "Where are you?"

"I'm at Edna Pratt's house. Can you come over here?"

Danny pinched the bridge of his nose.

"You're where?"

"Edna Pratt's house, the lady who died on Saturday."

"Why?"

"Long story. Are you free?"

Danny glanced at his friends. Two of them were currently throwing popcorn into the air and trying to catch it in their mouths. Somehow, the thought of being with Jo was doubly appealing. Danny knew that he could go. His friends would help themselves to the food, enjoy the game, and let themselves out when they were done.

"How soon do you want me?"

"Ten minutes ago."

"I'll do the best I can."

There was an odd look on Danny's face when he got there, but Jo was too excited to worry about it right then. Taking him by the hand, she led him to the dining table and told him to sit down.

On the wide surface she had laid out a row of photographs, six in all. Some of the pictures were older looking than others, five in black-and-white and one in color, all 8 x 10 enlargements.

"Tell me what you see," she said, taking a seat across from him.

Pursing his lips, he studied her face for a moment and then looked down at the photos in front of him.

"What am I looking for?" he asked.

"Impressions. Thoughts. Talk to me about these pictures. Are they real? Fake? Doctored by a computer?"

Danny shook his head, refusing to cooperate.

"Who are the people in the picture," he asked, "and what are we doing in the home of a dead woman?"

With a frustrated sigh, Jo realized she would have to elaborate somewhat if he was going to be of any use to her at all. She explained that Edna's daughter, Senator Sally Sugarman, had hired her to come and clear out all of Edna Pratt's belongings, get the house listed with a Realtor, and sell her car.

"We sort of made friends when she came to town," Jo said, "and she was looking for someone to help, and I, uh, I had some free time this week. So I took the job. In fact, I'll cut you in if you want. I'll need some help with the heavy lifting when the time comes."

"Sure," Danny said, still sounding confused. "Whatever you need."

"The main reason I'm here, though, is because I'm going to prove to the police that Edna was murdered. I think these pictures are a pretty good start."

"Why? What are they?"

Jo thought for a minute, and then she stood.

"Come with me," she said, knowing if she showed him the hidden compartment under the bathtub, he might be more inclined to follow her leap of logic.

She led him to the bathroom, pointed under the tub, and told him where to press the tile. Sure enough, it tilted as it had before, and the lid came off.

"Whoa," he said, bending down to peer inside the hole. "What is this?"

"A secret compartment."

He stared up at her, and she could almost see the wheels turning in his brain. She knelt down there beside him and held his gaze.

"Danny," she said slowly, hoping he would trust her in this. "Edna's death was not an accident. I really do think someone killed her. And I think this hiding spot helps to confirm my suspicions. The stuff on the dining table came from in there. And I think if we can figure out what it is, we'll be able to figure out why someone wanted her dead."

At first Danny had a hard time concentrating on what Jo was telling him. She was so beautiful, just so beautiful, and he couldn't understand why he hadn't really thought much about it before. How had he gone so many years without really seeing her vivid green eyes, her sweet lips, her long neck? How had he not kissed the faint freckles on her nose or run his hands through her gorgeous head of hair? He had fallen and fallen hard. With her being so animated right now, everything about her so *alive*, it made it even more difficult to concentrate on what she was saying. More than anything, he wanted to stop her talking and shout "I love you! I love you! Don't you understand? I love you!"

But he held his tongue. And as she talked and gestured and pulled him into her enthusiasm, he had to force himself to focus on what she was saying. He knew she must have thought he was dense. But she just smelled so nice and looked so good, it was all he could do not to take her in his arms and kiss her.

He wanted more than anything just to kiss her.

Danny closed his eyes, thanking the Lord that Bradford had taken off, leaving the opportunity for them to work out a new kind of relationship—eventually. Chances were, Jo loved Danny too; she just didn't know it yet. He opened his eyes and pushed such thoughts from his mind. There was time for all of that later. Right now she needed him to help her with this puzzle.

And what a puzzle it was. Jo was going on and on about Edna Pratt, insisting that the old woman's death had been a murder and not an accident. As he tried to follow her logic, he realized that the way she had invested herself in the situation was so understandable it was almost predictable. Once he figured out what was really going on, he tried to explain it to her as gently as possible.

"Listen, Jo," he said, leading her back into the living room and forcing her to sit on the couch. "Let's think this through. Edna Pratt was a devotee of household hints, particularly Tips from Tulip."

"Yes."

"She was following a number of those tips Friday night when she made a fatal mistake."

"No—"

"Stay with me here," he said, not letting her object. "If Edna made a fatal mistake while following your tips, then her death was indirectly caused by you. At least that's how it feels. But you don't have to think that, Jo. Everyone makes mistakes now and then. You can't do this."

She shook her head, frustration creating a furrow in her brow.

"Why are you second-guessing me?" she demanded. "Can't you give my theory a chance at least?"

"But don't you see?" he said. "To satisfy your own conscience, her death *has* to be a murder. Because if it was an accident, then you'd be indirectly culpable—and that would be too difficult to swallow. Let it go, Jo. Maybe it really was just a simple mistake by an old woman, nothing more. The car was a coincidence. The argument you overheard was a television left on too loud."

Danny's words sat there between them. He felt terrible for what he'd had to say, but she was so worked up he really didn't think he had much choice. In the long run, it seemed the kinder thing to do.

"Thank you," she said finally, her voice much more calm.

"You're welcome," he replied softly.

"No, I mean thank you," she continued, her voice growing stronger, "for the amateur hour at the psychiatrist's office." She sat forward, eyes blazing. "Listen to me, Danny Watkins. I don't need your pop psychology to explain away some irrational urge I have to justify culpability."

"Jo, I—"

"I'm not an idiot. I know what I'm seeing. There are things about this woman's death that don't add up. Yes, part of it is just my own gut instincts. But instincts are a good place to begin. You can either be my friend and go with me on this, or you can get out of here and leave me alone."

Danny swallowed hard, surprised at the rage in her voice. He knew she'd had a tough few days—a tough year, really. Maybe he had been wrong to try and nip this in the bud. At least she was showing some enthusiasm for something—and in the wake of her failed wedding, wasn't that a good thing?

Besides, he admitted, no way was he going to walk out of here now.

"Okay, Jo," he said finally. "I will suspend my disbelief for the moment and listen to your reasoning."

"Thank you."

"As long as you understand that I'm not on board with what you're saying about the woman's death. Not at all."

"Fair enough. Come look again at the pictures. I promise you, they'll change your mind."

Jo led Danny back to the dining room and waited as he sat in front of the photos. She moved behind him and watched over his shoulder as, one by one, he picked up each shot and studied it extensively. Jo had tried to place them in what seemed like chronological order based on the clothing and the nature of the pictures, but she wasn't sure if she had gotten it right or not.

The first picture was old and faded, the edges frayed, a posed portrait of a man sitting stiffly in a chair. He looked to be in his late fifties or early sixties, with silver hair and mustache, his stern expression typical of the photos of that era.

"This is a daguerreotype," Danny said softly. "One of the earliest forms of photography."

"How early?" Jo asked.

"Probably the late eighteen hundreds. Maybe eighteen-fifty at the earliest. It's in pretty good condition, except for the edges."

He set it down and picked up the next one. It was a picture of about ten soldiers, probably Civil War era, resting beside some cannons. The soldiers seemed to be wearing the torn and dusty uniforms of the Union army. There was nothing very remarkable about the photo other than historical interest in the subjects.

"This one looks vaguely familiar," Danny said, putting down the Civil War shot and picking up the next one. It was a shot of a woman in a street car, looking directly down at the photographer. "Do you recognize her?"

"No," Jo said. "Should I?"

"She was a minor celebrity of some sort," Danny said, "though I can't place who she was right now. Something about her face, though, is recognizable. I'd swear I've seen this picture before."

Sturdy and middle-aged, the woman in the photo wasn't attractive but there was something quite arresting about her piercing, exhausted gaze. Her image stood out much more vividly than those of the men who were sitting on the streetcar beside and behind her.

The fourth photo was obviously from a sporting event, probably the Olympics. It featured a man about to thrust a javelin, with several rows of spectators clearly visible behind him. Though also black-and-white, the contrast was greater, the image sharper, than the others. Danny said that judging by the quality of the print, it probably dated to the 1930s.

The next photo was in color, though the colors were muted and dull.

"I'd say this was an early version of Kodachrome," Danny told her, turning the picture toward the light. "Probably from the nineteen-forties."

In the shot, a group of men, all wearing overalls, were standing near a field of some crop.

"What are they growing there?" Danny asked.

"Looks like sugarcane to me," Jo replied.

All of the men sported mustaches and straw hats, their skin worn and tanned like farmers.

Finally, he picked up the last photo, a shot of a family sitting on a front stoop. There were several adults and two children, a girl of about nine or ten and a boy a year or so older. They were all dressed in the clothing of the 1950s or early '60s. The picture was nothing special, a black-and-white image probably taken after church one Sunday as they sported their pillbox hats and spiffy suits.

"Okay," Danny said, setting down the photos. "What do you want to know?"

"We've got pictures here," Jo said, taking the seat across from him again, "that cover a range of about a hundred years, right?"

"Sure," Danny said, looking back and forth at the six enlargements in front of him. "Give or take a few years."

"Then look at them again," Jo said, a gleam in her eye. "Tell me what they all have in common."

Danny frowned at her but seemed to accept the challenge as he once again turned his attention to the photos. It took him a little while, but finally it was like a lightbulb went off over his head. His eyes widened and he gasped.

"The man!" he said, picking up the oldest photograph, the one he had called a daguerreotype. "This man. He's in every one of these pictures!"

Jo nodded, grateful he had finally caught on.

"Always about the same age, the same guy," she said, grinning. "Silver hair and a mustache."

She pointed to each of the pictures in turn, from the daguerreotype where he was posing for a portrait, to the one where he lounged as a Civil War soldier, to the one where he sat on a streetcar behind a woman, to the one where he was in the stands at a javelin throw, to the one where he stood among the farmers beside the sugarcane, to the one where he clustered on the front stoop with the family.

"Wanna take it one step further?" Jo asked.

"What?" Danny replied.

She reached to the chair beside her, where she had rested the painting she also found in the hidden compartment under the tub. It was a small framed print of an oil painting that depicted the Nativity. The print was quite lovely, with Mary and Jesus at the center of the picture, both bathed in white light. Looking on were several animals along with a small group of men, including Joseph. In the upper left corner, one of the men partially hidden in shadow had silver hair and a mustache.

Not knowing what else to do, Danny laughed.

"This guy's been around a good while," he said, not knowing what to make of it. "Either that, or somebody's been pretty clever with a camera and a paint brush."

"So you agree that something weird is going on?"

He sat back and blew out a slow breath.

"Fine," he said. "You win. I'm convinced there are some things here that deserve a closer look."

The maroon velvet notebook was just as confusing as the photos and the painting. It held about fifty pages, each written on by hand. Danny sat beside Jo as they perused the pages, trying to make sense of the odd scribblings and notations that covered each page.

The writings looked like scientific formulas combined with mathematical equations, but Jo kept insisting the formulas made no sense. Danny had to defer to her in the matter, since neither math nor science had been his best subjects in school.

"This is the symbol for sulfur," she said. "And this is gold, and this is mercury. But I don't understand the equations here."

"How about the drawings?" He flipped through several more pages. "Such strange doodles. A lizard on fire? Half men, half women? It's bizarre."

"Hey, Danny, maybe we should run it past one of my old science professors at the college. I bet Dr. Langley would look at it for us and tell us what it means."

"Good idea."

"But we'll make copies first—and of the pictures too. I think the originals need to be locked up somewhere safe."

"I agree," Danny said, surprised to realize that he was already almost fully on board with Jo's theory of murder. Certainly, there was *something* odd going on here—something that needed to be explored in the context of a woman's death. "Do you have a safety deposit box?"

"I can use my grandparents'. If we make all the copies tonight, we can lock the stuff away first thing in the morning."

"Sounds good," Danny said, looking at his watch, surprised to see that it was nearly ten P.M. "But where can we go to make copies at this hour?"

"How about the campus library?" she said. "They'll be open, and there's something else I want to do there anyway."

The library parking lot was rather empty for a Monday night. Once inside, the place was quiet. So they wouldn't have to struggle with loose change, they used the copier nearest the reference desk, which worked with a counter instead.

Danny made copies of the six photos, put those aside, and then started copying each of the pages of the handwritten book. He looked as though he was on a roll, so Jo excused herself.

Carrying the Nativity painting, she went to the reference desk, held up the print, and asked the librarian if by any wild chance she recognized it.

"No. I'm sorry, but I don't," the woman said softly, studying it. "It's very interesting, though."

"I wonder if there's someway to find out who the artist is," Jo said, knowing if this didn't work, she could always contact the college's art department.

The librarian directed Jo to a group of art-related books, suggesting that she flip through the pages and see if she could spot that particular painting—or something similar. Jo thought it would be worth a try, so she carried the books to a table near the machine where Danny was working, settled down, and got to work. Briefly, her mind went back to college days, when she would study for hours on end, embracing the quiet and the knowledge contained in this place.

A little while later, Jo offered to switch tasks with Danny, knowing her job was certainly the more interesting of the two. As he went through the art books, Jo completed the tedious job of photocopying the notebook, paid for the copies, and then joined him at the table. Neither of them found the painting, though they wrote down the names of several artists who seemed to do similar work.

Feeling frustrated, they decided to call it a night.

Danny was quiet in the car, and Jo was glad. She had plenty of things on her mind to keep her occupied. First order of business was planning out the next day because she didn't want to waste a minute in hunting down the truth about the odd things they'd found in the hidden compartment.

"I'll make appointments with Professor Langley in the science department and somebody over in art," she said. "I hope they can see me tomorrow."

"Hope so."

"In the meantime, I'll make a copy of Edna's key for you so you can come and go as you need."

"You sure that's okay?" he asked. "I mean, Edna's daughter hired you for this job, not me."

Jo smiled.

"Yeah, well, I'm subcontracting," she said. "I have it on good authority that you're a trustworthy guy."

She smiled at him, and after a moment he smiled back. There seemed to be something wistful in his expression, and for a minute she had the disconcerting feeling that he had something important to tell her.

The look passed, however, as he focused his attention on the road. Jo gazed down at the print in her lap, wondering who the man with the silver hair was, and why he seemed to be popping up all over the place.

Simon stole a bicycle.

He didn't like being a common thief, but desperate times called for desperate measures.

The bus he had taken ended up being one that made a large loop around Jacksonville. Sitting quietly in the very back row, Simon had managed to stay on board for three go-arounds, the driver not even noticing he was there. Each time, Simon had crouched low in his seat as they drove past the pay phone where he had made the call to Edna's house. Each time, he had seen no cops nor detected any sort of police activity.

Maybe the call hadn't been traced after all.

Finally, on the fourth time around, he steeled his nerves, waited until one stop past the one where he'd gotten on, and disembarked.

He was tired. His feet hurt. His *brain* hurt.

His intention was to make his way back toward Wiggles' house but not actually go inside. If the cops had traced the call, they might review his prison record and connect him with Wiggles and get a lock on his location. Better to spend the night nearby, where he could watch the house and see if the cops ever showed up. If they didn't, he'd probably be safe to go back there in the morning.

On the way he passed a bicycle, a battered, navy blue Schwinn with a torn seat. It was locked up, but the person who locked it had merely wrapped the chain around a post. Glancing around to make sure he wasn't being observed, Simon simply lifted the bicycle and slid the lock over the top of the post, leaving it hanging from the frame as he climbed aboard and took off down the street.

Simon hated stealing. But so much had gone wrong lately that he needed a break. People who didn't properly protect their belongings deserved to have them stolen anyway.

And riding a bike sure was easier than walking.

It was quite dark by the time he neared the house. Wiggles' car was in the driveway, and through the front window Simon could see the flashing of the television screen. No doubt Wiggles was sitting there with a little frozen dinner, food all over the front of his shirt as he shakily tried to get most of it to his mouth. That was the hardest part about rooming with a man who had tremor problems—the eating. It was hard to watch him and enjoy your own food at the same time.

Simon pedaled over the train tracks, aiming toward a utility structure in the field beyond Wiggles' house. He rode up to it and then climbed off the bike and pushed it around to the back, hiding it by laying it down in the weeds. The structure obviously belonged to the electric company, as signs on all four sides proclaimed "Warning! High Voltage!" But Simon knew he would be safe enough as long as he didn't stick a fork in a metal plate or something. He mounted the six-foot-high chain-link fence, carefully swung his leg over, and came back down on the inside. He stepped from the fence onto a concrete platform and then found himself a relatively comfortable spot leaning against the little building, his bottom on cement, his back against cinder block.

He was getting too old for this.

While hundreds of thousands of dollars sat in the bank farther north, Simon was huddled in the dark next to an electrical way station, waiting to see if the cops would raid his friend's house looking for him.

Still, if Simon possessed anything, it was his unflagging optimism. Somehow, deep in his gut, he knew this would work out okay. He was like a cat, always landing on his feet, counting mightily on those nine lives.

He leaned against the cold wall, tucked his hands under his arms, and tried to be thankful that the fence would protect him from any stray creatures that might go sniffing around in the night. He settled in for the long haul, comforting himself the way he always had—in the knowledge that somewhere, two thousand miles away, Edna was thinking of him. Despite what she may have done, at least he always knew that Edna loved him.

Still, it was going to be a long night.

## TIPS FROM TULIP

*Dear Readers, this week as we feature classic letters from the past, enjoy this exchange from 1975.*

---

### Dear Tulip,

I'm looking for a cookie recipe that's simple to make but tastes great. A neighbor we don't know very well has invited my husband and me over to her house for a "swapping party." I'm not a very good cook, but we'd like to bring a nice plate of cookies for swapping. Any suggestions?

*Signed,*

*Doesn't Get Out*
*Much in Ohio*

### Dear Doesn't,

The easiest cookie recipe I know requires only two ingredients: a bag of chocolate chips and a can of chow mein noodles. Following package directions, melt the chips in a double boiler. Then stir in the noodles. Drop spoonfuls of the mixture into small heaps on waxed paper and allow them to cool. Voilà, these confections may look a little strange, but they taste great.

By the way, be a Smart Chick! Please, please make sure of your hostess' intentions. Before you melt the chips, double-check to make sure that it's COOKIES you'll be swapping. If it's not, this is one party you'll want to miss.

*—Tulip*

# 16

Jo sat at her kitchen table and flipped through the paper as she did every morning, looking for her column. Sometimes it was edited down for size, and she liked to keep an eye on the omissions, at least in her local area. Luckily, today's column was there in its entirety. She read it as she ate a bowl of oatmeal, considering the words of her agents as she went.

The second letter was about the wasted cleaner that sits at the bottom of spray bottles. Tips from Tulip recommended to Wasteful in Waukeegan that she drop a few marbles in the bottom to raise the liquid high enough to get sucked into the squirter.

*So don't lose your marbles,* it said, *just look at the pennies you're saving in cleansers!*

Jo hesitated, a sort of internal groan going off in her mind. What woman in this day and age would take the time to find marbles and drop them into a cleanser bottle just to salvage the last half inch of liquid? Answer: A woman who's old and cheap. Everyone else would simply toss it and buy a new one.

Jo went on to the third letter, where Twice as Nice wrote to suggest that old handbags could be recycled by cutting up the leather and using them as elbow patches on jackets.

It had seemed so clever at the time. Yet now, as Jo thought about it, she realized most women didn't sew these days—and even if they did, leather elbow patches on jackets weren't even in style anymore!

She set the paper down and blinked away sudden tears. Exactly how long had she been so disconnected from reality?

*Long enough to run this column into the ground,* she answered to herself.

*Lord, what do I think I'm doing? Of course this stuff isn't relevant anymore.*

She put the paper away without reading the rest of the column. She'd seen all she needed to see.

Jo rinsed out the half-eaten bowl of oatmeal and put it into the dishwasher, ran a damp cloth over the table, and dropped the newspaper into the recycle bin. Then she stomped back to her bedroom to get dressed for the day. As she did, she thought about today's women, the desired demographic, and knew that their lives were filled with all sorts of challenges she had never addressed. Child care. Working wardrobe. Office politics. Cell phones. Computers. Soccer moms. The Internet.

She pulled on her grungiest cleaning clothes, ready to put in a few hours at Edna's house. Jo promised herself that as she worked, she would think very hard about how to include some or even all of the above in her new approach.

She still hadn't heard a word from Bradford, but between thinking up a new direction for her household hints and investigating the murder of Edna Pratt, Jo knew there was plenty to occupy her mind anyway.

Simon jerked awake, the hot morning sun already beating down on his face. It was a little after seven A.M., and he realized he must have drifted off a few hours before.

Stiffly, he stretched out his legs, wondering how it had come to this. He was too old to spend the night sitting against hard concrete. He was too old to be hiding in wait to see if the police were going to show up and arrest him.

The original plan was to stay there and keep watching until noon, but suddenly Simon had an irresistible urge to get up, go in the house, grab a bite, and take a hot shower. After that, he would stretch out on Wiggles' couch and try to get back to sleep. He'd had a very rough night. To heck with the police.

The trip over the fence wasn't nearly as easy as it had been the night before. Then, he had been driven by fear; now, he could barely move he was so achy. Slowly, he managed to make it over the top, but he slipped and fell the last few feet, landing flat in the grass on his bottom. It was a miracle he hadn't broken a hip!

Leaving the bicycle in the weeds, he limped home, glad to know that Wiggles would probably sleep a few more hours himself. Simon crept into the bathroom and got under the hot spray, grateful at least to have somewhere to stay. He couldn't keep going like this, though.

Something had to give, one way or another.

Danny reached the studio before Tiffany, eager to have some time to work on the photos Jo had given him. As he walked past her desk, he glanced at the day's schedule, which was light. Commission-seeker that Tiffany was, she wouldn't be too happy, but that worked fine for him, as he was paid by the hour.

He put away his things and then brought the six photos into the lab and scanned them in one by one. After that, he pulled up the most modern of the bunch, the shot from the '50s or '60s of the family all dressed up and gathered on a front stoop. On the computer screen he was able the enlarge the face of the silver-haired man until he could find some irregularities in the pixels surrounding it. From what he could tell, the image had definitely been added to the scene.

One by one, he did the same with each of the pictures, growing more and more impressed with the deft handiwork involved. Whoever had doctored these shots was a very good photographer. But Danny was better, and he could spot the small problems with shadow and depth and detail that indicated the pictures had been altered.

Finally, he chose the sharpest, most straight-on image of the man's face and enlarged it to a full 8 x 10 size. He printed off a few copies, knowing he and Jo would need them in their pursuit of the truth.

"Oh Danny Boy," Tiffany sang from the doorway, her usual greeting.

"Hey, Tiff," he replied. "How's it going?"

She came in and tossed her purse into the filing cabinet, complaining, as he had expected, about the day's light schedule.

"Maybe it's good, in a way," she said. "Your ten o'clock is handicapped, so that might take some extra time."

"Handicapped?"

"According to his mom, he's in a wheelchair. Cerebral palsy, I think. She wants the standard package, so you might have to maneuver your props around a bit."

"Thanks. I'll see what I can do."

Tiffany started the pot of coffee in the break area and then paused as she passed Danny's desk again.

"Danny?" she asked. "Why do you have a photo of Emma Goldman on your desk?"

"Who?"

"Emma Goldman," she said, pointing to the photo of the woman on the streetcar, the one he had vaguely recalled as being some sort of minor celebrity. "I did a report on her for American history. She was a big union organizer back in the nineteen-twenties."

Danny picked up the picture and studied it, finally remembering why he'd recognized her. Just a few months before, he had gone to Moore City with his sisters to see the touring production of the Broadway musical *Ragtime.* Among the posters hanging in the hallways of the theatre had been huge blowups of actual photos from that era. Danny realized now that he had seen this very picture! He remembered it because he had thought it was a good example of irony in photography, the way she sat there on the streetcar with a poster of Uncle Sam directly over her shoulder, a sharp contrast to her own antigovernment stance.

Quickly, Danny went online to do a Google image search for the name "Emma Goldman." It didn't take long to find the exact photo, described as *Emma Goldman on a Streetcar, 1917. Recent gelatin silver print from original glass negative.* The photographer was unknown. Danny printed it out and then set it beside the one he already had.

"Well, would you look at that," he muttered.

Sure enough, the photo from the Internet was exactly the same— except that the seat behind her was empty! The silver-haired man was nowhere to be found.

"So what's up?" Tiffany asked. "What are you doing?"

Danny snapped back from his thoughts and gave her an innocent smile.

"Nothing," he said. "Just doing a little photography research."

He decided to see how many of these originals he could find online. He went back to Google and this time typed in "Civil War photos." He knew he might have to slog through a bunch of pictures, but he was determined to hunt down the original shots if it took him all day.

Jo had a good morning despite the rough start. As always when she cleaned and organized, she found herself moving into some other state of consciousness, a place where everything was under control and order reigned supreme.

She started in Edna's guest bedroom/sewing room, systematically going through every drawer, shelf, and closet to throw away, box up, give away, or set aside for a yard sale every single item she came across. Today she had thought to bring along tiny stickers and a pen, and she priced the yard sale items as she ran into them, placing them in a large box on the floor. She figured she could hold the sale either this Saturday or the next, depending on how soon she could get an appraiser to price out anything that might be of value.

At nine fifteen she took a break and sat down with the phone book, going through antiques and appraisals until she found someone who was willing to come out the very next morning. They made the appointment, and then she called Marie's real estate office to tell her she wanted to list a house for sale. Marie wasn't in, so Jo left a message; she wanted to deliver the news in person. Finally, she called the newspaper and placed a description of Edna's car, offering it at five hundred dollars above the price Sally Sugarman had suggested. This way there would be some room for negotiating and the buyer might feel he had really gotten a deal.

When she was finished with the more practical phone calls, Jo turned her attention to the college, calling first the science department and then the art department. As it turned out, a professor in the art department could see her in about two hours. Her old chemistry professor wasn't in, so she left a message.

In the meantime, she ran a few quick errands, first to the hardware store to have a key made for Danny and then to the bank to deposit her check from Sally and to put the original photos and notebook into the safety deposit box. When she arrived back to Edna's house, the next-door neighbors were in their yard, a woman playing in the leaves with two small children.

Jo watched for a moment, remembering that this was the neighbor who had first spotted Edna's dead body and called the police. She headed for the fence and gave a wave, wondering if she might be able to get any useful information from the woman.

They chatted for a good while. Jo explained who she was and what she was doing. The lady was friendly, if a little nosy, saying that her name was Betty and that she had only just moved there in the past year. She had met Edna over the fence one day, much like this, and in talking she learned that Edna frequently swam at the Y.

"I know an opportunity when I see one," Betty said, glancing toward the kids as they began raking a pile back to its original height. "A good, consistent workout buddy was exactly what I needed. I decided to join the Y too so we could go together. The timing was perfect because my husband doesn't head off to work until nine, so he could be here with the kids in the mornings while I would go work out."

Edna and Betty had started driving to the pool together each day, becoming more than acquaintances but not exactly good friends.

"We would talk in the car, coming and going, of course," she said. "But swimming isn't exactly a social activity. Things remained polite but friendly. She wasn't the nicest person in the world, and a bit of a pill as a neighbor—but I sure never expected to find her dead on the floor!"

Jo nodded, shuddering at the image of Edna in her tomato-juice-filled shower cap.

"She wasn't very neighborly?"

Betty rolled her eyes.

"Well, like this," she said, gesturing toward her children, who were laughing and screaming as they played. "The noise of my children drove her crazy. But they're just running in the yard, just being kids."

Jo nodded, thinking of poor Sally, Edna's daughter, wondering how it must have felt to be the child of woman who didn't like the sounds of children. No wonder Sally was bitter.

"Did you hear an argument last Friday night, the night Edna died?"

"The police asked me that too. I told them that with the window unit air conditioner, we don't hear a thing at night."

"Did Edna have many friends?" Jo asked, hoping to hear news of a silver-haired man.

"A few," Betty replied. "Simon was at her house a lot, of course, and the ladies from her club dropped in from time to time."

Jo tried not to react too enthusiastically.

"Simon?"

"An older gentleman. You don't know him?"

"Sort of sixtyish?" Jo asked. "With silver hair and a mustache?"

"Yeah, that's him. I don't know if he was her boyfriend or a relative or what. I never saw them holding hands or anything, but they sure spent a lot of time together. She was pretty vague about it when I asked her. I was surprised he didn't come to the funeral."

Jo's heart leaped. More than likely she now had a name for the man in the photos—and that name was *Simon*, the same name the women at the funeral had been whispering about.

"What about this club of hers?" Jo asked, thinking of Mrs. Chutney and Mrs. Parker. "They played Bunco or something?"

"Bunco?" Betty replied, laughing. "Not that I know of. According to Edna, it was a women's investment club. Simon was helping them make some wise choices."

Jo blinked, her mind reeling.

"Were they earning a good return?" Jo asked.

Betty glanced at her kids and lowered her voice.

"Rumor has it," she said, "that this guy Simon has the Midas touch. Apparently, everything with him turns to gold, if you know what I mean."

Jo nodded, wishing Danny were in on this conversation.

"If we weren't living paycheck to paycheck," Betty continued, "I think I would have invested with them myself."

"So where does this Simon fellow live?" Jo asked.

"I don't know," Betty replied. "Being new to the area, I'm not familiar with the whole town. But I don't think Edna ever said."

"How about his car?" Jo asked, hoping she didn't sound too persistent. "What kind of car does he drive?"

Betty excused herself to pick up her daughter, who had fallen short of the leaf pile and banged her knee. By the time she had comforted her and returned to the fence, Jo's mind was filled with even more questions.

"What kind of car?" Betty asked, considering. "I don't think he had one, from what I saw. Edna usually drove him around."

"He's got the Midas touch but doesn't own a car?" Jo asked.

Betty shrugged.

"Sometimes older folks don't like to drive."

"But he was only in his sixties. That's not old."

"Mom!" the boy yelled, in a tussle with his sister over the rake.

"I don't know," Betty said, hurrying over to settle the fight. "I never saw him driving."

"Has he been around since she died?" Jo asked.

Betty picked up her son and distracted him with a big pine cone.

"Come to think of it," she said, looking as if she was ready to head inside, "no. I haven't seen Simon around for a couple days."

# 17

"Awesome wheels, dude!" Danny said, rolling the boy toward the standard blue background.

When the mother and son arrived for their photo shoot, she confirmed that the child had cerebral palsy and that he would have to stay in the chair because of the straps that helped hold him upright. Danny had cleared away the table and props, glad to work with what he'd been presented. At least the wheelchair was cool looking, very state-of-the-art.

"My...chair...is...new," the boy said in a garbled voice. "I...can... pop...wheelies."

Danny laughed, glad to see a glint of mischief in the kid's eyes. If he could capture that spark, they could get some excellent photos.

"You'll have to shoot him from the neck up," the mother said. "Can we drape something directly behind him so the wheelchair doesn't show?"

Danny hesitated, surprised at her request. He'd had a handicapped friend in college, a paraplegic, and from what he'd learned in that relationship, a disabled person's chair is often very much a part of who they are.

Still, the customer's always right. He took out the fabric he usually draped under babies and covered the back of the chair with it, tucking it in behind the kid's shoulders. He adjusted the lights and the camera and then snapped a few shots. Finally, he swung the TV screen toward the anxious mother.

"How's that?" he asked.

She studied the image for a minute and then shook her head.

"It still looks obvious that something's there. Can you go in closer and just get his face?"

Danny did as she asked, zooming in. He tried to get the kid to smile, but it wasn't easy.

"That's better," the mother said, looking at the screen. "You can't see the stupid chair at all."

Danny tried to snap a few more pictures, but the spark was completely gone from the boy's eyes now.

Even though the mother was pleased with the pictures he was taking, Danny felt himself growing upset. Finally, he called Tiffany into the room and asked if she would stay with the child for a minute.

"There's some paperwork I need for you to do down the hall," he said to the mother. "Come with me, if you don't mind."

Tiffany looked at him oddly as he led the woman out of the studio, closing the door behind them. He brought her out to the empty waiting area and waved his hand toward the couch. She sat, looking confused.

"Ma'am," he said, sitting across from her, "I don't mean to be disrespectful, but I wonder if we could talk for a minute about your son."

"What about him?" she asked defensively.

Danny offered a silent prayer for wisdom and then let out his breath.

"I don't pretend to know how hard it must be to raise a handicapped child, but I do know one thing. Whenever you try to hide that chair or call it 'stupid,' it's like you're insulting your son himself."

"What?"

He took a deep breath and tried again, lowering his voice.

"Am I correct in assuming he's always been in a wheelchair—and probably always will be?"

"Of course."

"Then that chair is an extension of who he is. It's his legs. It's his mobility. If I can be so bold, in a way it's his whole world."

She was silent, her forehead wrinkled into a frown.

"Please, ma'am, don't try to hide that chair in these pictures. Why don't you celebrate it? Why don't we get some full-length shots, even? Why don't we let your son know how good-looking he is in it? It's not stupid to him. It's like a part of his body. It's his ticket to freedom."

Speech over, he sat back, hoping he wouldn't take big heat for this conversation from his boss. All the woman had wanted was some simple shots to put in her Christmas cards. Instead, he had turned it into a federal issue.

Still, the look on her face told him she was considering all he had said. After a moment, tears formed in her eyes.

"No one ever said that to me before," she told him, reaching up to wipe a tear that spilled onto her cheek. "But you're right. That chair isn't his enemy; it's his friend."

"Exactly," Danny replied. "So what's more important? That you hide the chair in the photos or that you show your son you embrace it as much as you embrace him?"

She nodded, a new determination on her face. Fortunately for him, she was the kind of person who was willing to learn and change. So many folks might have taken what he'd said and stormed out of there, furious.

"Let's go try again," she said softly, reaching out a hand to him. "And thanks. You've really given me something to think about."

Jo had to go home and change into something nicer before heading over to the college. She made it to Lancaster Hall just a few minutes before her appointment, easily finding the office of Archibald Pike, the dean of Arts and Humanities.

She tapped on the door and the man looked up, a bald fellow in his fifties with a warm manner and an easy smile. She introduced herself and thanked him for seeing her on such short notice.

"Not a problem," he said. "I had an appointment with a student at this hour, but she canceled just before you called."

"Well, I sure appreciate it. This shouldn't take long."

She sat where he indicated, in a padded chair next to his desk. Reaching into a tote bag, she pulled out the print of the painting of the Nativity and held it out to him.

"I'm trying to get some information about this print," she said. "The artist, the date, the value—you know, just the standard stuff."

He took it from her and looked at it, nodding almost immediately.

"That's funny," he said. "You're not the first person to ask about this same picture recently."

"I'm not?"

He shook his head.

"No, in fact, I loaned out our slide of it to a colleague a few weeks ago because he wanted to study it."

"Who was that?" she asked.

"Professor McMann, over in the history department," he said. "Same thing. He described this picture in detail and asked what I knew about it. I let him go through the slides until he found the one he was looking for."

She didn't reply but made a mental note to pay a little visit to Professor McMann.

"Let me see if I can find the slide," he told her, standing and going to the shelf. He pulled down a fat notebook, inside of which were pages of slides interspersed with pages of text. The man hummed to himself as he flipped through until he found what he was looking for.

"Here it is," he said, coming back to the desk. "*The Nativity* by John Singleton Copley."

"When was it painted?"

"About 1776," he replied. "Copley was a well-known portrait artist in the colonies in the seventeen hundreds. Just before the American Revolution, he moved to Europe, gave up portraiture for the most part, and began working on more historical subjects instead, like this one."

Jo nodded, scribbling notes in the little notebook she kept in her purse.

"Do you know where the original of this painting is located?" she asked.

He scanned the text and then nodded.

"Says here it was acquired by the Museum of Fine Arts in Boston in 1972," he said. "I have no idea of the value of the original, but certainly this print of yours has no great value beyond the nice frame. You could probably sell it for twenty or thirty dollars."

"How could I get a look at the original?"

"Well, here's the slide," he said, pulling the small white square from its sleeve. "To see it in person, I suppose you'd have to go to Boston and look at it there, if they even have it in their active collection."

He handed her the slide and she held it up to the light, vaguely surprised to see the silver-haired man in the painting. Somehow, she had assumed he was painted in later by a forger. *Then again,* she thought as she handed the slide back, *someone could have tampered with the slide as well.*

"If you want to see the museum's collection," he said, "you might go online to their database. You'd be surprised how many images have been uploaded there."

"Thank you, I will," she said.

She picked up the print and looked at it again.

"May I ask you another question?" she said.

"Of course."

"When an artist paints a picture like this, how do they decide to use these particular faces? Do these people just come out of their imagination, do they go by some historical record, or do they set up this scene with models and pose it out?"

"More than likely the latter," the professor said. "Chances are that these were simply local folks who had a biblical look to them or an interesting face. Copely would have brought them into his studio, one or two at the time, posed them in a way that would relate to the painting as a whole, and then worked on their part of the picture."

Jo nodded, looking into the eyes of the kindly professor.

"So even though this painting depicts an event from two thousand years ago," she said, "you're telling me that the faces in the picture were probably people who were alive two *hundred* years ago?"

"More than likely, yes," he said, smiling. "Just as our movies today might use actors to depict historical figures. It may be the man we know as Mel Gibson, but he's playing the part of William Wallace in *Brave-heart.* We may recognize Dame Judi Dench, but she's posing as Queen Elizabeth in *Shakespeare in Love.*"

He went on with several other examples, but she got the point: If the painting was genuine, then the man with the silver hair had been alive and serving as an artist's model in 1776.

Danny was exhausted but happy, thrilled with how the sitting with the handicapped boy had gone after talking with the mother. She really was a good woman, and once they went back into the room, her whole attitude had changed. Danny got a number of great shots of the kid grinning from his chair, the glint fully visible in his mischievous eyes. When Tiffany sat down to make her sales pitch, it wasn't even necessary. The woman bought the deluxe package—and thanked Danny again for his honesty and wisdom as they were leaving.

After the door closed behind them, Danny went back to the lab to give Jo a quick call on her cell phone. She sounded a little out of breath and said she was jogging from one side of the campus to the other, hoping to pop in on a history professor by the name of McMann. She had also heard from her chemistry professor, who told her to leave the photocopy of the notebook for him to go through later.

"I've got lots to tell you," Jo said. "But the most important thing is that I might have an ID on the silver-haired guy in the pictures from Edna's next-door neighbor. According to her, a silver-haired man named Simon has been around a lot, and he was either a friend or boyfriend of Edna Pratt."

"I've got lots to tell you too," Danny replied. "I was able to track down two of the original photos on the Internet, and in both cases, the man simply isn't there. He was definitely added in later using trick photography."

"I thought so. Too bad things don't seem quite as cut-and-dried with this painting."

"No?"

Jo described her visit with the art professor and the information she'd been given there. As she talked, Danny sat at the computer, went online, and typed in the artist's name and the name of the painting.

It showed up in a number of databases, and in every case, the silver-haired fellow—he would have to start thinking of him as Simon—in every case, Simon was there in the painting, in the upper left corner, his face half hidden in shadow.

"Maybe this was a look-alike ancestor," Danny ventured. "The face is fairly obscured."

"Maybe," Jo said, sounding skeptical. "But I still want to talk to the museum and verify whether that person is in the original painting or not."

When their conversation was finished, Jo hung up the phone, dropped it into her bag, and slowed her jog to a walk. No need to be out of breath when she walked into the professor's office.

She reached the chemistry building first, so she went inside and slid the packet of photocopied papers under her former professor's door. The explanation she had given him over the telephone was that she'd found some old papers containing what looked like scientific formulas, but that she couldn't make heads or tails of the data; before she threw the papers out, she'd said, she just wanted to make sure they weren't important. He promised to get back to her on it by the end of the day.

Simply walking through the chemistry building brought back a rush of happy memories. The smell of formaldehyde was strong throughout the halls, reminding her of the years she spent here earning her degree. Though her major was home economics, Jo had minored in chemistry.

She exited from the other end of the building, and then it was just a little way farther to the history building. Jo didn't know Professor McMann, but she hoped to find him inside.

Unfortunately, his office door was closed with no light visible from underneath. Disappointed, she consulted the scheduled taped to the wall, and saw he was teaching a history class at that moment in room 204. Glancing at her watch, Jo knew the hour would be up in just a few minutes. If she hurried, she might be able to collar him after class.

The classroom was easy enough to find, and she stood in the hall waiting for the bell, listening to him teach about Patrick Henry. He sounded younger than she expected, and once the bell rang and the students cleared out, she stepped into the room to see that he couldn't have been more than thirty or thirty-five at most. He was handsome in a quiet sort of way, with straight brown hair and frameless glasses. She tried not to smile when she noticed that there were leather patches on the elbows of his suit jacket. She supposed that with professors, that look never went out of style.

"Dr. McMann?" she asked, stepping toward the podium. He had been gathering together his papers, and he barely looked up as she approached. "Hello, my name is Jo Tulip. I wonder if I could speak with you for a minute."

He tucked the papers under his arm and nodded.

"Problems with the assignment?" he asked.

"No," she smiled, "I graduated a few years ago. Well, six years ago, to be exact. But thanks for the compliment."

He adjusted his glasses and gave her a slight perusal. Then he smiled.

"What can I do for you?" he asked. "I'm afraid I have to be somewhere soon, but I do have a minute."

"May I walk with you? We can talk as we go."

Together, they left the classroom and then the building, walking side by side.

"I was given your name by Dean Pike in the art department," Jo said. "I went to see him to ask about a particular painting, and he said you recently inquired about the same one. *The Nativity* by John Singleton Copley? I wondered where you had seen the print and why you were asking about it."

He hesitated in his walking. Surprised, Jo hesitated as well, noting the strange look that came over his face.

"Why do you ask?" he said, lowering his voice and glancing one way and then the other.

"It's kind of a long story," she said. "Do you mind telling me why you wanted to know about the painting?"

He took a deep breath, held it, and then let it out.

"Not here," he said finally. "Later."

"Later?"

He ran a hand through his hair, blowing out a slow breath.

"I have to advise on a dissertation right now," he said, glancing down at his watch. "Can you meet me in, say, an hour? How about over there. By the student union."

Jo hesitated, wondering why he was being so weird. She knew he had to go, but she wondered if she could wait a whole hour to hear what he had to say!

"Sure," she said finally. She really didn't have a choice. "Whatever you want."

He nodded, looking into her eyes for the first time.

"I'm sorry, what was your name again?" he asked.

"Jo. Jo Tulip."

He reached out a hand for a shake, his fingers lingering just a moment too long in hers. His deep brown eyes connected with hers, and Jo felt an instant attraction, like a spark flickering at the base of her neck.

"Jo," he repeated. "Okay. I'll see you at the union at two o'clock."

Simon slept on the couch until well after noon, finally awakening to the sound of Wiggles slamming some pots and pans around in the kitchen. Though Wiggles was, of course, always uncoordinated, Simon had a feeling he was being extra loud in an attempt to send a message.

Simon sat up and wiped his face with his hands, feeling about a hundred years old. Everything hurt, from the roots of his hair to the bottoms of his feet. He was wiped out—but at least the police had never shown up.

Slowly he stood and yawned, and then he made his way to the doorway of the kitchen, where Wiggles was busy trying to cook some eggs. He had spilled some of the egg mixture down the front of the pan, and now they were making smoke as they burned away in the flames of the burner.

"What's eating you?" Simon asked.

Wiggles gave him a dirty look and continued scraping the eggs in the pan.

"You are," he said. "Our deal. You're supposed to do the dishes. Look at this mess."

The sink was overflowing with dirty dishes. An inch-long brown roach scurried across the top.

"You're right. I'm sorry," Simon said. He certainly didn't want to push his luck. The last thing he needed was to get kicked out. "I had a really late night last night. I'll do 'em as soon as I finish eating."

"You bet you'll do 'em," Wiggles said. "Or you're out of here for good."

Simon nodded, knowing that Wiggles was near the boiling point. Over the years of visiting there, he had come to know the man pretty well—not to mention the time they had already spent sharing a cell. That taught you a lot about a person, for sure.

After changing his clothes, Simon returned to the kitchen, taking juice and a package of frozen sausage from the freezer. Silently, the men worked side by side to finish making breakfast. Simon fixed the sausage in the dirty microwave, and then he slipped some bread into the toaster.

Once the meal was on the table, they sat across from each other and ate, their smacks and burps the only sound in the room. When Simon was finished, he wiped his mouth and told his friend the eggs had been utterly delicious.

"Thanks," Wiggles said begrudgingly, trying to pick a piece of sausage from the front of his shirt. "I try."

"Remember the eggs in the joint?" Simon said, breaching their unspoken rule about not discussing their time in prison. "Did we ever figure out what made them so very, very yellow?"

Wiggles laughed, spewing juice down his chin.

"I don't think they was eggs at all," he said, reaching for his napkin. "I think they was yellow-colored, egg-flavored slop."

They shared a laugh, and it suddenly dawned on Simon that there were actually two people in this whole world he could count on: Wiggles and Edna.

Somehow, he just had to get her on the phone and find out what had happened after he left Friday night.

# 18

Danny had a long break between appointments, so he was glad when Jo called and asked if there was any way he could come over to the campus.

"I'll be talking to Keith McMann, a history professor, at two o'clock," she said, "and I'd love for you to be there. Looks like it might be important."

Before leaving the studio, Danny called his mother, who answered in her usual cheery voice. She said she was just heading out the door to go to the Ladies League luncheon.

"I figured you would be," Danny told her. "I wonder if you could do me a favor while you're there."

"Sure, honey. What do you need?"

He walked to the fax machine and placed an enlargement of Simon's face into the tray.

"Soon as we hang up, I'm going to fax you a picture of a man. Would you mind discreetly showing it around to see if you can get any information on this guy?"

"What is he, wanted by the FBI?"

Danny forced a laugh, though for all he knew, the guy could be.

"It's a long story," he said. "Jo got a job clearing out the belongings of that woman who died, Edna Pratt. We need to locate this man because we found some things we think belong to him."

Well, it was a lie that wasn't really a lie. They did need to locate the man, and chances are the photos and the notebook were his—or at least were connected to him in some way.

"All right, but do it now," she said. "As it is, I'm already a few minutes late."

They hung up and Danny sent the fax. Then he gathered his things and told Tiffany he'd be back in time for the next appointment.

He couldn't find a parking place near the student union, so he ended up having to park in the far lot and then walk a bit to get there. By the time he arrived, Jo was sitting at one of the outside picnic tables with a man of about thirty, tall and handsome and exactly the kind of guy she usually went for. Add to that he was probably quite intelligent, and it was a double whammy. Jo always was a sucker for brains.

From a distance Danny could see her laugh and then absently slip a lock of hair behind one ear in that feminine way she had. He knew she wasn't consciously flirting, but suddenly a stab of something painful shot directly into his heart.

Danny had known he would have to give her time to get over Bradford before he brought up the subject of his own feelings for her. But never in his wildest dreams had it occurred to him that she might move on this quickly to someone new.

He approached the table, trying not to let his emotions show all over his face.

"Danny!" Jo said, giving him a smile as warm and genuine as the one she had given the professor. "We were just talking about you."

"Oh?" Danny asked, introducing himself to the professor before taking a seat beside her.

"Keith heard your family perform at the town festival."

*Keith.* So already they were on a first-name basis.

"Regeneration, right?" the man said. "You guys are great."

"Thank you."

They talked for a bit about the group and their music, and Danny found himself calming down somewhat. At least the guy was friendly—and it didn't hurt that he was a fan.

"Anyway, Keith," Jo said finally, "we didn't want to hold you up too long. We just wanted to find out about your interest in this painting."

"Why do you want to know? If you don't mind my asking."

"It's a long story," Jo said casually. "We're putting someone's affairs in order, a woman who recently passed away. This was among her possessions, and we're just a bit confused by it. When we asked Dean Pike for more information, he said you were asking about the same picture recently. We figured there must be a connection, and that maybe you could shed some light on things for us."

Jo pulled the print from her tote bag and set it on the table. McMann picked it up.

"Yes, that's the one," he said, studying it.

"And you were asking about it because…" Danny prompted.

"I saw it and thought it was simply beautiful. I wanted to get a print of it for myself."

Danny felt Jo kick him lightly under the table. Surely there was more to the story than that.

"Where did you see it?" Danny pressed.

"At a history lecture I was giving. It was on display there, and I thought it was magnificent."

Danny wasn't sure what to ask next. The coincidence was just too great not to have more of a story behind it.

"A history lecture?" Jo said. "Where?"

"At a women's club."

Danny tried not to show any reaction.

"Tell us more about this women's club," he said.

The guy hesitated and then spoke.

"Well, it started a few months ago. One day a man came up to me after a class—like you did today, Jo. He said his name was Simon Foster and he was in need of an expert in history."

Jo glanced at Danny and he gave her a slight nod. Now they had a last name for this Simon fellow. Foster. Simon Foster.

"He had a few photographs he wanted information about, histori-cally speaking," the professor continued. "We went through the pictures, and I identified them for him. He had a shot of the Civil War and one of some depression-era farmers. A mid-twentieth-century Olympics. Things like that."

"Emma Goldman?" Danny asked, earning a quick glance from Jo.

"Yes. On a street car."

"So how did all of this lead to your interest in the painting?" Jo asked.

The professor looked from side to side, a red blush inexplicably creeping into his cheeks.

"He asked me if I would come to a women's group and give a short lecture about the photos. I wasn't interested until he said he'd pay me two hundred dollars. Two hundred dollars—for a half hour's work! He said he would have the prints put into PowerPoint and all I would have to do is show up and speak about the era that each of the photos represented.

It sounded easy enough to me. I can talk American history in my sleep. And I could always use a few extra hundred bucks."

"So you went?" Danny asked.

"Yes," he said, no longer making eye contact. "The meeting was at a lady's house, very lovely, with tea sandwiches and punch."

"Was the meeting at the home of a woman named Edna Pratt?" Jo asked.

He coughed and then shook his head.

"I don't think so. It was on Lagnaippe Street. Chutney was the name, I believe."

"Chutney?" Jo asked. "Iris Chutney?"

"Yes, I think that was it."

Danny and Jo knew Iris Chutney from church. She was an older woman, a widow who lived alone in a big house in one of the town's most exclusive neighborhoods.

"Anyway," McMann continued, "I gave my lecture. It went fine. I collected my check."

"And the painting?"

"The painting was there on display that night, a print like this one. I fell in love with it. Something about the lightness of Mary and the baby, contrasted with the shadows and the darker clothing on the people around them. And that moon through the window. When we consider the Nativity, we always think of the star of Bethlehem, but this artist chose to feature a full moon instead. That intrigued me. I'm very in tune with the different phases of the moon."

Danny sighed, sorry to learn that beyond getting the last name of Simon, this interview was going to be a dead end. He felt that this guy was holding back something, but he wasn't sure how to find out what it was.

"Okay, so what is it you're not saying?" Jo asked, surprising both of the men. Danny was impressed she'd had the nerve to ask.

Keith McMann put down the print and put his hands on the edge of the table, leaning forward. Sure enough, the blush had spread to his whole face.

"I think I was a pawn in some elaborate joke," he said softly. "In fact, I've been so embarrassed about it, I haven't told a soul what happened."

"What did happen?" Jo asked breathlessly, also leaning forward. Danny thought she was leaning in just a little too close.

"About halfway through the lecture," the professor said, "I looked up at the screen, at the shot of the farmers next to the sugarcane. It struck me that there was something odd about the picture, something different. I continued with the lecture, but when it was over and Simon Foster was distracted, I went to his computer and ran through the presentation slides. The photo had been altered. The whole lot of them, actually. The man had inserted himself into every one of the pictures!"

This time, Jo gripped Danny's knee under the table with her hand.

"What did you do?" she asked.

"I didn't want to embarrass the guy, but I was quite confused by it. The more I thought about it, the more it bothered me. The next day, he wouldn't return my calls, so I went to the address that was listed on his check and confronted him."

"And he said…?"

"He just laughed and apologized. He said he and a few of the other ladies were setting up an elaborate practical joke on Mrs. Parker. He said it was hard to explain but that if I wanted to come back the following night to her birthday party, all would be revealed at that time."

"So did you go?"

He shook his head.

"No," he said dismissively. "I believed him. Never thought of it again."

"But you still pursued the painting."

He shrugged.

"I couldn't get it off my mind. When I tried to contact Simon Foster again to study the print more closely and possibly get the name of the artist, again he didn't call me back. So I approached Dean Pike instead."

Jo and Danny looked at each other, both obviously wondering the same thing.

"So where does Simon Foster live?" Jo asked. "We'd like very much to get in touch with him ourselves."

Jo wanted to go there right away, but Danny asked her to wait for him. The address wasn't exactly in the safest part of town.

"I just have a few more appointments and then I'll be free," Danny said, looking at his watch. "Why don't I pick you up when I'm done?"

Reluctantly, she agreed.

"Come and get me at Edna's," she said. "I'll continue working on the house until then."

The afternoon passed quickly—Jo finished the sewing room and moved on to the bedroom—and soon she and Danny were in his car, driving toward the address the professor had given them for the silver-haired man in the photos named Simon Foster. According to Keith, Simon lived in a seedy long-term motel at the edge of town, a place ironically called the Palace.

Jo had never been there before, but she knew the area. It was in an old, industrial section of town, dotted with abandoned buildings, a few warehouses, and a sprawling trailer park. The hotel was at the end of a dead-end street, a blond brick building with a torn and faded awning over the main entrance.

The smell of stale smoke and mildew assaulted them as they went in the door. The front desk was unattended, so they rang a buzzer next to the counter, and eventually an older gentleman shuffled into the room.

"Help you?" he asked. "We don't rent by the hour here."

Danny stepped forward, looking offended by the man's insinuation.

"We're not trying to check in," Danny said. "We're looking for one of your guests. A man by the name of Simon Foster?"

"Foster," he replied, spitting toward the trash can. "Ain't seen him since Friday."

"You mean he checked out?"

"Not really. He just left. Might be back. His room's paid for through the end of the month."

"But you think he's gone for good?"

"Probably. When I got here Saturday morning, his key had been dropped in the slot. Housekeeper said the room was stripped out. Guy took all his stuff—not to mention every light bulb and roll of toilet paper in there."

"Is that normal," Danny asked, "for someone to pay for a room and decide to leave early?"

The old man chuckled, which turned into a hacking cough. When he was finished, he spit again and then spoke.

"This ain't exactly the Hilton," he said. "Costs a lot less per day if you pay by the month. Nonrefundable, though, if you decide to leave early."

"So you have a lot of transients here?" Jo asked.

The man smiled, showing several empty sockets where some of his teeth should have been.

"Folks around here do tend to come and go," he said, nodding. He turned and started to walk away, as if their business was complete.

"Could we ask a few more questions?" Jo said.

"Time is money," he replied.

Jo didn't know what he meant, but quickly Danny stepped forward and gave the guy a ten-dollar bill. Again, they were rewarded with a toothless smile.

"What else you want to know?" he asked, pocketing the cash and stepping back toward them. "You two cops or something?"

"No," Jo said, offering no further explanation. "Did Simon ever bring any guests here?"

The man seemed to consider her question.

"There was one woman," he said. "Older lady, grayish blond hair. Kind of plain looking, big nose."

Jo nodded, certain he was describing Edna.

"I figured she was his pigeon," he added.

"Pigeon?" Danny asked.

"Yeah. Two Eyes? Square? Shaky Mom?"

Danny and Jo looked at each other and then at him.

"Simon was the Mack," he said slowly, as if that explained everything. Jo felt as though he were speaking in a foreign language. "At least from what I could tell. Though he might have been working it alone. I never saw him with a drag team."

"I'm sorry," Jo said, "but we don't understand these terms you're using. What's a drag team?"

"A con. The guy's a con artist. The Mack is the boss of a con."

Jo's pulse surged.

"What's a pigeon?" she asked.

"The victim," he replied. "Little old ladies are always the easiest to fleece. That's why it's called a Granny Game."

Jo looked at Danny, a number of things suddenly moving into focus in her brain.

"What makes you think Simon Foster was a con artist?" she asked.

The old man shrugged.

"I been around enough to know it when I see it. Shoot, he tried to double-fold me when he checked in."

"Double-fold?"

The guy grinned, and Jo could tell he was enjoying this. Judging by the sounds coming from the back room, he didn't have much else to do except watch television anyway.

"I'll show you," he said.

He went around the counter, opened a drawer, and reached for a metal cash box.

"Don't watch," he said, so Jo and Danny averted their eyes, looking at each other instead. Soon, the man came back around the counter and gave them a nod.

"You be me, I'm you," he said. "I'd like a room, please."

Danny looked confused, but Jo understood what he was saying.

"That'll be two hundred dollars for the month," she said, playing the part of the innkeeper.

Nodding, the guy pulled a big wad of cash from his pocket, held his thumb across the front of the wad, and carefully counted out two hundred dollars in twenties. Then he pulled the twenties from the wad and handed them over.

"Now," he said. "I just gave you two hundred dollars, right?"

"Right."

"Are you sure?" he asked.

"You counted it right in front of us," she said. Nevertheless, she counted the bills out onto the counter, coming up with only one hundred and sixty dollars when she was done.

"How'd you do that?" Danny exclaimed. "I watched you. There was no sleight of hand."

"I fixed the wad," he told them. "Two of those twenties were folded in half, so they got counted twice. Classic con. Since I counted out the money right in front of you, you assumed I gave you the right amount."

Jo had to laugh. What an amazing trick!

"Vendors do it at football games and carnivals all the time," he said. "You buy a hot dog, give him a ten, he counts out your change using a few folded ones, you take it back and stick it in your pocket and don't bother to count it because you saw him count it and so you think it's correct."

He took the money back from her, moved behind the counter, and locked it into the box.

"Anything else I can help you folks with today?" he asked.

Jo looked at Danny, knowing they'd already learned more here than they'd bargained for.

"I think that'll do," Danny said. "Thanks for all of your help."

"No problem."

They started to leave, but Jo paused at the door.

"Excuse me, but can I make a suggestion?" she asked, unable to resist.

The old guy nodded.

"Sprinkle a little baking soda on the carpet in here, let it sit for about fifteen minutes, then vacuum it up. That should help eliminate the musty smell."

"Yeah?"

"While you're at it," she added, "you might cut up a few apples and set them out in bowls on the counter. That'll suck up some of the smoke."

"Thanks," he said. "What are you, like Betty Crocker or something?"

She smiled.

"Something like that."

# 19

Danny and Jo were quiet in the car, each lost in thought.

"I think we should go to the police," he said finally, and she nodded.

"I was just thinking the same thing."

He turned onto the road that would take them to the police station, feeling an odd heaviness settle in around his heart. Up until now this had all been fun and games. Once they brought the information they had to the chief, everything might change.

Still, the cops needed to know what he and Jo were pursuing. More than likely, Simon Foster had been working some sort of con game on Edna Pratt before she ended up dead. It all sounded very fishy, especially considering Jo's certainty that the woman's death had not been an accident.

Danny's phone rang, and a glance at the screen told him his mother was calling.

"Hey, Mom, what's up?"

"What's up?" she said. "Why don't you tell me? Thanks for making me a pariah!"

"What?"

"A pariah! All I did was whip out this fax and start passing it around, and the next thing you know, half the group of women simply got up and left!"

Danny looked at Jo, his eyes wide.

"Are you kidding me?"

"No. Well, maybe I'm exaggerating a little. But it was at least six or seven of them. Can you tell me, please, what I did that was so awful? I feel like an idiot and I don't even know why."

"Mom, I'm so sorry. I didn't expect that kind of reaction. Jo and I were just trying to figure out who he is."

"What's going on?" Jo whispered sharply, but he waved her off.

"Mom, who walked out? Did you know them?"

"Of course I do. They're friends." She rattled off the names, several of which he recognized, including Iris Chutney, the woman Professor McMann had mentioned.

Danny thanked his mother for the names and for her efforts, despite the bad reaction. They talked long enough for her to calm down a bit, and he promised her he would explain everything very soon. Once he hung up the phone, he told Jo what his mother had said.

"I think the con was bigger than just Edna," Jo replied. "I think a whole group of women were being conned by this guy. I think Simon Foster was a sharp character who blew into town and started up some kind of crazy scheme and tricked a local expert like Keith McMann into making him seem legitimate. I think something went wrong last Friday night and Simon killed Edna and skipped town. That's my theory. What do you think?"

Danny put on his blinker to turn into the police station parking lot.

"I think you should spell it out just that way for the chief," he said.

Chief Cooper didn't seem to be in the best mood, considering that they had caught him practically on his way out the door. Still, Jo was glad he agreed to sit down with them. They went into his office and shared their thoughts and what they had learned. When they were finished, he shook his head slowly.

"I'm sorry, folks," he said. "But nothing has come to light in this office about any sort of swindle or con going on. No one has reported anything. No money has gone missing. And there's a perfectly logical explanation for Edna Pratt's *accidental* death. I don't see on what grounds I could proceed with any of this."

Danny reached into his pocket and pulled out his wallet. From there, he extracted a folded piece of paper. He unfolded it and set it on the desk in front of the chief.

"How about you go into your computer and look up the name Simon Foster?" he said. "That's his picture, right there. That's what he looks like."

"That's all you got, a face and a name? No social? No date of birth?"

"Sorry. That's it."

The chief studied the picture for a minute, looked at Danny, and frowned.

"I'll send it through," he said tiredly. "But if I do, then can I go home?"

"Absolutely," Danny replied.

The chief turned to the computer at his desk and painstakingly typed in the information using one finger. After a few minutes, he exhaled slowly and spoke.

"Foster's an alias," he said. "Real name's Kurtz. Simon Kurtz."

Jo blinked, knowing she had recently heard or seen the name Kurtz somewhere.

"Is he a wanted man?" Danny asked.

"Nope. Has a criminal record, but no outstanding warrants. Hold on."

He pressed a few more keys and a new screen came up in front of him.

"Okay, well, the prison thing is a matter of public record. Go do your own research on the Internet. I suggest you start with the state of Florida."

"They've got prison records online?" Jo asked.

"With photos and everything," the chief replied. "You can't escape the long arm of the law."

He gave them back their photo and stood.

"Okay, I'm going home now," he said. "Sorry I couldn't help you more."

"You won't even consider the possibility that Edna Pratt was murdered?" Jo said.

"On what grounds, Miss Tulip?" he asked, not unkindly. "Because you have a hunch? I don't care if you are the Smart Chick. It's not enough."

It was getting dark by the time they came out of the station. Danny apologized that he had to abandon Jo in order to go to music rehearsal at the church.

"In the meantime," he said, "why don't you go online and see if you can find Simon's prison records?"

"I'll do that and more," she replied, sounding determined. "I heard or read the name Kurtz somewhere in the last few days. I feel sure it was at Edna's house. I'm going to dig back through the paperwork I've already boxed up to send to Sally. That name's really bugging me."

They drove a few miles in silence and then Danny took a deep breath, hoping Jo would read his words simply as concerned friendship.

"Look, Jo," he said, "I don't think it's safe for you to be there at Edna's at night by yourself. I wish you'd wait until morning."

He expected an argument, but she simply nodded.

"I know what you mean," she told him. "Why don't I call Marie and see if she'll meet me there? I want her to look at the house anyway, so we can start the ball rolling on getting it sold."

Jo made the call to what sounded like a very eager Marie, who agreed to come right over.

After she hung up the phone, Jo turned to Danny and smiled.

"Thank you," she said.

"For what?"

"For believing me. I know you were probably humoring me at first, but you still went through with my investigation. And now I can tell you believe me. It means a lot."

"You're welcome," he said. "And for what it's worth, I think you are definitely the smartest of the Smart Chicks."

By the time Danny and Jo reached Edna's, Marie was already sitting there in her car in the driveway, waiting for them. If she didn't succeed in her real estate career, it wouldn't be for lack of trying.

Danny promised Jo he would meet her at her house later, after practice was finished. Then he watched her jump from his car, give Marie a quick hug, and head into the house with her.

Deep inside, he felt a physical ache, acknowledging the growing possibility that even if Jo found out how he felt about her, she might not ever feel the same in return. It hadn't struck him until today when they were meeting with the professor that Danny wasn't her "type" at all and never had been. For the last two days he had been thinking in terms of "when" they might move from friendship into something more.

Now he had to wonder if he needed to change that "when" to "if." *If.*

Putting it out of his mind for now, Danny drove toward the church, taking just a few minutes to hit a fast-food drive-through on the way to get a burger and fries, supersized. He knew his sisters would give him grief about the unhealthy choice—they already thought he was a Neanderthal when it came to food—but he had missed lunch, so he was starving.

Despite all of the concerns weighing heavily on Danny's mind, band practice was fun, as usual. Regeneration rehearsed in the church's old sanctuary, a vast improvement over the years they had spent practicing in the family's garage. They usually had the building to themselves on Tuesday nights, but this time there was a group of people in the main sanctuary, decorating for the new sermon series.

"Oh, no," Danny's mother said when she came back from a restroom break. "Iris Chutney is in there. How awkward."

Danny sat up straight behind his drums, knowing this might be an opportunity to talk with the woman whose name kept popping up in the course of the investigation.

The moment they were finished rehearsing, Danny pulled his mother aside and asked if she would mind calling Mrs. Chutney into a small side room and staying there while Danny spoke with her.

Danny's mom looked relieved, as he felt certain she was confused and embarrassed by the whole incident.

Soon, Danny found himself in one of the Sunday school rooms, sitting in a circle of chairs with his mother, who was being too chatty in the face of her nervousness, and Mrs. Chutney, who looked as though she might bolt any minute. Praying for guidance, Danny took a deep breath and began.

Gently, he explained that he was trying to get some information about a man, a fellow named Simon Foster, who had recently moved to Mulberry Glen and was doing some business with some of the women there in town. Danny was making a few educated guesses as he spoke, but judging from the look on Mrs. Chutney's face, he was hitting pretty close to the truth.

"Now that Edna Pratt has passed away," Danny said, "Simon Foster has disappeared, and I'm trying to figure out where he might have gone or what happened to him. I wondered if maybe you had some dealings with him, and what you could tell me."

To his surprise, Mrs. Chutney suddenly burst into tears. Danny's mom quickly moved over beside her and put an arm around her shoulders, pulling her close as the woman sobbed. Danny retrieved a box of tissues from beside the door and handed them over, and for a few minutes all that could be heard in the room was sobbing and sniffling and soft murmurings of comfort. Finally, Danny's mom looked up at him, an imploring expression on her face.

"I know this is difficult for you," Danny said to Mrs. Chutney. "But it's important. What can you tell me about Simon Foster?"

The woman took a ragged breath and swiped at her face with tissues.

"Not much," she whispered finally. "Just that I'm afraid we were a foolish bunch of old women—with nothing to show for it now except broken hearts and ruined hopes. I can't tell you the promises he made…"

She started wailing again, and Danny patiently waited out her sobs.

"What sort of promises?" he asked finally, but she shook her head and closed her eyes.

"I can't tell you," she said. "I won't tell."

He tried to think of a different approach.

"What do you know about Simon?" he asked. "Was he a friend of Edna Pratt's?"

She blew her nose loudly.

"He was a friend of Edna's grandfather," she said. "They were buddies when they were young."

"Edna's grandfather?" Danny said. "But Simon is only in his fifties or sixties."

She closed her eyes and spoke softly.

"He is older than you'd think," she said. "Much, much older."

Danny thought of the photos, of all of the doctored pictures that featured Simon at different, recognizable points in time. Was it possible he had convinced these women that he had actually been around when each of those photos was taken? Danny quickly did the math in his head. If the oldest photo had been taken in the mid 1800s, and the guy had been in his sixties at the time, that meant he was now over 200 years old! More than that, throw in the painting, and he'd be closer to 300!

Danny tried not to gasp, realizing that the reason for the photos and the painting was to convince these women that he *was* that old. He had probably been peddling some sort of pills or antiaging cream or something, telling them that if they used it, they could keep from growing old, as he had. Why else would he want them to think he had lived for centuries?

"How do you know he was a friend of Edna's grandfather?" Danny asked, hoping to start simple and move on from there.

"Edna had a photo of herself as a little girl, with him standing behind her and next to her grandfather."

"Did she remember him from when she was a child?"

"Yes. Of course."

Danny thought about that. *Edna* remembered this man from when *she* was a child? That meant one of two things: Either she was mistaken, or she was lying.

"Was the photo she had a family scene, on a front stoop, like from the fifties?"

"Yes," she gasped. "That's the one."

She opened her mouth as if to say more, but suddenly the door swung open and Mrs. Louise Parker appeared in the doorway. According to Danny's mother, Mrs. Parker was one of those who had walked out of the meeting when she saw Simon's picture.

"Iris!" she said. "What are you doing?"

Danny was devastated to see Mrs. Chutney pull back into herself and close her mouth. He knew this conversation was over.

"I was asking her about a man named Simon Foster," Danny said bravely. "Do you know him?"

If she did, she wasn't showing it in her face. She simply shook her head, reached out for Mrs. Chutney's hand, and pulled her up from the chair.

"I'm sorry, but Iris and I have to go."

Just like that, the two women were gone. Danny and his mother looked at each other, eyes wide.

"Don't ask, Mom," he said, shaking his head. "It's just too complicated to explain."

Simon couldn't stop pacing. Wiggles had gone out drinking, so he had the house to himself—a rare luxury. As good as his word, Simon had done all the dishes and taken out the trash. After that, he'd dug around in Wiggles' rusty old tool cabinet, coming out with a hack saw and half a can of spray paint. Then he retrieved the stolen bicycle from the the field nearby, sawed off the lock, and spray painted it a completely different color. Now all that remained was to kill time until the morning, when he could call the bank and see if the checks had cleared and the money was available for withdrawal.

Last night's misery—and today's resulting stiffness and pain—had convinced him that this was a risk worth taking. He was going for broke. If the money in the bank was free and clear by tomorrow, he was going to do what he needed to do to claim it. Someway, somehow, Edna had changed her mind and hadn't gone to the police. He just knew it, deep in his gut.

Though it was too early to go to bed, Simon was bone tired. He changed into pajamas, brushed his teeth, and laid the sheets out on the couch. He slid his suitcase from under the easy chair, reached into one of the hidden pockets, and pulled out his favorite picture, one of him and Edna as children. He held it tenderly, wondering if she could still remember that day as vividly as he could.

It was a Wednesday in June 1954, and their father had been released from prison the day before. The three years their dad had spent in the joint had made him thinner and more short-tempered—but it had also made him more extravagant. When he came home, he told everyone, relatives and kids included, to get dressed up because they were heading out for a steak dinner, a true luxury in those days. To this day, Simon wondered how he had paid for it.

Their mother had seemed beside herself, thrilled to have her husband home again, optimistic that everything was going to be easier for her, now that she didn't have to be a mother and the breadwinner at the same time. It had been a happy family day, filled with laughter and celebration. Their neighbor snapped the photo of the whole group out on their own front stoop, and in the picture Simon and Edna stood side by side, brother and sister, friends for life.

A month later, their mother went upstairs and hung herself by the sash from her bathrobe.

In the suicide note, she said simply that life was "too much." Simon and Edna never knew what that meant, exactly. How much is too much? Would they also someday have "too much" too?

After that, they held on to each other even more tightly. Their father was an okay guy, a little short on parenting skills but he did the best he could. Saddled with two children, he could have taken the easy route and unloaded them onto someone else. Instead, he decided to pull them into the grift. Within months, the three of them were traveling carnies, working the cat rack or the milk bottles, using every trick they knew to separate the customers from their cash.

Their dad had learned a lot in the joint, and he worked hard to pass the knowledge along to his children. Edna was the perfect shill, enthusiastically winning the games as an example for the customers, then quietly returning her "prizes" at the end of the night. Simon's role was a little less defined, but from one night to the next it might include running some three-card monte in the back, playing the shell game, or even doing a little pickpocketing.

They stayed with the carnival until Edna was seventeen and she fell in love with a mark. She ran off with him and reinvented herself, in one quick civil ceremony, leaving behind forever Edna Kurtz, carnie tramp, and becoming Edna Evans, housewife and mother. She distanced herself from her family and her past, and Simon didn't blame her. Given the chance, he might have done the same thing too. Now she was Edna Pratt, twice widowed and no one even the wiser to the truths about her past.

Simon hadn't stuck around the carnival for very long once Edna was gone. He was tired of busting his hump for small change, tired of seeing his father drink away what little money they did manage to bring in. When his dad finally died from liver failure, Simon took off for bigger and better things. Soon, he was working cons his father never dreamed of, big-time stuff, cons that took brains and planning and teamwork.

Simon and Edna stayed in touch. When Sally was born, Simon was allowed to come around, as long as he promised never to breathe a word about Edna's carny past. There was something about having a baby in the family that made Simon feel hopeful, as though something there could still be redeemed. Conning was the only way he knew to make a living, but his hope was that this family legacy would end with his generation.

When Sally was a toddler, Simon entered into his biggest con game yet—only to find that one member of the drag team was actually an undercover cop. Simon got fifteen years and served seven in a cell with Wiggles, who was in for grand theft auto. Simon's life since then had been a series of other cons—some successful, some not so successful— until the biggest one he ever thought up, the one he came to Mulberry Glen to pull off.

If only Edna hadn't messed everything up.

Jo peeked out of the back window, hoping to see Danny walking across the dark lawn from his house to hers. It was taking him so much longer to get home than she expected—and she really wanted to talk to him! She dropped the curtain and returned to the papers she had spread on the table. She couldn't wait to show him what she'd found.

The evening had been an interesting one, to say the least. Marie was thrilled to get the listing, especially because she had already listed another home on the block just a few doors down. So, while she thoroughly examined, inside and out, the home she would be putting up for sale, Jo went through Edna's papers.

Jo was determined to remember where she had seen the name Kurtz—and when she found it, everything came rushing back. Kurtz was the name on Edna's birth certificate—her maiden name—which meant that Simon Kurtz was, most likely, a relative, probably Edna's brother or a very close cousin. There was a boy with Edna in many of her childhood pictures, a boy who could easily have grown up to look like the man they knew from photographs as Simon.

Jo recalled her conversation with Sally after the funeral, when she asked Sally if her mother had known anyone by the name of Simon.

"I used to have a relative named Simon," Sally had said, "but he died when I was a child."

Died? Unless there were two Simons in the family, that was more than likely not true. The question now was whether Sally was lying—or if she had been lied to by others.

Jo wanted to call Sally and ask her more about the relative named Simon, but she didn't want to push things too far. Sally had already made it clear she didn't think her mother had been murdered—and that such reasoning, if pursued, could mess up her chances in the upcoming election. Jo was afraid that if Sally knew she was still pursing this notion, then she might fire her from the job of settling Edna's affairs—thus ending Jo's access to Edna's home and possessions.

Tomorrow Marie would be bringing over the real estate contract for the house, so Jo decided to wait until then, using that as an excuse to call Sally for her fax number, and slip in a few of her questions as nonchalantly as possible. It seemed like a plan, anyway.

"Jo, you home?" a familiar voice called, and Jo realized Danny had come in through the front door.

"In the kitchen," she called.

"Why was your door unlocked?" he scolded as he entered. His eyes were sparkling, and for a moment Jo was captivated by the intensity of his expression. Danny always did have beautiful eyes.

"Why did you come in through the front?" she countered.

"I was running so late, I just parked here instead of at my house. But you really should lock your door."

"Well, sorry," she said. "I wasn't thinking. At least I kept the doors locked at Edna's house—and I left there when Marie did, just to be safe."

"Good," he said, going to the fridge and helping himself to one of the cold sodas she kept on hand just for him. "Boy, do I have some developments for you."

"I've got some for you too."

She went through hers first, showing him the photos and papers on the table, talking about her ideas and theories. Her most interesting "find" of the evening was a photograph, the smaller version of one of the photos they had discovered in the hiding place under the tub. It was the picture that showed a family all dressed up and sitting on a front stoop. In the small version of the photo, however, there was no silver-haired mustached gentleman standing in the back row—just an empty wooden wall. Jo had brought the original photo back to her house, along with the doctored enlargement of the same thing, and Danny set them on the table, side by side, looking from one to the other.

"Kind of creepy, isn't it, to add yourself as an adult to a picture you're already in as a child?"

"But it works," Jo said. "If you didn't realize that man and that boy were the same person, you'd just think they were similar-looking relatives."

"That's true."

Jo had also gone online to the Florida database of prisoners and printed out a whole bunch of information about Simon Kurtz. Sure enough, the police chief had been right: The records were simply there for the finding. This man's crimes were on display for all the world to see.

All of Simon's convictions were for crimes that fell along the lines of fraud, theft, and deception. There wasn't a violent offense on the list, though, which gave her an odd feeling. If Simon hadn't killed Edna, then who had? Suddenly, Jo felt an urgency to get to know the women this man had somehow fleeced. Could one of them have been angry enough to kill? If so, then why was it that *Edna* was dead and not Simon?

When she and Danny had gone through everything she found, it was his turn to share about his conversation at the church with Mrs. Chutney—and the odd behavior of Mrs. Parker.

"I think we need to pay a visit to Mrs. Parker," Jo said. "Ask her straight out what she's trying to hide. Maybe we'll talk to both women and show them these two photos, side by side."

"I've got more," Danny added, "other originals I found online before Simon had himself inserted into them. They make pretty convincing evidence when you look at them this way."

"Let's do it tomorrow," she said. "Soon as you get back from Moore City."

Danny studied her beautiful face for a moment and then smiled.

"You like to stir the pot, don't you, Jo?"

She grinned.

"Oh, Danny. Stirring the pot is what I do best."

## TIPS FROM TULIP

*Dear Readers, this week as we feature classic letters from the past, enjoy this exchange from 1979.*

---

**Dear Tulip,**

How can I get out stubborn grass stains? My teenage daughter has been having fun with her new boyfriend at the local park. They must like to play football or something, because when she comes home, the backs of her clothes are always covered with grass stains. Help!

—*Green in the Midwest*

**Dear Green,**

Removing grass stains can be difficult. Try dabbing the stains with rubbing alcohol. If that doesn't work, try sponging on white vinegar. If that doesn't work, try rubbing in toothpaste. Launder as usual, but don't dry the clothes until the grass stains have been completely removed, lest you set the stains.

Mom, be a Smart Chick! A teenage daughter with a new boyfriend and grass stains on her back sets off all sort of flags for me—and I don't mean the kind they toss out in football. I doubt it's baseball, either, though she's probably well toward third base at this point, if you know what I mean. Talk to your daughter about sexual limits, and if she won't confide in you, bring in a trusted friend or relative to help you help her.

—*Tulip*

## 20

The next morning Jo awoke with an odd heaviness on her heart, a vague feeling of disquiet that lingered over from sleep. She opened her eyes and sat up in bed and then it hit her: Today was Wednesday, the day she would have returned back from her honeymoon.

Today was the day her life as a married woman was supposed to have begun in earnest.

She swung her legs over the side of the bed and sat there for a while, wondering if Bradford had kept the same return time for his flight from Bermuda. If so, then he'd be arriving at the Moore City airport around ten or eleven this morning. She wondered if he would drive to Mulberry Glen to seek her out to talk—or if he'd head the other direction, to his apartment in New York, and continue to pretend there was nothing to talk about.

"I don't get it, God," Jo said, looking up at the ceiling. "How does a man walk out on a wedding and then not even explain himself to the bride?"

Part of her hoped he would show up today so that at the very least she could have some closure. Another part of her felt that she'd be happier if she never saw him again for the rest of her life. What was there to talk about, anyway? That he didn't really love her? That he'd saved them both from a huge mistake? She didn't want to hear it, not any of it.

Then again, once she was dressed in her cleaning clothes and ready to head to Edna's, she scribbled out a note and taped it to her front door, just in case. It said, "If you're looking for Jo Tulip, go to 387 Weeping Willow Way."

At least that way, if he did come looking for her, he'd be able to find her.

She got a very early start on Edna's bedroom and bathroom. Going through all of the stuff was really quite distracting—fun, even—and she added a box for small collectables and things that she thought might bring a better price on eBay than at the yard sale.

The appraiser showed up promptly at nine, and Jo went slowly through the house with her, taking notes as the woman talked. There were only a few pieces of furniture of any value, and even those weren't that extraordinary. After the woman left, Jo scheduled a pickup from a consignment shop for those pieces, and then she returned to the busy work of slowly packing up Edna's possessions. She was making very good time.

She had just finished with the master bedroom and bathroom when Marie came by with the real estate contract. Jo looked it over, saying she would fax it to Edna's daughter when she ran home for lunch.

"Thanks again for this opportunity," Marie said, picking up her briefcase and reaching for the doorknob. "I really appreciate it."

Jo went outside with Marie as she pointed out where the For Sale sign would eventually go in the yard, and then she walked with her to the other house Marie was representing on the same street. It was across the street and down three, a modest ranch home like Edna's, but with faded cedar shingles and a much older roof.

"This looks like a real fixer-upper," Jo said, taking in the sight of the run-down house and its weedy yard. "I bet Edna's house sells first."

"Yeah, I've been trying to talk the owners into making some minor improvements, but they have already moved halfway across the country. They just want to get it sold, even if they have to take a loss."

Jo knelt down to examine a giant brown splotch in front of her.

"These stains really mess up the look of the whole driveway."

"I know."

"You've got a couple of choices for getting rid of them, if you want." Marie smiled.

"Ah, Jo, I should have known better than to bring you over here. Don't go inside, or you'll end up giving me enough household hints to keep me busy for a week!"

Jo laughed.

"I think it would make a big difference," she said, waving again toward the splotches. "You want to take notes here or not?"

"Fine," Marie said, putting down her briefcase and taking out a pen and notepad. "Go ahead."

"Step one," Jo said. "Wet down the stains with a hose and then, believe it or not, sprinkle them with lemon Kool-Aid. Cover them with plastic, let them soak for about fifteen minutes, and then scrub with a brush and rinse. The stains should be gone."

"And if they're not?"

"Then you try step two. Get some oven cleaner, spray it on kind of heavily, let it sit for fifteen, and then rinse."

"You think if I do that, the driveway will look better?"

"I think if you do that, the driveway will look like new."

"Well, thanks, Jo. If my showing this morning doesn't pan out, maybe I will give it a try. Not exactly in the job description, but then again, I'm getting desperate."

"As long as you're fixing things up, you might throw a few potted plants in that area by the garage."

Marie's showing would be any minute, so Jo told her goodbye and walked back to Edna's. As she did, she saw that there was a big van in the driveway, and a man pounding on Edna's front door. Jo called out to him, and as he turned toward her, she read the words on the front of his uniform: Mulberry Glen Animal Home.

Oh, no.

Simon ran a finger under his collar, hoping he wasn't sweating in the Florida morning heat. He needed to look calm, cool, and collected. First, though, he had to make the phone call that would determine—or perhaps seal—his fate.

He had borrowed Wiggles' car this morning, aware that his friend hadn't arrived home until the wee hours last night and would probably sleep half the day. Still, just to be safe, Simon had left a note on the kitchen table, along with a ten-dollar bill: *Wiggles, had to borrow the car, hope this covers your trouble. Be back in about an hour. Simon.*

He knew Wiggles would be mad, but he figured the ten bucks would ease his pain. And if Simon were lucky, he'd get back to the house before Wiggles even woke up, and then he could toss the note, pocket the cash, and his friend would never even have to know the difference.

Just to be prudent, Simon picked a different pay phone from the one he used last time. He found a quiet convenience store several miles from the house and just down the street from a small Florida bank. Heart pounding, he dropped in the coins and dialed the automated system that would tell him the status of his bank account. Once he was into the system, he typed in his account number and passcode.

After a moment, an automated voice responded.

"Your checking balance is four hundred thousand dollars and zero cents. Funds currently available for withdrawal are four hundred thousand dollars and zero cents. For recent checking activity, press one. For recent savings activity, press two…"

Simon hung up the phone, hardly able to catch his breath.

The checks had cleared! The money was his for the taking!

Unless…

Unless it was a trap.

He paced back and forth, took some deep breaths, and tried to calm his heart. He swore that if he could just get this money, he would give up grifting for good. No more games. No more cons. He was done.

Simon thought about what he could do with four hundred thousand dollars to go legit. He'd take a hundred thou and buy a little house, twenty more for a car, and sock the remainder away, living the rest of his days on what was left. Maybe get a little part-time job to supplement his income. Be a normal person for a change.

The more he thought about it, the more excited he got. Maybe he could talk Edna into moving down to Florida too. If she sold her house, they could add that to the hundred he was gonna spend and buy something twice as nice. They'd get a place with a pool, maybe. That would convince her—her own swimming pool!

He dropped in more coins and dialed Edna's number. It rang and rang and then went to the machine. His mind raced, trying to think of some sort of encoded message he could leave.

"This is a church call," he said after the beep. "It's a brush, right? We'll talk."

Then he hung up the phone, confident Edna would understand what he meant—but no one else who might hear the message would.

Part of him wanted to wait until he got her on the phone before he took the next step. But a bigger part of him knew there was no time to lose.

He had to take the next step. Go for broke. It was now or never.

Leaving the car there beside the phone, he strolled the half block to the bank. Once inside, he told the teller he wanted to open an account.

She led him over to a desk and began entering information into a computer. He gave her one hundred dollars in cash and two legitimate forms of ID. When she asked, he supplied his date of birth and social security number. For an address, he provided Wiggles' house as his street address, but requested that all mail from the bank go to his PO box—the PO box he renewed annually but hadn't even taken a peek at in at least three months.

He kept the box for a variety of reasons, like this today. The last thing he needed was for Wiggles to get wind of his windfall. The guy was a friend, but a friend with an open palm, to be sure.

The only lie Simon gave the teller was the telephone number. When asked, he simply supplied a nonexistent number, explaining that he had just moved to town and the phone hadn't yet been installed, so it might not work for a few days.

As he spoke, he could hear the voice of his father, saying *Stick with the truth as much as possible, Simon. Lie only when necessary. Otherwise, you'll end up shooting yourself in the foot.* It was advice he always tried to follow.

Everything went through fine, just as Simon had hoped. Luckily, there was nothing that might flag him as an ex-con—or a fugitive on the run. He looked like a nice, normal guy in an Armani suit, just getting his finances in order.

When she finished with the paperwork, he asked for a notarized letter with all of the information so that he could transfer down the funds from his old bank. The bank had a notary on the premises, of course, so within fifteen minutes he had the letter in his pocket and he was on his way. They told him where he might find a Federal Express office, so he drove there straight away and sent the letter off.

It was done. At this point, one of two things was going to happen.

If the police weren't currently looking for him, then in a few days he would get the funds. If the police *were* looking for him, the simple banking trail would lead right to Wiggles' door—and to an arrest.

Ah, well, it was too late to turn back now.

Simon hurried home, eager to get back his ten bucks and change out of his suit before Wiggles even knew he had left. As he did, he had to keep himself from smiling.

He still needed to talk to Edna. But the way things were looking, he just might get away with this after all.

Jo had forgotten all about the dog.

Of course. Of course. Today was the day the dog had been scheduled to arrive. How could she have forgotten?

Only three weeks ago, she and Bradford had gone together to the private animal shelter in town and picked out their new pet—a precious two-year-old chocolate lab. They had scheduled for the shelter to deliver the dog the day they were to return from their honeymoon.

How pathetic it all seemed now, this strange attempt to construct a fairy-tale life. Husband and wife, cute dog, small-town home. But a few things had gone wrong along the way—namely, that the groom was missing from the picture!

Jo closed her eyes, remembering the moment they first spotted their pet. It was a dreary, rainy Saturday, the kind of day when it seemed best to sit around and do nothing, but Jo and Bradford had braved the weather because they very much wanted to run this particular errand. As they walked down the row of cages at the shelter, dog after dog thrust themselves against the wire, whining and begging and barking to be adopted.

But not Chewie. He simply sat at the back of his run, watching them, daring them to take him home. He was bedraggled and put-upon-looking, to be sure, but he was also very quiet and mellow. When Jo asked if there was any chance he was sick, the attendant just laughed.

"Chewie's healthy as a horse. He just gets a little nervous when it rains."

"Why is his name Chewie?" Jo had asked, afraid she might be getting more than she bargained for. The last thing she needed was a dog that chewed up the furniture or something.

"I think he was named after Chewbacca, from Star Wars," the man said. "Least, that's what the family said."

"Cool," was Bradford's reply. He was a big sci-fi fan. "We'll take him."

Signing the papers and paying the fee was almost like adopting a child, and guiltily Jo had toyed with the idea of bringing the dog home that day. But then she knew she would have to find something to do with him during her final wedding preparations—not to mention she'd have to find someone to take care of him during the honeymoon. Better that he remain where he was for the next few weeks. The shelter was willing to keep him there for an extra fee, so it had all worked out fine.

Until now.

Now, there was a man at Edna's door, clipboard in hand, asking Jo to sign for this particular delivery.

"I went to your house and saw your note," he told her. "I figured you left it there for me."

"I'm so sorry," Jo said, shaking her head. "Since we adopted that dog, everything has changed."

Face burning with humiliation, Jo explained about the wedding and Bradford taking off when it came time for the vows. She said she understood that they probably couldn't refund her money, but that she wouldn't be taking the dog after all.

"Well, I'm the one that's sorry," he said, still holding out the clipboard. "He's yours now, whether you want him or not. We're just a seasonal shelter. He's one of the last to go and then we're closing down until the spring."

"What do you mean?"

She tried to argue with him that she couldn't take the dog. He was polite but persistent, saying if the dog really was that much of a burden, that maybe she should call the pound.

In the end, she lost the fight. She was angry about it until she got another look at him, huddling in his cage, looking for all the world like the sweetest, gentlest, most easygoing dog in the world. Maybe it wouldn't be so bad. Maybe she could find someone who would take him off her hands.

Maybe Danny would like to have him.

Jo signed the clipboard, waited as the guy released the dog from the cage, and then accepted the leash as he handed it to her.

"Enjoy your new pet!" he said before climbing back into the van and driving away.

"Yeah, thanks," she muttered softly.

On top of everything else in her life, this was exactly what she didn't need.

# 21

Jo held the leash while the dog went potty in the yard, making a mental note to buy a pooper-scooper ASAP. When he was finished, she awkwardly led him inside, closed the doors to the living room, and set him free in there while she went to the kitchen, got out the phone book, and called the pound.

She explained the situation and wasn't surprised to learn that all of those rumors from when she was a kid about what they did to doggies who didn't get adopted were true. As much as she didn't need this right now, she just couldn't be responsible for the death of a perfectly healthy canine.

She dug around in Edna's dishes until she found a bowl, which she filled with water. There was no food in the pantry, but she recalled bagging up a can of tuna, so she found it, opened it, and scooped it out on a plate next to the bowl. Pooper-scooper and dog food. The checklist was already growing.

Finally, she opened the living room door so that the dog could come into the kitchen. He jumped up and down, the first signs of excitement she'd seen in him. Jo felt her scowl turn into a smile as she knelt down to his level and accepted his affection. He wanted to be her friend. And he did have beautiful brown eyes.

"Okay, Chewie, why don't you eat?" she said begrudgingly.

He didn't hesitate, wolfing down the tuna and then slurping noisily from the water. As he did so, she decided to go out back and walk the chain-link fence, checking for holes. At least Edna had a fence. Jo had nothing at her house except the split rail across the back.

What was she going to do?

Once she verified that the fence was safe, she let the dog out back to run around for a while. He really was jumpy and happy, far different from the meek creature they had first spotted at the shelter. While he ran and played and chased squirrels, she decided to take a peek into Edna's small shed, the one structure she hadn't yet examined.

It was filled with a push mower, some tools, and a few big boxes. There was a box with a paint can and a few other odd items in it, and Jo hoped the paint would match the beige interior of the house. If she decided to do some touch-ups before Marie started showing the house, she knew the paint would come in handy. She had told Marie to give her at least a week before actively putting the house on the market, but Jo had been moving through things so quickly she might be able to revise that estimate.

Chewie found a spot near a tree where he settled down to take a breather, so Jo brought his water bowl outside and decided to let him stay there for a while. Then she went inside, washed his dinner plate, and went into the living room.

"No!" she yelled as soon as she entered the room.

It took a minute for her to figure out what had happened, but when she did, she wanted to scream again. Apparently, in the small amount of time she had spent on the phone with the pound, Chewie had managed to completely dismantle the couch and rip up an entire couch cushion. The stuffing was everywhere, little white puffs of foam rubber that made it look as if it had snowed.

"Chewie!" she yelled, and a moment later she could hear him thrusting himself against the back door screen trying to get to her.

She marched into the kitchen, ready to yell, but as soon as he saw her he just sat down, eyes wide, looking as innocent as any creature ever had. Jo didn't know much about dogs, but she had a feeling that yelling at him now, so far after the fact, would have no impact. He wouldn't even understand what he had done wrong.

Before she could decide what to do, the telephone rang. She answered it, half expecting it to be Danny. Instead, it was another man's voice.

"Yes, hello," he said, "this is Pinkerton Jewelers, in Moore City. I just wanted to let you know your order is ready."

"My order?"

"Yes. Is this Edna Pratt?"

"Uh," Jo hesitated, wondering what kind of an order Edna might have placed at a jeweler. Somehow, Edna didn't exactly seem the jewelry type. "No. This is a friend. But I can take a message."

"Good. Would you tell her the order's been ready for pickup for two days? The man who placed it said it was a rush job, so we got it done on time, but then nobody ever showed to pick it up."

"The man?" Jo asked, heart pounding. "You mean Simon?"

"I don't know his name. Gray hair, mustache? He was insistent that it be done by Monday, and here it is Wednesday and we haven't seen him."

"I understand." Jo reached for pen and paper. "Can you give me the address of your store? We'll send someone right over to get it."

As Jo wrote down the address in the city, she told herself that this was just part of her job description, part of putting Edna's affairs in order for her daughter Sally. But she knew it was more than that. It was a lead in her investigation.

Maybe.

Danny walked down the long hall surrounded on all sides by teenagers. This Moore City high school was a lot bigger and newer and fancier than Mulberry Glen's modest little one where he had gone yesterday. Today he was on an errand for himself, not Jo, procuring the job of photographer at their upcoming Homecoming dance.

He had already presented his bid to the student council, been offered the job, and signed the papers on the spot. That's what he liked about students; they didn't waste a lot of time. Now he just had to find his way back through this maze of hallways and he would be on the road to home. As he went, he read some of the posters they had hanging on the walls: *If you can dream it, you can become it,* one said. *Imagine the possibilities and claim your future,* declared another.

Yeah, right.

Danny wondered if anyone ever thought about those posters and what they were teaching the children. Lofty hopes and ideas were good, he supposed, but what happened when the dream didn't match the reality? "If you can dream it, you can become it?" Says who? He had dreamed it for years and years—not to mention worked his tail off—and he still hadn't become much of anything. His whole family was a study in unrealized dreams, for that matter, from his mother with her failed family band to his sister who wanted to be a professional stage magician and instead spent her time doing kid's birthday parties for chump change.

Danny was starting to think he never would be a successful photographer, one who did more than hold up rubber duckies and take snapshots of babies. Even this dance he had gone to so much trouble to secure would be a miserable night of cocky guys, self-conscious girls, raging hormones, and teenage angst. Danny could think of a few better ways to spend an evening.

Feeling fully miserable by the time he left the building, he didn't even want to answer his cell phone when it rang. It was Jo, probably calling to see when he'd be back so they could go visit the two ladies.

Somehow, he just didn't feel up to it right now.

"Hello?" he said, trying not to sound preoccupied and distant.

"Are you still in Moore City?" Jo asked breathlessly.

"Yeah."

"Super. There's an errand I need you to run."

Sure enough, Simon made it back to the house before Wiggles had even stirred. He quietly put the keys in the tray, took care of the money and the note, and then changed from his suit into more comfortable clothes.

He needed to talk to Edna.

Trying not to make much noise, he threw together a quick breakfast sandwich in the kitchen, and then he went out back to see if the paint job had dried on the stolen bicycle. It had. It looked a little lumpy, but it would do.

He climbed on and took off, finding the road to the gas station pay phone much quicker via bicycle than when he had gone on foot.

Once there, he parked the bike, climbed off, and made the call. He was running out of change, so this time he decided that he would give it three rings and if she hadn't answered by then, hang up. There was no need to leave another message.

He dialed the number, feeling his heart soar in his chest. This was going to work out fine, he just knew it. Edna would come to Florida and the two of them would make a new life for themselves.

"Hello?"

Simon hesitated, knowing the voice was not Edna's. It sounded like the same person who had answered the phone the other day. This time, he spoke in his normal voice rather than trying to disguise it.

"Is Edna there?" he asked.

"I'm sorry, no," the woman said, sounding strange. Who was she?

"Can you tell me when you expect her back? I left a message on her machine."

"Um," the woman said, and suddenly Simon wondered if this was his niece, Sally, in town for a visit with her mother. He couldn't imagine who else it could be. "Do you have some business with Edna?"

"Yes," he said, "business," and then suddenly his heart was in his throat. Was something wrong? Had Edna become sick or hurt—or arrested? "Is there something wrong?"

The voice at the other end hemmed and hawed for a moment and then spoke.

"I'm sorry, but Edna Pratt passed away. She had an accident."

"An accident?" Simon demanded. "When?"

"Sometime last Friday night. They...um...found her dead Saturday morning. She had fallen and hit her head. I'm working for her daughter this week, trying to put her affairs in order. Is there a message you'd like me to pass along to her?"

The pounding in Simon's head was so loud he couldn't even hear what she might have said next. In shock, he hung up the receiver, one thought crowding out all of the others:

Edna was dead.

His sister was dead.

Blindly, he got on the bike and started pedaling, pedaling as fast and as hard as he could. He didn't even know where he was going, but after a while he found himself at the beach, where the sidewalk ended in sand.

Dropping the bicycle there, he stumbled out toward the water, finally collapsing into a sobbing heap near the tide line.

Edna was dead, and he knew what happened.

She hadn't had an accident. She'd had *too much*, just like their mother. Life was too much.

Edna had killed herself.

Simon closed his eyes and pictured Edna as he had seen her Friday night, the night everything went wrong.

"I'm going to the police, Simon," she had said. "I just want to give you fair warning."

They had fought about it, long and hard.

But she was adamant. She'd already spent the afternoon cleaning house, literally and figuratively, putting her things in order before she went to the cops and revealed all. When Simon finally understood that all the arguing and pleading and begging in the world couldn't change her mind, he asked simply that she wait as long as possible before she called them.

"Noon tomorrow," she had said. "That should give you enough time to get away. I can't wait any longer than that."

"But, Edna, don't you love me?" he had demanded, tears in his eyes. It wasn't just that all of their hard work would be for naught, or that he had to kiss almost half a million dollars goodbye. It was that his sister, his own blood, was turning on him.

"Yes, I love you," she had said, tears in her eyes as well. "But this is something I just have to do. I can't live a lie anymore."

In the end, Simon realized now, she couldn't do it after all. Rather than turn herself in, rather than rat out her big brother, Edna had taken the easy route and killed herself.

Just like their mother.

Simon sobbed, big gut-wrenching tears he had never cried in his life. He would miss Edna more than he'd ever missed his father or mother. Most of all, he would miss knowing she was *there*, that somewhere in this empty world where everyone was only out for themselves and what they could get, he would miss knowing he had someone who loved him.

"Why, Edna?" he cried, his voice lost in the swell of the waves. "Why?"

He curled into a ball and cried, crying for every hurt he'd ever felt in his sixty-two years of life. Finally, when he had cried himself out, when he couldn't cry anymore, he simply lay there on the sand, watching the sea gulls, understanding now why the money had remained in the bank, untouched. It was his now, free and clear.

He'd give it all away tomorrow if only that could bring her back.

Jo felt like an idiot. The call with the jeweler was still so fresh on her mind that when the next call came, she just figured it was another business matter. It wasn't until the man reacted with such shock to the news of Edna's death that Jo realized it might be Simon, the man everyone was looking for.

The phone had gone dead, so she hung it up and pressed star sixty-nine. Unfortunately, it said that the call could not be identified because it was from out of the area. Frustrated, Jo hung up the phone and ran to the kitchen, replaying the messages on the machine. He said he had left a message, and sure enough, it was there.

*This is a church call,* the same voice said. *It's a brush, right? We'll talk.*

Such a strange message. Jo remembered the conversation she and Danny had had with the innkeeper of the Palace and all of the crazy con game terms that guy had used. She wondered if he could decipher this message for her now.

Jo wanted to pay the man a little visit. Before letting Chewie into her spotless car, however, he needed a bath. She brought him into the bathroom and washed him in Edna's tub with some of Edna's leftover shampoo, something that would have worked fine had the dog not chosen every minute or so to brace himself and shake furiously. By the time she was finished, there were water droplets on every single surface of the bathroom and her clothes were soaked.

After giving the dog a thorough towel drying and then a quick few minutes with a blow-dryer, Jo took a few minutes to wipe everything down. She would have to stop at her house for a change of clothes, but then it was on to the Palace for some help.

"Come on, Chewie," she said, grabbing her keys and the answering machine. "We're going for a ride."

Danny had a bit of trouble finding the jewelry store. The place was tucked away on a side street, a little hole-in-the-wall he drove past twice before spotting.

Once he found it, he still had to park, which took another ten minutes. Finally, he got to the store, went inside, and asked for the order for Edna Pratt.

"That'll be two hundred and fifty dollars," the man said, reaching under the counter for a manila envelope and then handing it over.

Danny swallowed hard and dug out a credit card, hoping very much that someone would pay him back for this from Edna's estate. This was two hundred and fifty dollars he could not afford to lose.

"Plus tax," the guy added. "Comes to two hundred sixty-seven dollars and fifty cents."

While he rang it up, Danny dumped out the envelope onto the counter, curious about what he was buying. Two women's pins slid out—though one was a stained and faded metal while the other was a shiny gold. Both pins were identical in size and shape, an image of a just-blossoming rose.

"I don't know why this guy pressured us to hurry and then didn't even pick it up on time," the man said, waiting for the credit card slip to spew from the machine. "It's been ready since Monday."

"Yeah, he, uh, he had to go out of town," Danny said.

"He's usually waiting at the door when we open, ready to pick up his order."

Danny studied the gold pin, thinking there wasn't really anything remarkable about it.

"Usually?" he asked, trying to sound nonchalant. "How many orders have you done for him?"

The machine sprung to life, the credit card approval obviously having gone through. The man tore off the printed sheet and slid it toward Danny with a pen.

"This is about the tenth one, I guess," he said. "Always the same thing. He brings me some cheap metal trinket and tells me to replicate it exactly in gold."

"So he brought you this," Danny said, holding up the metal rose, "and you made him this?" holding up the gold rose.

"Yeah," the man said. "I don't know what it's for. But the work's been pretty steady, so I'm not complaining."

Jo was actually glad she had the big dog in the car. When she had come to this hotel the first time, Danny had been with her, making her feel safe and protected. Now that she was alone, she was starting to have second thoughts. It really was a seedy part of town.

She clipped the leash on Chewie's collar and climbed out, glad to see he was behaving. With her free hand, she scooped up the answering machine. Then she tucked some money in her pocket and went inside.

As before, the counter was deserted, and as before, she rang the buzzer. As soon as the man came out from the back, though, Chewie started barking.

"Whoa!" the guy said, stepping back. "No dogs allowed, lady. No pets of any kind."

Jo set the machine on the counter and knelt down to calm Chewie. She got him to stop barking, though he kept his body on full alert, a low growl escaping now and then from his throat.

"I'm not checking in," she said. "Do you remember me from the other day?"

"Uh, sure," the guy said, still looking uncertainly toward the dog.

"Smell it?"

"Excuse me?"

"Smell it? I did the baking soda in the carpet like you suggested and put out the bowls of apples. The housekeeper was afraid of getting fruit flies, though, so she threw the apples out."

Jo nodded, stifling a smile.

"It definitely smells better in here," she said. "I think it made a real difference."

The place was still a little rank, but he was right: It wasn't as bad as it had been before.

"Anyway," she said, "I was wondering if I could get a little more help."

"You still looking for Simon Foster? Ain't seen him."

Jo pulled out a ten and set it on the counter in front of him.

"Time is money, right?" she said, meeting his eyes.

He took the ten and pocketed it.

"What do you want to know now?"

She lifted the plug from the answering machine and handed it to him.

"I want you to listen to a message and tell me if this sounds like Simon to you. He's using some kind of code. I wondered if you could tell me what he's really saying."

The man hesitated before plugging in the machine.

"Ten bucks for telling you if it's him," he said. "Another ten if I can explain what he's saying."

"Fine."

He plugged the machine in behind the counter and she pressed the buttons to make the message play.

*This is a church call,* the message said. *It's a brush, right? We'll talk.*

When it was finished, she pressed the stop button.

"Yeah," the old guy said. "That's Simon, far as I can tell."

Jo reached into her pocket and came out with two fives. She gave them to the man, and he told her to play the message one more time. She did, and when it was finished, he nodded.

"He's saying two things here. A 'church call' is a discussion about a con. Like, when you're ready to get the team set up, you sit down and go over the plans. That's a 'church call.'"

"What's a brush?"

He shook his head, chewing on his lip.

"A brush is usually a hand signal," he said, demonstrating with a sweep of his hand. "It means, 'The game is called off. Permanently.'"

# 22

Jo wasn't sure what to do with Chewie while she paid a visit to Mrs. Chutney. She didn't dare risk putting him inside her house, as he might eat one of her couch cushions. Finally, she decided he could go back to the fenced yard at Edna's. She dropped him off, made sure he had some water, and then kept going. She checked her voice mail as she drove, surprised to hear that she had a message from the handsome history professor.

"Hey, Jo, it's Keith McMann. I hope you don't mind; I looked you up in the phone book. I was just thinking about our conversation and wondered if maybe you'd like to get together and talk about it some more. Well, to be honest, I was just thinking that maybe I could take you to dinner. I hope you don't think I'm too forward. I don't even know if you're seeing somebody. I'm not. But now I'm rambling, so I guess I'll go. Call me back when you get a chance. Bye."

The message ended without leaving a number. The second message, not surprisingly, was also from Keith.

"Keith McMann again. Sorry, I guess if you're going to call me back, you need my number."

He gave the number and then said goodbye a second time.

Smiling to herself, Jo decided that was one call she would return later. For now, she dialed Danny's cell phone to ask how things had gone at the jewelry store.

"Long story," he replied mysteriously. "I'll show you when I get back to town."

Finished with that call, Jo turned onto Mrs. Chutney's street and drove slowly, looking for the right house.

She knew it was rude to pop in on someone unexpected, but that was the whole point. The more likely she was to catch Mrs. Chutney off guard, the more information she might be able to get out of her.

She parked in the street and then took the long stone walkway to the front door. The trees in the yard were just turning to their fall colors, complementing a lush row of yellow rose bushes. It was all so beautiful that by the time Mrs. Chutney answered the door, Jo had to bring her mind back to the task at hand.

"Jo Tulip!" Mrs. Chutney said, looking truly perplexed. "How are you, dear?"

Jo smiled, hoping she'd come at a good time.

"Hello, Mrs. Chutney," she said. "I'm sorry about popping in like this. I wonder if I could speak with you for a moment."

The woman momentarily looked confused, but she stepped back and held open the door politely.

"Of course," she said. "Come in. Is this regarding the Christmas pageant?"

Jo didn't reply, letting the woman hold onto that notion until they were inside and seated. For the Christmas pageant last year, Mrs. Chutney had loaned Jo's committee several gorgeous tapestries that they had carefully fashioned into capes for the wise men, so it was a natural assumption as to why Jo had come calling today.

"Actually," Jo said once they were across from each other in the formal living room, "I just wanted to talk to you. And I need to show you something."

"Would you like a cup of coffee?"

"No, thank you. This shouldn't take long."

Jo reached into her tote bag and pulled out the photo of Edna as a child, with everyone posed on the stoop. She handed it over to Mrs. Chutney, who immediately stiffened up.

"I know you've seen this photo," Jo said quickly. "And I know you know the man in the upper right corner."

Mrs. Chutney did not respond.

"I wonder, however, if you've seen this version of the same picture. The *original* version."

Jo handed her the smaller picture, the one without Simon added in. Mrs. Chutney studied them both for a long while, speechless.

"Mrs. Chutney, you and the other ladies were the victims of a con game," Jo said gently. "I'm not sure why no one will talk about it, but the proof is coming out anyway."

Jo pulled out the other two pictures for which Danny had found the originals and gave them over as well, along with their corresponding, doctored versions. Mrs. Chutney stared at them all, her face white as a sheet.

"He brought in experts," Mrs. Chutney said softly. "An art historian. A history professor. Local people with sterling reputations who I know would not have lied."

"They didn't lie," Jo said. "They were duped as well."

Mrs. Chutney studied the pictures even longer, but to Jo's relief, she didn't start to cry.

"I *told* Louise we needed to put a stop payment on our checks," she said softly. "But she was afraid that would mess everything up—especially now that we were so close. She said we needed to trust Simon, that we would surely hear from him by the end of the week."

"As far as I can tell, Mrs. Chutney, Simon is long gone. Your money is probably long gone as well."

She nodded, closing her eyes.

"We were such fools. No one lives forever."

Her statement sat there between them while Jo tried to puzzle that one out.

"Immortality?" Jo asked finally. "Is that what he was promising you?"

Mrs. Chutney' eyes snapped open. She gathered the photos into one pile and held them out to Jo.

"Darling, I'm sorry, but I can't say anything more right now. Let me talk with the other women first. We took a vow. I'm sure you understand."

Jo didn't understand, but she could tell from Mrs. Chutney's posture that the interview was over. The woman stood, and Jo had no choice but to follow suit.

"I tell you what," Jo said. "My house, tonight, seven o'clock. Anyone who is willing to talk to me about this can show up there. Then you can decide how to proceed as a group."

Jo started to give her address, but Mrs. Chutney stopped her.

"I know where you live, dear. I was friends with your grandmother."

"Then you know you can trust me," Jo said. "Why don't you tell me what's going on?"

Mrs. Chutney simply pursed her lips and led the way to the front door.

"My house, tonight, seven o'clock," Jo said. "I'm trusting you to spread the word."

Simon was lost. He had ridden the bicycle to the beach in such a frenzy that now he couldn't even figure out how to get back to Wiggles' house.

It didn't matter. He could ride around all day and not care.

His sister was dead.

Almost like picking at a wound, Simon insisted on going back over in his mind the origins of this last con. He just couldn't understand where it had all gone wrong.

The idea for the game actually started several years ago, when Simon was visiting with an old buddy, a guy named Moses whose specialty was insurance fraud, particularly helping shady homeowners collect more than was rightfully theirs. The man was putting together a bogus portfolio of "proof of possession" when Simon stopped in to shoot the breeze and see if there were any good games floating in the wind and looking for another member.

Simon didn't get any work out of the visit, but something happened while he was there that had never completely left his mind. The guy had been going through art catalogs, trying to choose some lesser-known works that could have feasibly been owned by the homeowner—and lost in the fire that was going to burn his home to the ground. He ran across one painting, and he held it out toward Simon, laughing.

"Hey, buddy, I know you're getting old," he said, "but I didn't know you were this old."

He was pointing toward a painting of the Nativity, one where a small group of men were looking down at Mary and the baby. One of the men in the painting looked almost exactly like Simon.

"Weird, huh? That guy could be your double."

Simon studied the painting, something stirring in the back of his mind. That he looked like a character in an old painting was just a coincidence, but in his world, a good coincidence never went unexploited.

Simon had taken down the information about that painting and hung onto it, knowing that someday he would come up with a way to use it to his advantage. It wasn't until probably two years later when he met a talented young computer technician whose specialty was fake documents and doctored photos that everything began to come together in his mind. As a part of his preparations for the con, Simon had his hair cut exactly as the man's in the painting and then he grew a mustache. By the time he was done, the resemblance was close enough that he knew the right kind of mark—the gullible, hopeful kind—would fall for his claims hook, line, and sinker.

By the time Jo got back to Edna's, Chewie was gone. Jo wasn't sure what had happened, but the gate was swinging open and there was no dog to be found.

She was more upset than she thought she'd be. Not knowing what else to do, she ran next door to Betty's house and knocked.

"Oh, hey," Betty said, standing in the doorway as her two children watched a blaring TV in the background. "Would you like to come in?"

"No, thank you. Have you seen a dog around? A cute chocolate lab?"

"No, but I did hear some barking earlier," Betty said. "Is he yours?"

"Sort of," Jo replied. "I was keeping him in Edna's backyard."

"The doggie opened the gate," the boy said, suddenly appearing at his mother's side.

"What, honey?" Jo asked, leaning down.

"The big brown doggie was really smart. I watched him open the gate."

Jo looked up at Betty, who shrugged.

"Where were you when you saw the doggie open the gate?" Betty asked.

"I was in my room, playing," the boy replied. "But I could see through the window. The doggie kept chewing the latch, and then it popped open, so he went out."

"Do you know where he went?" Jo asked.

"He's probably just hanging out in the neighborhood."

Jo hit the ground running, calling for Chewie as she made her way down the street. She whistled and called and looked but saw no sign of the animal. Finally, as she was almost back to Edna's, she could hear barking and children's laughter. She looked up, and across the street at the playground she spotted a brown lab, climbing up the ladder of a children's slide. Jo froze, watching in amazement as the dog reached the top of the ladder, sort of hunched down, and slid down the other side. The kids who were there squealed with joy and cried, "Do it again, dog! Do it again!"

Jo crossed the busy street and ran over to where they were playing, knowing for sure it was Chewie the closer she came.

"Chewie!" she cried, scolding him.

He looked up at her and ran over happily, as if he was completely innocent of all charges. Again, she hesitated to fuss at him, because he probably wouldn't even understand what she was mad about.

"He's quite an amazing animal," an older woman called from a nearby bench. "The kids have been having great fun with him."

"I'm sorry about that," Jo told her. "He's new, and I didn't realize he could get out of the gate."

"Oh, I've known a few dogs like that," she said. "They're much smarter than we give them credit for."

Jo reached down and impulsively hugged the dog, whose tail swung back and forth in delight.

"No harm done anyway," the woman said. "I believe he just felt it was his duty to patrol the area and make sure things were in good order."

Jo thanked her, led Chewie back to Edna's, and brought him inside, blocking him in the kitchen this time where there weren't any couches to demolish. While he rested on the tile, catching his breath, Jo ate the lunch she had packed, forced herself to focus, and stared at the telephone.

She needed to talk to Bradford.

It wasn't just that she couldn't handle the demands of an active dog right now. It was that this shouldn't have to be solely her responsibility. She had already been saddled with facing her friends and trying to pick up the pieces of his abandonment. This dog was simply the icing on a very bad cake.

Jo dialed Bradford's home number first but got no answer. She hung up when the machine answered and tried dialing her parents' house instead. She got her mother, who sounded out of breath and distracted, as though she were just heading either in or out.

"Is this a bad time?" Jo asked.

"No, I have a second," she said, the usual amount of time Jo was allotted when she called. "What can I do for you?"

Jo exhaled slowly, trying not to dump her anger toward Bradford onto her mother.

"I just wondered if either of you have heard from Bradford. There's a situation here that needs his attention."

"He called a while ago," she said. "He got back from Bermuda this morning."

Jo was too stunned and angry to respond. So he really had no intention of coming to Mulberry Glen and talking to her and trying to straighten this out.

"He and your father had a talk," Helen continued, oblivious. "And it looks like Bradford may be putting in for a transfer to Chicago."

"A transfer?"

"It's a little uncomfortable now, you know, for Bradford and your father to be working directly with each other."

"Oh. Of course."

"Now, darling, don't sound like that. It'll all work out in the end."

Jo could feel the muscles in her jaw clenching shut.

"Do you know if Bradford has any intention of calling me and discussing what happened at the wedding?" Jo asked.

"Oh," Helen said, as if that were a novel idea. "I don't know. I'm sure he knew you and I would be speaking."

Jo's pulse surged.

"Mother, he owes me an explanation," she said fiercely. "And not through someone else. Face-to-face."

"Well, then, why don't you give him a call? You could probably reach him on his cell."

She just didn't get it. Why did Jo think she ever would?

After she hung up with her mother, she dialed Bradford's cell phone, her heart in her throat as it rang. He answered after a long while, and Jo knew he must have been staring at the number on the screen for a few rings, trying to decide what to do. The big chicken.

"Hello?" he said.

"Bradford," she replied, wishing she had been more prepared before dialing. "It's Jo."

"Hi," he said. "How's it going?"

She counted to ten.

Very slowly.

"That's all you can say to me?" she asked finally. "How's it going? How do you think it's going?"

"You're angry."

"No, Bradford, I'm not angry. I love being publicly humiliated. I simply adore looking like an idiot, being abandoned in the middle of my own wedding."

"Yes," he said slowly, "I guess I deserved that."

The man was an absolute, utter... She didn't know what. There weren't words for what he was. Not decent words, anyway. Suddenly, she wanted nothing more than to be done with the conversation.

"Look," she said, "we have a problem. Remember the dog we picked out together? The animal shelter delivered him this morning, and they wouldn't take no for an answer."

"Oh, wow," he said. "That's too bad."

"I am in no position to care for a dog right now," she said, glancing over at Chewie, who seemed to know she was talking about him. He perked up his ears, wagged his tail, and then rested his chin on his front paws. "So I need to know what you want to do about it."

"Gee, Jo, wish I could help you out. But it looks like I'll be moving soon, and I can't take a dog with me. You understand."

You understand.

Sure.

Suddenly, she understood a lot.

"So you're not going to do anything to help," she said. "Fine. Do you have anything useful to say to me about what happened? Any last words that you'd like to offer before I hang up?"

He was quiet for a moment.

"Just that in the last few days, I really had some time to think."

"Yes," she said, "I understand thinking is a popular sport in Bermuda."

"Don't be sarcastic, Jo. I had some time to think, and I decided that maybe we moved things along too quickly. I don't want to give up on us completely. I just think we need to slow it down."

She wished she could reach through the telephone line and strangle him. The nerve of him, to think he had even the slightest chance with her after all that had happened.

"Slow it down," she repeated, her free hand curled into a fist. "Good idea, Bradford. Why don't I start by ending this phone call? That should slow things down significantly."

She set down the phone without waiting for a reply. Then she laid her head in her hands and waited for tears that didn't come. Was she all cried out? Or, when it came down to it, did she just not care anymore? She had to admit that less than a week after Bradford walked out on her, she was still feeling more angry and embarrassed than heartbroken. That had to be significant.

After a while, Jo could feel a presence next to her, and she opened her eyes to see Chewie standing there, his shoulder at her knee, his head resting gently in her lap.

"Ah, Chewie," she said, rubbing him behind the ears. "Maybe Danny was right all along. Maybe I didn't really love Bradford after all."

# 23

When Danny arrived at Edna's house, Jo wasn't there. Eager to talk to her, he drove toward home, passing her on the road. She was Rollerblading, and in her hand was a green leash attached to a big brown dog.

"Hey!" he called, slowing the car and rolling down the window. "Who is this?"

"This is Chewie," Jo replied, rolling her eyes. "Long story."

"Okay. Can't wait to hear it. Are you headed to Edna's?"

"Actually, I'm going to pick up some dog food first. But can I meet you at Edna's in, say, half an hour?"

"Sure. That'll give me time to do something first anyway. See you there."

He drove off, curious about the dog but eager to keep his attention on the investigation. He had a feeling that things were about to become much more clear.

After a stop at the library and a call to his sister Denise, Danny was back at Edna's, waiting for Jo, when she rolled up the drive. She put the dog into the backyard, locked the gate, and then tied it shut in a complicated knot with a rope.

"Expecting Houdini?" Danny asked, climbing from his car.

"Hah," she replied. "You have no idea." She gave a terse explanation about where the dog had come from.

Danny reserved comment. While he couldn't imagine Jo Tulip as the mother of any creature who might make a mess, he was secretly glad to see her with a little canine protection. The dog might come in handy for her own personal safety.

"Anyway," she said tiredly as they went inside the house, "why do you look like the cat who ate the canary?"

He would have sat on the couch next to her, but it was missing a cushion. Instead, he took a seat on the ottoman to her right, eager to lead her through his thought processes. Since picking up the gold pin that afternoon, he had done a lot of thinking and had come up with a theory, which had then been confirmed by his magician sister and by what he had found at the library.

"What is it?" Jo asked, her eyes on his, a slight smile to her lips. "Tell me what you've learned."

He sat back and crossed his arms.

"Alchemy," he said triumphantly.

"Alchemy?" she asked, shaking her head.

"The science of turning metal into gold. Also, some believe, the secret to eternal life." As she processed what he had said, he reached into his bag and pulled out a stack of books on alchemy he had taken from the library. "You studied chemistry, Jo, so you know basically what alchemy is. Half science, half mysticism, it's been around for thousands of years. Studied by kings and chemists and philosophers, it's suppos-edly the ancient art of securing both immortality and great wealth through 'transmutation.' Legend has it that someone who possesses the secrets of alchemy can turn ordinary metals into gold and they will never die."

Jo nodded.

"Some famous scientists believed in alchemy, didn't they?" she asked.

Danny opened one of the books and flipped through the pages.

"Roger Bacon, Nicholas Flamel, Sir Isaac Newton, Carl Jung. They all dabbled in alchemy, even when it wasn't legal. Newton almost died from mercury poisoning because of his secret experiments."

Jo exhaled slowly, running a hand through her hair.

"So how does this fit in here?"

Danny leaned forward.

"We know Simon was working a con game on some rich but gullible women. I think his whole con centered around alchemy. He used the photos and the painting to prove he had already achieved immortality himself. As for the ability to turn metal into gold, well, look what I got from the jeweler."

Danny opened the envelope and handed Jo the metal pin.

"Last week, Simon Kurtz brought this to the jeweler and ordered an identical one to be made in gold," Danny said. He pulled out the gold version and handed her that as well. "The jeweler told me that Simon has placed a number of orders with him lately, and that every single time he has brought in some sort of metal trinket and had it duplicated in gold."

"Keep talking," Jo said, studying both items.

"On the way home, I was wondering why a person would do something like that. Then I started thinking that maybe these were props in a very elaborate trick. I called Denise and asked her how it could be done, exactly, and what she said made perfect sense."

Jo looked up at him expectantly.

"Let's say Simon wants to convince some rich widow that he has the power to turn metal into gold. He tells her to bring him some trinket, some small worthless item, and he'll prove it to her. Once he has the trinket, he says he needs a few days to mix up some of the secret formula or something. In the meantime, he takes the trinket to an out-of-town jeweler and has a duplicate made in gold."

"I'm with you."

"When they get back together, he brings out the trinket and the magic formula. Right in front of her eyes, he drops the metal trinket into the liquid, stirs it around, and pulls out the golden duplicate."

"But why go to all of that expense? I don't understand."

"Because she takes back the trinket, now golden, and brings it to her trusted jeweler. He examines it and pronounces that it's real, through and through. What she doesn't know is that at the bottom of the pot, hidden by the liquid, is the original trinket. She thinks she witnessed magic, when all she really saw was a simple switch."

Jo sat back, her eyes wide. Danny could tell she was coming on board with the idea.

"So," she said slowly, "first he makes them think he can turn metal into gold. Then, with the painting and the photos, he leads them to believe that he's been alive since the seventeen hundreds. He dupes local experts into validating his claims, and then he tells these women that they, too, can have the Midas touch and can live forever. They, too, can know the secrets of alchemy—for a price."

"Right."

"But, Danny, who would be gullible enough to really believe that?"

"Who indeed? What about Sir Isaac Newton? What about all of the alchemists through the ages? What about a few women in this very town who are old and alone and afraid to die?"

Jo's eyes met his and she nodded.

"I think you've hit the bull's-eye, Danny," she said. "In fact, I may even have found the special liquid he used for supposedly transmuting the metal into gold. It's in a paint can in the shed."

Jo led the way out back, where the dog was nearly frantic with joy to see them, knocking over his water bowl in jubilation. While Danny knelt and rubbed him behind the ears, Jo ran to the shed and came back out with an unlabeled paint can, an ornate silver and marble container, and a long, silver spoon.

"These were all together, in a box. The 'magic formula.'"

There on the back porch, she pried open the paint can to reveal a strange, sparkly liquid. They stared at it for a moment as Jo went through a sort of scientist's checklist.

"Viscous, odorless, opaque," she whispered. "I'd almost guarantee this is nothing more than some sort of ionic liquid, probably with a dye added for opacity. Or maybe a petroleum distillate. Or a synthetic latex."

"Whatever you say, Jo. Can you run a few tests, analyze it, and figure out what it is?"

She shook her head.

"I could do a few rudimentary things here," she said. "But defining an unknown is not as easy as you think. We'll have to send it out to a lab, one with some very high-tech equipment."

*The irony,* Simon thought as he finally rolled the bicycle into Wiggles' driveway, *is that Edna died while involved with a con that was supposed to provide eternal life.* As he thought about that, he finally understood the appeal of his own con: Nobody wants to die—particularly not those who are already frail and failing and alone.

Rolling the bicycle around to the back, he remembered the rules his father had taught him years ago, rules about why elderly women were the most perfect pigeons.

They often had significant savings, for one thing. For another, they were trusting and lonely and a bit socially isolated. Finally, they were always reluctant to go to the police once all was said and done. Not only would doing so be horribly embarrassing, but many elderly women feared that if their families found out how they had been duped, there would be serious consequences—like losing control of their own finances or even being placed in an old folks' home. To most of them, it wasn't worth it, and so they kept quiet.

The perfect pigeons.

Simon dropped the bike and went inside just as Wiggles was getting ready to go out.

"You look like death," Wiggles said, reaching for his car keys. "What happened?"

Simon realized he hadn't cleaned himself up after spending several hours on the beach. He was dirty, sandy, and tired, and his eyes were still swollen from crying. He knew he was a sight.

"Yeah, I've had a rough day," he said, for some reason reluctant to tell Wiggles that his sister had died. As long as he didn't say it, maybe it wasn't real.

"Well, I'm going down to the Surf and Turf for all-you-can-eat shrimp night. Wanna come?"

Simon looked at Wiggles, probably the only true friend he had left in the world.

"Sure," he said tiredly. "Can you wait while I hop in the shower? It'll just take a minute."

"I'll wait," Wiggles said. "But if we get there too late for the early bird special, you gotta pay the difference. For both of us."

Simon sighed, heading for the shower. What difference did it make? Two days from now, he'd be filthy rich.

Danny sat on the couch beside Jo's test kitchen, watching as she pulled on an apron and some rubber gloves. When they'd arrived there, she had a few messages on her voice mail, including one from the science professor saying he could not decipher the notebook and that he had a feeling it was just nonsense. There was also a call from Iris Chutney, saying that no one would be coming to Jo's that night but that the club was having a private meeting and deciding what to do. If they could agree, they would come over the next day at noon, if that was all right.

Since that left the evening clear, Jo decided she would run a few simple tests on the viscous liquid. At the very least, she said she should be able to draw some basic conclusions.

Danny was just enjoying watching her work. He sat on the couch, Chewie curled at his feet, a part of him pretending that this was their life, together, as husband and wife.

What would it be like to be married to Jo Tulip?

It would be beyond any expectation for marriage that Danny had ever had, that was for sure. To marry someone who had been a friend first had to be the very best possible scenario for a happy life. All that remained was how to help her realize, without scaring her off or risking the friendship, that there were deeper feelings involved here than she ever realized.

"Stop watching. You are making me nervous," she said.

Smiling, Danny turned his attention to the book in his lap, one of the ones on alchemy. Together, they both felt that they were on the homestretch of understanding what was going on with this con game—even if they still had no clue why Edna Pratt ended up dead.

"Chewie, get off the couch!" Jo said, glancing toward the dog. He had been curled at Danny's feet, but in the last half hour he had decided to take over the bottom half of the couch instead and make himself at home there.

After she fussed at him, though, he climbed off, found a spot on the rug, and settled down again.

"Smart dog," Danny said, glancing up from his book. "He knew what you said."

"Yeah, a smart dog for the Smart Chick," Jo replied, pouring a little of the chemical into a glass. "Just what I need."

Jo's theory was that the liquid was a substance known as molten salt. That was a salt, like sodium chloride, but one in which the cation was bulky and oddly shaped, and the anion was something soft, like tetra-fluoroborate. Being oddly shaped and soft, the ions in molten salt didn't stack well, giving them a strange, almost mystical appearance. It also helped that molten salt was viscous and odorless because it had no vapor pressure. If Jo were pulling off a trick like this, she decided, that's what she would use anyway.

So far, her theory held true as far as the solubility of the liquid went. She still wanted to check the pH, but she had a feeling that a dye had been added because the compound was an interesting deep blue color. With the right equipment, she would probably be able to identify the exact dye. Rather than go to that trouble, however, Jo decided simply to conclude her rudimentary analysis by determining the freezing point and boiling point of the liquid. With the data she had gathered, she would at least be able to preliminarily confirm or reject her theory. If the police became involved, they could have it sent to a lab, which would use expensive, specialized analysis equipment—such as infrared, nuclear magnetic resonance, neutron activation analysis, X-ray scatter, thin-layer and gaseous chromatography, and more—to analyze the compound more completely.

Jo worked for several hours, finding enormous comfort in the presence of Danny and even Chewie. The whole scene reminded her of days past, when she was the one hanging out on the rug, her grandmother sitting in the chair, and her grandfather working in the lab area.

*The more things changed, the more they stayed the same*, she thought. And, oh, how things had changed.

The phone rang around 9:00 P.M. It was Keith McMann, following up on the message she had never found time to return.

"You must think I'm a babbling idiot," he said, "leaving two messages like that."

"Not at all," she replied, bracing the phone against her shoulder so she could continue to work as she talked. "I thought it was cute."

"So, how about it? Would you like to go out sometime?"

Jo glanced over at Danny, who seemed to be thoroughly immersed in the book on his lap.

"Thank you so much for asking," she said. "I'm very flattered. But the truth is, I'm kind of in dating limbo right now. Going through a breakup."

"Ah. The musician?"

She glanced again at Danny.

"No, Danny's just a friend. This was…well, it's been a big mess. My fiancé left me at the altar. On Saturday."

"Saturday. Last Saturday?"

"Yeah."

"Ouch. I'm so sorry. How big of an idiot is he?"

Jo smiled.

"A really big idiot," she replied. "I think he's out of the picture for good, but I'm not up to starting something new just yet. Why don't you hang on to my number and give me a call in a month or so?"

"A month or so. Hmm… I don't know if I can go that long without looking into your beautiful green eyes again."

Jo was both startled and secretly pleased with his boldness. Her ego had taken such a bruising on Saturday that it felt good to be admired by a handsome and intelligent man.

They ended the conversation a few moments later, and after she hung up the phone, she began whistling as she worked.

"Do you mind?" Danny snapped, strangely irritable. "I'm trying to read here."

"Sorry."

She went back to working in silence.

When her final test was run, she pulled off the gloves and apron, sealed the remaining liquid back in the can, and looked over at her two companions.

Chewie was back on the couch, snoring soundly. Danny, too, was asleep, the book open on his lap, the light still shining over his shoulder. Somehow, at that moment, all of the mess with Bradford and her mother seemed a million miles away.

Reluctant to disturb the scene but knowing they all needed to get to bed, she walked over to Danny and shook him awake with a hand on his shoulder. He opened his eyes slowly, and as he focused in on her, she felt an odd sort of surge, like a longing mixed with safety mixed with something she couldn't identify.

"Time to go home, sweetie," she whispered. Then, unable to stop herself, she leaned down and kissed his cheek, thanking God that she had such a dear friend in her life, one who had always been there for her—and always would.

The all-you-can-eat shrimp at the Surf and Turf wasn't sitting well. Simon sat up on the couch, his mood as sour as his stomach.

There was one angle he hadn't covered, one phone call he knew he ought to make. Wiggles had gone to bed early, and Simon could hear deep snores coming from the bedroom. The man was down for the count, for sure.

Simon didn't want to use Wiggles' telephone for a business call, so despite his exhaustion and his upset stomach, he pulled on a pair of pants, took Wiggles' car keys, and headed out the door. This shouldn't take more than a few minutes, and Wiggles would never be the wiser.

The streets were dark and quiet, and as Simon neared the pay phone, he was reminded of the horrible call this afternoon, when he got the news about Edna. Putting that out of his mind for now, he dropped in the last of his change and dialed the home phone number of Angus Young, his inside man at Golden Acres Retirement Village.

Angus answered with a muffled voice, and Simon realized he must have been asleep.

"Angus?" he said, making sure he had the correct person.

"Yeah?"

"It's Simon."

That was met with a long, cold silence.

"Simon," the man's voice said finally, his tone sounding angry and disappointed. "I thought you fell off the end of the earth."

"No, I just found it necessary to go out of town for a while. I suppose you've heard the news about Edna."

"Yeah, that's too bad. I know you two was close to each other."

Simon looked away, trying not to tear up again.

"The thing is," Simon said, "I haven't talked to anyone there in town since I left. I wonder if you could tell me the general mood at the retirement village."

"The mood?" Angus asked. "The mood is getting desperate, if you really care to know. There's lots of whispering and meeting and threatening going on. I don't think they're gonna stay quiet about things much longer."

"Really."

"Yeah, really. You shoulda called some of 'em, Simon, kept them calm. Mrs. Louise is holding them off as long as she can, but it's a fight she's about to lose. There's this girl, Jo Tulip, going around and asking a lot of questions. People are starting to panic, thinking you ripped them off."

"What about the police?"

"The police? What about them?"

"Are they…looking for me?"

Angus sighed loudly.

"I already told you, ain't nobody talked yet. But soon as they do, you can bet everybody'll be looking for you—police, FBI, you name it."

"You think I should call some of the women and assure them that everything's right on schedule?"

"I don't think nothing. I don't care what you do. I'm just glad to see you're gone, wishin' you'd be done and out of here."

Simon didn't blame Angus for his attitude; after all, he *was* being blackmailed. And good thing, too, because he had been a valuable help in the last few months as the con came together.

Simon had first spotted Angus while visiting some wealthy potential pigeons at Golden Acres, and that night he showed up at his house with his proposal: Angus would keep an ear to the ground at the home, let Simon know who the wealthiest residents were and what people were saying about him. In return, Simon would withhold from Golden Acres management—not to mention the local high school—the interesting tidbit that Angus's real name was Fred Jackson and that he had done fifteen years in the Florida state penitentiary for murder one. Simon knew this because their prison terms had intersected. The scar that ran from Angus's nose to his chin had come compliments of a fight in the lunchroom one day, between Angus and another inmate. Simon could still remember the sight of that guy using a food tray to try to shut Fred up permanently.

"Is this thing over yet, or you coming back to finish things off?" Angus asked.

Simon hesitated, knowing he was a thorn in Angus's side—a very irritating thorn. While he knew he had the upper hand, he sure didn't want to press his luck.

"Just keep your ears open," Simon said. "What I do from here is my business."

"What about Jo Tulip?" Angus asked. "I know her, from the school. She's a pretty sharp girl. I think she's close to figuring some things out."

"Then you'd better turn your attention in her direction," Simon threatened. "Because if the cops get wind of this game before I get my money, the first person I'm bringing down with me is you."

## TIPS FROM TULIP

*Dear Readers, this week as we feature classic letters from the past, enjoy this exchange from 1982.*

---

**Dear Tulip,**

Can you break a calculator by changing the batteries? For several months now, my checkbook hasn't balanced. I seem to be short about $50 every month. My nephew, who handles my bank deposits for me, says it's because my calculator batteries are so old. My neighbor bought me some new batteries last month, but that only made things worse. This month I'm short almost $100! I hope I haven't ruined the calculator by changing the batteries.

—*Not Adding Up*
*in Los Angeles*

**Dear Not,**

There are two ways you can damage a calculator with batteries. First is if you mix batteries (old with new or two different brands). To avoid that problem, use only what comes in a pack together. Second is if you allow the batteries to corrode. If that happens, use mild sandpaper or an emery board to scrape off the corrosion and then wipe out the inside of the battery compartment with a dry paper towel. If the corrosion is significant, you may not be able to save the appliance.

In your case, however, I don't think you have an issue with batteries at all. Be a Smart Chick! I suspect the problem lies not with your calculator but with that calculating young man who takes your deposits to the bank.

—*Tulip*

# 24

Not knowing what else to do, Jo let Chewie sleep on a blanket on the floor in her bedroom. When she awoke the next morning, however, he was pressed up next to her, sound asleep, on the bed. Jo didn't know what to think about that—though she was glad she had taken the time the day before to give him a bath.

Before doing anything else, Jo spent half an hour getting the house ready for company—dusting, vacuuming, setting up the coffee machine and a tray of treats. The house was already spotless, but it felt good to run over it again just in case.

Jo had a lot going on that day, including—she hoped—a meeting with the women's club at noon and her radio show at 2:00 P.M. She also wanted to drop off the forms she filled out applying for a full-time teaching position at the high school. She brought Chewie along with her, noting that he really seemed to love riding in the car. Once Jo was there, she cracked the window and ran inside the brick building, glad that it was cool enough outside so that he would be fine.

Simon opened his eyes, knowing that today was the day the bank would get his notarized letter requesting the funds from his account. He had included a return overnight express form, prepaid, so if all went according to plan, tomorrow he would receive a bank check for nearly half a million dollars. That meant that as long as nothing went wrong in the next twenty-four hours, he would be home free. Tomorrow he would probably spend the entire day on Wiggles' front steps, waiting for the delivery.

Of course, so many things could still go wrong. The pigeons, for one thing, might not remain silent much longer. According to his conversation with Angus last night, in fact, it was time to do some damage control. If only he had known sooner that Edna didn't go to the police, this whole thing would have turned out much differently

Simon got up, dressed, and rode the bike to the pay phone, where he dialed Louise Parker, the one he considered the ringleader. Louise had obviously had both wealth and beauty in her youth, and though the wealth remained, the beauty had long since faded. She still carried herself as if she were something to look at, however, which was kind of sad. She had been making a play for Simon since the day they met.

Throughout the con, Edna had confided to the other women that Simon was her grandfather's best friend, a man she remembered quite well from her childhood. To keep up that pretense, for propriety's sake, Simon didn't even stay at Edna's house but instead rented a room in a fleabag motel across town.

Once the con was rolling and the women were starting to take the bait, Edna announced to the group that she had taken the magic formula and felt wonderful, as if she really were going to live forever. Once a shill, always a shill.

Now that Edna was dead, of course, Simon had some explaining to do. He should be able to wing it, as he only needed to string the women along until his bank check arrived.

Simon dialed Louise's number, relieved when she answered rather than letting it go to the machine.

"Louise, it's Simon," he said enthusiastically. "I've had the hardest time getting hold of you!"

She was angry. He let her rant for a few minutes, but when it sounded as though she was winding down, he spoke. His voice warm and apologetic, he explained that he'd been called out of town unexpectedly on business, but that it had all worked out for the best because while he was away he had spent some of his time perfecting the formula—which meant it would work better than ever.

"But it doesn't work at all!" she cried. "Edna Pratt is *dead*. If it worked, she couldn't have passed away. No matter what kind of accident she had, she shouldn't have died."

Simon closed his eyes, feeling a surge of guilt for what he was about to do. Simon rarely felt guilty about anything, but at this moment even he was ashamed of himself.

"Oh, but Louise, that's partly why I had to go away. I learned that Edna lied. She lied to all of us. She never did take the formula like she said. She wasn't as honest and upstanding as we all thought."

"I knew it!" Louise said, eager to pounce on a common enemy.

*Forgive me, Edna,* Simon thought. *But a man's got to do what a man's got to do.*

"Edna wasn't like you, Louise," he said. "You're the kind of woman I know that I can trust. Edna didn't believe in me; she only pretended that she did. But you really do. I know that you do."

"What are you saying?" she cooed breathlessly.

"I'm saying that I've been alive now for two hundred and ninety-one years and I've never met anyone quite like you, Louise. A little patience is all you need, and then I'll be back with the formula, you can take it yourself, and we'll be together forever. Just think about that—we'll never be separated by death. And since we can change metal into gold, we'll always have money and our needs will always be met. Just don't tell anyone about us—not yet, anyway."

That should calm her down and shut her up for a day or two, which was all he needed to be free and clear.

"Oh, Simon," she whispered after a moment's silence. "You don't know how long I've waited to hear you say all of this."

Jo ran into Angus as she was leaving the school, and he walked with her all the way out of the building, simply making conversation. He was much more animated than usual, almost agitated. Certainly, he didn't seem like himself. Once outside, he walked with her all the way to her car, a little startled when Chewie began barking from inside.

"Big dog like that," he said, "can sure mess up your house. Where do you keep him at home?"

"So far he goes wherever I go," she replied. "But if he's going to stick around, I guess I'll have to break down and install a fence."

"Really?" Angus said. " 'Cause I do odd jobs on the side. I'd be happy to come over and give you an estimate on that."

"On putting a fence around the yard?"

"Yeah, I could come over tonight, take a look, give you an idea of what it would cost. Where do you live?"

If he weren't being so pushy, Jo wouldn't have thought twice about their conversation. As it was, something about his demeanor was giving her the creeps.

"I'm not ready for that yet," she said. "First I have to decide if I'm keeping him or not. And right now I have to run."

"That's right," Angus said, stepping back from the car. "You're having some kind of meeting at your house at noon, aren't you?"

Jo's pulse surged.

"How do you know about that?"

"I, uh, I did a shift for a friend over at the retirement village last night. You know how old folks like to gossip. They got nothin' better to do."

Jo nodded, wondering what else he wasn't telling her.

"What kinds of things are they saying?"

He took another step back, shrugging.

"I don't know. I just heard it mentioned that some of them were going over there to your house. Well, you have a nice day. If you want me to give you a price on a fence, let me know."

"I'll do that," she replied.

Then she got in the car, locked the doors, and drove away.

Danny knew Tiffany was mad at him for canceling the noon appointment. But he needed to be at Jo's when the women's group showed up, and if that meant one less customer at the studio today, then that's just how it would have to be. He assured Tiffany that she was such a schmoozer that she should be able to reschedule the appointment without too much trouble.

He made it to Jo's fifteen minutes early, surprised to see that there were already several cars in her driveway. When he got inside, there were about five older women there, sipping coffee, nibbling cookies, and making small talk.

"Oh, Jo," one of them said enthusiastically, "I just have to tell you, I followed your tip for roasting a juicy chicken, and it really does work."

Jo thanked her, flashing the same beaming grin she always gave when someone praised her column.

"I must have missed that one," one of the other women said. "What was it?"

"It's so simple," the first woman said. "When you roast a chicken, stuff an apple inside of it first. It makes it much more moist."

"Do you eat the apple?"

"No. Just throw it away. But you'll be amazed at how much better the chicken is."

Danny tuned them out as they continued to talk about cooking, which led to a discussion of the small kitchens in the units at Golden Acres. From what he could tell, about the only one of them who didn't live at the retirement community was Iris Chutney. Two more cars arrived, so that by 12:05 there were nine women in the room. Danny was shocked that there were so many. Iris Chutney was there, but Danny was disappointed that Louise Parker, the unofficial head of the group, was not. From what he had seen so far, none of the other women made a move without her consent.

By 12:15 it was obvious she wasn't going to come. He and Jo brought up some folding chairs from her basement and put them in the living room next to the couch. Then they asked everyone to have a seat as the meeting was about to begin.

"Ladies," Jo said once they were quiet, "Danny and I want to thank you for coming today. I know it wasn't an easy decision for any of you to be here."

Danny looked around the room, noting that the friendly joviality from earlier was gone. These ladies suddenly looked quite serious—and very, very wary.

"It has come to our attention," Jo said, "that your group has made some recent investments about which you are concerned. To put it bluntly, since Edna Pratt's death and Simon Foster's disappearance, you must be wondering if you've been had."

There was a collective gasp, but no one said a word.

"I'm sorry to tell you that from what Danny and I have discovered in the last few days, it looks as though there are definitely some unscrupulous things going on here. But until one of you decides to go to the authorities and tell them what happened, nothing is going to change."

The women remained silent. Jo looked to Danny, so he took over.

"Let us make some educated guesses here," Danny said. "You have been introduced to the mystical secrets of alchemy."

They did not respond.

"You have seen ordinary metal turn into gold, right in front of your eyes," Jo said.

At this, several of the women actually nodded.

"You have been promised immortality," Danny added. "And you believe you know a man who has already achieved immortality and has the proof."

Several more nods, accompanied by some very defensive expressions.

Jo held up a piece of paper, a printout taken from the Internet, showing a mug shot and prison record.

"This man is named Simon Kurtz," she said. "You may know him as Simon Foster. He is sixty-two years old and has served time in prison for counterfeiting, forgery, and consumer fraud. It's a matter of public record, in case you think we're making this up. In short, he's a con man, and all of you have been victims of his latest con."

The astonishment in the room was audible. Suddenly everyone was talking at once, and the piece of paper was being passed around frantically.

"My son will be furious with me!" one of the women cried.

"Where is our money?"

"I knew it was too good to be true!"

"What can we do?"

Once Danny could get them to calm down, he and Jo listened as Iris Chutney explained how it had worked.

It started with Edna Pratt, she said, who had come to her and Louise one day and said that she knew a man, a very dear and trusted acquaintance, who had shown her the most remarkable thing. Edna would let them in on it, she said, if they would promise not to tell anyone.

Danny and Jo shared a glance, and he realized they were both thinking the same thing: So far, they had given Edna the benefit of the doubt, assuming she was just a pawn in her brother's game. Now they understood the truth of the matter, that Edna had also been working the con. She was just as culpable as Simon. That had to have something to do with the fact that she ended up dead—probably murdered by her very own brother.

"Sure enough," Mrs. Chutney said, "Louise and I went to Edna's house one night, met Simon, and watched him turn metal into gold. Then he showed us some pictures that proved how old he was."

"Don't forget the painting," another woman added. "I didn't trust those photos, but when I saw the painting, I knew it was true. I have a degree in art history, you know."

Mrs. Chutney gave the woman a silencing look and then continued.

"Simon said the secrets of alchemy were passed down to him more than two hundred years ago, when he was 62 years old. He took the formula at that time and never turned a day older than that, even though time continued to pass. He said there was one formula for transmuting gold and another for transmuting the body, and that they were both very expensive to make. He told us that if we could raise a million dollars, he could make enough of the formula for everyone."

"A million dollars?" Jo cried.

"We were allowed to share this with only our closest, most trusted friends," Mrs. Chutney said. "Louise and I thought about it, and we decided that if we could find ten people who would each give a hundred thousand dollars, then we would have our million. Simon said that with that much money, he could make enough formula for ten people."

"A hundred thousand dollars *each?*" Jo asked in dismay.

"As of last week, we were almost halfway there," Mrs. Chutney said. "Then Edna died and Simon disappeared, and we didn't know what to think."

"But you had already given Simon your money?" Danny asked.

"Four of us had. But the rest were ready to come on board pretty soon. He was supposed to do another demonstration of the metal into gold first for the ones who hadn't seen it."

Jo reached into the bag next to her chair and pulled out the metal pin Danny had retrieved from the jeweler.

"Was this the item he was going to transmute?"

"Yes," one of the women said. "It's mine. Simon told me he needed it ahead of time so that he could do some measurements and calculate how much of the formula would be necessary for the transmutation."

"I'm sorry," Jo said, reaching into the envelope and producing the second pin. "The truth is, he just needed enough time to bring it to a jeweler and have a duplicate made in gold. Using an old magician's trick, he was going to make it look as if he was changing one into the other right in front of your eyes."

Pandemonium broke out in the room. Several of the women began to cry.

"Ladies," Danny said, trying to get them to quiet down. "The police can help you if you'll let them. May we give them a call?"

The women took a quick vote. It was unanimous.

Before they had a chance to change their minds, Jo rushed into the kitchen to get the police on the phone. Danny was relieved because once the cops opened an investigation about this fraud, then they might be willing to take a second look at Edna's death as well.

Jo returned to the living room a few minutes later, assuring them that the police chief himself was on his way. The women talked and cried among themselves until there was a knock at the door, and then it was flung open.

Louise Parker stood there, eyes wild, breathing heavily.

"Ladies!" she cried, holding up one hand. "Not a word to anyone! I've spoken to Simon, and he's assured me that everything is right on schedule."

Iris Chutney stood, visible trembling.

"Too late, Louise," she cried. "We've already spilled the beans. The police are on their way."

# 25

Jo had to leave for the radio station before the chief was ready to start taking statements. She told him they were welcome to use her home until they were finished, but he said no thanks, that he wanted all of the women to relocate to the police station where they could do it more officially. His deputies took the names and addresses of the ladies present and then began herding them toward their cars.

Poor Louise Parker was beside herself. Though it had taken a while to convince her of the truth, once she was presented with all the evidence, she had finally given in. Now she was clamoring for justice more vigorously than the rest, even inviting the police to trace back the phone call she had received from Simon a little while before.

While Jo was glad that the scam was finally getting some official attention, she felt really bad for Sally Sugarman. The Texas senator was not going to be happy when she learned what had happened. Then again, if Edna was indeed murdered, surely Sally would want justice to prevail in the end. Maybe if the story stayed local, the voters in Texas would never have to know the truth about Sally Sugarman's mother or uncle—or the swindle they had tried to pull.

The chief thanked Jo before leaving and asked her to come by the station later as well to give her own statement.

"I'll come as soon as my radio show is over," she said. "In the meantime, I'm just glad you're willing to consider that Edna's death wasn't an accident after all."

She started to climb in the car, but he stopped her.

"Whoa, whoa, whoa," he said. "I'm not going there. We're investigating a con game, not a murder. None of this evidence leads me to change my mind."

"But, Chief, you see what the woman was involved in. Whether she was a victim or a perpetrator, you can't tell me her death isn't suspicious considering all that has come to light."

He glanced toward the last car full of women and then looked back at Jo.

"And who killed her, Miss Tulip?" he asked, lowering his voice. "Do you think one of those sweet ladies did her in?"

"They might have," Jo said defensively. "Money can be a powerful motivator."

"Yes, but none of those women even knew they were being swindled until today. So much for a motive."

"What about Simon? He could have killed his sister. He had motive."

"You're the one who told him Edna was dead. Why would he try to call her on the phone if he had killed her? Nope, as far as I'm concerned, Edna Pratt was doing some housecleaning, mixed the wrong chemicals, passed out, hit her head, and died. End of story."

"What if someone wanted to test her immortality?" Jo asked. "What if they wanted to check their investment, make sure it was genuine?"

The chief shook his head, taking a step back.

"I'll keep an open mind," he said. "But we won't open her death as a murder investigation unless we get some hard proof or a confession."

A confession would be good! That was what Jo prayed for as she drove toward the radio station. It was about ten miles outside of town, a right turn off of the highway and then down a long dirt road. She reached the small brick building just fifteen minutes before she was to be on the air, the closest she had ever cut it.

Her laid-back producer didn't seem concerned, however, which only served to remind her what a small-town market this was. If she hadn't shown up today, he probably would have just put on a "best of" tape—and no one listening would have even cared.

Jo grabbed a bottle of water, sat in the booth, spread out her papers, and waited for her cue. They had done some promos last week, and every advertisement they had run promised that today's subject was camping.

Oh, boy. How relevant to the average American woman.

The clock ticked straight up to two o'clock, the producer pointed at her through the glass, and she was off and running.

"Hello, friends, it's camping time. Want to keep ants off the picnic table? Forget the bug spray. Just put the table legs in water-filled coffee cans and you're good to go! Stay tuned for more Tips from Tulip after this."

The music cued up and Jo sat back in her chair, catching her breath and focusing for the show. Even when it was an off topic like this one, she still enjoyed it. Maybe she really should work on increasing her radio exposure.

The hour went by quickly. One caller suggested pouring some rice in a tackle box to keep out moisture. That gave Jo an opening to suggest that whenever little ones come along on a fishing trip, the hooks should be kept in a childproof container, like an old medicine bottle.

One caller wanted to know how to get sap off a tent, and Jo went through the process of rubbing the sap off with margarine and then cleaning with a light dish soap.

"Here's my favorite tip for the campsite," she said, "one you'll thank me for later. Bring along a hula hoop and a shower curtain, rig it up on a tree branch, and you have an instant dressing room. Throw in an inflatable kiddie pool, and it becomes your own private bathtub."

She told one caller how to make waterproof matches by dipping match heads in candle wax, and then she suggested that every camper should bring along the perfect fire starter in a plastic bag: cotton balls dipped in petroleum jelly.

"They don't take up much room," Jo said. "And you'll be really glad you have them if it rains and all your kindling gets wet. Speaking of kindling, save the lint from the dryer. It's flammable, makes perfect fire starter, and, best of all, it's free."

Mildew was a big topic, so she went through the steps for getting mildew off a tent.

"Trust me, folks, you don't want to clean your tent with harsh chemicals, like bleach or even ammonia. It needs a little more tender loving care than that."

As Jo went down the list of dos and don'ts, she couldn't help but think of Edna, with her fatal mix of bleach and ammonia. Someone else had to have combined those chemicals on purpose when Edna wasn't looking. But who? How? When?

All along Jo had had a hunch that Edna's brother had killed her. Now, however, she was starting to doubt that theory. Edna's death had hurt Simon in this con game, not helped him. All of his victims were turning on him, and apparently he was on the lam. Plus, he called her after her death, as if he thought she were still alive. So why did he leave town? Was he the one Jo heard Edna arguing with the night she was killed?

Suddenly, Jo had a thought, and it was so all-consuming that she could barely finish the segment. When they went to a commercial break, she told the producer she'd be right back, ran outside where she could have some privacy, and called Danny on her cell phone.

"I've got forty-three seconds," she said quickly once he was on the phone. "Call the chief and ask him to call the coroner. Danny, every time I think about Edna inhaling those fumes and passing out, I wonder how someone could have mixed them right there in front of her without her even noticing. But what if those chemicals were mixed *after* she was dead? What if someone whacked her on the head to kill her, and then, to cover it up and make it look like an accident, poured bleach into the ammonia? Tell the chief to make sure the coroner examined Edna's lung tissues. Because if she never inhaled those fumes, then his theory about her passing out from the homemade mix of cleaners just doesn't hold water. Gotta go!"

Jo made it back to the booth just in time, and she went immediately to a call so she could catch her breath.

"Tips from Tulip, you're on the air."

"I want to know how to keep our sleeping bags from getting all musty smelling over the winter," a woman said.

"Well, I'm glad you asked," Jo replied, consulting her notes and trying not to sound flustered. "I've got three suggestions for you. First, store them in a cool, dry place, like a closet—never the basement. Second, when you're finished with them for the season, don't roll them up too tightly or they won't have room to breath. Finally, when you do roll them up, slip a fabric softener sheet down inside. Follow those three steps, and your sleeping bags should keep smelling fresh all year long."

Danny finished at the studio, gave his statement to the police downtown, and then rushed home, afraid of what he might find once he got there. Jo had asked if she could lock Chewie inside his guest bedroom during the meeting at her house and the following radio show. He had agreed, not really thinking, but now all sorts of questions ran through his mind, primarily: Was the dog really housebroken?

When he came inside, Chewie began barking immediately. Danny had to admit that it was fun to come home to something other than a quiet, empty house. He went to the back bedroom and opened the door to find the dog, tail wagging furiously. It didn't look or smell as if there had been any accidents. On the other hand, there was something odd all over the top of the bed. After petting Chewie and rubbing him behind the ears, Danny stepped closer to see. Yellow blobs littered the surface of the bedspread, and after a moment, he realized what they were: little pieces of foam rubber.

"Hey, boy, where's the pillow?" Danny asked. As if in reply, Chewie's stomach growled loudly. Danny's stomach was growling, too, so he led Chewie to the kitchen and set about making himself a bagel. He called Jo as it was toasting.

"How's Chewie?" she asked. "Did he survive there by himself?"

"Yeah. I think he ate one of my good foam rubber pillows, though," Danny replied, reaching for the leash, which Jo had left on the table. He clipped it to Chewie's collar. "There's tiny pieces of foam all over the bedspread."

Jo apologized profusely, promising to buy him a new one once all of this mess with Edna was over.

"He sort of has a thing for pillows," she said. "I forgot to tell you."

"No harm done."

"Good. Because until I get a fence, I may need to put him over there again."

"Whatever you need Jo. *Mi casa es su casa*, you know that."

Danny glanced over at the dog and yelled, dropping the phone. He lunged for Chewie but wasn't quick enough to stop him from gulping down an entire package of cream cheese from off the table.

"News flash," Danny said when he came back on the line. "He's got a thing for cream cheese too. You might want to keep an eye out for that silver packaging to pass. Otherwise, you'll have to call a vet."

They moved on from talk of the dog to planning their next moves. Jo was on her way to the police station, she said, so Danny described his experience with giving his statement. As he talked, he looped Chewie's leash over a chair and settled for spreading his bagel with butter.

"What did the chief say about Edna's lungs?"

"He called the coroner while I was there," Danny said. "Maybe by the time you get there, they'll know something."

"Okay, well, depending on what happens, I guess once I'm finished at the police station, I'll head back over to Edna's and work some more. I'm ready to be done with that job—especially since I have feeling that Sally Sugarman is going to be firing me real soon anyway."

"Yeah, I know what you mean. Want some help?"

"You know it. I think we make a good team."

*That we do.*

Once Danny hung up the phone, he sat at the table, and took a bite of his bagel. Chewie was looking at him so longingly, however, that Danny relented. He carefully set half of it on the floor.

"Okay, boy," he said gently. Chewie went to town immediately, making quick work of the whole thing. By the time Danny had taken three bites, Chewie was completely finished eating and looking at him for more.

"Let's go outside," Danny said.

He led the dog out back and waited patiently while Chewie did his business. As Danny waited, he looked through the trees at Jo's house, feeling a longing deep in his soul.

"Father, I know You want the best for me," he prayed softly out loud. "And I don't think You would put someone like Jo in my life and give me these feelings of love for her unless You had something very special in mind. Please give me the patience and goodness and insight I need to bring this relationship in the direction You see fit. Thank You for the blessing of an amazing friendship. If it's Your will, please work on her heart to make it something much, much more."

He hesitated and then added, "And keep Keith McMann out of the picture, will You? Competition is the last thing I need."

Jo was in the right place at the right time.

That's what she decided as she sat quietly in the corner of the police station and listened to all that was going on. The officer who was taking statements was tied up at the moment, but while Jo sat and waited her turn, the whole place seemed to spring to life. From what she could tell, the cops had located a joint bank account for Simon Kurtz and Edna Pratt—and just in the nick of time too, because the bank had already closed out the account, issued a bank check for the balance, and put it in an overnight delivery envelope to be delivered to Simon the next day!

The chief spoke excitedly into the phone—from what she could tell, going back and forth between the DA, a judge, and the bank's lawyers—as he worked out the legalities that would force the bank to hold that envelope. Once he was finished, he banged down the phone triumphantly and said to another cop, "Not only did we stop the money, but we got an address too!"

After that, almost everyone, including the chief, disappeared into a different part of the building, so Jo was no longer privy to the breaking news—or the excitement. Still, she felt gratified to know that they might be able to collar Simon Kurtz very soon. She hoped there was still enough of the swindled money left over in the bank account to reimburse the women at least somewhat.

Eventually, Jo was invited into a small room to give her statement. The officer seemed weary but diligent, taking care to do a thorough job. He let her tell her story and then asked some clarifying questions. When they were finished, he thanked her and walked her out.

"Any chance I could talk to the chief?" she asked.

The man smiled and shook his head.

"He's pretty busy," he replied. "Right now I think you'd have a better chance of getting an audience with the Pope."

Simon walked up the front steps, a brown bag clutched in each hand. Feeling spontaneous, he had sprung for the two-dish special at the China Dragon restaurant, bringing home enough takeout for him and Wiggles both. Once inside, he cleared off the messy kitchen table and then set out two plates, some utensils, and all of the Chinese food. He knew Wiggles would be home soon, and he wanted to surprise him.

More than likely, this was the last night he'd see his friend for a while. Simon had made a radical decision. Rather than settle down in Florida and go legit, as he had planned, Simon was going to take the money when it arrived, head straight for the airport, and use his remaining cash to buy a ticket somewhere out of the country. He hadn't done his homework, really, but if he didn't need a passport, he thought Brazil might make a great place to live. He could settle there quite cheaply, get in on a little con action now and then, and maybe even meet a senorita or two. All in all, not a bad deal.

Except for one thing. Edna wouldn't be there.

An ache suddenly gripped deep inside of Simon's chest, like a vise. He held onto the back of a chair, face white, breathing shallow, almost as if he were being crushed. In his pain, the enormity of the situation hit him anew: Edna really was dead.

The physical ache subsided, but the emotional one did not. Finally, he pulled out the chair and sat, tears once again filling his eyes. As the General Tsao's Chicken and Beef Lo Mein went cold on the table, Simon sat there and cried.

Jo and Danny worked for the rest of the afternoon. He and his buddies had a standing basketball game every Thursday night, so Jo wanted to get as much time from him as she could before he headed to the Y.

So, while Chewie played in the yard outside, Jo and Danny emptied closets and sorted items and packed boxes. Jo kept listening for the phone, hoping she'd hear from the chief and hoping she wouldn't hear from Sally. The phone remained silent in both cases, and in the quiet they were able to get through the living room, the second bathroom, and the kitchen. That left only the attic and the basement and they would be done. Jo couldn't believe how much they had accomplished.

As they worked, they kept tossing around different ideas about who might have killed Edna Pratt. During a break, Danny took one of the markers and made a list down the side of a box: Simon, Louise Parker, Iris Chutney, all the rest of the women.

"I can't say why," Jo told him, "but put down the name Angus. I just have an odd feeling."

"Angus Young? The janitor?"

"Yeah. I was at the school this morning, and he was acting really weird."

Danny wrote out the name, nodding.

"You know," he said, "now that you mention it, he was asking me some strange questions about her death the day after it happened."

"I suppose," Jo said slowly, "that you might include Sally Sugarman. It's a bit of a stretch, but if she had gotten wind of what her mother was involved in, she might have tried to nip it in the bud by having the old lady killed. Certainly, there was no love lost there."

Danny added her name to the list.

"Who else?" he prodded. "How about the history professor, Keith McMann."

"Write him down if you want, but I think he's was just an unwitting pawn in Simon's game."

"How about the old guy at the Palace? He sure knew a lot about con games."

Danny wrote *Innkeeper*.

"The next-door neighbor?" Jo asked, grasping for straws. "Betty."

"I doubt it, but sure," Danny said, writing the name.

When he was finished, he sat beside Jo on the couch, missing cushion and all, and together they stared at the list.

"I know who did it," she said finally.

"Who?"

"Bradford. My almost husband."

"Bradford? He didn't even know Edna Pratt."

"So? Let's frame him, and then he'll get arrested and go to prison and I'll never have to see him again."

Danny glanced sideways at Jo.

"Nah," he said, "that's just cruel. Bradford's way too pretty to go to prison."

Jo giggled.

"He is pretty, isn't he?" she said. "He'd be a big hit on the old cell block."

They laughed, and Jo realized that it felt good. She reached down and took Danny's hand in hers. She entwined her fingers with his and squeezed, hoping he knew how glad she was that he was there for her.

She didn't know what she'd ever do without him.

# 26

Jo knew she wouldn't be falling asleep anytime soon. It was bedtime, but her mind was still racing. She wanted to take a walk, so she called Danny, and though he sounded tired, he agreed to a short jaunt around the block. Jo was glad, as she didn't think it would be prudent to walk alone.

Together, with Chewie between them, they made the bigger block, both of them quiet as they strolled past Edna's dark, empty house. In the distance, a dog barked, and though Chewie's ears perked up, he did not respond.

Across the street and down a ways from Edna's house, Jo spotted the real estate sign for the other home Marie was representing for sale. *The place looks a bit neater at night,* Jo thought, and then she did a double take as she realized that the place *was* a bit neater. Even in the moonlight she could tell the big rust stains were gone from the driveway, and a small grouping of potted plants had been artfully placed along the front wall.

Good for Marie. Jo was always secretly tickled when friends took her household hint advice.

When their walk was over, Jo thanked Danny for walking with her. Then, rather than going to bed, she went into her home office, the best place to be when her brain was on hyperdrive and the night stretched endlessly before her.

She let Chewie come along, but she also brought a roll of aluminum foil. Once they were inside the office, she pulled out about five feet of the foil, tore it loose from the roll, and laid it on the couch. She put a blanket on the floor for the dog, settled down at the chair, and reached into the basket of reader mail.

Jo had been working so hard this week to solve Simon's con and Edna's murder that she had given short shrift to the problem that was sitting squarely in her own lap: her column! She decided to brainstorm with herself, thinking of different ideas that might work to bring this dying art form back to life.

She had been going through reader letters for fifteen minutes or so when the dog stood, stretched, and decided to relocate to the couch. He jumped up onto it and landed on the aluminum foil, which made a horrible crinkling noise. He leapt back down to the floor, circled a few times, and then glared at Jo, almost insulted that she had subjected him to such a frightening indignity.

She laughed.

"Serves you right, boy," she said. "Maybe now you'll stay off the couch."

He went to his blanket, worked for a while to get it just so, and then collapsed into it. Jo watched the whole thing, wondering if it might not be so bad to have a dog around permanently. They had gotten off to a bad start, but he was a sweet dog and a smart one. Maybe if she had a fence installed and bought him his own bed and some chew toys and things, they might find themselves happily cohabitating. He certainly brought a feeling of security and comfort—and companionship. Jo had never had a pet before, but she was starting to understand the attraction.

Turning her attention back to her work, she put away the letters and reached for a pen and some paper. She wrote down the names all of the icons of the household hints business and what they had done to stay relevant. Martha Stewart, despite all of her legal problems, had positioned herself as a purveyor of elegance on a budget. Heloise stayed in the public eye primarily because she continued to write a razor-sharp column in a national women's magazine. The Fly Lady—one the biggest up-and-coming household hinters—used the Internet as her primary medium, dedicating herself to helping the organizationally impaired.

Jo's agent was correct that she needed a website too, and she decided to find a webmaster very soon. Besides that, she thought she might talk to a publicist—and a speaker's bureau. Surely she could begin to make herself more of a household name, no pun intended. Suddenly, she felt very determined, knowing she would not go down without a fight!

Jo picked up the latest issue of the newspaper and flipped through it, skimming the articles and trying to get a feel for modern culture. As she did, she jotted down all sorts of crazy ideas of how she could proceed, sort of brainstorming with herself.

*A reality TV show?*

*Focus groups?*

*Stay-at-home-mom support groups?*

*Women's retreats?*

*Creative projects for latchkey kids?*

*Working-mom luncheons?*

She kept thinking and kept writing, and soon she had filled an entire page with different directions she could go. She was particularly intrigued by the idea of a reality television show—not that it would be easy to get such a thing on the air, but she ought to look into it, at least. In her fantasy of how that could work, she decided she could create her own catchphrase, something like "Your Hint Takes the Cake!"

Smiling to herself, Jo was suddenly overcome with exhaustion. It had been a long and complicated day and the need for sleep was finally catching up with her. She put away the pen and paper, turned off the light, and then simply grabbed a pillow and blanket from the closet, moved to the couch, ditched the foil, and lay down. She could hear Chewie readjusting himself at her feet, and something about him being there made her feel safe and complete.

Jo awoke to pitch-black darkness and an odd sound sending tingles down her spine. In an instant, she remembered she was out in the office. Then she realized Chewie was growling.

One glance at the softly illuminated digital clock across the room told her it was 4:37 A.M. She sat up and put a hand on Chewie's back, softly whispering words of comfort.

But she didn't feel comforted. He continued to growl, and Jo stood, moving silently to the window. Peering out, she saw movement along the back of her house, and from what she could tell, it looked as if someone was trying to break in.

Lucky for her they didn't seem to realize she was out in the office. She only hoped she could keep Chewie from barking.

Heart pounding in her throat, Jo reached for the phone and dialed 911, muffling the receiver so the touch tone beeps couldn't be heard. When an operator answered, she whispered sharply that someone was trying to break into her house. The operator quickly took her information and then told her to hold on while he contacted the police. While he was doing that, she grabbed her cell and dialed Danny's number. He could get there a lot quicker than the cops could, if the intruder decided to turn his attention toward her.

"I'm coming right over," Danny said after she explained.

"No!" she whispered sharply. "That's too dangerous. Just stay on the line with me, in case."

"All right, but I'm getting dressed," he said. "Haven't you got some acid out there, or something you could use as a weapon?"

"Hold on," she whispered. "I'll check."

She set down the cell but kept the regular phone to her ear, listening as the 911 dispatcher gave her address to the police. She silently crept over to the chemical storage area and grabbed a spray can of toilet bowl cleaner, a substance that would be sure to stop anyone in their tracks. Then she returned to the window, shocked to see the intruder working on her back door knob.

Chewie couldn't take it any more. He barked loudly and then barked again. Jo pulled her face from the window just as the intruder turned and looked her way.

"That's it, I'm coming!" Danny said through the phone, and then she could hear it drop.

"Please hurry!" she said to the 911 operator as she dared to peek from the window again. This time, she saw the intruder running toward the backyard—the direction that Danny would be coming from. Steeling her nerve, she opened the lab door and let Chewie out, hoping he might be able to protect Danny.

In the distance, she could hear a siren.

"I'm going out there," she said to the operator.

Against his protests, she dropped the phone and returned to the chemical storage area, tossed the can of toilet bowl cleaner, and grabbed a squeeze bottle of acetone and a butane lighter.

Jo ran outside, turning toward the back.

Chewie was barking furiously and a man was yelling. Jo ran toward the noise, praying that Danny and the dog wouldn't be hurt.

By the time she reached the fence, the intruder was face down on the ground in Danny's yard, Chewie was standing on the man's legs, barking, and Danny was poised with a baseball bat.

"He didn't see the split-rail fence!" Danny cried when he spotted Jo. "Landed flat as a pancake and Chewie was all over him! Good dog!"

Jo squirted the acetone all over the man's back and hair, knowing the cold wetness and the flammable smell would be a bit of a shock and ensure his cooperation—even if the threat wasn't genuine. He didn't have to know that the acetone was evaporating too quickly in these conditions to actually be flammable.

"Mister, that's acetone I'm pouring on you, and I've got a lighter in my hands," Jo cried. "Don't move or you're toast. Literally."

"I'm not going anywhere," the man mumbled. "Lord help me."

When she could see the flashing lights out front, she handed the lighter to Danny and ran to get them, telling the two cops who responded to the call that they had already apprehended the suspect out back. They ran with her and took over.

"This guy smells like lighter fluid," one of them said, gesturing for Jo to pull off the dog.

"More like nail polish remover," amended the other.

"It's acetone," she said. "I had to think of something that would keep him still until you got here."

The cops laughed.

"I'm sure the big dog and the baseball bat didn't hurt either," one of them said.

As they cuffed the man, Jo knelt down to calm the still-barking dog, not surprised to see lights coming on in several of the surrounding homes. Putting both arms around Chewie, she buried her face against his shoulder.

"Good boy. That's a good boy," she cooed. Finally, once he was calm, she stood and put her arms around Danny, who held her close.

"All right, buddy," one of the cops said, "stand up."

They pulled the man to his feet, and as he turned around, Jo recognized him.

"Angus!" she cried, pulling away from Danny, dismayed to see that her intruder was the scar-faced janitor. "What are you doing here?"

He shook his head, unwilling to speak.

"Did you kill Edna Pratt?" Jo demanded.

Angus' eyes widened.

"Kill her?" he said, seeming genuinely surprised. "The newspaper said her death was an accident."

It was a long night.

Danny was tired of answering questions, tired of going through his version of what had happened. But the chief himself had gotten out of bed to come down to the station and question Angus. According to him, the coroner had declared Edna's death a possible homicide earlier in the evening after analyzing some of her preserved lung tissue and finding no evidence of caustic fumes having been inhaled. Not surprisingly, Jo had been right all along. Edna was murdered. The bleach and ammonia had been combined *after* she was dead.

Jo seemed relieved that the cops were finally going to take the matter seriously and do something about it. The chief was in with Angus Young for a long time, and when he came out, he, too, looked exhausted.

"So is Angus the murderer?" Jo asked when they saw him. Danny and Jo had been hanging around in the inner waiting area in hopes of speaking with him.

"I don't know," the chief replied. "On the one hand, he's got some serious prior convictions."

"Prior convictions? You mean he's been to prison?"

"Yep. His real name isn't even Angus—it's Fred Jackson."

"Fred Jackson?"

"Uh-huh. On the other hand, he has a pretty good alibi for the night Miz Pratt died. We'll have to check it out, of course, but if it's true, then he wasn't the one who killed her."

"What was he doing at my house tonight? Was he going to hurt me?"

The chief raised both hands as if to say, "Who knows?"

"He says he was just looking for information, trying to see how close you were to learning the truth about Simon's con."

"Simon Kurtz?"

"Yep. Says he was being blackmailed by the man. Apparently, Angus got his jobs at the school and at Golden Acres with a fake résumé, fake name, and fake identification. He was working there under false pretenses, and Simon knew that. It's pretty complicated."

When Danny and Jo were ready to leave the police station, the chief suggested they go out the back way because there were reporters in the main lobby. Apparently, the coroner, afraid it might look as if he had made a bad call in the death of Edna Pratt by first saying it was an accident, had held a late night press release announcing that his own further study had confirmed that the death was, by all likelihood, a murder instead. The middle-of-the-night brouhaha at Jo's house had somehow been connected to Edna, probably from speculation by a neighbor or two, and now the reporters were out in full force, trying to figure out what the story was, exactly, behind Edna's death and Jo's intruder, and how the two were connected.

The chief seemed furious, especially since Simon Kurtz was still at large. His efforts at damage control seemed to include stringing along the reporters, keeping them at bay until the man could be apprehended.

By the time Danny and Jo left the police station, slipping out the back way and to Danny's car unnoticed, the sun was just coming up. Reluctant to part ways, they decided to go for breakfast. Rather than drive around trying to find somewhere that might be open, they headed for a sure thing, the 24-hour pancake house out by the interstate. For Danny, the lack of ambience from the orange plastic seats, vinyl-top tables, and ceiling-mounted television droning from the corner disappeared with the first cup of coffee, it was that good.

As he sipped his coffee and Jo studied the menu, Danny watched her across the table, thinking she was beautiful even with her hair a mess and circles under her eyes. It struck him suddenly that hers was the face he wanted to grow old with. He wanted to spend the rest of his life looking at her across the breakfast table.

"So what are you doing today?" she asked. "You working at the studio?"

He nodded.

"Regeneration is playing this morning at a women's breakfast over at Cornerstone Church," he said. "I'll be going to the studio after that."

"Cornerstone Church," Jo replied. "From what I recall, that was Edna Pratt's church."

Danny watched her whole face cloud over. He hesitated and then reached out to put a hand over hers.

"Don't do this, Jo. You hardly knew her."

Tears filled her eyes. She blinked, sending them down her cheeks.

"But she was a fan, Danny. She read the column every day. She collected her favorite tips in a little notebook. Somehow I feel that I *owe* her something."

"You've given her what you owed her. You've convinced the police of the truth. They'll take it from here."

"So why do I feel so sad?"

His heart pounded, wanting to say the first thought that sprang into his head: *Because love is staring you right in the face and you don't even see it!*

"Because it's been a tough week, Jo. Because in the last seven days you've had to be an expert at a crime scene, get the image of a dead body out of your mind, recover from a failed wedding, get abandoned yet again by your parents, investigate a murder, deal with a surprise pet, and face down an intruder in your own backyard. I'd say you need to go home and put on one of your favorite old movies, watch it, and have a good, long cry. I think you'll feel better after that."

She smiled at him through her tears.

"Why do you always know the right thing to say to me?" she asked.

"Because I love you."

His statement sat there for a moment, totally unplanned, totally unavoidable, totally horrifying from his point of view. Why had he spoken so soon?

He held his breath, but from the look on Jo's face, she didn't even understand what he was saying. She merely smiled and patted his arm and said, "Thanks, Danny. You know I love you too."

Jo couldn't get over how hungry she felt. Maybe confronting potential murderers in the middle of the night did something to the appetite. She only knew that when the waitress brought the modest cheese omelet she had ordered, she asked for a side of pancakes. In companionable silence, she and Danny ate, and she felt grateful to the core that he was there with her. He was such a rock.

When the waitress brought the pancakes, she lingered oddly, looking at Jo. Her behavior was so strange that finally Jo looked up at her questioningly.

"It *is* you!" the woman said. "Are you Jo Tulip?"

It wasn't often that Jo ran into a fan who recognized her, but it was always fun when it happened. She wiped her mouth with her napkin, sat back, and smiled.

"Yes, I am," she said. "Do you read my column?"

"Column?" the woman asked. "What column? I'm talking about the TV."

She pointed across the room. Jo turned to look, shocked to see a photo of herself on the television screen. It was one of her publicity photos, and underneath was the caption, "Jo Tulip of Tips from Tulip."

"What?" Danny cried, equally surprised.

They both got up from the table, crossed the room, and stood directly under the television set, where they could see and hear what was going on.

It was a news story, and they were calling "household hints expert Jo Tulip" a hero.

A hero?

"Miss Tulip apprehended the suspect about four-thirty A.M. this morning as he attempted to break into her home here on Oak Street."

They cut to the reporter, who was standing in front of Jo's house. From all appearances, it looked like a live report.

"Armed with flammable liquid and a butane lighter, Miss Tulip and a neighbor held the suspect at bay until police could arrive to take over at the scene and make an arrest."

"A neighbor!" Jo laughed, poking Danny in the ribs. "That's you."

"Shut up," he teased.

"In custody is this man," the reporter said, and then a mug shot appeared on the screen, a younger, unscarred version of Angus Young. "Fred Jackson has been working at both Mulberry Glen High School and the Golden Age Retirement Village in Mulberry Glen under the name of Angus Young. In truth, he is a convicted felon, having served a ten-year sentence in Florida State Penitentiary for first-degree murder."

Jo gasped. The chief had said Angus was an ex-con, but she had never dreamed his crime was murder. The scene changed to a shot of the Golden Acres sign.

"Those who worked with Jackson here at Golden Acres describe him as a kind and gentle man who was good with the residents. There are no suspected incidents of foul play at the facility, and police have not released any information about Jackson's motivation for the murder of

Edna Pratt. The chief of police in Mulberry Glen is expected to give a statement to the press in the next few hours. In the meantime, this is Suzie Chin, reporting from Mulberry Glen. Back to you, Jim."

The television switched to a different story, and Jo and Danny both realized that everyone in the place was staring at them. Then they all applauded.

"Breakfast is on the house, honey," their waitress called. "Good for you for being so brave!"

Jo swallowed hard and looked at Danny, eyes wide.

"I guess we're heroes," she said, grinning.

"I guess we are," he agreed.

"Or at least I am," Jo added. "You're just a neighbor."

## TIPS FROM TULIP

*Dear Readers, this week as we feature classic letters from the past, enjoy this exchange from 1994.*

### Dear Tulip,

Do you have any clever craft ideas for old wine bottles? Since my husband retired last year, we seem to have a lot of them around the house, and I'd love to use them to do something creative with my grandchildren.

—*Crafty in Colorado*

### Dear Crafty,

Kids love sand art, so you might try that. You can purchase colored sand at any craft store. Gather a few small funnels and some long, pointed sticks (chopsticks work well). Using the funnels, the children can layer the sand in all sorts of creative ways, poking the sticks into the sand along the sides to create patterns. Be sure to fill sand to the very top before you cork or seal it off, otherwise the sand inside will get jostled and lose its design.

Please be a Smart Chick! If there are a lot of wine bottles around, that means there's been a lot of wine. Your husband may have a drinking problem. Check the phone book for your nearest Alcoholics Anonymous chapter, and by all means solicit the help of your church and your loved ones to get both of you through the challenging road of recovery that lies ahead. Don't bury your head in the sand!

—*Tulip*

# 27

Danny reached Cornerstone Church at the same time as his mother. Together they began unloading their equipment, bringing it into the fellowship hall where the breakfast would be held. Once they had brought everything inside, he slipped into the bathroom to shave and change clothes, glad he kept an electric razor in his car's glove compartment for just such a situation.

His mom was full of questions about the news report she had seen on TV that morning. As they set everything up on the stage at the end of the room, he explained quietly, though he had to start over each time one of his curious sisters arrived.

Fortunately, Danny realized, since he had been identified as only a "neighbor" on the news report, none of the women at the banquet would know of his involvement. That saved him from more repeated explanations, for which he was quite grateful once they opened the hall doors and women began pouring inside.

Edna Pratt's murder was the topic of the day. It was all the church women could talk about as they stood waiting in line for the buffet. Regeneration wouldn't be playing until after the meal was over, so Danny listened a bit from his table near the buffet line, curious to hear what the gossip might be. From what he could tell, most of the women hadn't known Edna personally. They were just shaken by the thought that someone—anyone—in calm little Mulberry Glen could have been murdered.

"I praise God that Edna came to know the Lord just before she died," one of the women said. "Murdered or not, I sleep easier at night knowing that's one soul that went straight to heaven."

The comment struck Danny as odd. Edna had come to know the Lord *just before she died?* How did this woman know that?

She was standing behind the buffet table in a white apron, scooping out hash browns onto each plate. Danny leaned over and asked his mother who the woman might be, and she replied that it was Cora Pepperdine, the pastor's wife.

When she ran out of hash browns and went into the kitchen, Danny excused himself and followed her.

"Need help carrying something out, Mrs. Pepperdine?" he asked, trying to act as if he belonged there.

She flashed him a worried smile as she lifted the foil covers on several containers, saying that that wouldn't be necessary since apparently the hash browns were all gone.

"I hope no one is disappointed," she said. "I guess I made the serving sizes too big. And call me Cora, please."

"Well, the line's almost finished anyway, Cora," he replied. "And there's still plenty of other food out there."

He didn't want to hover, but he didn't want to leave either. Mostly, he wanted to engage her in a conversation.

"Would you like some help taking out the trash?" he offered, gesturing toward the overflowing cans.

"Good idea."

They chatted as they bagged the trash and carried it outside. She asked about the band and he complimented the facility and the next thing he knew, they were at the dumpster, tossing in the big plastic bags.

"Before we go back inside, may I ask you something?"

"Of course."

"I couldn't help but overhear you say that Edna Pratt came to know the Lord just before she died. Were you friends with Mrs. Pratt?"

"Her late husband was a member here," the woman replied, "but she hardly ever came."

"Then how do you know she found faith there at the end?"

"How do I know?" she asked, smiling shyly. "Because I was there."

Simon zipped the suitcase shut, picked it up, and set it beside the door. Wiggles was still asleep, his snores practically rattling the windowpanes throughout the house.

Breakfast was a simple bowl of cereal because Simon didn't want to make any noises or smells that might wake up his roommate. Better that Wiggles sleep for as long as possible. That would make this day easier.

They had already said their farewells last night anyway, over reheated Chinese food. Wiggles had come home to find Simon crying about Edna and had turned out to be a pretty good friend. There weren't a lot guys who could sit there and watch another guy cry, but Wiggles hadn't seemed bothered by it. In fact, he shared the sad story of his own sibling's death, giving strange comfort to Simon in the universality of his suffering.

Today, after he finished eating, Simon would go outside and sit on the front stoop. The overnight delivery truck should arrive by ten A.M. at the latest. After that, Simon would take the money and run—straight to the airport, straight out of the country. He had pretty much decided on Brazil, though if it turned out that he would need a visa, his second choice was the Cayman Islands. Banking was easy there, where he could go by a number rather than a name.

There wasn't much Simon would miss by leaving the country. He had always struggled within himself between the two kinds of cons a person could choose from: the way he was raised, doing mostly small cons, and the way he had tried to earn money as an adult, doing mostly big cons. Each method had its pluses and minuses, but Simon had a feeling he was done with both types of cons for a while—at least until his money ran out. He'd spent the last year working so hard, and what had it brought him? A sister who'd found religion and decided to come clean, spoiling the whole game for both of them.

He could still picture Edna's face last Friday night when he got to her house. She had called and said she had an urgent matter to discuss with him, but the news she hit him with when he got there was something he wasn't prepared for in any way.

"I've had a big change in my life," she told him. "Today I accepted the Lord Jesus Christ as my personal Savior."

Simon knew lots of folks who had taken the Lord Jesus Christ as their personal Savior. He met them all in prison, where Bible study was a nice alternative to boredom and a religious conversion always looked good to the parole board.

But what good was Christianity in the outside world? Most of the inmates he knew who became Christians while on the inside went right back to the their old lives once they were out. The best Simon could tell, all religion did in the real world was complicate things the way it had complicated the con with Edna.

In hindsight, Simon supposed, he should have seen it coming. When he first came to town and convinced his sister to get back in the game, she had really hesitated. Edna hadn't worked a con in the forty years since she ran away from the carnival and reinvented herself. But Simon convinced her to do it, promising money and excitement and a whole new life together. Edna was bored with being a widow, bored living in Mulberry Glen, bored by knowing her own daughter couldn't stand the sight of her and hardly ever visited. Finally, Edna relented. But as her friends and acquaintances got sucked into their little game, one by one, she hadn't seemed to be enjoying herself. Where Simon drew excitement and pleasure from clever deception, she seemed only to grow more withdrawn and guilty.

In the end, all it had really taken for her to change her ways was a kind word from the pastor's wife and a few well-chosen Bible verses.

"The Lord has washed me clean as snow, Simon," Edna had told him that night. "All of my sins are gone. Do you understand that? They're gone, simply swept away, through the power of prayer and the redemption of Christ. Yours sins can be gone too, Simon, just by letting the Holy Spirit into your heart."

He let her make her pitch. But when she was finished, he told her he wasn't interested. It was after that that she dropped her bombshell.

"Well, then, you need to know," she said, "at noon tomorrow I'm meeting with my lawyer to turn myself in. What you do between now and then is completely up to you."

He realized that she had called him over there to give him fair warning. She was telling him that the con was off, and that he could either disappear on the double or stick around and end up getting arrested.

It broke his heart, and he cursed God, if there was one, for being more important to his sister than her own flesh and blood. How could she turn on him like that? Hadn't they always stuck up for each other? Hadn't he always been there for her?

Simon tried convincing her for over an hour, but she wouldn't budge. Even his stories about the misery of prison wouldn't dissuade her.

"My sins have been forgiven," she kept saying, "but that doesn't mean I can continue to sin. I have to make this right, no matter what the cost."

Her mind was made up. In the end, despite his anger, they had hugged goodbye—a long, tender hug that Simon knew might have to hold him for a good long while. From now on, he would be just another ex-con on the run, and his sister would likely be spending the next few years in jail.

After telling Edna goodbye, Simon had walked to the main road and caught a bus back to the hotel and packed up his things. At first he planned to get as far away as he could as quickly as possible. But the more he thought about it, the harder it was to leave. He ended up staying awake all night, trying to figure out some way to get out of town *with* the money. At least the bank had Saturday hours. In the end, he had caught the bus to the bank, gone inside as soon as it opened, and attempted to make a withdrawal. It hadn't worked, but that had still given him several hours to get away. He assumed Edna had gone along as planned, meeting with her lawyer at noon and confessing to their crimes. Little had he known, though, somewhere between the time he left her house and the next morning, that she had committed suicide. He wouldn't have predicted that, given her emotional state when he left, but one never knew. Before their mother killed herself, she made a batch of cookies and changed the kitty litter.

You could never know what someone else was really thinking.

Exhaling slowly, Simon stood and carried his bowl and spoon to the sink, setting them down without even bothering to wash them. Then he went outside and waited for the delivery, knowing that as soon as it came, his life would forever be changed.

To avoid the reporters camped out in front of her house, Jo parked at Danny's and went home across the backyard. She picked up Chewie on the way, who had once again been stashed in Danny's guest room. Jo knew she was taking advantage of Danny's hospitality, but she just couldn't bear the thought of Chewie running loose in her own home when she wasn't there. There was no telling what he might eat!

Chewie was delighted to see her, of course, practically knocking Jo over in his enthusiasm. She led him to her house on the leash, letting him stop at almost every tree to lift a leg. Once they were home, she slipped in through the back, went into the kitchen, and gave Chewie a nice big bowl of dog food. He wolfed it down while she checked her telephone messages.

There were plenty.

Her favorite was from her agent, who sounded more excited than he had been in a long time.

"Hey, doll!" he exclaimed. "It's Milton. Looks like you just got your fifteen minutes of fame. Call me right away so we can figure out how to use it to our advantage."

The other calls were from reporters or friends, each wanting to pump her for information. Jo decided to ignore all but Milton. She called him back and they mapped out a strategy for how to proceed. He was going to put several things into motion right away, including trying to get her some television appearances and responding to an offer of a book deal.

"You need to start putting together a 'Best of' collection," he said. "Go through the old columns and think about how you would organize them into a book. I don't know what kind of advance we're talking about, but if you're gonna try to put something out, it would be nice to strike while the iron's hot."

Jo felt a bit guilty once she hung up. It was one thing to fight her column's demise with grit and determination. It was quite another to capitalize on a tragedy just to make a buck.

She tried to think it through as she showered and dressed for the day. She was just buttoning her shirt when the phone rang. Letting it go to the machine, she listened until she heard Danny's familiar voice.

"Hey," she said, picking up the phone. "Shouldn't you be on stage whacking a drum right now?"

"In about five minutes," he said. "I had to talk to you first."

"What's going on?"

According to Danny, they now had a whole new perspective on Edna Pratt's last days.

"What do you mean?"

"I mean, I just had a significant conversation with Cora Pepperdine. The pastor's wife here at the church."

"Several weeks ago," Danny said, "Cora had heard rumors that Edna Pratt was offering some of the older widows in the church a chance at 'eternal life on earth.' Feeling concerned, Cora had paid a visit to Edna to talk about it. Edna had been very closemouthed during the whole encounter, but as Cora was leaving, she made Edna a promise. She said, *If you really want eternal life, Edna, I can tell you how to get it. It's not something you can earn or buy or wish into existence. It's a gift and it comes through the blood of Jesus Christ. Call me if you want to know more.*

"Edna must have been thinking it over ever since," Danny said, "because last Friday morning she called Cora and asked if she could meet with her again. According to Cora, Edna Pratt had been reading the Bible, and she was feeling strongly convicted in her heart."

"But, Danny," Jo said, "don't you think this was just another swindle? It would have been easy for Edna to fake some sort of conversion if it would get the pastor's wife off her back."

"Here's the thing," Danny replied. "On Friday afternoon, Cora presented the plan of salvation and prayed with Edna, who seemed to genuinely come to faith. Afterward, Edna was crying and saying how evil she had been and how much she needed forgiveness. Cora assured her that God had given her that forgiveness the moment she asked for it, but then Edna said—are you ready?"

"What? What?" Jo prodded.

"Edna said, 'I have to set things right. I have to go to the police and make them understand what I've done.' When Cora started asking questions, Edna just clammed up and said she had to talk to someone first and that the truth would all come out in the end."

Jo sat there for a moment, thinking about the implications of what Danny had just told her.

"Edna was going to confess her part in the con," Jo said softly. "She was going to own up to it, hoping to set things right. She was going to blow the whistle on the whole game. That means her brother must have been the one to kill her."

"Maybe not," Danny replied. "What if she warned him first? What if she told him what she was planning to do and gave him a chance either to convert and confess along with her or get out of town? That would explain why he disappeared right in the middle of the con. He got out while the getting was good."

Jo nodded to herself. That would also explain why Edna had been in the middle of housecleaning and beautifying when she died. She was putting all of her ducks in a row before valiantly marching off to jail. Had she not been murdered Friday night, chances are Edna would have shown up at her lawyer's office on Saturday at noon, ready to tell all.

"It makes sense," Jo said.

Danny had to go, as they were calling him to the stage. Jo hung up the phone, thinking of what they had learned.

If Edna was killed because she was going to confess, then whoever killed her was someone who needed to stop her from making that confession. Jo thought again of Edna's daughter, Sally, a woman whose political career took precedence over everything. She blinked, thinking also of the older women who had been duped—any one of which would have been mortified to see the truth come out in that way.

Jo got out the phone book and looked up the medical examiner's office. She had to go through several people, but finally she was connected with the coroner. She gave her name and reminded him how they met at Edna Pratt's crime scene. Then she asked if he would mind answering a few questions about the autopsy.

"If I can," he replied.

"If Edna Pratt didn't pass out from fumes," Jo said, "then that means she was pushed down where she hit her head against the window. Am I correct?"

"Not exactly. She had no other bruises or marks that might indicate she was pushed. So my theory is that she was bludgeoned on the head with something dull and square. I made some good drawings of the fatal head wound when I was doing the autopsy, and though at the time I felt certain the shape matched that of the windowsill, further study has shown that perhaps it was something else squared-edged, like a piece of wood or metal. Obviously, once she was dead, the killer hit that same implement against the widowsill, to make it look as if Edna had fallen and hit her head."

"Could a woman have done it?" Jo asked.

"Not an older woman, unless she was abnormally strong. But a young woman, certainly. Especially in the heat of the moment."

Jo thanked him and hung up, a sudden image coming into her mind. She recalled walking with the police through the crime scene, explaining the different oddities in the house. Jo closed her eyes, remembering the felt-covered brick on the coffee table.

Simon heard the truck before he saw it. As it came around the bend, he stood, heart pounding at the sight of the familiar purple-and-orange logo.

The money was here.

He walked to the edge of the driveway, watching as the driver put the big truck into park but left the motor running. The man climbed down from his high seat, went around back and reached inside, leaving the doors open. Then he came around to Simon, an envelope in his hand.

"Howdy," he said. "Are you Simon Foster?"

"Yes, I am," Simon said, reaching out to take the envelope.

Once he took it from the guy, he saw that there was a gun in the driver's other hand, aimed directly at him.

"Then you're under arrest."

Suddenly, five men in full SWAT gear spilled out from the back of the truck, each of them with guns trained firmly on Simon. He put his hands into the air, wondering for a moment if he were still asleep and this was just a dream.

Then they had him down on the ground, one foot against his back, two men pulling his hands together behind him for the handcuffs.

Simon felt a crushing weight in his chest, more than just the weight of the cop's foot. It was the weight of betrayal and lost dreams and a dead sister.

It was the weight of his own greed.

When Jo arrived at Edna's house, she left Chewie in the yard and ran inside to dig through some boxes, trying to remember what she had done with it. She finally found it in the bottom of a trash bag: a brick, wrapped in green felt, with some steel wool affixed to the bottom.

She pulled out her cell phone and dialed the police station. Once she identified herself, they put her directly through to the chief.

"Miss Tulip?"

"Chief!" she cried. "I may have found the murder weapon."

She went on to describe the item, reminding him of what she had said at the crime scene, that Edna was probably using the brick as a sander while fixing the water rings in her coffee table.

"It's heavy, it's square, it's dull, and I bet you anything it was sitting nearby when someone came here to kill her."

"Have you touched it?" he asked.

"Yes," she replied. "On Saturday, and then when I came here to clean out the house for Sally Sugarman. It's in a box now."

"It's covered in felt, you said?"

"Yes. Green felt."

"Probably wouldn't hold a print anyway, but it's certainly worth a look."

He asked if she could bring it straight to the coroner's office, which was downtown about a block from the police station.

"The coroner can measure it, at least," he said. "Compare it to the measurements of the wound site. And you never know, there might be some latent prints there."

She agreed to bring it right over, and then they hung up. She ran into the kitchen, retrieved a plastic bag, and carefully put the brick inside.

Before leaving, Jo ran out back to check on Chewie, dismayed that he had turned over his water bowl yet again. Pausing to think, she ran back into the sewing room, pulled out Edna's bundt pan she had put in the yard sale pile, then brought it into the kitchen, and filled it with water.

"Here you go, boy," she said, carrying it outside. She set it down on the grass, grabbed a wooden stake from Edna's tomato plants, and drove it into the ground right in the center hole of the pan. "Just try to knock that over."

In the car, Jo realized that life with a dog might yield all sorts of new possibilities for her column. Already, she had dealt with several frustrating situations, using her ingenuity to solve each one.

"That's why they call you the Smart Chick!" she said out loud to herself.

Then she drove as quickly as she could to the coroner's office.

# 28

Regeneration finished their set to enthusiastic applause. They took their bows, and then Danny slipped off to the side to close the curtain. The women's group was going to have a meeting now, so the family would have to dismantle their equipment quietly and carry it from the stage through the back exit.

He had some spare time before he had to be at the studio, so he helped his sisters with all of their stuff before loading his own. By the time everything had been put away, his mother was standing in the parking lot, divvying up the love offering the women had given them.

Each share came to only forty-three dollars, and Danny wondered briefly if it had been worth it. Considering the time and trouble they'd gone to—not to mention the quality of their music—they were worth much more than that.

Aggravated, Danny told his family goodbye and climbed into his car. Before he could pull out of his parking space, however, the passenger door opened and his mother plopped down into the seat next to him.

"Wait a minute, Danny," she said. "I need to talk to you."

"What is it, Ma? I have to get to work."

"What's going on?" she asked. "You seem upset."

He put the car in park, hesitated, and turned off the key. It was a cloudy day, dark and oppressive, and he wondered if his life would always be like this—lots of hard work for very little money and some big dreams that were never going to come true.

"How do you do it, Ma?" he asked her. "How do you collect these penny-ante love offerings when you know what our shows are really worth? How do you keep plugging away with the band when you know that your goals and dreams are never going to come true?"

That was probably more than she had expected to hear, Danny realized. But he was tired and frustrated, from the situation with Jo to his career as a photographer. Soon, something somewhere was going to have to give.

"You're right," his mother said softly. "I did have big dreams when I was younger. I just had to rethink things, is all."

"*Rethink* things? How do you reconcile your desire to be a big music star with the knowledge that you just made forty-three dollars from a morning's worth of talent and hard work? It's crazy."

"Yeah, it is," she admitted. "I guess I just tell myself that the Lord knows what He's doing. Maybe you need to surrender."

"But how?" Danny demanded. "How do you surrender something you want with every fiber of your being? How do you give something over to God's control when you still have to spend every waking moment trying to make it happen for yourself?"

She exhaled slowly, reached out, and patted his hand.

"Ah, Danny," she said, "it's so hard to explain. Part of the peace I have comes from knowing that God is using me, no matter how limited the fashion. Given the choice, I would rather have performed this morning for an audience of thousands. But today God put me up in front of about sixty women, and so that's what I did instead. Hopefully, a song we sang or a story we shared touched someone in there in ways we can't ever understand. Don't you see? That's much bigger than anything I might have planned because that's letting God use me for His purposes."

Danny closed his eyes, wondering if he could ever be as surrendered as she was.

"But why would God give me the desire to be a professional photographer if He wasn't going to let that dream come true?" he asked softly.

"You *are* a professional photographer, Danny."

He shook his head.

"You know what I mean. I want the big leagues, Ma, the *Scene Its* and the *National Geographics* and the recognition and the respect. Do you know how hard it is to snap pictures of drooling babies all day and pretend I'm making some kind of art?"

"You're touching people's lives, honey. Can't that be enough?"

*Touching people's lives.* Danny thought of the kid in the wheelchair and how he had stood up to the boy's mother. Maybe in some small way, he was doing some good in the world. But what about doing good for himself, for his career?

"As a man, I can't let this go," he said slowly. "My dreams are just too big. Too important to me."

He expected her to sympathize. Instead, she simply pursed her lips and then opened the door.

"You need to surrender your ambitions," she said. "And while you're at it, you need to surrender your relationship with Jo as well."

He looked at her, surprised that she knew.

"What?" she asked. "You didn't think your sisters would tell me? Like they had to? I've known for a long time."

He had to laugh, hating that the women in his life seemed to know him better than he knew himself.

"What if I tell her I love her and she says she doesn't love me back?" he whispered.

"Sur-ren-der, Danny," his mother replied slowly. "God will work it out." Then she climbed out of the car and got into her own and drove away, leaving him there in the parking lot, alone.

"I believe we have a match," the coroner said, peering into his microscope. "Good job, Miss Tulip."

Her hunch had been correct. The killer had used the brick to kill Edna. Chances are, the coroner said, this brick had also been used to make the dent in the windowsill as well.

"You'll call the chief and let him know?" Jo asked.

"I'm calling right now," he replied, one hand already on the phone.

When she was finished there, Jo drove back to Edna's, wondering if they would ever know who's hand had wielded that brick. It must have been a crime of passion, a spur-of-the-moment impulse followed by a quick bit of damage control that included pouring some bleach into the ammonia, or vice versa. Considering the danger of the fumes, the murderer must have had to cover his or her mouth and nose and then run away as quickly as possible once the deed was done.

It also had to be someone Edna had let come into her home voluntarily. More than likely, it was someone who balked at the notion that Edna was going public with what she'd done.

Which brought Jo back around to the same list of suspects she'd had before.

*Who killed Edna Pratt?*

There was a strange car parked in the driveway of Edna's house when Jo got there, a shiny white Chrysler. Jo parked along the street and headed up the walk, hearing Chewie barking furiously from the back-yard. Jo wasn't quite sure what to do, but the front door swung open before she had to make a decision. Sally Sugarman was standing there, and she didn't look happy.

"For starters," she said, "would you explain to me why there's a dog in my mother's backyard?"

"He's mine," Jo replied defensively. "I had to run out for just a minute, so I left him here."

"Well?" Sally said, stepping back from the doorway. "Come on in. I guess we need to talk."

Jo hesitated, feeling strangely afraid. She glanced toward the house next door, relieved to see Betty peeking from behind a curtain. At least if Sally did her in, there would be a witness who saw Jo going inside.

She mounted the steps and went through the door, putting her keys and purse on the small front table. Sally gestured toward the couch and then sat on the chair beside it.

"Murder," Sally said once Jo had sat down. "The police are telling me my mother was murdered."

"She was hit on the head by a felt-covered brick," Jo replied. "Then whoever did it set things up to make it look like an accident."

"You knew I didn't want you to pursue this," Sally said softly. "You knew this had the potential for derailing the entire election for me. But you did it anyway."

Jo glanced toward the door, wishing someone would walk in.

"Your mother was murdered, Sally," Jo said. "Even if you hated her, you can't tell me that whoever did it shouldn't be caught. Election or not, you can't tell me your mother doesn't deserve justice."

Sally stood and began pacing.

"My mother deserved a lot of things," she said. "But I don't know if justice was one of them. Certainly, I never had any justice growing up. Do you know what she would do if I spilled my glass at the dinner table, or accidentally tracked mud into the house? She'd spank me and send me off to bed without any supper, my only real 'crime' being a typical kid. Her clean floors were more important to her than I was."

"I'm sorry, Sally," Jo whispered. "That must have been difficult for you."

"The sad thing is, all those years, I kept expecting her to change. As a teenager, as an adult, somehow I just thought that one day she might turn to me and say, 'I love you' or 'I'm proud of you.' But no. Even when I was elected a senator for the state of Texas, all she had to say was that the skirt I was wearing on television made my hips look big. Can you imagine?"

Sally started crying, the tears spilling freely down her face.

"You know," Jo said, "your mother may not have encouraged you to your face, but she was forever bragging about you to everyone else."

"You've told me that before."

"It's true. I used to avoid her in the grocery store because I just didn't have the time to stand there and listen to her go on and on about 'my daughter the senator this' and 'my daughter the senator that.'"

"Really?"

"Really. She was proud of you, Sally, even if she never let you know."

Sally dabbed at her eyes.

"What is it about you, Jo, that makes me pour out my heart?" she asked finally. "Do you know what my first thought was when the police called last night to tell me that my mother had been murdered?"

Jo shook her head.

"I thought, 'It serves her right.'"

"It serves her right?"

"Had I been a braver person, I might have killed her years ago myself."

The room was silent except for Sally's weeping. Jo didn't know what to make of it, whether Sally was trying to make a confession or just unburdening a bitter heart. Before Jo could form a reply, her cell phone began ringing from her purse.

She excused herself and answered it, surprised to hear the voice of Keith McMann, the handsome—and persistent—professor from the college.

"I wonder if you have a minute to get together with me," he said. "It's not a date. I need to ask you a favor."

She looked over at Sally, who had found a tissue and was cleaning herself up. Suddenly, she wanted more than anything to be out of that house.

"Sure," she said. "Where do you want to meet?"

"Wherever you want," he said. "Pulio's? I could buy you lunch."

The popular campus hangout was convenient, and it would probably be half empty at this hour of the day.

"Okay. I can be there in ten minutes."

After Jo hung up the phone, Sally seemed like a different person. She had stopped crying, and now she was standing and walking around the room, peeking into all of the boxes.

"I'm sorry," Jo said. "I have to leave in a minute. Something urgent has come up."

"That's okay," Sally replied. "I assume you'll keep the things I told you here confidential."

Jo didn't reply. If Sally murdered her mother—or had had her murdered by someone else—then nothing she had said was confidential.

"I have some boxes in the bedroom I was planning to send to you," Jo said instead. "And everything in the sewing room is tagged for a yard sale, if you want to look through that."

"You've accomplished so much so quickly," Sally said. "I'm very impressed."

Jo shrugged.

"A friend helped me," she said. "Together we've really made some progress."

Sally nodded, seeming at loose ends. Jo wondered why she had come.

"The police wanted me here to ask me some questions," she said, as if she could read Jo's mind. "I guess I need to get down to the station."

"Guess so."

"Come on," Sally said. "We can walk out together."

Simon knew the drill. He remained silent, almost in a daze, as they photographed him, printed him, and locked him in a cell. He didn't speak a word to anyone, not even when they brought him into an interrogation room and started peppering him with questions. It wasn't until they said the word "murder" that he seemed to snap out of it.

"What?" he asked, focusing in on the detective.

"Why did you murder your sister?"

Simon tugged at his ear, wondering if he had heard correctly. "Why…what?"

The detective put his hands on the table and leaned forward.

"Why did you murder your sister?"

Simon's head started spinning. Edna had been *murdered?*

"I didn't," he replied. "She killed herself."

"Killed herself," the detective repeated sarcastically, glancing at the other cop. "By whacking herself in the back of the head?"

Simon's heart pounded.

"My sister committed suicide, did she not?"

"No, she did not. You hit her in the head with a blunt object. Why'd you do it?"

Simon's mind was spinning. Someone had killed Edna. Someone had done her in.

"I…why do you think it was me?" Simon asked.

"I'm asking the questions here. Were you mad at her, Simon? Was she going to tell the cops all about your little con game?"

Simon didn't know what was going on here. All he knew was that Edna was dead by someone else's hand, not her own.

*Not her own.*

Simon didn't know why that made his heart soar. He didn't know why tears of joy sprang into his eyes. Most of all, he didn't know why the pressure in his chest returned, tighter than before. No matter how guilty he may seem to these cops—no matter, even, if he ended up going to prison for a murder he didn't commit—just knowing she hadn't taken the easy way out, that she hadn't had "too much" as their mother had—made all of the difference.

Before he realized it, Simon was on the floor, the pressure in his chest unbelievably tight. He thought someone was sitting on him or pressing him down, but when he opened his eyes, all he could see was the two detectives, their faces swimming above his, their mouths moving but no sound coming out. He saw something roll into his peripheral vision, some kind of machine, and instinctively he knew it was a defibrillator.

Simon was having a heart attack.

He closed his eyes, unable to breathe. Then everything around him simply went black.

# 29

Keith McMann was more handsome than Jo remembered, with one dimple in his cheek when he smiled. He was in the restaurant when she got there, sitting at a table beside the window. He rose until she was seated and then sat again himself.

"Thanks for coming," he told her. "I went ahead and ordered a pepperoni pizza for us. Hope that's okay with you. I'm a little pressed for time."

"Sure," she replied, though pepperoni wasn't really her preference. "What did you need to see me about?"

He rolled his eyes, and Jo could tell that he was embarrassed.

"I saw your picture splashed all over the TV this morning," he said. "And I realized you might be able to help me. I hope you don't think it rude of me once you hear my request."

Jo studied his face, thinking she'd be happy to help out anyway she could, feeling surprised at her rather gut-level reaction to this man. Less than a week ago, she had been about to exchange lifelong vows with Bradford. Now she was already sitting here with someone else, thinking how very good-looking he was?

What was wrong with her?

"I'm coming up for review with the university," he said. "From all indications, they're going to promote me from assistant professor to associate professor. This is part of the tenure track, something I've been working toward all along."

"I understand," Jo said, nodding. Among her grandfather's chemist friends, academic standing had always been a frequent topic of conversation.

"This...um...problem with Edna Pratt's murder and the whole con game and everything..."

"Yes?"

He shook his head, taking a sip of tea.

"Well, it's not going to do me any favors. The university hates scandal of any kind. I'm afraid if I get lumped into this whole thing in the media, then not only will my promotion be at risk, but the job I have now will be at risk as well."

Jo's pulse surged. *The university hates scandal of any kind. Would he have killed Edna to keep her from going to the police?*

"Keith," Jo said, reaching for her water glass, "are you asking me to keep your name out of this? Because I can't lie to the police."

"Oh, gosh, no," he said. "I've already been contacted by them, and I gave a statement about what happened and everything. They were very nice."

"What is it, then?" she asked. "What do you want me to do?"

He leaned forward, looking at her hopefully.

"You're just so media-savvy, Jo. I wondered if you could tell me how to keep myself and the stories of my involvement in this thing off the news and out of the papers."

Simon could hear screaming.

No, it wasn't screaming. It was a siren.

He opened his eyes, understanding that he was inside an ambulance. To his right was a man in white, probably a paramedic. To his left was a uniformed policeman.

Simon closed his eyes, realizing as he did so that he was probably dying of a heart attack.

Was this how it had been for Edna? Did she have any warning before she was killed? Did she lay on the floor in the dining room, her head in massive pain, conscious for even a few seconds before she passed, understanding that she wasn't going to live?

Most importantly: If she had, had she been comforted by her new-found faith?

Simon didn't like to think about eternity. Life on earth was hard enough without the prospect of eternal damnation. As far as he was concerned, God had pulled the ultimate con: Believe in Me and you'll have eternal life!

Yeah, right. That "eternal life" was about as real and available as the immortality-on-earth he had sold to the women of Mulberry Glen.

He opened his eyes again, looking around at the tools that were keeping him alive. Was this what it came down to in the end, all of these machines, working to keep his heart pumping?

The pain was so far beyond anything he had ever felt that he could hardly breath. There was a mask over his face, and for a moment Simon thought maybe it was choking him. He reached up to take it off but the paramedic stopped him, held down his hands, and spoke words of comfort.

Simon couldn't hear much of what he said.

"Almost there. Hold on. Just a minute."

The screaming lessened. The feeling of motion ended. Suddenly, instead of the ambulance, he was looking up at the clear blue sky. Had he just sat on the front stoop this morning, waiting for his check to arrive? What had gone wrong? How and when?

Was he really going to die?

The blue sky turned into a white tile ceiling. Simon felt a piercing in his arm and he knew he'd been given some kind of shot. He was floating then, floating through the carnival, watching his father calling out for people to play the game.

"Time for some ring toss. Just land a ring around a bottleneck and win a great big prize!"

Each week, one of Simon and Edna's jobs was to sit down after closing and go through the rings in the ring toss game, making sure that almost every single one of them had a clear stripe of glue on the inside of the circle, just enough to make it impossible for the ring to fit on the neck of the bottles. Simon's dad kept the three ringers, the sample rings that were slightly bigger than the others and always landed correctly. But the rest of the rings were rigged. People would plunk down their money and try and try and try to get the rings around the bottles' necks. But it never worked because the game had been fixed.

This thing that seemed so simple was actually impossible.

Jo and Keith talked easily, finding common humor in the world of academia. When their pizza came, Jo tried to make some suggestions as to how he could avoid the media.

"The problem," she said, "is that if they get a look at you, then they'll be all over it."

"What do you mean?"

"You're not...exactly...unfortunate-looking. Television to an attractive person is like a heat-seeking missile to a fire. It will find you. If you're really concerned about it, you should probably get out of town until this thing blows over. That would be the safest move if you need to avoid reporters at all costs."

He seemed flattered by her compliment.

"That's funny," he said. "Because when I saw your photo on television this morning, I thought to myself, 'She's made for that medium.' Even in a still picture, you have quite a presence on screen. Heat-seeking missile indeed."

Their eyes met and held. Oh, yes, there was definitely a spark between them.

But the spark was misleading. The more they talked, the more Jo decided she might not be interested in him after all. Yes, he was good-looking, and yes, he was smart. But he was also a bit too self-absorbed, talking endlessly about his work, his home, his life. Twice he quoted Taoist sayings, and Jo got the distinct feeling that he was more New Age talk than anything substantial. When she mentioned her Christian faith, he just smiled.

"I've done an historical study of all religions," he said. "And I've come to the conclusion that all are valid. All say the same thing, just in different ways. My yin to your yang."

Jo didn't bother arguing with him. In her experience, religious arguments only served to entrench people more deeply into their own positions. Better she simply love the Lord with all of her heart, and love her neighbor as herself.

Finally, despite their differences, when they were finished eating, the professor reminded her that he's be calling in a month or so, to officially ask her out on a date.

Jo merely smiled, knowing that when he did call, she would decline.

"Thank you for lunch," she told him before leaving. "And good luck with the media."

"We'll see how it goes," he replied. "After all, the journey is the reward."

Jo had turned off her phone during their lunch, and there were three messages waiting for her when she turned it back on. She had heard from Danny, the police chief, and her agent, Milton. All three were calling to say that there would be a press conference at 6:00 P.M. in the main auditorium of the township building, and that all parties related to the case were encouraged to attend. In the chief's message, he added that Simon Kurtz had been apprehended in Florida and was now in the temporary custody of the Florida state police.

Jo returned Danny's call, but he was in the middle of a photography sitting and couldn't really talk.

"That's all right," Jo told him. "Will you be home before the press conference? We can ride over together."

"Yeah, sure."

When Jo arrived at Edna's house, a news van was parked out front. Milton had told her to remain accessible to the press, but Jo wasn't ready to be interviewed just yet. She drove right past, peeking to make sure that Chewie was okay in the backyard. From what she could see, he was fine, sitting in the shade of a big tree.

She went home, knowing that if she wanted to come across in the media as articulate and intelligent, she would have to do some more reading about alchemy. Somehow, Jo's education in chemistry had never included much about the topic. Fortunately, Danny had left the books he'd gotten from the library in her home office. She settled down there and started skimming. The things she learned were fascinating.

According to what she read, no one knew for certain the origins of alchemy, only that it had been around for a long, long time. From ancient Egypt to China to everywhere in between, the popularity of alchemy had come and gone throughout history, at some times being banned and other times being celebrated.

The symbols of alchemy throughout the ages were quite prevalent. Jo flipped past a lot of sketches and paintings, many of them similar to those in the velvet-covered notebook, most of them violent and disturbing. The images were so strange: Men and women bonded together, lions eating the sun, winged mermaids holding chalices. Architects and other artisans had inserted alchemical symbols in a number of public structures. Gothic cathedrals had facades full of alchemical symbols. Even the great Notre Dame in Paris featured an alchemic image: a woman with a lizard engulfed in flame.

No wonder Simon Foster thought this stuff was ripe for a con game. From what Jo read, it sounded as though he wasn't even the first person to attempt this particular con. Supposedly the scientist Nicholas Flamel had been spotted in a Paris coffeehouse some 400 years after his "death." No doubt, some lookalike person had tried to pass himself off as Flamel, bilking gullible Parisians and fooling them into believing that he had achieved immortality, just as Simon Foster had tried to do.

The final irony of all of it, though, was that in 1941, Harvard scientists did finally succeed in turning mercury into gold. Using a particle accelerator, they bombarded mercury with radiation until its chemical structure actually changed. Unfortunately, such a process was so expensive that it cost much more to conduct the experiment than the resulting gold could ever be worth. Jo looked up from the page, thinking about that. For centuries, men had tried to achieve the impossible. Once they did, it was useless to them.

She skimmed some more, flipping pages, until she ran across references to "Taoist alchemy" and "yin and yang." Jo blinked, thinking of Keith McMann and his adherence to Taoist beliefs. She leaned forward, reading about the transformation of the physiological structure and function of the body, "while at the same time effecting parallel changes in the mind and spirit." Sounded exactly like something Keith would say.

Was it possible he was an alchemist, that he believed these things as a part of his religion?

If so, then he must have lied about what happened that day at Iris Chutney's house. In her gut, Jo had a feeling that Keith hadn't gone there to validate the photos.

He had gone there to validate alchemy.

When Danny finished his final sitting, he learned that Jo had called back a second time.

"She sounded kind of frantic," Tiffany said. "She said to tell you she had an errand to run and that she'd see you at the press conference instead of driving over together."

"Frantic, what do you mean?"

Tiffany shrugged.

"I don't know. She said she was looking through some books you left at her house and saw something really important, and that she had to go talk to somebody."

"Who?"

"I don't know. But she said she'd be cutting it close and for you to go on to the press conference. She'll see you there."

Danny tried dialing Jo's cell, but it went straight to the message, which meant she had turned it off.

*Please, Lord, don't let her be foolish. Don't let her put herself in danger.*

Jo rang Iris's doorbell, her pulse surging when she heard footsteps from inside. This time, once Iris saw who was at her door, her expression was much more guarded. The poor woman had been through a lot in the last few days, including the public humiliation of having her name leaked to the press as one of the victims.

"Mrs. Chutney," Jo said. "I'm so glad you're here. May I come in and speak with you for a few minutes?"

Mrs. Chutney hesitated and then stepped back to wave her in.

"I'm very tired, Jo," she said. "Please make it quick."

They went into the living room and sat, but this time there was no offer of tea or cookies. Jo was glad, as she wanted to get straight to the point.

"I think I may know who murdered Edna Pratt," Jo said. "But I need some information from you first."

"The police already have two suspects in custody," Mrs. Chutney said. "Angus and Simon. Do you mean there's someone else?"

Jo nodded.

"I was just doing some reading about alchemy. Much to my surprise, I saw that alchemy is very intermixed with the Taoist religion."

"Oh? What does that have to do with anything?"

"I need you to tell me about a meeting you had here, where Professor Keith McMann came and authenticated Simon's photographs."

"Yes?"

"What did he say, exactly?"

"He taught us all about alchemy. He's quite a scholar on the subject, you know. It was a fascinating presentation, tracing the history of alchemy from ancient times up to the present day."

Jo nodded, understanding now that her suspicion had been correct: Keith McMann had been brought in as an expert to authenticate alchemy. The ladies had bought into all he told them—hook, line, and sinker.

The bigger question was, had Keith participated knowingly in the con, or did he genuinely believe that what he was telling them was true?

Before leaving the studio, Danny put away his supplies for the weekend, trying not to worry about Jo. She was a smart woman. She could take care of herself.

Tiffany was lingering also, finishing up her paperwork, but then she planted herself in her favorite spot, sitting on the counter across from Danny's desk.

"So tell me about your weekend," Tiffany said. "Now that you're practically famous, you'll probably be kind of busy."

Danny laughed.

"Oh, yeah, I'm famous all right," he said. "I'm nationally known as 'the neighbor.'"

Tiffany twirled a lock of hair in her fingers.

"Not after tonight. Once you get up there for that press conference, everyone will know who you are. You might even get some groupies."

"Groupies," Danny repeated, rolling his eyes. "I doubt it."

"I'd be your groupie," she said.

Danny glanced at her, not surprised to see that she was fixing him with her sexiest gaze.

"So how about it, Danny?" she whispered. "Are you ever going to get around to asking me on another date?"

He sat back, knowing the moment of truth had arrived. *Let your yes be yes and your no be no,* the Bible said. Danny had always tried to follow that rule in other ways, being as honest and straightforward as he could with everyone in his life. This situation would have to be no exception.

"You're a beautiful girl, Tiffany, and a lot of fun besides. But the truth is that I only want to be your friend. The night we went for coffee wasn't supposed to be anything more than that."

She shook her head, clenching her jaw.

"You told me you liked my hair. You said it made me look sexy."

"I said it made you look hot."

"Right. Hot. Sexy."

"No, *hot.* Heat. It's so long and thick. We were sitting in an outdoor café on a night in August, for goodness' sake. We were drinking coffee. You looked hot."

She shook her head.

"Are you kidding me? You weren't coming on to me?"

He held up his left hand and placed his right hand on his heart.

"I promise. I think you're a great girl, but you're not the one for me. I'm sorry if I gave you the wrong impression."

She sat there, chewing on her lip, and then she rose and put both hands on the desk, leaning forward.

"You have no idea what you're missing," she proclaimed.

He nodded, swallowing hard. "I can imagine," he replied.

She stomped away, turning to look back at him from the doorway.

"I'm going to hate you for a little while," she added, "but for the sake of my commissions, I'll try to let it go. Eventually."

# 30

Danny got to the township building about 20 minutes early, glad to have settled things with Tiffany. The place was already packed, but as he made his way into the room, the chief waved him toward the front, where they had set up a long table with seven chairs behind it and seven microphones.

"You can sit there," the chief said, pointing to one end, "and Jo can go next to you."

"Who else will be up here?"

"Me, one of my officers, the coroner, Senator Sugarman, Louise Parker, you and Jo."

"Okay."

Danny sat, and soon he was joined by Mrs. Parker. Though he would have thought she'd feel humiliated to be there, she was, in fact, simply glowing from the attention. She was all dressed up with her hair and makeup just so, and she made a grand entrance as she strolled down the aisle and took her place at the table up front. The coroner came in and sat next to her, and from what Danny could tell, she was actually flirting with him. Go figure.

Jo wasn't there yet, so Danny tried again to reach her on her cell phone. He didn't bother leaving a message but simply disconnected the call. Then he kept his eyes on the door, watching for her to arrive.

If she drove fast, Jo could pick up Chewie from Edna's house, get him over to Danny's, and still make it to the press conference with a few minutes to spare. She would have liked to skip Chewie altogether, but the press conference might drag on for hours, and she didn't think the dog should be left outside at Edna's for that long.

Jo's heart was still racing after her discussion with Mrs. Chutney, and more than anything she wanted to talk to the chief, to tell him that Edna Pratt might not have been killed by Angus or Simon—she might have been murdered by Keith McMann.

Jo tried to think of a reason why Keith would have killed Edna.

To test the theory of immortality?

Out of anger when he learned this whole thing was just a con?

Whatever his motivation, at the very least Jo had now proven that Keith McMann was both a scholar of alchemy and a liar. Surely, when the chief reviewed Keith's statement to the police, he would see that there was cause to bring the man in for further questioning.

Jo glanced at the clock and picked up her cell phone as she drove, dialing Danny.

"Where are you?" he demanded when he answered. "Everyone's here but you."

"Tell the chief I should just make it." she said. "I have to stop at Edna's and get Chewie. Can I put him in your guest room?"

"Of course. But where have you been? Who did you go talk to?"

"It's a long story," she replied. "But I think I know who killed Edna."

Danny pulled the chief aside and gave him Jo's message that she was on her way. The room was packed, with reporters filling the front few rows and townspeople in the rest of the seats and standing all along the back and the sides.

"If we get any more people in here," the chief said to Danny, "we'll be violating the fire code."

"Listen, I don't know what you'll be announcing," Danny said, "but I was just talking to Jo. She said she knows who murdered Edna, and it isn't either of the two men you have in custody."

"She's right that it wasn't Angus," the chief said. "His alibi checked out after all."

"But Jo says it's not Simon either."

"That's not true," the chief replied. "We found a witness who saw him get on a bus near Edna's house last Friday night. He had motive and opportunity."

"Jo says it was Keith McMann, the history professor over at the college."

"That guy? He couldn't hurt a fly. What makes her think it was him?"

"I don't know, but she'll be here soon. She'll have to tell you about it herself."

Jo pulled into Edna's driveway and jumped out, the car still running.

She almost stepped in a pile of dog poop, and as she hopped over it, she was glad to pick up the glint of silver. She leaned forward to look closer, thrilled to see that the cream cheese package seemed to have passed fully intact, thank goodness. That was one less thing she had to worry about.

Her relief was short-lived, however, when she got to the fence and saw that the gate was hanging open on its hinges.

Chewie was gone.

Had she forgotten to tie off the latch? She could have sworn she had done it when she first put him out there.

"Chewie!" she called. This was the last thing she had time for.

She ran next door and knocked, but no one was home. She ran toward the end of the block, praying Chewie would be across the street, on the slide, but the park was empty.

Jo didn't know what to do. She had to get to the press conference. She had to explain to the chief about Keith McMann.

One time around the block, she decided, and then she would leave and come back to deal with this later. Chewie was a bright dog. He would be all right on his own for a while.

Jo ran past Edna's house in the opposite direction, calling for Chewie as she went. She almost missed him, but something in the shadows over to the right caught her eye.

"Chewie?"

She ran up the driveway of the vacant house, the one with Marie's For Sale sign in the front yard. There, against the garage door, lying in a crumpled heap, was her dog.

"No!"

Jo ran to him and felt for a pulse but she couldn't find one. She wasn't even sure how to feel for a pulse on a dog. Finally, she pressed her ear against his chest and there she could faintly hear the rapid, irregular beating of his heart.

"You got here much sooner than I thought."

Jo spun around to see Keith McMann standing behind her. Before she could react, he grabbed her, one hand on her mouth, the other around her chest. She kicked and struggled, but he dragged her around the side and into the door.

He threw her into the garage, where she landed on the her hands and knees on the cement. She started yelling for help, but the next thing she knew, he had gripped her by the arm and held a gun to her head.

"Shut up!" he hissed. "Shut up!"

Jo began trembling. This man had already obviously poisoned Chewie. There was no telling what he might do to her now.

"What did you do to my dog?" she demanded.

"Took a little cue from Tips from Tulip."

"What?"

"You had an item the other day about harmful house plants. From what I recall, dumb cane paralyzes the vocal chords and can even asphyxiate you."

"You fed my dog a dieffenbachia plant?" Jo asked, aghast.

"Don't worry, he'll sleep it off. If it doesn't kill him."

"What do you want with me?"

"The notebook. Where is it?"

"The notebook? What notebook?"

"Red velvet cover, filled with notations. I know you brought it to that chemistry professor at the college. Where is it now?"

"I only brought him a photocopy," Jo said. "The original is in my safety deposit box at the bank."

Jo realized that it hadn't occurred to her to turn the notebook over as evidence of the con to the police.

He let her go and paced, though he kept the gun trained firmly on her. She spun around and pulled her legs up under her, trying to make herself as small as possible, ignoring the scrapes on her knees and hands.

Absurdly, she thought of the other night, when Danny tripped on the fence and scraped himself.

*Please, Danny,* she thought urgently. *Find me now.*

"The bank's closed until tomorrow," he said. "You'll have to call your chemistry professor and get the copy instead."

"Why do you want it?"

"Because it holds the secrets!" he cried, the gun trembling in his hand. "Because Simon promised it to me."

"Where did he get it?" she asked, hoping to keep him talking.

"He first received it in the late-seventeen hundreds," he said, his expression utterly serious. "It was given to him by a renowned alchemist. He has guarded it carefully for more than two hundred years, just waiting until he could find an apprentice worthy of the knowledge it contains."

"And you're that apprentice?" Jo asked.

Even in the dim, yellow light of the garage, Keith McMann did not look crazy. Intense, yes. Insane, no.

"I am," he replied. "I have devoted my life to the study of alchemy through the ages. When Simon approached me and told me he knew its secrets and was willing to share them with me, my lifelong dream had been answered at last. I won't leave town without those notes."

Jo studied his face. Was there no way to convince him that Simon was a first-rate con man, that the professor had been sucked into Simon's lies, just like the women had? Surely, Keith had seen the stories on the news.

"How do you explain the mug shots of Simon Kurtz?" Jo asked. "What makes you think he was anything more than what the newspeople are saying he is?"

"Because it's all an elaborate ruse," he whispered. "Because Simon fabricated his own past just in case any of this came to light. He always has a fail-safe. The secrets are too important to risk being revealed."

Jo's trembling had calmed somewhat. She figured he would let her stay alive until they had acquired the notebook.

"Dr. Langley says the notebook is gibberish," Jo said. "He says it's nothing but obscure symbols and nonsense notations."

To her surprise, Keith smiled.

"Of course he said that. Only a true devotee of alchemy can understand what those symbols and notations mean. That's how we've guarded our secrets through the centuries."

Jo hoped her professor hadn't simply tossed the pages in the trash. Her mind raced, trying to think her way out of the situation.

"Where's your phone?" he demanded.

"In my car. At Edna's."

"We'll have to use mine, then."

He glanced around, obviously looking for something. The garage was completely empty, however, except for a box of items over in one corner.

Still keeping the gun pointed at Jo, he went to the box, reached inside, and pulled out a hose.

"This'll have to do," he said.

Kneeling behind Jo, he roughly pulled her wrists behind her back and wrapped the hose around them. He brought the rest of it around to the front and wrapped it around her ankles and then her legs.

"That was you I heard arguing with Edna on Friday night, wasn't it?"

He shrugged, grunting with the effort of wrapping the hose around Jo's body.

"She called and told me she was going to confess everything to the police the next day," he replied. "I tried to talk her out of it, but she wouldn't listen to what I had to say. I came over, figuring I could talk some sense into her in person."

"Didn't work, huh?"

He jerked the hose tightly, pinching her skin.

"The stupid woman was going to tell the police that she and Simon were involved in a con. She never understood that it was real. She never believed it at all."

"So you hit her with the brick."

"Just to shut her up!" he hissed. "Then at least I was free to search her house for the notebook."

"But you didn't find it."

"No, I didn't find it. By the time I was finished looking, I realized she was dead."

"So you put a dent in the windowsill, mixed some chemicals that would make it look like an accident, and then left."

"That's about right," he said. "Since then, I've been waiting to hear from Simon, waiting to learn where he had put the notebook for safe-keeping. Then when you said you were settling Edna's affairs, I realized that *you* had it, and that you didn't even know what it was."

Danny was getting worried. The press conference was rolling along in full force, and there was still an empty seat beside him. He could see why Jo might be a little longer than she had predicted, but this was getting ridiculous.

At the far end of the table, the chief was doing a good job of fielding questions. Danny was surprised to hear him say that though Simon Kurtz was in custody in Florida, he was currently in the hospital there, under full police watch.

"Why in the hospital?" one of the reporters asked. "Was he injured during the arrest?"

"No," the chief replied. "He was having some heart troubles, so he was admitted for evaluation."

"Senator Sugarman," another reporter said, "Simon Kurtz is your uncle. Do you know him well?"

Danny had been impressed with the senator throughout the conference. She was a real pro at a microphone, articulate and intelligent—and evasive when necessary.

"Simon was a part of my life, off and on, when I was a child," she said. "I vaguely remember him. When he went to prison I was only six years old. My mother told me that my Uncle Simon had died. I wasn't aware that was a lie until this week."

That earned a sympathetic gasp from the audience. Danny was impressed. He supposed she had shared that nugget of information to protect herself from the critics who might say she had hidden some potentially explosive facts about her family from the voters. To a politician, an uncle in prison could never be a good thing.

"Danny," another one asked, "do you think Jo Tulip will be able to get any household tips from this whole experience?"

The audience laughed.

"From what I know of Jo Tulip," Danny replied, leaning toward the microphone, "she can get tips out of everything."

"Open your mouth," Keith commanded when he was almost finished. He wrapped the final section of hose around her face, gagging her with it. "Good. Now, understand something. I'm going to get the phone from my car down the street. If you make one sound while I'm gone, when I get back I will put a bullet in your dog. Are we clear?"

Jo nodded, eyes wide.

She watched as he tucked the gun in his waistband, peered cautiously out the door, and then quietly opened it and slipped out.

Jo was alone in the garage. Working quickly, she did the only thing she could think of: She started wiggling. The hose, being cylindrical, was bound to give way if she could just shake it off. Sure enough, though at first she could only move her neck and her ankles, soon she was able to move her legs and her waist. Finally, she spit the hose out of her mouth. It slipped down her shoulders, and then she pulled her hands free.

She had done it.

Danny had a feeling that something was wrong. Much to the chief's dismay, he excused himself from the table right in the middle of a reporter's question. Then he made his way through the room and outside, where he dialed Jo's cell.

Her phone rang a number of times but she never picked up. Danny ran to his car, a sense of desperation suddenly overwhelming him.

He decided to start with his own house because that's where Jo was headed with the dog. Driving as quickly as he could, he made his way through town, running a few stop signs along the way.

When he finally got there, he screeched to a stop in his own driveway and ran inside.

The dog wasn't there.

Jo ran to the door of the garage and peeked out, shocked to see Keith only about ten steps way. She was trapped.

Moving quickly, she dragged the hose to the door, stretching it across the bottom where she might be able to make him trip.

Sure enough, as he opened the door and stepped inside, his feet were caught on the tangled rubber. He moved quickly, however, reaching for Jo and bringing her down with him as he fell.

"Thought you could escape, did you?" he spewed.

She scrambled away from him, trapped in the front corner of the garage. Now she had really done it.

He managed to stand, pulling out the gun and pointing it at her. With the other hand, he pressed some buttons on the phone then set it on the ground and slid it in her direction.

"Now, just press the call button," he commanded, trying to catch his breath. "Tell Dr. Langley that you need the notes you gave him and that your good friend Dr. Keith McMann will be stopping by in just a little while to pick them up."

Hands shaking, Jo took the phone and pressed the button. Listening as it dialed, her mind raced. She knew that as soon as the call was over, she was as good as dead.

"Hello?" the professor said.

"Dr. Langley? It's Jo Tulip," she said, trying to keep her voice from trembling. "I need to ask you something."

"Sure," he replied. "What can I do for you?"

"You know those notes you looked through for me? The ones you said were just a bunch of junk? I-I need to get those back."

"Oh, I'm sorry, Jo," he said. "After we talked, I threw them away. I thought that's what you wanted me to do."

Jo's mind raced, her heart pumping furiously.

"Super," she replied, glancing at Keith. "Listen, could I send someone to get them right now?"

The professor was quiet for a moment.

"Didn't you hear what I said?" he asked. "I threw them away."

"Excellent," she replied. "I can't get over there right now, so I'm going to send someone else, my good friend Dr. Keith McMann. Do you know him?"

"Keith McMann? From the history department? Of course I know him, but I'm telling you, Jo, I don't have those notes."

"Okay, hold on," she said. She looked up at Keith. "He wants to talk to you."

She handed him the phone. She hoped he would be distracted enough by the confused professor on the other end of the line that she would be able to get away.

Unfortunately, before speaking into the phone, Keith stepped closer and held the gun directly at her head.

Again, she was trapped.

Working backward, Danny drove to Edna Pratt's house a few blocks away. Relief flooded through him as he spotted Jo's car in the driveway. But the relief turned to confusion when he found that the car was running and the door was open, but Jo was nowhere to be found. He reached inside and turned off the ignition, a prayer for her safety stuck somewhere in his throat.

"Hello, Bob? Keith McMann here."

Jo watched his face as he listened to what was being said. Glancing around desperately, she looked at the nearby cardboard box, the one where he had gotten the hose. Jo thought the box was otherwise empty, but in the bottom she could see a few empty packs of lemon Kool-aid and a bottle of oven cleaner.

God bless Marie. She had left these items here after getting the stains off the driveway.

Taking a deep breath, Jo rolled away from the gun, knowing it was time to go for broke since she was about to die anyway. She reached the box and grabbed the oven cleaner. Spinning around, she saw that Keith was right behind her.

With a deep, guttural yell she let him have it, right in the eyes: a long, solid spray of Oven Off.

He screamed and dropped the phone, grabbing at his face.

"Call the police, Dr. Langley!" Jo screamed. "Send them to Weeping Willow Way!"

Then she ran from the garage. Adrenaline pumping, her intention was to scoop up Chewie and carry him all the way to her car. He only weighed 50 pounds or so. She could do it.

But when she came out of the garage, Chewie was gone.

Danny hung up with the police, who said they were sending a car right over to investigate the strange disappearance of Jo Tulip. He was just slipping the phone back into his pocket when he saw movement from up the street.

"Chewie?" Danny cried.

The dog was coming toward him, but he was walking strangely, weaving back and forth, falling down and getting up again. Danny wanted to run to him and help, but his first thought was rabies. He froze, not knowing what to do.

Suddenly, a figure appeared in the darkness on the road behind the dog, also coming in this direction. It was Jo!

"Danny!" she hollered. "Start your car!"

Without hesitating, he did as she said. He jumped in and started it up and drove to her on the road. She was hysterical, sobbing, saying something about Keith McMann coming after them with a gun.

Together, they lifted the dog into the backseat, but before they could get back in the car themselves, a gunshot rang out, striking the vehicle directly on the front bumper.

"Go! Go!" Jo said.

On the road in front of them stood Keith McMann, a gun in his hand, his face shiny with some sort of white foam.

They jumped into the car and Danny slammed it into reverse, pressing the gas pedal all the way to the floor. He steered the best he could backward, spinning out in a driveway so he could take off again, forward this time. Another shot rang out, shattering the windshield, and then suddenly, one police car whizzed past, and then another.

Danny drove to the end of the street, screeching to a stop once he thought they were safe enough to see what was happening. He climbed out of the car, listening at the shouts of the police. Soon, from what he could tell, they had apprehended McMann without more gunfire.

Everyone was safe.

Danny looked again at Jo, but she had climbed into the back and was cradling Chewie's head in her lap.

"What's wrong with him?" Danny asked.

"He was poisoned," she said, crying. "Please, Danny, take us to a veterinarian. I can't lose him. He's my second-best friend in the world."

# TIPS FROM TULIP

*Dear Readers, this week as we feature classic letters from the past, enjoy this exchange from 2002.*

---

**Dear Tulip,**

Do you have any recipes that call for fruitcake? Like I do every year, I baked fruitcakes for all of my neighbors. The problem is that when I went to deliver them, no one was home. I could never seem to catch them at home the entire Christmas season. So now I'm stuck with lots of leftover fruitcake. How can I keep it from going to waste?

—*Fruity in Massachusetts*

**Dear Fruity,**

First, try making a trifle. Cut the fruitcake into cubes. In a trifle bowl or individual parfait glasses, layer the cubes several times with vanilla pudding and whipped topping. Allow it to set in the refrigerator before serving. You might also tear some of the fruitcake into small pieces and leave it outside for the birds and squirrels.

But maybe you should be a Smart Chick! Next year, toss the fruitcake recipe and try baking some other holiday favorite instead. Chances are, your neighbors will be more likely to open the door if they see you coming with a tray of brownies or fudge.

—*Tulip*

## 31

Danny sat at the kitchen table, drinking his morning coffee and looking out across the yard toward Jo's house. He had seen her cutting through earlier with her backpack and her Rollerblades, but even when she stopped to put a note in the gnome, he didn't come out and tell her he was awake. Once she was gone, he had retrieved the note, which said, simply, "Chewie's doing okay. Still at the vet. Went Rollerblading."

They had taken the dog to the emergency veterinary clinic last night, where his stomach was pumped and he was intubated. The doctors had been quite confident that he had already seen the worst of it, but they wanted to keep him there until this afternoon, just in case. They said there should be no lingering effects.

From there, Jo and Danny had gone, once again, to the police station. If they had been heroes before, they were positively stars now. After they had given their statements, the press corps had come out in full, interviewing Jo about how she solved the mystery of who killed Edna and how she had made her escape. The morning's headlines had a field day with that one: "Household Tip Expert Discovers New Use for Oven Cleaner."

Danny had been so impressed with Jo last night as she spoke to the interviewers. She was poised and beautiful, and as the police chief watched from the sidelines, Jo made sure to give him full credit for everything he had done in this case and more.

"It makes me feel so safe," she had said, "to live in a community like Mulberry Glen. We have a top-notch police department, led by a very talented and hardworking man, Chief Harvey Cooper."

When all of the excitement had finally died down, Danny brought Jo back to her car and then followed her home. Even though Keith

McMann was now behind bars, Danny wanted to make sure that she was safe.

He had hardly slept all night. Instead, he kept thinking about Jo and how close she had come to death. He realized that no matter what happened, he had to tell her how he felt about her. He had to do it today.

Putting his cup in the sink, he decided to bike over to the park and find her. Maybe they could talk there.

It was time to go for broke.

On the way he glanced down Edna's street, where he saw Sally Sugarman out in front of her mother's house. He took the curve so he could say hello, and she smiled warmly as he rolled up.

"There's the star of the hour," she said. "From what I understand, you were Jo's knight in shining armor last night."

He shrugged.

"She saved herself," he told her. "I just provided the transportation."

They talked for a few minutes. Sally had returned her rental car last night, deciding not to sell Edna's vehicle after all, but to keep it for her teenage daughter. Sally was leaving today, driving all the way to Texas, the boxes of her mother's photos and papers and other keepsakes already tucked securely into the trunk and the backseat.

"If you don't mind," she said, "would you tell Jo to cancel the classified ad for selling the car? I added a bonus in her check, to cover the percentage I had promised her."

Sally said that from what she could tell, the job was just about finished. She had already written out a check for the balance that she owed and left it on the kitchen counter.

"I'll be calling her," Sally said. "But please tell her I said thank you for everything that she did. Thank you, too, Danny. On behalf of my mother, thank you."

Jo rolled down the sidewalk as fast as she dared, realizing as she went that she was missing Chewie. She was counting the hours until 2:00 P.M., when she would be allowed to pick him up. She'd already spoken to the animal hospital this morning, and they said that the tube was out and he was doing beautifully. She had also called a fencing company and

arranged for them to come next week and fully fence in the yard—
though with an extra gate at the back for Danny to come through.

Compared to last week, this next week should be a breeze. This afternoon, a policeman was going to accompany Jo to the bank, where she
would take out the alchemy notebook from her safety deposit box and
hand it over as evidence. Tonight she hoped Danny would be free to
help her finish up Edna's house.

Tomorrow would be a much-needed day of church and rest, and
then Monday would begin a new era for her, new opportunities with her
career, new household tips to explore.

Feeling better, Jo sailed along in the morning breeze. It was a sunny
fall day, the autumn leaves a rich array of deep oranges and yellows and
reds. Jo skated down the path through the park, taking the detour to the
cemetery. When she reached her grandmother's grave, she pulled from
her backpack a bottle of hydrated lime. On her hands and knees, she
sprinkled it around the headstone. Hydrated lime was nontoxic to
humans but deadly to weeds.

As she worked, Jo talked to her grandmother. She knew her grandmother couldn't really hear her, but there was still something comforting about the one-way conversation.

Today Jo felt as though she was on the verge of understanding something important. She hadn't slept well all night, and now an odd sort of
undefined emotion hung over her. This morning Bradford had called,
and their conversation had been short and strained. He said he needed
to talk to her, in person, after all.

"Why, Bradford?" Jo had asked tiredly. "So you can explain why you
ran out of our wedding?"

"No," he replied. "So I can explain why we were getting married in the
first place. There was...more to it...than you realize."

That wasn't what she was expecting to hear, and though she tried to
press him for more details, he said that was something he could only
discuss in person. Against her better judgment, she agreed to meet with
him next week. She had a feeling he was only acting to soothe his own
aching conscience, but she would let him have his say if it made him feel
better.

Now, something hurt, deep inside, and she wondered it was the pain
of pure loneliness.

"Why do I make such dumb choices when it comes to men?" she
asked her grandmother. "As if Bradford wasn't bad enough, for a while

there I was considering going out with *Keith*. A murderer, and a nut to boot. What's wrong with me, Nana? Am I blind or just stupid?"

The air was still. Jo finished sprinkling the lime and put the container away. She sat there on the grass, wishing her grandmother were here to talk to. Jo tried to think back, tried to remember the conversations they had had about love when she was a teen.

*You're going to have a hard time in life, Jo Jo, if you don't stop keeping people so far away, outside of your heart.*

Jo hadn't understood what her grandmother meant at the time. Jo had friends. She let people into her heart all the time.

She closed her eyes, thinking of her parents and the cruel way they would uproot her life without a moment's notice. Maybe over the years, Jo had learned to "connect" with people without really connecting at all. Maybe over the years, Jo had guarded her heart so carefully that these days almost no one got in.

*Especially not God*, she could almost hear her grandmother say.

"Not God?" Jo asked out loud. "I worship. I pray."

*Let Him in.*

Jo was so confused. For the first time in her life, she realized that maybe this was a struggle she couldn't handle alone. She closed her eyes and prayed, asking God to show her what she should do.

Simon awoke with a start, a steady beeping sound coming from somewhere near his head. He was hurting, deep in his chest, but it was different than before.

He felt coherent now.

He tried to make a sound but nothing came out. That's when he realized that there was tube down his throat. There were tubes everywhere. Tubes and wires and beeps.

A man stepped over to the bed, gray hair, black shirt. Collar. A priest. The man wore the collar of a priest.

"My son," he whispered. "Do you know the story of the thief who hung on the cross beside Jesus?"

Simon couldn't answer. He only blinked, feeling a terror gripping deep inside his soul. Glancing frantically around, he saw a uniformed policeman standing guard nearby.

"There were two thieves crucified with Him that day," the priest continued, "and one of them mocked Jesus. But the other defended Him, saying 'This man has done nothing wrong!'"

Beep, beep, beep…beep.

The hesitation in the beeps terrified Simon. He looked up at the priest, eyes wide.

"He asked Jesus to remember him once he got to heaven. And you know what Jesus said? He said, 'I tell you the truth, today you will be with Me in paradise.' Do you understand what that means, my son? It means you must ask Jesus to remember you. It means it's not too late to commit your soul to heaven."

Ask Jesus to remember him? But how? Simon couldn't talk. He couldn't move.

Simon closed his eyes, picturing Edna last Friday evening as she told him about her own miraculous transformation.

"You can't really understand unless it's happened to you," she had said. "But faith is such an amazing thing, if you'll just take that step."

A voice was chanting now and Simon opened his eyes, realizing that the priest was giving him the last rites. Simon wasn't Catholic, but he thought it couldn't hurt. Most assuredly, he was about to die. One thought pierced him through the fog: What if the ultimate con—God's con—hadn't been a con at all, but the truth?

What if Edna had been right?

Simon closed his eyes again, knowing that whether this heart attack killed him or not, he wanted to believe. What had the thief said to Jesus?

*Remember me,* Simon prayed suddenly. Then again, praying even more firmly, as if his brain were shouting: *Remember me, Jesus! Please!*

After he prayed, hot, sudden tears rolled from Simon's eyes. Tears of shame, of forgiveness, of joy. As he slid slowly toward unconsciousness, he had one final thought:

*This thing that seemed impossible was actually so simple.*

Danny didn't see Jo at the park, so he kept going down the path, hoping to catch her at the cemetery. He knew her routines so well that he could almost set a clock by her.

He was feeling anxious about this encounter, but when they finally spotted each other, the smile she gave him reached into every single chamber of his heart. He loved her. It was time to tell her so.

"Jo," he said, gesturing toward a nearby bench. "Let's sit down. I have to tell you something."

"Before you do," she said, "I have something to tell you too. I've been doing a lot of thinking, a lot of praying, and I just realized something."

Danny's pulse surged as they sat. She took his hands in hers, and on her face was an expression he'd never seen before. Could it be, was it possible, that Jo had realized she loved him too?

"Yes?"

"Danny, I've decided that I'm going to give up men for a while."

He swallowed hard, blinking.

"You're what?"

"I'm going to give to up men, give up dating. I'm making bad decisions, doing something wrong, and it wasn't until today that I realized that this isn't just about boy-girl stuff. It's about me. It's about my own fears of intimacy."

Quickly, Danny could feel his hopes tumbling to the ground. Yet, deep inside, he had to tell himself that this wasn't a bad thing. It was time for Jo to tear down those walls inside.

He would just have to be patient.

"For how long?" he asked, hoping his voice didn't betray more than it should.

"Until I figure stuff out," she replied. "All I know is that I don't want to live the rest of my life like this. I need to find out why I keep making such poor decisions."

"Jo—"

"Danny, I *want* love in my life, I really do. But I've got some things to figure out first. Big things."

Danny studied her green eyes, wishing more than anything in the world that he could take her face in his hands and kiss her and tell her that he loved her, that he was the guy she'd been waiting for all along.

But it wasn't the time for that now. Despite this astounding turn of events, Danny realized that God knew exactly what He was doing—and that what he needed most now was patience. In his heart, through silent prayer, Danny surrendered.

"So what's the news you had to tell me?" she asked. "Go ahead. It's your turn."

Danny held on tightly to the hands holding his own. Friendship. For now, all he could have was her friendship. He looked longingly at her lips, and then back at her eyes. Her beautiful eyes.

The eyes of his love, his friend.

"I was just thinking," he said, inhaling deeply and then letting it back out, "that you and I make a good team. That's all."

She smiled, reaching up to tenderly touch his face. Then she sat there close beside him and rested her head on his shoulder.

"We do make a good team, Danny," she repeated, patting his arm. "Truly, I don't know what I'd ever do without you."

They sat there for a long time in a comfortable silence, Danny's heart soaring with love for this woman. He thought of the argument they had had last week, when he was trying to talk her out of getting married. When he had described what a marriage should be, Danny realized, he'd been talking about them and what they could be to each other.

"Hey, Jo?" he said now. "How about we meet back up this afternoon, go down to the hardware store and stroll around, and then maybe pick up some rocky road and an old Doris Day-Rock Hudson movie?"

It took her a minute, but then she sat up straight and laughed out loud.

"You're too much, Danny," she said. "How I like to spend my free time, my favorite ice cream, and my favorite movies. I get your point."

They shared a smile.

*No, I don't think you do,* Danny thought.

*But you will, Jo.*

*In time, you will.*

# about the author

**M**indy Starns Clark's plays and musicals have been featured in schools and churches across the United States. Originally from Hammond, Louisiana, Mindy now lives with her husband and two daughters near Valley Forge, Pennsylvania.

Mindy's fast-paced and suspenseful inspirational writing—with a hint of romance and a strong heroine—are sure to delight readers everywhere.

Visit Mindy's website at www.mindystarnsclark.com to see a photo of the *real* Chewie and learn how he made his way into the pages of a novel.

And don't miss Jo and Danny's adventures in the next exciting Smart Chick Mystery, coming soon.

# other books by
# mindy starns clark

## THE MILLION DOLLAR MYSTERIES

### A Penny for Your Thoughts

Philanthropy investigator Callie Webber has a new work assignment: Go to Philadelphia and present an old family friend of Tom's (her employer) with a check for $250,000. When Callie goes to his office, check in hand, she discovers him dead on the floor. At Tom's request, Callie moves into the family's home and begins a murder investigation. But it's a dangerous place to be, for the family has secrets they would rather not have uncovered.

Callie's only hope is that God will help her use her investigative skills to discover the murderer and escape the web of deceit that surrounds her.

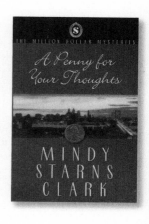

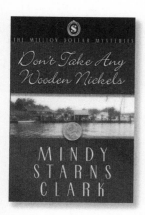

### Don't Take Any Wooden Nickels

Working to provide quality work clothes to women who can't afford to buy their own, Callie becomes involved with one young woman trying to come out of drug rehabilitation—just as she's charged with murder.

What appears to be a routine investigation in her sleepy waterside village suddenly becomes complicated amid international intrigue, cutting-edge technology, and deadly deception. In a desperate moment at what could be the end of her life, Callie cries out to the God who is as close as a whispered prayer.

### A Dime a Dozen

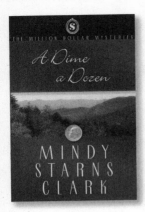

In Book 3 of this exciting inspirational suspense series, Callie investigates a charity in North Carolina's beautiful Smoky Mountains. While there, a migrant worker mysteriously disappears. Now Callie must find out why someone wanted him out of the way. But will the villain strike again?

Callie puts her new romance with Tom in peril as she pursues leads that will either bring to light a heart of darkness or end her hope of happiness. Trusting in God, she forges steadily ahead through a mire of clues, believing His hand will hold hers along the way.

### A Quarter for a Kiss

It's April, spring is in the air, and Callie and Tom have just spent a wonderful few weeks getting to know each other after years of a telephone-only relationship. But as their time together draws to a close, they are called to the hospital bed of mutual friend Eli Gold, who has just been shot.

Eli asks Callie to find out who is responsible for the shooting and begs Tom to help her. The search leads Tom and Callie to the beautiful island of St. John in the Virgin Islands. There they face a sinister enemy who's willing to do anything to keep his identity secret and the past deeply buried.

### The Buck Stops Here

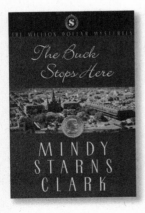

When Callie learns that the man she loves is somehow connected to the man who killed her late husband, she confronts Tom. But he informs her that his hands are tied by the National Security Agency and he can tell her nothing.

Despite the secrecy surrounding Tom and the NSA, Callie decides to find out for herself exactly what is going on and how Tom may have been involved in her husband's death. Using her investigative skills, Callie throws herself into the most important mystery she has ever attempted to solve.

Will their affection be able to stand the strain? And what was God's plan in bringing Tom and Callie together—marriage or merely answers for her questions about Bryan's death?

# A Letter to Our Readers

Dear Reader:

In order that we might better contribute to your reading enjoyment, we would appreciate your taking a few minutes to respond to the following questions. When completed, please return to the following:

Andrea Doering, Editor-in-Chief
Crossings Book Club
401 Franklin Avenue, Garden City, NY 11530

You can post your review online! Go to www.crossings.com and rate this book.

Title _____ Author _____

**1  Did you enjoy reading this book?**

❑ Very much. I would like to see more books by this author!

❑ I really liked_____

❑ Moderately. I would have enjoyed it more if_____

**2  What influenced your decision to purchase this book? Check all that apply.**

       ❑ Cover
       ❑ Title
       ❑ Publicity
       ❑ Catalog description
       ❑ Friends
       ❑ Enjoyed other books by this author
       ❑ Other _____

**3  Please check your age range:**

      ❑ Under 18    ❑18-24
      ❑ 25-34     ❑ 35-45
      ❑ 46-55     ❑ Over 55

**4  How many hours per week do you read?** _____

**5  How would you rate this book, on a scale from 1 (poor) to 5 (superior)?**

_____

Name_____

Occupation_____

Address_____

City_____ State_____ Zip_____